WHEN THE *GENESIS* reappeared in open space, it was only 328,000 feet from the surface of a planet. Almost devoid of power, their inertial dampeners were out of operation, so the sudden deceleration jolted most of the crew and passengers off of their feet.

It took them several seconds, but as they started to regain their composure, Billy asked Nicholas, "What just happened?"

"IN ALL MY YEARS, I've never seen that kind of destruction. The only way we'll ever identify any of the people that were in there is if Linda can do DNA tests on the ashes."

"I'm afraid my news isn't much better, but we do have one reactor that's still online," Billy said. "The problem is that it's not very large, and it's not connected to the power distribution system. However, I've come up with a way to use it. I've already printed out the changes that need to be made. When they're completed, we should have enough power to maneuver the ship closer to that planet."

"How long do you think it'll take us to make the repairs and get back underway?" Larry asked.

"That all depends on what we find on the planet...."

TOR BOOKS BY KEN SHUFELDT

Genesis
Tribulations

TRIBULATIONS

Ken Shufeldt

A TOM DOHERTY ASSOCIATES BOOK
NEW YORK

This is a work of fiction. All of the characters, organizations, and events portrayed in this novel are either products of the author's imagination or are used fictitiously.

TRIBULATIONS

A Tor Book
Published by Tom Doherty Associates, LLC
175 Fifth Avenue
New York, NY 10010

www.tor-forge.com

Tor® is a registered trademark of Tom Doherty Associates, LLC.

ISBN 978-0-7653-6558-3

First Edition: January 2012

Printed in the United States of America

0 9 8 7 6 5 4 3 2 1

ACKNOWLEDGMENTS

Many thanks to my world-class editor, Robert (Bob) Gleason, whose capacity for patience is only surpassed by his ability to impart sage advice.

TRIBULATIONS

PROLOGUE

THE BEGINNING

AT THE TIME, Larry Sheldon hadn't thought that much about the call he got from the Logos high council to make an emergency trip to Iraq to retrieve an artifact they had found.

When Larry had delivered the artifact to the research team at Glen Eyrie, he had no way of knowing that his actions would set in motion events that would forever change the course of human history.

Dr. Billy Evans had also been a member of the ultra-secretive evangelical society called the Logos. At the time of the accident, he had been leading the elite team of scientists at Glen Eyrie who were studying the ancient sarcophagus that Larry Sheldon had brought back from the battlefields of Iraq.

The sarcophagus had been used by Evevette to bury her husband, Adamartoni, over a hundred thousand years ago.

Adamartoni and Evevette had been ancient space travelers from the planet Theos. Their spaceship's power center had failed during a desperate resupply mission to their fleet, which had been engaged in a battle to the death with the Apollyon Empire at the center of the universe.

When they had been unable to repair their ship, they had journeyed to the nearest planet in search of help. While they were exploring the planet, a massive earthquake had damaged their shuttle-craft beyond repair and had permanently stranded them on Earth.

The humans they found on Earth had been extremely primitive and had lacked any form of technology. With no way to repair their ship, they had been forced to live out their lives on Earth.

In addition to being highly intelligent, Adamartoni and Evevette had been extremely long lived, by human standards. Over the ensuing centuries, their family interbred with the local population, and that had been responsible for the acceleration of humanity's development.

Their family had managed to build a fairly advanced civilization before they died. After their deaths, however, barbarian hordes had destroyed most of what they had accomplished.

The Theos had been an extremely religious people, and Adamartoni and Evevette had made sure that they had documented their beliefs and a chronological history of their family before they died.

Over the centuries, the texts had been either lost or destroyed; however, before the originals had disappeared, they had provided the basis for many of the Earth's formal religions and had been directly responsible for the foundation of the ultrasecretive evangelical society called the Logos.

As Dr. Evans's team studied the sarcophagus, they had discovered that its entire surface was covered with microscopic text.

Evevette had realized that what they had built was going to fall to the barbarians, and she had used the virtually indestructible metal of the sarcophagus to try to ensure that their words weren't lost to their descendants.

The text on the sarcophagus included everything they had ever written. But even more importantly, it provided the details of Adamartoni's final warning to his descendants.

The warning had come from a vision that Adamartoni believed was from God, and it told of a coming catastrophe that would destroy the Earth, and of a young couple who would ultimately save mankind from extinction.

WHEN BEN AND Mary West had taken refuge at Glen Eyrie, they had set in motion the next step in the chain of events in the long saga of Adamartoni and Evevette's legacy.

Shortly after they had arrived, Mary had gone into labor, and Dr. Billy Evans had delivered the baby for them. In a spur-of-the-moment decision, they had named the baby Billy in honor of Dr. Evans.

While he had been treating the baby, Dr. Evans had accidentally injected the baby with the recombinant DNA they had extracted from the body in the sarcophagus. The injection had produced amazing changes in Billy's body, and when they were complete, he was unlike any human that had ever been born. His intelligence was beyond measurement, and his body was capable of regenerating itself with remarkable speed.

Billy's parents had been lifelong friends with Rob and Beth Bustamante. When Rob and Beth's only child, Linda Lou, had been born, she needed an operation to save her life, but there hadn't been any blood available.

Even though Billy was still an infant, Ben and Mary

had let the doctor use some of his blood for Linda Lou's transfusion. The transfusion had saved her life, but it caused the same changes in her body that Billy's had gone through.

When their transformations were complete, a unique bond had been formed between them, and they became the first two instances of what might be the next stage of human evolution.

When the Logos found out what had happened, they started to follow their development. It hadn't taken very long for the Logos to come to the conclusion that Billy and Linda were the couple that Adamartoni's final words had foretold.

The Logos high council was determined to do everything in their power to help fulfill Adamartoni's prophesy. To make sure that nothing got in the way of that goal, they gave Larry Sheldon full access to their considerable resources so he could make sure that Billy and Linda would reach their full potential.

From that day on, Larry Sheldon had followed, guided, and even manipulated them, as they had grown up together; however, he had never divulged the secret of their transformations.

DREAMS

As Billy West dreamed, his mind was retracing the events of his life. He remembered how hard he and Linda had worked to hide how different they were from everyone else. How Pastor Earl Williams had helped them understand it was alright to be different, and that God had a plan for them.

He relived the frustration they had felt when their

teachers couldn't keep up with their development, and how quickly they had progressed when the school had given them computers and Internet access so that they could study at their own pace.

Billy remembered their experiences at the university the summer before they were supposed to start high school: As they had worked to learn everything they could, the professors, and Larry Sheldon, had recognized how brilliant they were and had allowed them to take achievement tests to finish their formal educations during their summer stay at the university.

Then he recalled the shock on their parents' faces when they had explained what he and Linda Lou had accomplished during the summer. How they struggled to help their parents understand who, and what, they were. How much alike they had become, but so different from virtually everyone else in the world.

He remembered the blur of events that had followed their summer at the university, and the premonitions that were constantly in their minds. He would never forget the day when it had all finally become clear, when Larry Sheldon had briefed him on the coming catastrophe.

His heart ached as he thought of how much he had missed Linda Lou while she was at the Mayo Clinic working on her residency. He remembered the friendship he had formed with Klaus Heidelberg as they labored to develop the technology necessary to save the human race.

His mind was flooded with conflicting emotions as he remembered the exhilaration he had felt when they had been able to develop the advanced power and the necessary technology to build the ships.

His feeling of exhilaration had been replaced by frustration as they had frantically raced to build the ships they needed. Then the utter devastation he had felt when

Klaus Heidelberg died from an infection he had caught from a terrorist attack victim.

Finally, he remembered the chaos of their final hours on Earth as they struggled to overcome the riots and the terrorist attacks so that they could save as many people as they could. How the leading edges of the asteroid swarm had surprised them, causing them to fall far short of their goals to fill their ships with evacuees.

The last thing he remembered before he woke up were the feelings that God had shared with him as he had watched the destruction of Earth.

1

WHEN BILLY WEST woke up, he opened his eyes to a wondrous sight: Open space filled his entire field of view, and his mind was struggling to understand where he was. As his mind cleared from the night's sleep, he remembered they were on board their spaceship, *Genesis*.

Once he was fully awake, he smiled to himself as he remembered their wedding night. He turned his head to look at his new bride, Linda Lou, whose head was resting on his shoulder as she slept. As he was enjoying watching her sleep, she began to stir. She opened her beautiful dark brown eyes to an amazing sight. The walls of their room were still transparent and allowed her to see the grandeur of space.

She lifted her head off Billy's arm.

He said, "Hi you."

She smiled and said, "Hi yourself, husband."

As she replayed their first night together in her mind, she felt his mind touch hers.

"I love you so much. Last night was everything I dreamed it would be," Billy said.

"It was neat. Wasn't it? Space is so beautiful. I thought it was awe-inspiring when we used to lie on the grass and look up at the stars, but this is amazing. Are you ready to get up and go and eat some breakfast?"

She felt his answer in her mind and told him, *That's a much better idea. We can eat later.*

A COUPLE OF hours later they showered and went down to the main galley for breakfast.

Richard Patterson spotted them as they entered and wished them a good morning. He asked, "How do you like married life so far? Wait, you don't need to tell me. You're both glowing. I just hope you're always as happy as you are today. Why don't you take that open table over there, and I'll be right back with your breakfast?"

As they waited for their meals, Richard's wife, Shirley, brought them a pot of coffee and their silverware. "Congratulations again, and you both look so happy. It almost makes me believe that we may have a chance for a decent life yet."

"We're very happy," Linda said. "And we both think that we'll all have a good life. It may not be anything like we could have imagined, but it'll be a good life nonetheless."

"How can you be so sure? Things definitely don't look good right now."

"I know they don't, but I believe there are truly wondrous adventures ahead of us."

"Here's your breakfast," Richard said as he sat their meals down.

"That was quick," Billy said. "I meant to tell you the other day, you guys are doing a great job running the galley."

"Thanks. I'm afraid we don't know much, other than how to run a café, but we always try to do our part."

"You're definitely doing your part."

"We'd better let these two newlyweds eat their breakfast," Richard said. "I just saw some soldiers come in. We'd better get busy, because those kids can eat like horses."

Billy and Linda Lou ate their breakfast in what looked like complete silence. In reality, they were conversing in their own special way. When they finished eating Billy asked, *I'm going to the lab to work on finding us a destination. Would you like to come with me?*

No thanks, I need to get down to the hospital and get back to work. There are over a hundred people waiting to see a doctor.

I didn't realize that we had that many people who were injured.

They're not all injured. Most of them just have your normal everyday health problems.

When Billy reached his lab, he reviewed the ship's logs for any issues. When he was finished, he leaned back in his chair as he contemplated what their initial destination should be.

Since it was technically the closest one, several of the other scientists in the fleet wanted to try to reach the Canis Major dwarf galaxy. He'd strongly disagreed with them, however, because it was in the process of being pulled apart by the gravitational forces of the Milky Way.

It had taken him several hours, but he finally decided on the Sagittarius dwarf elliptical galaxy. The problem was that although it was relatively close as stellar objects go, it was still over four light years away.

As he pondered the immense distances they would need to travel, he realized that they needed to find a way to exceed the speed of light.

As he tried to think through the problem, it brought back memories of a conversation that he and Klaus Heidelberg had had on the subject. He had told Klaus that he thought faster-than-light travel was feasible, even though Albert Einstein's theories didn't support his thinking.

Klaus had been a close friend of Einstein's, and he had assured Billy that Einstein had believed it was possible. Thinking of Klaus made him remember how much he missed having him around.

After he had spent a few minutes remembering Klaus, he said a quick prayer for him and resumed his work.

He called up the schematics of the ship on his computer screen so he could study them. While they were building *Genesis,* he had Nicholas Stavros add a set of massive magnetic projectors in the bow of the ship. At the time, he didn't know exactly how he was going to utilize them, but he had felt that he would at some point.

He spent the day deep in thought, and when he finally looked up from his computer, it was after 6:00 PM. He had worked through lunch, and he realized he was starving. He saved his work and went to find Linda, so they could eat dinner together.

He found her in the hospital, where she had just completed an evaluation of John Tyler. John had passed out during their wedding reception the previous night, and he had to be rushed into surgery. Linda's boss and mentor at the Mayo Clinic, William Robbins, had performed the microsurgery necessary to repair several congenital defects in his heart.

Linda greeted Billy as he entered John's room. "I'm glad you're here. I just finished examining John, and he's making a good recovery from his surgery. I think he'll be able to resume some light duties in eight weeks or so."

She turned back to John and said, "You don't know how lucky you are. Without the advances in microsurgery that we've made in the last two years, you probably wouldn't have survived, and if you had, you would have been laid up for several months, instead of several weeks."

"Actually, I understand more than you could ever know. The doctors at Walter Reed had told me that the surgery wasn't even possible. In fact, it was the reason I got out of the military."

"The last few days have been pretty exciting for you," Billy said. "You've got a new baby boy, and you're going to get your health back. How are Millie and Adam doing?"

"I only got to spend a few hours with them before I had my problem, but this is the happiest we've been in many years. We can't thank both of you enough for all that you've done for us."

"No thanks needed," Linda said. "Besides, if it hadn't been for you, our entire team might not have made it."

"It's great that you're going to get your strength back, because I'm going to need your help," Billy said.

"No problem, you can count on me. If you don't mind, I do have a couple of questions. Do you think we'll be able to find a new home, and how long will it take us to reach it?"

"I've selected our first place to search, but at our present speed, we won't be able to reach any destination for many years."

"That doesn't sound very promising. I would hate to think of Adam growing up without ever being able to run and play in the sunshine."

"It's too early to think like that. I'm working on some things that may allow us to cut some time off of our travel, but it's too early to talk about them yet."

* * *

MOST OF THE living quarters had kitchens, but they hadn't worked out the logistics for everyone to pick up the food they needed, so everyone was either eating in one of the ship's galleys or they were picking up their meals and taking them back to their quarters to eat.

Billy and Linda Lou liked eating with everyone, but they had decided that they wanted some time alone. As they sat eating, they had joined their minds instead of talking out loud. Billy had turned on the virtual reality system so the scene was quite a contrast of perceptions. They were sitting at a small table in front of the fireplace in their bedroom, but they were surrounded by open space.

The stars didn't twinkle in the vacuum of space, and the crystal-clear view was incredible. They could see the faint glow of the ships that stretched out for miles behind them, and the occasional piece of space junk that went speeding by.

They were already moving faster than any human had ever gone. The fleet had been under constant acceleration since they had left the rally point, and it wouldn't be too much longer before it reached its maximum speed.

At maximum power, the *Genesis* was capable of almost 60 percent of the speed of light, but the rest of the fleet was only capable of about half that.

"I don't know if I'll ever get used to the view," Linda said.

"It is awe-inspiring," Billy replied. "But I imagine we're going to see a lot of things that we never thought we would. Even though I'm responsible for much of the technology, I've got to admit that I'm somewhat astonished by what we've achieved."

"I know what you mean. I'm still struggling with our lives in general, but as bad as some of it has been, I'm still extremely grateful for what God has given us."

They had almost finished eating when Larry Sheldon called Billy on the intercom. "Our sensors have just picked up a ship, and it's about three hundred thousand miles behind us."

"Can you identify it?"

"I believe it's the president's ship, *Freedom*."

"The President of the United States! Are you sure?"

"I am, and that's not all! There're several other ships traveling with it. They're closing with us, but our sensors show that they're running dangerously close to an overload on their power systems."

"Signal the fleet to reduce our speed by 30 percent. That should be enough for them to catch up to us. At that speed, how long do you think it will take them to catch us?"

"Let's see, it shouldn't take more than twenty-four hours."

WHEN THE PRESIDENT'S ships were within a few hours of the fleet, Billy hailed them: "This is the *Genesis,* calling the *Freedom. Freedom,* please respond. *Freedom,* if you're receiving this, please respond."

He was about to hail them again, when they answered: "*Genesis,* this is President McAlister, on board the United States Vessel *Freedom.* Who am I taking to?"

"This is Billy West, and I'm glad you made it. How many other ships do you have with you, and what took you so long?"

"I'm glad we're finally getting to talk," President McAlister said. "I've heard so much about you from Larry Sheldon and Klaus Heidelberg. How are they doing?"

"Larry Sheldon is fine, but Klaus Heidelberg died just before we left."

"I'm so sorry. He was one of my most senior advisors and a truly brilliant man. I'll miss him."

"We all will. He was quite a man."

"He was, wasn't he? I'm sure that he would be proud of what you and Larry Sheldon have accomplished."

"It could have never happened without his help."

"I'm sure he would have appreciated the credit, but the last time we talked, he told me you're the only reason any of us made it.

"You asked me earlier how many ships we have in our group. We have forty ships, not counting the *Freedom*. We would have been here sooner, but we had to leave Earth in the wrong direction to avoid the incoming asteroid swarm.

"I'm glad you slowed down, we were running at over a hundred-percent load on the generators, and I was afraid we would burn them out. Luckily for us, you did such a great job designing the ships that they were up to the challenge. Did you pick us up on sensors, or did you slow down for another reason?"

"We picked you up on our sensors, so I gave the order to slow down."

"I'm sure glad you spotted us. As soon as we catch up, we'll assume the lead positions, and I'll take over. I appreciate you getting the fleet that far. It's a job well done."

Almost anyone else would have taken offense to someone taking over after they had brought the group that far, but it never occurred to Billy.

It took the *Freedom* and its sister ships the rest of the day to pass Billy's fleet. Once they had, they took up positions in front of the *Genesis*.

Once they were all in formation, the president radioed the fleet:

"Attention, attention, this is the President of the United

States, John McAlister. I'm happy to report the *Freedom*, which is my flagship, and the rest of the United States fleet, has arrived. I've assumed command and assumed responsibility for the continued planning and execution of our evacuation.

"My advisors have told me it's going to take a long time to reach another planet. However, you may rest assured that I'll do everything possible to ensure we all reach safety.

"I need to get an assessment of everyone's current status, so there will be a mandatory video conference at one tomorrow afternoon. All ship commanders should be prepared to present their current supply inventory so I can begin to assess our available resources. Again, thank you all for your cooperation in these trying times."

As THE MONTHS passed, President McAlister continued to consolidate his control over the fleet. He brought structure to the fleet, but his heavy-handed ways were beginning to grate on the nerves of several in Billy's group.

Meanwhile, Billy had been working almost day and night as he tried to develop his plans for a faster-than-light drive. Finally, he decided he had a solution and called his team together to discuss his plan.

He had Nicholas Stavros and his teams meet him in his lab for a briefing. He also invited John Tyler and Larry Sheldon, so he could keep them up to speed.

"Thank you for taking the time to meet with me," Billy said. "As many of you know, I've been working on a plan to allow us to exceed the speed of light."

"I didn't think that was possible," Nicholas Stavros replied. Nicholas was a brilliant young engineer, and he and his teams had been largely responsible for the construction of the American portion of the fleet. If you had been observing him, you might have thought that he was a teenager with ADD.

"That's what most of the scientific community believes, however, I've developed an approach that should allow us to break that barrier. I had talked with Klaus Heidelberg about it before he died, and he also believed it to be possible.

"It was his encouragement, and his suggestion that I read all of Stephen Hawking's research that kept me working toward a solution. Before he died, Klaus arranged for me to gain access to Hawking's unpublished papers, which has proven to be invaluable."

Klaus had mentioned it in passing, and Larry Sheldon had actually been the one who had gotten the papers for Billy, but he didn't say anything about it.

"What do you need us to do?" Nicholas asked excitedly.

"I've already uploaded the engineering changes that I need done."

"How do we get at them?"

"They're all stored on the central server, but I would like to walk you through them, before you get started."

Billy hit a button on the wireless remote he was carrying, and a holographic image of the bow of the ship appeared before the group.

"These things will never cease to amaze me," John said.

"It's pretty amazing, but it'll let me show you exactly what I need done."

Billy used the remote control to highlight the new power leads to the magnetic projectors, and the projectors' main plates.

"If you'll pay close attention to the highlighted areas,

you'll see the sections that I want to replace with the new formulation of the ceramic superconductors.

"Once we have replaced the marked areas, we'll add two more fusion reactors to power the projectors. I've got a new design for them as well, and the output from the two reactors should be a little more than twice the existing power of the *Genesis*."

"Wow, that's some upgrade," Nicholas exclaimed. "When can we get started? We've been going crazy since we ran out of new projects."

"You can begin whenever you're ready, but I would like to start no later than the end of the week."

"No problem. In fact, if you don't mind we'll get started this afternoon. How long did you estimate it should take us?"

"Using your team's previous work as a reference, I would say about thirteen weeks."

Later that night, Billy and Linda met their parents for dinner. They were going to meet them on the upper deck where they could eat under the starlit skies, but at the last minute Billy decided to meet them on the beach deck. When they got there, their meals were already laid out on a table by the water.

"I don't think I'll ever get used to all of this," Linda's dad, Rob Bustamante, said. "Here we are on a space-ship, hurtling through space, to who knows where, and we're about to have dinner on a beach that's identical to a South Pacific island."

"This looks scrumptious," Linda's mother, Beth, said. "Is that a lobster?"

"Yes it is," Linda replied. "I knew it was your favorite, so I had the Pattersons prepare one for you. I know the rest of you would rather have beef, so you'll be having some really good rib-eye steaks."

"How can we be eating all of this?" Ben West, Billy's dad, asked.

"We have plenty of food, and we also have the capability to raise more. The lagoon is stocked with all sorts of seafood, and you and Rob already know about the agriculture decks."

"We sure do, and thanks for letting us work on them," Rob said.

As they sat eating their dinner, a faint breeze suddenly moved over them, and they thought they heard the sound of distant thunder.

"Is that thunder?" Mary West asked.

"It is," Billy replied. "In another hour there will be a tropical rainstorm falling where we're sitting. I've engineered all the agriculture areas to have normal weather patterns, and the forest areas have all four seasons."

"It's great to see both of you, but what are you going to spring on us this time?" Ben asked.

"I would like to say that I don't have something to tell you, but I do," Billy answered. "You've all asked how long it's going to be before we can find a new home, and I have some news that will affect my answer."

"It's not bad news again, is it?" Beth asked.

"Not this time. I've been working on a way to exceed the speed of light. When we talked about this before, I told you it would be many years before we could reach any possible destination. If the new propulsion system works like I think it will, we should be able to cut decades, if not centuries off of our transit time."

"Does this mean that there's a chance that we'll be able to find another place to live?" Rob asked.

"I don't want to raise your expectations too high, but I do believe that it gives us a chance."

His statement set off an outburst of excited conversations from their parents. After several minutes the conversations started to die down, and Billy told them, "We'd better get going. It's going to start raining in another ten minutes."

"Would you mind if we stay?" Rob asked. "Beth and I just love the rain, and it's been a while since we've seen any."

"No problem, stay as long as you want. You know your way back to your quarters, don't you?"

"Yes, we do, and thanks for the great evening. We really enjoyed it."

LATER THAT NIGHT, Billy and Linda were lying in bed talking.

"I think our parents really enjoyed dinner," Linda said.

"They seemed to. I just hope I didn't upset them."

"I don't think they were upset, but you know how badly my dad wants to have a real home again. He's doing much better since you let him and your dad take over the agriculture decks. But he still struggles from time to time."

"I know he does, but I don't know what else to do."

"I don't think there's anything more you could do, but hearing that there's even a chance of a real home again helped. Do you really think you can exceed the speed of light?"

"I do, and if Stephen Hawking's theories are correct, we may even change dimensions."

"I'm sure I don't understand all of that, but if you do, it's good with me."

"Don't sell yourself short, you're just a smart as me, you're just not interested in the same things."

"I know, but I like to play the helpless young wife once in a while." She giggled as she snuggled up closer.

As they continued on their way across the Milky Way, the fleet had reached its maximum speed of 33 percent of the speed of light.

The fleet was stretched out over hundreds of miles, and at two miles long and hundreds of feet tall, the massive ships represented the largest moving objects man had ever built.

ELEVEN WEEKS LATER, Nicholas called to tell Billy they had finished the upgrades.

"We just finished connecting the new reactors to the magnetic projectors," Nicholas said.

"Great work, you've finished weeks ahead of schedule," Billy said. "Why don't all of you take a couple of days off, and then we'll set up a test."

"Thanks, we are pretty worn out. We've been really pushing it to finish early."

TWO DAYS LATER they met to discuss the testing protocol they would be using.

Billy put a holographic image of the bow in front of them and started the briefing.

"Even though we have cameras and sensors all along these areas, I want one of your teams stationed in each of these locations," Billy said as he highlighted the areas he was referring to. "If there are going to be problems, I think these are the areas where they might occur.

"Each of you will be carrying a remote kill switch to abort the test, if need be. If you observe anything that even remotely concerns you, I want you to stop the test."

"That seems simple enough," Nicholas responded. "Do

you have any idea what we should expect to see or feel from the test?"

"I have no idea. No one has ever even attempted this, so whatever we experience will be truly unique."

"Are you going to notify the fleet?" Larry asked. "You know how paranoid President McAlister is. He's going to think you've been hiding this from him."

"I hadn't intended to tell him until we had finished the test. To be honest, I'm afraid he would attempt to stop us if he found out. His advisors haven't been that good to work with so far, and I'm convinced that they'll try to stop anything that they can't take credit for."

"I agree with your decision. We can always beg for forgiveness later."

Larry Sheldon was used to being the maverick, and he was glad Billy saw things the same way. Even though the president was a member of the Logos, Larry wasn't at all comfortable with his actions up to this point. In the back of his mind, he knew he might have to deal with the president someday.

The ships that President McAlister had brought with him were still leading the formation, and he had positioned the *Genesis* in the center, just behind the *Freedom*.

Since the *Genesis* was the largest, most powerful ship in the fleet, the president wanted to keep it as close to him as possible. In fact, he was already working on a plan to seize control of the *Genesis*, so he could use it as his flagship.

Billy had the entire team meet him on the *Genesis*'s bridge for the test. Billy turned to Larry and said, "Since you were the closest to Klaus, I would like you to say a prayer for him, and then I would like you to initiate the test in his memory. Without his inspiration, I wouldn't have been able to pull this off."

"I know Klaus would be honored, but I also know he would say he really didn't have much to do with it."

When Larry finished his prayer, he reached over and tapped the screen to initiate the test.

For a second or two it didn't seem like anything was happening, and then a shimmering vortex of energy burst out of the projectors. It continued to grow and spin faster until it extended for almost twenty miles in front of the *Genesis*.

For a moment Billy thought they were going to hit the *Freedom*, which was forty-five miles in front of them; however, before he could reach over and turn the projectors off, the *Genesis* was sucked into the vortex and disappeared from sight.

WHEN THE CAPTAIN of the *Freedom* saw the *Genesis* disappear, he called President McAlister.

"Sir, the *Genesis* just disappeared into what looked like a tornado of light."

"What do you mean by disappeared? Did it blow up?"

"No sir, it simply isn't there anymore."

"Tell no one else, I'll be right up."

After the president's science team had analyzed the video of the *Genesis*'s disappearance, they decided it had suffered some sort of catastrophic malfunction and had been destroyed.

2

"WHAT JUST HAPPENED?" Larry asked. "Where did the fleet go?"

"I think we just broke the speed of light, and if that's true, we're already a long way away from the fleet," Billy said. "Give me just a moment, and I'll see if I can find them on our long-range sensors."

He worked for several minutes before he announced, "It's official. We're the first humans to exceed the speed of light. I had to go back through the sensor logs to find them, but before we were out of range the fleet was several million miles behind us.

"I had to update the sensor programs to compensate for the anomalies we're experiencing. But as close as I can tell, our effective speed is roughly twice the speed of light."

"Impossible," Nicholas exclaimed. "I know we added a lot of additional power, but we don't have that much."

"If we were still in our own dimension you'd be right, but I'd already theorized that the supposed laws of physics might be materially different in what I'm going to call the fifth dimension."

"How did you come up with the idea of multiple dimensions?" Larry asked.

"Actually, I didn't develop the theory. Kaluza and Klein

first theorized a fifth dimension in 1921. But it was a book called *The Grand Design*, co-written by Stephen Hawking and Leonard Mlodinow, that convinced me to study everything I could find on string theory."

"It's a good thing that you understand it, because I can't get my mind around it."

"I didn't say I totally understand it, I just said it's where I think we are. How are the new fusion reactors holding up?"

After Nicholas had checked with the team that had been monitoring them, he told Billy, "Everything is going according to the plan. How long are you going to run the test?"

"Since we aren't having any problems, give me another thirty minutes, and then we'll start back."

Billy spent the time running tests and making sure they had enough data for him to continue refining the projectors. When he finished, he had Nicholas reverse their course.

When they thought that they were within thirty minutes of the fleet, Billy told Nicholas, "You can begin reducing power to the projectors."

For the next fifteen minutes, they gradually reduced power until Nicholas reported, "The projectors are offline, but we are still in your fifth dimension."

"So I see," Billy remarked. "This wasn't something I had anticipated. I'm going to need a little time to sort this out." He had plenty of data to work with, so he didn't think it would take very long. He worked day and night, but after two days he still hadn't figured out a solution to the problem.

Finally, Linda called him in his lab. "What's going on? I haven't heard a peep out of you in almost two days. What are you working on that's so important that you can neglect your poor wife for so long?" she said with a giggle. "Didn't your test work?"

"It worked, but now I can't figure out how to get us out of this dimension. Sorry about neglecting you, I got wrapped up in this and lost track of time. Are you up for dinner? I haven't eaten anything in two days except for some crackers."

As they sat in the galley eating, Linda said, "It's not like you not to know exactly what was going to happen. I'm sure it won't take you very long to figure it out."

"At first I didn't think it would, but I haven't had any luck so far. Klaus would have been very upset with me. He was always telling me to slow down and to not be so cocksure.

"I could just kick myself. I'd even considered testing the projectors out on the *Imagination*, but then I decided to go ahead on the *Genesis*. I just hope I haven't gotten us trapped in another dimension."

IT TURNED OUT the answer hadn't been that easy to figure out, and Billy worked on it for almost four months before he found a workable solution.

When he finally figured it out, the actual solution had been fairly simple: All he had to do was to reverse the polarity of the magnetic vortex to reverse the process. The problem was that the projectors were going to have to receive a massive surge of energy on the return trip.

His realized that his overconfidence had almost resulted in disaster, and this time he was going to be extra cautious. He ran the test scenarios until he was absolutely sure the redesigned system could withstand the tremendous surge of energy.

When he was satisfied he had his plan of attack figured

out, he called the team back together so he could brief them.

"I've already stored the system modifications in the central server," Billy said. "You shouldn't have any problems making the upgrades, but it's imperative you follow the plans exactly.

"The system has to be perfect, because I've estimated it'll have to withstand an energy surge that's roughly equivalent to three times the energy it took us to jump dimensions."

"Whoa, that's some surge," Nicholas exclaimed. "Are you sure we can deliver enough power to generate the field?"

"We'll only have to generate about a third of that amount, the rest will be the result of the dimensional transition. Going in, the energy was expended into open space, this time it'll feed back through the vortex to us."

Billy took the time to point out every modification on the holographic image. When he was finished, he asked, "Are there any questions?"

After such a detailed briefing, he hadn't been expecting any questions, but Vladimir Demetrius stood up and asked, "Sir, shouldn't we add some additional power to the reactor complex feeding the projectors?"

"That won't be necessary. As I said, the power requirements to generate the field will be relatively modest on the return trip."

Vladimir was a brilliant young Russian. He had just completed a double doctorate program at MIT when Nicholas found him. He had been pleased when he had managed to add Vladimir to his team, and the young man had proven to be as valuable as Nicholas had hoped. Nicholas had already come to trust him enough to put him in command of the fusion reactor upgrades, which allowed Nicholas's team to take care of the control computer upgrades.

Once they got started, Vladimir drove his team even harder than Nicholas, and they were finished well ahead of schedule.

"THAT WAS THE last of the planned upgrades," Terry Flint said. "Is there anything else we need to do?"

They had already restarted the upgraded fusion reactors, and the five members of their crew were bathed in the reactors' green glow.

Vladimir stood staring at the reactor for several seconds as he tried to get his mind around the tremendous energy that was contained behind the magnetic containment fields. The two fusion reactors were generating more power than all of the old Earth power plants put together, but he just wasn't sure it was enough.

He had worried about Billy's plans from the moment that he had seen them. Even though Billy had tried to reassure him, he still had a nagging feeling in the pit of his stomach that Billy wasn't right.

His ego wouldn't allow him to believe that someone could know more than he did. He had spent all of his young life as the smartest person in the room, and he still believed he was.

"How much superconducting cable do we have left?" Vladimir asked.

"We have a little over nine thousand feet," Terry said. "Why do you ask?"

Vladimir ignored his question while he was doing the math in his head. The central reactor core was located in the exact center of the ship, and it was just over eight thousand feet from their location, so he knew there was enough cable to carry out his plan.

"Take what we have left and connect it to the main power junction. Then run the cable up here, and we'll splice it into the projectors' main power leads. That way we can bridge in the rest of the *Genesis*'s power if we need to," Vladimir said.

"That's not on the plans," Terry replied.

Vladimir saw that Terry was worried about it, so he told him, "It's okay. I received the additional changes last night."

It never occurred to Terry that anyone in their group would ever lie about anything, let alone something that was this critical. It took them a couple of hours to complete cross-connecting the reactors, but they were still finished several hours ahead of the other teams.

When all the upgrades were completed, Billy gave the crews the day off before they attempted to reenter their own dimension.

The next day, Billy and Nicholas were standing on the bridge as they waited for everyone to reach their assigned positions for the test.

Vladimir and his team were in the auxiliary reactor room so they could keep an eye on the magnetic projectors. Just before the test was due to happen, Vladimir decided to send Terry Flint to the bridge.

"Take this note to Nicholas Stavros," Vladimir said. "You need to hurry because they're about to initiate the test."

While they had been on their way down to the reactor room, Vladimir had suddenly realized that his unauthorized modifications might cause unforeseen complications. He knew that he was going to be in big trouble for making them, but he was determined to come clean, even if it caused him to lose his position as a team leader.

When everyone was in place, Billy did the honors and hit the button to start the projectors. When he did, the vortex of magnetic energy formed and started to spin up.

Just like their previous attempt, once the vortex had fully formed, the *Genesis* was pulled into it at a tremendous speed. Just as Billy had predicted, the power feedback was immense, but he had taken it into account. What he hadn't taken into account were Vladimir's unauthorized changes to his plans.

The redesigned system would have easily carried the load; the junction where they had cross-connected the power systems, however, was not up to the task. Instead of the projector's reactors receiving the power feedback, the main power systems received the full brunt of the surge. The massive surge caused it to suffer a catastrophic power overload.

When the main reactors fried, it caused an unbelievable surge of energy back to the projector's reactors. The last thing that Vladimir and his team saw was an immense burst of what looked like thousands of lightning bolts as the electricity arced all over the reactor room.

Vladimir had been half-expecting a problem, so he had his hand poised over the kill switch when Billy triggered the projectors. When he saw the initial surge, he reacted immediately, but even as he hit the emergency shutdown, they had all died.

His quick reaction had saved the ship, but the overload had destroyed most of the ship's reactors, leaving it almost completely devoid of power. Their only remaining useable power source was a small reactor that provided backup power to the life support systems.

When the *Genesis* reappeared in open space, it was

only 328,000 feet from the surface of a planet. Almost devoid of power, their inertial dampeners were out of operation, so the sudden deceleration jolted most of the crew and passengers off of their feet.

It took them several seconds, but as they started to regain their composure, Billy asked Nicholas, "What just happened?"

"I'm not sure. Everything was going as planned, and while the power feedback was immense, it was well within the expected tolerances."

As Nicholas frantically scanned the logs, he saw what had happened. He turned to John Tyler and told him, "Take a team and check on the people in both reactor rooms."

Nicholas turned back to Billy and said, "Somehow the energy surge reached our main reactors as well as the projector reactors. I've sent a team to check on the people in both areas, but I doubt that anyone could have survived. The energy released would have incinerated virtually everything in both areas."

"How could that have happened? I was very careful not to interconnect any of the systems. There should have been no way for the surge to reach the main reactors."

"Give me a few minutes while I check a few things, and maybe I can answer that for you," Nicholas said as he continued to work feverishly. It was indeed only a few minutes before he told Billy, "I've verified that the plans the teams used didn't include any cross-connections."

As he was about to continue his explanation, John reported back in. "I've just finished searching the projector reactor room, and I'm pretty sure they're all dead."

"What do you mean you think they're dead?" Billy asked. "Either they're dead or they're not!"

"All I can tell you for sure is that the stench in here is terrible. The only possible signs of Vladimir and his team are some piles of ashes. My best guess is that's all that's left of them. I'm on my way to the main reactor room, but I imagine that I'll find the same thing."

As Nicholas and Billy struggled to understand what had happened, the only surviving member of Vladimir's team spoke up.

"Vladimir sent me up here with this note for you," Terry said as he handed the note to Nicholas.

Billy saw the blood rise in Nicholas's face as he read the short note from Vladimir. "That explains everything: Vladimir had them cross-connect the reactors!"

"That wasn't in the plans," Billy said. "What in the world made him to do that?"

"You would have had to have known Vladimir to understand. However, it sounds just like him. He was a brilliant young man, but he had never learned even a modicum of self-restraint. He was one of those people who believed their own press clippings, and he firmly believed that he could do no wrong. I even find it hard to believe he sent this note with Terry. He must have realized that he had made a big mistake. I just wish he had called us on the intercom. We could have avoided all of this."

Billy took over one of the other consoles so he could begin assessing the situation. The first thing he needed to figure out was what sort of resources they had left.

While he worked, Nicholas Stavros, John Tyler, and Larry Sheldon each took a team of men to survey the physical damage to the rest of the ship.

Several hours later they all met back on the bridge. When Billy heard them come in, he looked up and said, "Good. You're all back. Larry why don't you go first."

"My group just finished inspecting the outside of the hull. It looks like we got lucky, because we couldn't find any breaches."

"We've done our initial assessment of the main reactor areas, and they're a complete loss," Nicholas said. "The heat from the overloads destroyed everything in there. If it hadn't been for the secondary containment fields, we would have lost a lot more people.

"One of the walls had a ten-foot-wide hole in it that looked like it had been melted by a high-power laser. The heat was so intense that even the equipment that's identifiable will never function again."

"I couldn't do the technical level of assessment that Nicholas did, but the projector reactor room was in the same condition as what he just described," John said. "In all my years, I've never seen that kind of destruction. The only way we'll ever identify any of the people that were in there is if Linda can do DNA tests on the ashes."

"I'm afraid my news isn't much better, but we do have one reactor that's still online," Billy said. "The problem is that it's not very large, and it's not connected to the power distribution system. However, I've come up with a way to use it. I've already printed out the changes that need to be made. When they're completed, we should have enough power to maneuver the ship closer to that planet."

"How long do you think it'll take us to make the repairs and get back underway?" Larry asked.

"That all depends on what we find on the planet. Unless we can get some help down there, I don't know whether we can repair the ship. We've got a lot of work to do before we can even think about repairs. The first thing we need to do is scrap the old reactors."

"Isn't there some way we can repair them?" Nicholas asked.

"I'm afraid they're a total loss, which means we're going to have to start from scratch. We're also going to need to replenish our fuel supply."

They continued talking for several hours before Nicholas and his crews left to start wiring in their surviving reactor.

THE NEXT MORNING Billy used the ship's intercom to update the passengers and crew.

"Good morning everyone, this is Billy West, and I would like to give you an update on our situation.

"As you may have already heard, we weren't successful in our attempt to reenter our original dimension. Unfortunately, our ship has suffered severe damage to its reactors, and at this point, we aren't going to be able to continue our voyage.

"We've stabilized the situation, and the ship is not in any danger at this point. We've been lucky enough to be stranded near a habitable planet. In the next few weeks we're going to attempt to reach the planet, where we hope to be able to find enough materials to make our repairs.

"I have no way of predicting whether we're going to be successful, but I can promise you that we'll do everything possible to resume our journey.

"I'll be giving you periodic updates, and if you have any questions just enter them on one of the consoles, and I'll attempt to answer them as time allows."

"That sounded pretty grim," Linda said. "I thought you said everything was going to be alright?"

"I think that's still true. But, if we can't find what we need on the planet, we're not going to be able to fix the ship."

* * *

WHILE THEY WERE working on the repairs Billy decided to take an inventory of everything they had on board.

As always, Nicholas had done a meticulous job of logging in every single item they had brought. But when Billy got down to the area marked WEAPONS LOCKER, the records showed that nothing had ever been stored there.

When had completed the rest of the inventory, he decided to go and check out the weapons locker. He knew that Nicolas Stavros would want to know, so he asked Nicolas to meet him in the cargo area.

"If the ship's manifest doesn't show anything for this area, it's probably empty," Nicolas said. "We were very careful to log in everything we brought on board."

Nicholas unlocked the door and they went inside. The storage area was nine hundred feet by fifteen hundred feet, and it was completely filled with an impressive array of weapons.

"Well, so much for having a record of everything," Nicholas remarked dryly. "General Medley and I had discussed what he intended to do with this area, but we never finalized the plans. It looks as though he went ahead anyway."

"So you did know what he had in mind?" Billy asked.

"In general principle, I did. He wanted to make sure that he had at least a few examples of every infantry weapon that he could lay his hands on. He was a little obsessed with it, so I imagine that we're going to find some pretty exotic weapons in here. It's too bad that he didn't make it, he could have easily explained everything."

They spent a few more minutes walking the storage area, until Billy told him, "There's no sense in us wasting any more time in here. Larry and John can make better sense of this than we ever could. I'll give them a heads-up, and they can figure out what to do with all this stuff."

IT HAD ONLY taken Nicholas's crews ten days to make the reactor modifications so they could have at least minimal propulsion.

The one small reactor wasn't powerful enough to allow them much speed, but at least they could maneuver. Billy moved the *Genesis* into orbit around the planet so they could start looking for the resources they needed.

While they had been surveying the planet's surface, Billy and Linda had begun having premonitions again. As the weeks passed, the premonitions had grown stronger and stronger. Finally, on the night before Billy was due to brief the ship's crew and passengers again, they both dreamed that they were going to suffer another catastrophe of some sort.

"I had a really disturbing dream last night," Linda said.

"Me, too," Billy said. "Mine was about what seemed to be a king who could have been taken right out of medieval history. I was trying to convince him that his people were in danger. In the dream, I was becoming extremely frustrated because I couldn't get him to believe me."

"I had the same dream, but I can't seem to remember what the danger was."

Billy thought about it for a moment and said, "I can't either, but I remember being very worried about whatever it was. The only other thing that I can remember was that it seemed cold all the time."

"Given what we have experienced so far, when God gives us insight to coming events, we need to be prepared to deal with whatever the event is going to be."

Later that morning, Billy called the teams back together

so they could go over what they had been able to discover so far.

"Thank you all for your hard work. I just wish that I could tell you that we're done, but I'm afraid we are just getting started. As most of you know, we've just completed a detailed study of the planet.

"What we've discovered so far is going to present a problem for us. The planet has abundant resources, and I have no doubt that we'll be able to find the mineral deposits that we need; however, the inhabitants have almost no technology. From what we've been able to discern so far, their civilizations are approximately where Earth's were in the late fifteenth century."

"But that means they haven't even discovered electricity yet," John said.

"They haven't even discovered steam power yet," Billy said. "I did see some evidence that they have gunpowder and probably some very crude firearms."

"What's next?" Larry asked.

"I've identified the two main cities on the planet. There's one in the northern hemisphere and one in the southern hemisphere. I think we should try to contact whoever is in command in both cities. My best guess is that they're being controlled by different factions, but we won't know for sure until we can make contact."

"How are you going to do that?" Larry asked.

"At some point we'll contact them in person; however, if their development is where I believe it to be, we're going to have to be careful not to panic them.

"We need some more specific information about them, so I think that our next step is to construct several unmanned drones. That way we can get a closer look at their societies without letting them know we're watching."

"A couple of my guys worked on the last generation of drones that we were using in South America," Nicholas said. "It shouldn't take them very long to build you several of them."

It only took three weeks to build the drones, and when they were finished, they deployed them over both groups.

The drones carried acoustic as well as visual surveillance equipment. They could record a conversation from a couple of miles away, and the video equipment could deliver crystal-clear images from many times that distance.

Once the drones were deployed, they spent almost five weeks gathering data about the people they were intending to contact. As they had expected, they couldn't understand the language of either group.

They had already discovered that the north had many of the materials they were after, so once they had enough data to start, they began to study the surveillance tapes from the northern hemisphere's culture.

They soon discovered that their language was very similar in structure to the Old Norse language.

Much as languages had evolved on Earth, several variations or dialects had developed in the northern hemisphere, but they found that differences between them were subtle enough to be able to translate most of them.

Billy and Linda had no problem becoming fluent in the north's languages. Like most things, linguistics came very easily to them.

Billy realized that the rest of their people would have to struggle to learn the languages, so once he had gained a thorough understanding of them he built miniature translators for the rest to use. He knew that most of the crew and passengers were already struggling with everything that had happened so far, so he changed the translation of the northern kingdom's name to Norseman, and the southern kingdom to Nubian, to give them something familiar.

Once they had their landing teams properly outfitted with the translators, they brought them together to brief them on what they could expect to encounter when they met the locals.

They spent the first ten minutes showing detailed videos of their first stop. They had decided that their first meeting would be with the king of the northern hemisphere.

They had learned from their initial research that both areas were controlled by monarchs, but Billy had decided to listen to their premonitions and meet with the king of the north first.

Much like the feudal societies of Earth, this culture was a mixture of military and religious authority, and superstitious beliefs. In addition, like those times on Earth, all the planet's societies were in a fairly chaotic state.

"Does anybody have any questions about the video?" Billy asked.

"Why did you choose the north instead of the south?" Larry asked.

"There were several reasons, but the biggest reason was that the north has the minerals that we need. In addition to that, Linda and I have the feeling they're who we need to work with."

Larry had enough experience working with Billy and Linda not to ask any more questions. He knew that they were probably referring to some sort of message from God, but he also knew that the rest of the group didn't need to know that.

His background with the Logos, and his mission to help Billy and Linda fulfill their destinies, had trained him to trust in what God was sharing with them. In the back of his mind, he wished that God would touch him as directly as He had them.

"How many men do you want on the first mission?" John asked.

"I thought it should be you, me, and Larry. I don't want them to think we're a threat. Besides, I know that both of you can handle yourselves if we get in a jam."

They had more than enough men, so John didn't understand why he was insisting on such a small team. "Fine, if that's what you want, but I think we should take some more men. We have no idea how they are going to react, and we already know that they're violent people by nature."

"I can understand your concerns, but I'm willing to take the chance. You and Larry can bring whatever equipment you think is necessary, but I don't want to show up with a large force.

"I have a few more details that I want to take care of, so let's plan on making our first visit in three days."

WHILE THEY HAD been studying the planet's surface, they had also been surveying the galaxy they were in. They were still having premonitions of danger, but Billy hadn't found anything on the planet that concerned him.

Once he had finalized his plans for their first visit to the planet, he decided to spend a little time scanning the data they had collected on the galaxy.

He had only been studying the data for a few hours when he first spotted the anomaly. It was still in the far reaches of this solar system, so it took him another hour to make a positive identification.

As he realized what it was, he got that same sickening

feeling he had gotten when Larry Sheldon first told him about the approaching asteroid that destroyed Earth.

The initial survey hadn't been detailed enough to determine the level of risk, so he programmed their long-range sensors to gather some more data. He wanted to make sure of what they were looking at before he told anyone what he had found. As he considered what to do next, he decided to put off their first trip to the planet until he could figure out how much trouble they were in.

Once he had enough data, he could see it was a massive meteor, and that it had a large swarm of smaller meteors traveling with it. He ran its current course through the computer to try to determine if it was going to be a problem.

After it had processed the data, he had the computer select the plots with the highest probability and sat down to study them. He quickly saw that it was going to be close, but there wasn't much of a chance the meteor swarm would make a direct hit on its current pass.

Billy knew that the biggest problem with projecting the level of risk was that the meteor's course was constantly being altered by its interaction with celestial bodies along the way.

That night he had his first dream about the meteor's interaction with the planet. The dream was so disturbing that he decided to try to model some additional scenarios for the meteor's path.

Using *Genesis*'s massive supercomputer, he ran literally millions of different possibilities. Virtually none of them had the meteor impacting the planet on this pass, but several of the simulations put the odds of it impacting on subsequent passes at over 70 percent.

The meteor had been passing by the planet for millions of years. But for some as yet undetermined reason, its course had been radically altered, and several of the model's projections were predicting it would strike the planet within the next few years.

It wasn't anywhere close to a certainty, but the odds were such that he knew he was going to have to make some contingency plans. He was convinced that they weren't in any immediate danger, so he decided to go ahead and meet with the king.

LARRY SHELDON AND John Tyler were both used to being leaders, not followers, but they had both been willing to follow Billy's lead.

Working with Nicholas, they had finally decided on the equipment they wanted to take along on the mission. They still weren't confident, however, that three men were enough.

After studying the clothing the natives were wearing, they had outfits tailored to resemble what was normally being worn by the ruling class.

The only deviation they made was to wear lightweight body armor underneath the outfits for a little extra protection. The armor wouldn't be any help against swords, but it would stop a musket ball.

They wanted to be as heavily armed as possible without looking out of place. It had taken some ingenious thinking, but Nicholas had managed to build them a variety of weapons that were disguised to look like the weapons being carried by the locals.

Larry and John would be carrying both a short sword and a long sword. Each could function as a normal sword, but they could also be converted into different weapons.

With the touch of a button, the long sword could convert into a high-powered rifle, while the short sword could be converted into a machine gun. Billy would be carry-ing only a dagger, but it could be converted into a small pistol.

If it came down to hand-to-hand combat, Larry and John were confident their advanced hand-to-hand com-bat training would let them defeat anyone they encoun-tered. They were concerned about Billy's lack of formal training, but they didn't have time to try to train him.

When they all gathered in the ship's massive landing bay, Linda was struck by how much like Vikings they looked. Even though she wasn't going along, she had already learned the various languages on the planet.

"Please don't take any unnecessary chances," Linda said.

"You know me," Billy said.

"I do, and that's why I said it." She looked directly at Larry and John and said, "I expect you two to take care of him."

"You can count on us, but you have to realize that it doesn't always go as planned," Larry replied.

"I do, and that makes me like it even less."

They had intended to use the *Imagination* to make the trip to the planet's surface, but the damage caused by the reactors had made it impossible to get it out of the hanger where it was stored. Instead, Nicholas had built a shut-tle to make the trip. If it was fully loaded, it could trans-port a hundred people, but on this trip, there were only going to be the three of them.

It was about half the size of the *Imagination,* and at this point it wasn't much more than an empty shell, since they hadn't taken the time to outfit it with any amenities, or even separate compartments.

As the shuttle descended from orbit, they were struck

by the unspoiled beauty of the planet. Their destination was the capital of King Ivan Peterovan's kingdom. His castle was at the end of an enormous fjord that extended for several miles inland. The fjord and castle were set in the middle of the highest mountains in the northern hemisphere.

The castle sat at the base of the highest peak on the planet. The colossal mountain was just over thirty-two thousand feet tall, and like Mount Everest on Earth, the peak was in a constant state of winter. As they descended over the peak of the mountain into the valley below, a storm with sixty-five-mile-per-hour winds caused a complete whiteout.

"Boy that's some storm," Larry said. "It's a good thing we have radar to fly by."

Billy's first thought had been to land outside the walled city, so they didn't unduly alarm the inhabitants; however, after he had studied their culture for a while, he had decided that they needed to try to impress them.

He had quickly seen that the only things the planet's two cultures valued were strength and bravery. If they were perceived as weak, they wouldn't have a chance of getting the king to help them.

The king's castle was located at the far end of the city. They had carved into the side of the mountain to make the back wall of the castle. When you first looked at it from the air, it looked like it had grown out of the mountain.

A sheer rock cliff extended several thousand feet above the highest point of the castle, rendering it virtually unapproachable from that side.

All the other approaches to the castle were guarded by moats that were almost a thousand feet wide. The castle walls were three hundred feet high, and the walls that surrounded the city were eighteen feet high, and all the walls had been constructed from the stoutest granite on the planet.

Even though there weren't any apparent threats to the city, the walls were manned by five hundred fully armed men. As they got closer, they could see that there were cannon ports every eighty-two feet, and that they covered every possible angle of approach to the city.

"It doesn't look like they leave much to chance," Larry said. "It would be suicide to attack this position."

John guided the shuttle to a landing in the courtyard in front of the main entrance to the castle. The castle's massive doors were over thirty feet tall and looked like they were covered with some sort of armor plating.

As soon as they had landed, they were surrounded by fifty armed men. Their weapons would have been considered quite crude by Earth standards, but they were still quite lethal. Each man was armed with a sword or a crossbow, and several carried what looked like muskets.

"They sure don't seem very friendly," Larry commented.

"Nor did I expect them to be," Billy said. "We'll definitely be viewed as enemies at the beginning."

"How do you propose to get to talk with their king?"

Billy didn't answer him. He turned on the external sound system and called to the men in their native language.

"We come in peace and mean you no harm. I'm Billy West and I request an audience with King Peterovan."

As they watched, they saw one of the soldiers talking to what looked like the officer in charge. When the soldier went running into the castle, the officer called to them.

"I don't know how you managed to get in here, but

you're not welcome here, and you must leave immediately. Failure to do so will lead to your immediate destruction."

"I can understand your concerns, but we must speak with King Peterovan on some urgent matters."

Instead of responding, they saw soldiers begin to take aim with several of the cannons they had in the courtyard.

"I don't think he was kidding," Larry said. "It looks like they're preparing to fire on us."

Again, Billy didn't say anything. He simply tapped the screen on the console to turn on the shuttle's defense shields. A few seconds later the soldiers fired their cannons at the shuttle.

When the cannonballs hit the shuttle's shields, they exploded in brilliant flashes of light. The explosions startled the men inside, but the shuttle didn't even shudder.

The soldiers kept firing for almost a full minute, but to no avail. Billy knew that they only respected power, so he told John, "Use the laser and take out a couple of those cannons. But be careful not to injure any of their men."

It only took a few seconds for the Petawatt laser to incinerate two of the largest cannons.

When the officer in charge saw them take out two of his cannons, he immediately ordered his men to cease firing. When the smoke had cleared, he walked up to the shuttle and said, "What manner of magic is this? Those were the most powerful cannons we have, and they had no effect." The officer added rather excitedly, "And what sort of a weapon was that?"

He looked a little perplexed and shaken when they didn't answer him, and he turned on his heel and entered the castle. Almost twenty minutes later, he returned with the king.

They knew in an instant that it was the king. You

could just tell by the way he carried himself. He was a little over seven feet tall and looked like he might weigh over four hundred pounds. His massive neck and shoulders flowed into the biggest set of arms they had ever seen.

If they had been trying to describe a Norse god, he would have fit the bill. Showing no hesitation at all, he strode up to the front of the shuttle and bellowed, "Who dares challenge King Peterovan?"

"We're not here to challenge you," Billy said. "We come in peace, and we seek your help."

"Hagar told me that you incinerated two of our cannons. How can you claim to come in peace?"

"Your officer made the mistake of firing on our ship. We come in peace, but we'll not allow anyone to attack us without a response."

"Well said, but how is it that I can hear you, but I can't see you? Come out here so that we can talk like men. I give you my word you won't be harmed."

"Thanks, we'll be right out."

"Alright, let's go out and see how this goes," Billy said. "John, why don't you stay here and keep an eye on them? If something goes wrong, you can use the laser. We're both wearing cameras and radios, and we'll leave them on so you can see and hear what's going on."

Billy lowered the stern cargo ramp and he and Larry walked out to meet the king.

Billy walked up to the king and said, "Greetings King Peterovan, I'm Billy West and this is Larry Sheldon. We come in peace, and we've come to ask for your help."

"Greetings Billy West, and where did you say you come from? I've never seen anyone who looks like you two, and I've certainly never seen anything like whatever that is you just got out of."

"We call it a shuttle-craft, and we're from a far distant land. If you can spare us a little time, I would like to try to explain why we're here."

"Excellent, this should be quite interesting. It's about time that we had a little excitement around here. Follow me and we'll have a drink and talk."

3

As they entered King Peterovan's castle, they were struck by how similar it looked to the European castles of the late fifteen-hundreds.

Their footsteps echoed down the hallway as they walked the rough-hewn stone floors, and they could smell the pungent wood fires that heated the castle.

The banners that hung from the thirty-foot-tall ceiling carried the crests of the kings that preceded King Peterovan's rule.

Unlike the monarchies of old on Earth, the kingdom didn't automatically go to the king's heir. When a king died, the kingdom would hold a two-month-long tournament to select his successor. The only benefit that the king's heir received was the automatic right to a spot in the final contest.

The final fight was always to the death, and it wasn't unusual for the king's heir to lose.

King Peterovan had been the first heir to win in seven generations. Luckily, his father had trained him to fight from the time he was old enough to hold a short sword. By the time his father died, King Peterovan was the fiercest warrior his people had ever known.

As they entered the castle's great hall, they felt like they had been transported back in time. The walls were covered with the shields of every king who had ever ruled the northern kingdom. Above each shield was a massive torch to illuminate it. The banners that hung from great hall's ceiling each represented a successful battle that had been fought by King Peterovan during his reign.

There was an eight-foot by forty-eight-foot wooden table that sat in the center of the room. It was flanked by a number of smaller tables, and in back of the tables, there was a large fireplace with a roaring fire.

The flames were almost seven feet high, and the heat coming from the fireplace was intense. The hearth stones in the front of the fireplace glowed dull red from the heat. The fire burned constantly, and was tended at all times by the slaves who were responsible for its care.

It was the most coveted position among the slaves. The slaves that watched over the fireplace got to sleep in the back of the room by the fireplace, however, the best part was that they got to eat whatever was left over from the previous night's feast.

The area where King Peterovan's castle was located was in a state of almost perpetual winter. The temperature rarely exceeded the freezing point, so life was hard for the general population. Much of their food, and all of their fresh fruits and vegetables, came from their trade with the southern hemisphere. They, in turn, provided the south with whale oil, coal, and crudely refined metals of all types.

King Peterovan walked to the head of the table, where his massive chair sat, and said, "Have a seat." He turned to the slaves and bellowed, "Bring food and drink, we have guests."

As the slaves scurried to bring the food and drink,

Billy and Larry sat down at the table. Behind them, the king's throne sat on a raised area of the room, making it the dominant feature of the room.

The throne, like the king, was massive, and quite impressive. As Billy looked around the room he noticed that there were guards stationed discreetly along the walls.

It was only a couple of minutes, but it seemed like forever, as they sat silently waiting for the food. As the slaves were scurrying to put the food on the table, the king bellowed, "Eat up. If you've traveled from afar, you must be hungry. You must tell me of the wondrous carriage that you arrived in. The captain of the guards said that it came out of the sky, and if that is so, you must be magicians or the devil's emissaries."

"We're not magicians or emissaries of the devil," Billy said. "What your captain saw was simply technology in action. We do have many things that may seem like magic to you, but I assure you it's not."

The king motioned for them to eat up, so they looked down at their plates to see what the slaves had brought them to eat. Billy and Larry quickly discovered they were big eaters, because there were boiled red-skinned potatoes, a slab of what looked like rare roast beef, and a whole chicken on their platters.

The only silverware they had been given was a knife. A large copper cup that was filled to the brim with a steaming beverage of some sort was placed beside each platter. Billy picked up the cup and took a small drink of the liquid. The spicy beverage burned Billy's throat, and it reminded him of a really alcoholic apple cider. He and Linda didn't normally drink alcoholic beverages, but he remembered John telling him that it would be absolutely required to try to fit into the cultures that they were going to encounter.

Billy wasn't concerned about having to drink the alcohol because his metabolism was capable of processing it at a much faster rate than a normal human. He knew that he could easily drink more than his fair share and not suffer any ill effects.

They ate and drank in relative quiet for the first twenty minutes, and then the king asked, "So, Billy West, tell me about your people. You seem awfully young to be the leader of your people."

"We're from a planet called Earth. We were forced to flee our planet before it was destroyed by an asteroid storm. We were attempting to upgrade our ship when we suffered a malfunction in its propulsion system, and now we are stranded in orbit around your world."

"What do you mean by, your planet was destroyed? What's a planet?"

"Let me see if I can explain."

Billy had brought several drawings of the solar system they were in, and he had thought to bring a drawing of Earth's solar system. He moved his plate aside and spread them out on the table.

He pointed to the king's planet and started to try to explain what he was talking about. "This is your planet, and this is your moon. This is your sun, and these are the other planets in your solar system."

Billy spent several hours trying to get the king to understand what he was trying to tell him, but he had little success. The only thing Billy had discovered was that they referred to their world as Midgard.

The king was definitely trying to understand, but by the time night had fallen, he had become increasingly frustrated with Billy.

Seeing the king's frustration, Larry caught Billy's attention and said, "If I might suggest, why don't we go outside so you can point out a couple of the objects you're trying to show the king?"

As they walked outside, Midgard's moon was just rising above the mountain's peak behind the castle. It was a full moon, and as the moonlight bathed the courtyard, the group stopped and Billy said, "The object you see over the mountain is the moon I was referring to. It's about two hundred thousand miles from Midgard.

"In the morning, your sun, Helios, I believe you call it, will rise, and it's ninety million miles from Midgard. There are three other planets in your solar system, but none of them is habitable. Two are too hot, and the other one is too cold to support life."

"How can you know these things?" King Peterovan asked, more than a little frustrated.

"I'm not sure that I can make you understand, but we have the ability to travel through the space that surrounds Midgard."

"I knew it, witchcraft, that's what it is. There's no other way you could know these things."

As Billy considered the king's reaction, he realized that he wasn't going to get through to him, at least not in one session. It wasn't that the king wasn't trying to understand, he simply couldn't grasp what Billy was trying to tell him.

So to keep from further frustrating him, he decided to change tactics.

"It's probably best that we continue this discussion at another time. If you can spare a few more minutes, I would like to get to the real purpose of our visit."

"I can, but I hope it will make more sense than what you've been talking about."

"I'm very sorry about that; however, I think that you'll find this to be a very straightforward proposition. We would like your permission to set up a small settlement and a temporary mining operation in your territory. We need to mine some of your raw materials so that we can repair our ship."

The king started to deny Billy's request out of hand, but he thought for a moment, and then he asked, "Where would this outpost be located?"

"The area we've selected is approximately eleven hundred miles to the north of the mountain behind us, and it doesn't appear to be inhabited," Billy said as he pointed to the mountain behind the castle.

"We call the mountain Jotunheimen, and I'm familiar with the area that you're talking about. It's part of my kingdom, but I'm afraid you haven't done your homework. We're used to the cold, but that area is much too cold even for us. I doubt that you and your people would last a week.

"Besides, why should I allow you to use any of my land?"

"I can understand your reluctance, but I believe we can make it worth your while. If I've understood the situation correctly, you currently have a trade agreement with Queen Amanirenas. I also know that this year's unusually severe winter hasn't allowed you to mine the necessary ore to meet your agreements. If you'll allow us to build a settlement in the location I mentioned, I'll guarantee that we'll deliver twice the refined metals you need to meet your agreements with the queen.

"Concerning the weather, I realize the climate in the area is less than ideal, but we'll be alright. Besides, what do you have to lose?"

The king was silent for a few seconds as he pondered Billy's offer. He knew he didn't have any other solutions to his trade problems, so he told Billy, "You have my permission, but I'm afraid you're going to regret settling there. I'll expect you to keep me updated on your actions while you are in my territory. When can I expect the metals that you've promised?"

"I promise to keep you updated. It's going to take us a few weeks to get started, but we should be able to begin the deliveries in about a hundred and fifty days."

They continued talking for another twenty minutes and then Billy said, "Now if you don't mind, we've had a long day, and we need to be getting back to our ship."

BILLY AND LARRY returned to their shuttle, and as they lifted off, the king watched in amazement. He pondered aloud, "Oh Lord, what have I done? Have I made a deal with the devil?"

Unlike the Norsemen they resembled, the king, and most of his people, believed in one god. Much of the rest of Midgard's population worshiped multiple gods.

Even though he was a religious man, King Peterovan was extremely superstitious, and he simply couldn't understand what was happening. There was no way that he could know the depth of the changes that his world was about to go through, but he sensed that something was about to happen, and as he returned to the castle, he thought to himself, "I've never been afraid of anything or anyone in my entire life, but I'm terrified of these people."

BEFORE THEY WENT back, Billy decided to take a closer look at where they were going to build their base. John was piloting the shuttle, and as they flew over Jotunheimen's peak, they once again encountered a blinding snowstorm that continued for hundreds of miles on the other side of the mountain.

As they approached the location of their proposed settlement, they found a break in the snowstorm. Unlike the rugged mountainous terrain where the king's castle was located, the countryside where they were going to build their base was as flat as a tabletop for over a thousand miles in all directions.

The full moon was reflecting off the snow, which made it very easy to see the landscape below. As they studied the terrain, all they could see was snow and ice.

"I see what the king meant," Larry said. "This is worse than Antarctica. I doubt that the temperature ever even reaches freezing."

"The current temperature is five degrees Fahrenheit," John said. "There's no way we can settle here."

"I know it's going to be hard, but the minerals we need are located directly below us," Billy replied. "Besides, this is the coldest part of the year. It'll get better in the spring."

As Larry studied the windblown wasteland below, he asked, "How thick is the ice down there?"

Billy turned on the ground-penetrating radar, and after a few seconds he said, "I don't believe it. It's over three hundred feet thick. I'll have to work out a different plan of attack, but minerals are definitely down there. I'll admit, it's going to be a bigger task than I had anticipated, but it's still doable."

"I'm glad you're so positive," Larry said. "I'm not even sure that we can survive down there."

Billy had them circle the location several more times, so he could do a complete assessment of the site.

"Ok, I've got everything I need. Let's get back to *Genesis* so I can get to work."

* * *

IT TOOK BILLY almost a week to finish updating his plans for their new settlement. When he was finished, he called Nicholas Stavros and his crews back together.

The room wasn't as full as before, because they had lost ten of their original team members when the reactors had overloaded.

He took a moment to lead them in a short prayer for their missing teammates, and then he started the briefing.

"Thanks for coming," Billy said. He turned on the holographic projector and picked up a laser pointer so he could point out the locations he was talking about.

"This is a representation of what the settlement will look like when it's finished. The mine shaft will be located right here, and it'll be protected by a magnetic containment field. The remainder of the compound will be protected by a twenty-five-foot-high electric fence.

"This is the blueprint for the building that will cover the mine shaft's elevator.

"We're going to have to dig down through three hundred feet of ice before we can even begin to tunnel. Once we're through the ice, we'll have to drill down about seven hundred and fifty feet deeper to reach the deepest deposits of the minerals we're going to need.

"Before you ask about the weather, I picked this location because almost all the minerals we need are available here."

"How many people do you think we're going to need to transfer to the surface?" Larry asked.

"Since the weather has turned out to be even worse than we had anticipated, we'll take as few as possible; however, if we're going to meet the schedule I promised

King Peterovan, we're going to need at least fifteen hundred workers."

Nicholas considered Billy's statements for a few seconds before he said, "We may need to transfer more people than that. We've had several more issues with our power distribution systems, and we're having a hard time keeping the life support systems working properly."

"You and I will need to spend some more time on that, but are there any other comments?"

"I do have one bit of good news," Nicholas said. "We've managed to salvage enough material from the two destroyed power centers to build an additional small reactor. That should give us enough power to expand the size of our settlement on the planet if we need to."

"If you can do that, why don't we just use the salvaged materials to build a new reactor for *Genesis*?" Larry asked.

"We could, but the reactor wouldn't be large enough to power our propulsion systems, and besides, we don't have enough superconducting material to repair the power conduits that were vaporized. Even if we could take care of all of that, we still wouldn't have enough fuel left to reach the rest of the fleet."

"Now that you've seen the plans, how long do you think it's going to take to get the settlement ready?" Billy asked.

"I think if we really work at it, we can have it ready to receive the first fifteen hundred people in twelve to fifteen weeks," Nicholas said.

"That's longer than I had wanted, but I guess it'll have to do. I think that wraps it up for now. We'll continue meeting at least once a week until we make the initial transfer. If any of you run into anything that we didn't account for, please give me a call."

* * *

THE NEXT DAY, they started work on the settlement. Nicholas managed to scrounge up enough parts to build an additional shuttle, but even with two shuttles to work with, it still took them several days to get enough people and materials moved to get started.

They spent the next twelve weeks building the main building. Meanwhile, they had successfully completed the first small fusion reactor that they needed to power the settlement.

As the king had tried to warn them, the area was one of the bleakest, most inhospitable to be found on the planet. Even worse, they had the bad luck to start construction during the winter months. The temperature rarely approached zero, and often was well below zero. Even on the days it wasn't snowing, the windblown snow caused almost constant whiteout conditions.

The teams working on the settlement had been outfitted with the best arctic survival gear they had; however, the brutal conditions had caused so many cases of frostbite that, before they had finished, they had to rotate almost half the original workers back to the ship for medical care.

When they had the first reactor online, they set up a magnetic field to protect the site where they were going to dig. The magnetic field was tuned to stop virtually anything, so it provided a measure of protection from the everpresent storms.

Once they were sure it was working, they started transferring the rest of the construction workers they needed. Far behind their original schedule, they worked day and night in order to transfer people as quickly as possible.

While Nicholas's crew was finishing up moving the

workers, Larry and Billy decided to make a visit to the new base.

"I don't mean to whine, but doesn't it ever stop snowing?" Larry asked.

"It should let up a little in about two months," Billy answered, "however, even in the middle of summer, it's not going to get much above freezing for more than an hour or so a day."

"I just wish we could have found a more hospitable location."

"I agree, but the mineral deposits that we need are here. How long do you think it'll be before we can begin work on the main mine shaft?"

"Nicholas's teams are finally starting to make progress, so I think we should be able to start in a couple of weeks."

After they had talked for a few more minutes, they decided to do a quick tour of the construction site. Even though they were dressed in arctic survival suits, the conditions were still just barely tolerable.

When they reached the edge of the magnetic shield, they were amazed at the sight of the snow flowing over the invisible force field.

"That's a really weird effect," Larry said.

"It is, but it sure makes you glad we managed to get the shield up. Even with the shield, these conditions are brutal." Billy turned to face Larry.

"Now that we have the bulk of the construction teams in place, Linda and I are going to relocate to the surface. I want you to stay on board *Genesis* and make sure everything stays under control."

"No problem, I can do that. When do you think we can start moving the rest of our people to the surface?"

"Now that we've experienced the conditions down here,

I've changed my mind. We're only going to move the fifteen hundred we need to operate the base. It makes no sense to subject the rest of them to these conditions."

A FEW WEEKS later, they completed the first phase of their base construction, and they were ready to start the mining operation.

The massive building that would house the mine shaft only contained three sections, and Billy and Nicholas moved to the center of the largest one to kick off their mining operation. They were standing on the twenty-foot-high platform that they had built to hold the Petawatt laser they were going to use to drill the vertical shaft for the mine.

In order to protect it from the hot gases it would produce while drilling, they had encased the laser in a magnetic containment field. At Billy's command, Nicholas fired the laser to begin drilling the tunnel through the ice.

The immense heat of the Petawatt laser easily cut through the ice and, as it did, superheated steam was being violently vented from the shaft. The same magnetic containment field that protected the laser also served as an exhaust tube for the superheated gases. The tube extended up through a hole in the roof of the building and then out through the base's main magnetic shield.

The steam was being vented at a tremendous rate and, within minutes, it had already reached an altitude of over twenty thousand feet.

From the outside, it looked somewhat like a volcanic eruption. The laser's normally distinctive hum was being overwhelmed by the roar of the steam, which made it very difficult for the work crew to hear one another.

"What do you suppose the temperature of that steam is?" Nicholas yelled.

Billy glanced at the control monitor and yelled back, "I show it to be a little over nine hundred degrees Fahrenheit."

"It's a good thing that you thought of the magnetic tube to handle the exhaust. Otherwise we would have been cooked alive."

Even though the ice was three hundred feet thick, it only took a few minutes to reach the ground beneath the ice.

When the laser reached the ground below, the material being vented changed to a bright red as the melted rock and dirt were being ejected. Their progress slowed, but it only took them another ninety-five minutes to penetrate the seven hundred and fifty feet that they needed for the vertical mine shaft.

WHILE THE WORK crews had been busy erecting the buildings, Billy and Nicholas had been working on the tools that they needed for the actual mining phase. Using the Petawatt laser to drill the initial shaft had gotten them off to a quick start, but they couldn't use it in the actual mining operation.

After they had considered their options, they built several sled-mounted magnetic projectors. The projectors could be pulsed at several hundred pulses a second, and they would be used to crush the rock so it could be removed and processed.

After the shaft had time to cool, Nicholas sent a group of men down into the shaft to begin the mining operation. Unlike most miners, they didn't have to use an elevator, because, much like the shuttles, the magnetic sleds could simply raise and lower the workers inside the shaft.

Their first tasks were to use the sleds to carve out the different chambers that they would need. The minerals were located at various depths, so they needed several chambers at various levels.

THE NEXT DAY, Larry returned to the *Genesis,* and John stayed on the surface to work with Billy and Linda.

"What's next?" John asked.

"I've asked Larry to come back tomorrow so that he and I can try to contact Queen Amanirenas," Billy said.

"Why? I thought that you had already made a deal with King Peterovan."

"I did, but I want to learn more about the queen and her people. It's always a good idea to get to know as much about a potential adversary as possible. Besides, I don't imagine she's going to be very pleased when she learns that we're helping out King Peterovan."

"Why should she care if you help him out? She'll still get the metals that the king promised her."

"While she does value the metals they're receiving, she knows that it's not going to be that much longer until the north has to throw in the towel and surrender to her.

"The northern hemisphere's climate has been cooling for many generations, and it's not going to be that much longer until it's completely uninhabitable. Even now, they're almost totally dependent on the south for their food supply."

They had found that while King Peterovan's kingdom was very similar to the Norsemen of ancient Earth, Queen Amanirenas's was just as similar to Earth's ancient Nubian culture.

As Billy had thought about it, he realized how eerily similar the two planets were turning out to be. Very few people on Earth had known that Homo sapiens had actually migrated from ancient Africa to all the other continents of Earth. It had been much the same on Midgard; however, neither King Peterovan's people, nor Queen Amanirenas's, would have ever acknowledged a common ancestry. It was true nonetheless.

They may have had a common ancestry, but their cultures had definitely diverged over the centuries. Unlike King Peterovan's people, the Nubians placed great value on continuity. Queen Amanirenas's family had been the ruling family for all of Nubian recorded history.

The queen wasn't imposing in the same ways as King Peterovan; however, at six foot three and weighing two hundred and thirty pounds, she was an impressive figure.

A fierce warrior in her own right, she was highly skilled in all forms of weapons and was a master of Nubian hand-to-hand combat techniques, but she was much more than just a warrior. She was also a brilliant tactician, and when her battle armor wasn't hiding her flawless ebony skin, voluptuous figure, and long black hair, she was a strikingly beautiful woman.

She was a highly effective ruler, but she was known to be a brutal adversary and wouldn't put up with any form of dissent.

Their society was well developed in comparison to King Peterovan's people, but, unlike the people of the north, they worshiped many gods. Various high priestesses held sway over the day-to-day lives of all the Nubian people, including Queen Amanirenas. She wouldn't make a move until she had consulted with the high priestess of the temple of Isis.

Unlike King Peterovan's people, the Nubians also had a good grasp of mathematics, astronomy, and chemistry. With that in mind, Billy felt sure that they would more easily understand what he was going to try to share with them.

4

"I THINK YOU should let me come along," John said.

"Not this time. I can't afford to risk both of you," Billy replied. "If something goes wrong, you'll be needed to carry on."

As their shuttle-craft was climbing away from the base, Billy marveled at how remote their outpost really was. Inside their protective shields, they could almost forget about the seemingly endless snowstorms.

They had only reached an altitude of fifteen hundred feet when the outpost disappeared into the blizzard that was beginning to sweep over the area.

The northern and southern continents were separated by four thousand miles of ocean, and an hour into their flight, the weather turned much warmer.

As they neared the coastline, they started seeing the fleets of fishing vessels that provided much of the food and trade goods for Queen Amanirenas's kingdom.

When they reached the coast, the terrain soon changed to the lush croplands and forests of date trees that lined the mighty river Norel. They turned and followed the river inland.

The queen's palace was located right on the river, about two hundred miles upstream. As the city came into view, they noticed the buildings on the east side.

"Are those pyramids?" Larry asked.

"Yes, they are, and they serve multiple purposes. The ones to the right are the burial sites for their previous kings and queens. The one that we're going to be visiting is the largest one, in the center of the city."

The pyramid sat in the exact center of the city and served as Queen Amanirenas's palace. It had taken almost ten years to construct, and it rose to a height of five hundred and three feet. There were only four entrances to the queen's palace, one on each side. The entrances were twenty-five feet above the ground, and could only be reached by the ramps that led up to them.

There were a hundred handpicked palace guards stationed at each entrance. To even be considered for membership in the palace guard, a soldier had to have had at least ten years of experience and have passed the most rigorous testing imaginable. The final test consisted of a battle to the death against four armed attackers. If the soldier survived, he was inducted into the elite palace guards.

"How do you think they're going to receive us?" Larry asked.

"Not very well, I'm afraid. They aren't used to having strangers visit them. They place great value on precious metals, so I'm going to try to impress them a little.

"I know that the queen is a devout worshiper of the goddess Isis, and that gold and scorpions have a special meaning in their beliefs, so I've brought a couple of solid gold scorpions to present as gifts."

When Larry landed the shuttle about fifty yards from one of the ramps, the guards couldn't believe their eyes. They had never seen anything like the shuttle, and they believed anyone who could fly must be one of the gods. Every one of one of them immediately knelt on one knee and lowered their heads in deference. They were all fearless warriors, but this was definitely not something they were prepared for.

When Billy and Larry saw what was taking place, they gathered their gifts for the queen and left the shuttle. As they emerged from the back of the shuttle, the captain of the guards stole a glance at them from the corner of his eye.

Billy had spent quite a bit of time considering how they should dress for their first meeting with the queen. At first he considered dressing like Nubian nobility, then he had considered emulating Nubian battle dress, but in the end, he decided to go with a copy of an ancient Roman centurion's battle dress. He wanted something that gave the impression of power, but he didn't want to make them think he was disrespecting them.

"I'm Billy West of Earth, and I request an immediate audience with Queen Amanirenas," he bellowed to the soldiers.

Still frozen in terror of what they believed to be gods, not one of the soldiers moved.

"Captain of the guards, stand and answer me."

The captain snapped to his feet. "The queen does not grant an audience to strangers."

"Take these things to her, and then return with her answer."

Billy walked over to the captain and handed him their gifts, a parchment with their introductions, and a brief explanation of why they were there.

Still without looking Billy in the eye, the captain took everything and ran up the ramp into the pyramid. Even then, none of the guards moved, and they remained still as they waited for the captain to return. Had Billy and Larry attempted to enter the pyramid, they would have immediately attacked, but since they hadn't made a move to enter, the guards remained in place.

Several minutes later, the captain returned and said, "If you'll follow me, the queen will see you."

The captain motioned to twenty of his best soldiers, and they quickly moved to surround Billy and Larry. He turned and started back up the ramp, and they followed him into the pyramid.

Unlike the weapons Billy and Larry had carried to visit King Peterovan, their weapons today wouldn't convert into anything else.

"I wish you had let me bring some better weapons," Larry whispered. "I feel completely naked with nothing but a sword and a dagger."

"Look around. Even if we had come fully armed, we wouldn't stand a chance if they decided to kill us."

When Larry glanced upward, he saw that there were at least fifty archers poised on the level above them. They hadn't made a sound as they had appeared, but their bows were all fully drawn, and they were ready to fire on a command from the captain.

Even though it was ninety-five degrees outside, as soon as they entered the opening, the temperature quickly moderated to seventy-five degrees.

The hallway's walls were covered with ornate murals depicting several of the gods the Nubians worshiped. Billy and Larry had gone almost a hundred feet, when the hallway opened into a large room.

There were over three hundred people in the room, not counting guards, and they were all dressed like royalty. There were tables with all sorts of food, and several servants were walking around with large pitchers of wine. Many of the people were resting on chaise lounges, and the sounds of multiple conversations filled the air.

A hush fell over the entire room when the crowd noticed their presence.

Except for a few of the soldiers in the room, most of Nubians had never seen a white man other than in paintings of their battles against King Peterovan's people.

Billy marveled at how similar the two races of people were, aside from the color of their skin. Like King Peterovan's people, the Nubians were large in stature by Earth standards, and they all looked to be in excellent shape.

The captain of the guards left them standing outside a large double door, and as they waited to see Queen Amanirenas, they could almost feel the stares.

Even if they hadn't been so different from everyone else in the room, Billy and Larry would have stood out due to their regal appearance. Their Roman battle dress was quite impressive, if not quite authentic. Normally, it would have been silver, but Billy knew that gold held a special place in Nubian culture, so their armor was a gold-colored alloy. Nicholas's group had developed this special alloy, which was twice as strong as original Roman armor, so they could have maximum protection if the need arose.

It seemed like forever, but it had only been a minute or so before the captain returned for them.

"If you'll follow me, the queen will see you now," the captain of the guards said.

The queen was seated on an ornate golden throne, and when she saw them enter, she motioned for them to approach her. When they were about fifteen feet away, they stopped and Billy said, "Thank you for granting us an audience."

"I have to admit I was intrigued by your note. I don't know how you managed to do it, but you must have done some research on our culture, because the gifts were perfect.

"But, that's not why I agreed to see you. Normally, I would have just had you killed, but it's not every day that someone arrives from the sky. So tell me, are you truly gods, or are you men?"

"We're men, and we're from a far distant place. If you'll allow me a few minutes, I'll try to explain who we are and why we are here."

He spent the next thirty minutes recounting their adventures to that point. He told her of their need to repair their ship, and how King Peterovan had allowed them to settle in the northern section of his kingdom. As soon as he had told her about their settlement, he noticed that she had gone quiet.

Since the meteor swarm wasn't an immediate problem, Billy hadn't intended to mention it. But he decided to tell her about it, to see if he could regain her attention. When he finished, he paused to gauge her reaction.

He was about to continue when she stopped him to ask, "Why did King Peterovan allow you to settle in his territory? He's not known for his benevolence, so there had to be something in it for him."

"You're right, there was. I've agreed to help him meet his commitments to you."

There were several seconds of silence before the queen screamed, "Why would you do that?" She didn't even give him a chance to respond before she continued her tirade. "I've got to tell you that I don't like you helping him out."

"I can understand your concerns, but, as I explained, his land contains the materials that we need to repair our ship."

"I don't doubt what you're saying, but it doesn't matter. You've taken quite a risk by coming here. All of my instincts tell me to have you executed and be done with it. Why should I allow you to continue aiding my enemy?"

"It was never our intention to help him against you, but we must repair our ship."

The queen paused for a moment while she considered what she was going to do, and then she told him, "That may be true, but I'm afraid you've miscalculated. I'm not going to stand by and let you destroy my plans for reuniting Midgard's people. You'll both be executed at first light tomorrow."

Momentarily stunned by the queen's pronouncement, Billy thought back to the research he had done on their customs and laws. "If I understand your laws correctly it's my right to challenge for the right of safe passage."

"I don't know how you could know that, but that's correct. Do you intend to issue a challenge?"

"I do."

"Since you know of the right of a challenge, you must also know that as the spokesperson, you have to be the one to issue the challenge. You're much too young to hold such a position in our culture, but since you seem to be the one in command, I'll accept your challenge if you issue it."

Larry's blood had run cold at the queen's pronouncements, and he knew in an instant what would happen next. He had trained most of his life for situations like this.

He knew Billy had at least some basic skills in several of the martial arts, and even fencing; however, Larry knew he'd never had to use whatever skills he had in real life. He had seen Billy do many truly unbelievable things, but he didn't want him to attempt this.

After he gathered his thoughts, Larry said, "Queen Amanirenas, it's my duty to stand for Billy West."

"It may be your duty, but it's not allowed. Our laws dictate that it must be the leader who fulfills the challenge."

"Then I issue the challenge," Billy said.

"I accept your challenge. Captain Gelloris will be my representative. The fight will be to the death, as our customs demand, and if you lose, your man dies as well. The contest will be held in the city arena in one hour. As the challenger you have your choice of weapons."

Without hesitation, Billy said, "I choose swords."

"Very well, but you may want to use one of ours; that puny thing you're carrying will be no match for one of our broadswords."

The broadswords the Nubians carried were massive weapons and weighed almost ten pounds. Billy's sword was fashioned after the last generation of Roman short swords. It may not have been as impressive as a Nubian sword but Nicholas had crafted it from a new alloy that he had developed. The alloy was about half the weight of weapon-grade steel and virtually indestructible.

"Thank you, but if you don't mind I will use the one I'm carrying."

"As you will."

The guards escorted them down the street to the arena. By the time they reached it, it was already packed to capacity. Word of the challenge had spread like wildfire and everyone wanted to see the visitors before they were killed.

Captain Gelloris was a renowned fighter, and he'd never even been seriously challenged in over one hundred combats. It didn't matter whether he was in the arena or simply in combat, he was a merciless killer.

The queen had often thought that he might make a suitable mate, when she was ready. She didn't believe he could defeat her in combat, but even so, he was a formidable man. As she prepared to address the arena, she thought to herself, "There's no need in putting this off any longer. After Gelloris finishes killing the intruder, I'm going to announce that I've decided to take him as my mate."

The captain of the guards led them onto the floor of the arena. He pointed to Billy and said, "You can wait here until they're ready for you. The combat will stop every three minutes so that you can rest."

He turned to Larry. "You may cleanse his wounds and give him water, but you're not allowed to do anything else. If you attempt to interfere in any way, the archers on the railings will immediately kill you. Do either of you have any questions?"

"Do I have to kill Captain Gelloris, or may he yield?"

"I can't believe you had to ask, but yes, you have to kill him. Trust me, he'll not ask you to yield. I probably shouldn't share this with you, but his fights rarely last past the first period."

The captain left Billy and Larry standing beside the bench that had been set up for them on the arena's floor.

The amphitheater was buzzing with excited conversations as the people sat waiting for the fight to begin. Everywhere they looked, there were bookies taking people's money.

They weren't betting on who would win, they were betting on how long the stranger would last. None of the bookies had even bothered to offer odds on the possibility of Billy winning the fight.

"He's a big man," Larry said. "And the sword he's carrying is massive, so you've got to be prepared for the blow. His size may actually give you a bit of a chance. You should be quicker than he is, but I just wish we had thought to teach you at least some basic hand-to-hand combat."

"Don't beat yourself up about it. When I decided to come here, I did some research. I've studied everything I could find on sword fighting and hand-to-hand combat techniques."

"Reading a book doesn't count for training."

"Maybe not, but it's all I've got, and believe it or not, I do pretty well at learning from a book."

Billy's immense intelligence and the unique way his brain processed information allowed him to not only memorize what he read, it allowed his mind to train his senses and reflexes to use the information. In a matter of hours, it was as if he had been practicing for decades.

The queen entered, took her seat overlooking the arena floor, and addressed the overcrowded amphitheater: "I've condemned Billy West and Larry Sheldon to death for trespassing on our lands. However, in the tradition of our people I've accepted the challenge for safe passage from Billy West. If he's successful, they'll be free to leave our lands. Otherwise they'll both die. As custom dictates, I've chosen Captain Gelloris to represent me."

She had to pause for a moment as the roar from the crowd filled the amphitheater. As the roar started to diminish, she gestured to the amphitheater floor and said, "You may begin when you're ready."

When Billy and Larry had put together their weapons and armor for the trip, they hadn't thought to include shields. Seeing that he didn't have one, the captain of the guards handed Billy his shield. Then he motioned for him to begin.

Billy took a deep breath and put on his helmet. He took a quick look around the amphitheater, drew his sword, and moved to meet Captain Gelloris in the center of the arena.

When they met in the center, Captain Gelloris saluted

Billy with his sword and said, "It's a shame for one so young to die, but die you will for challenging my queen."

Gelloris turned and saluted the queen, and then he turned back to Billy and said, "Prepare to die."

Gelloris moved fast for a large man, and before Billy was really ready, he made a vicious overhead strike with his massive sword.

Billy managed to block the blow with his shield, but the force of the strike drove him to one knee. The crowd immediately sensed a speedy end, and they stood and let out a roar of approval. Billy quickly regained his feet and spun away before Gelloris could strike again.

They traded several blows back and forth, but they both managed to block the blows with their shields. As the fight progressed, Billy came to the conclusion that Gelloris was much too strong to defeat with a normal attack.

Changing tactics, he started to circle him, and as he did, Gelloris turned to follow him.

Billy moved at lightning speed as he seemed to leap forward to strike a blow. Gelloris parried it and tried to swat him with his shield.

Seeing an opening, Billy used his martial art skill to slip under the blow and deliver a karate kick to his knee. The blow severely injured Gelloris, limiting his ability to move.

Gelloris limped after him as they continued to thrust and parry at each other. After what seemed like hours, the trumpet sounded to end the first period.

Glad for the break in the action, Billy returned to where Larry was standing. "Wow, he almost got me with the first blow. I know you warned me, but that was way more than I expected. I can't believe how strong he is."

"Where in the world did you learn those moves you're using?"

"They're a combination of karate, fencing, and kung fu. Tell me, do you really think that I have to kill him? I'm not sure that I can bring myself to do it."

"I know it's not in your nature, but yes, you have to kill him. It's not like you have a choice. The queen was quite specific in her instructions. The fight is to the death, and there can be no other ending. I'm sorry that you're in this situation, but we knew we were taking a risk when we came."

"I'm just sorry that I got you into all of this."

"No apology needed, I'm used to putting my life and the lives of others at risk. If we survive, you'll find that killing becomes easier as you go."

The horn sounded, and Billy moved back to the center of the arena. Gelloris again saluted the queen, and then Billy. This time, however, he didn't bother threatening him. He simply slapped his sword against his shield and moved to the attack.

Much like the first time, they went back and forth at each other for the first couple of minutes. Several times Gelloris used his brute strength to make Billy hastily retreat.

Just before the horn sounded to end the round, Gelloris managed to slam his shield against the side of Billy's head. The vicious blow sent his helmet flying across the arena.

When the blow landed the crowd let out a roar, and they all jumped to their feet in anticipation of a kill.

Billy was bleeding profusely, but he managed to scramble out of the way of Gelloris's next blow.

Groggy from the blow, all Billy could do for the rest of the round was keep moving and try to stay alive. By the time the horn blew, the entire front of Billy's uniform was covered in blood.

He staggered back over to Larry and collapsed on the bench.

"Sit up so I can take a look at your head," Larry said, clearly worried that he was about done. Billy managed to sit up, and as Larry started to wipe the blood off his face, he was amazed to find there weren't any open wounds.

"I don't understand. You were bleeding like a stuck pig."

"As I've told you before, I'm a quick healer. If you'll wipe the rest of the blood out of my eyes, I'll be fine."

It seemed like he had only just sat down when the horn sounded to start the next round. Billy had expected the same posturing as before, but Gelloris immediately moved to attack him with a vicious overhead strike.

The blow caught Billy out of position, and he had to block it with his sword instead of his shield. The force of the blow made his whole arm go numb, and he dropped his sword.

He immediately spun away from Gelloris, but Gelloris followed him as quickly as his injured knee would allow. With nothing but his dagger left as a weapon, the crowd again roared as they waited for the death blow to fall.

Billy drew his dagger and started to move around Gelloris while he was looking for a way to retrieve his sword. When he saw what Billy was trying to do, Gelloris moved back to the sword, put his foot on it, and waved at Billy to come and get it.

"Come to me, little man, and we'll end it now. I'll make it quick so you don't suffer. If you make me chase you, I promise that I'll make you suffer terribly before I kill you."

Seeing that Billy was in deep trouble, Larry took a single step toward them, and as he did, half a dozen arrows stuck in the ground in front of him. He froze in place, resigned to the fact his young friend was about to die. As he watched the fight move toward its inevitable conclusion, he thought to himself, what a shame it is for Billy to die for no real reason.

He had seen men killed in combat many times before, but this time it broke his heart to know that he was helpless to prevent it. He would have gladly traded places if he could have, but he knew that wasn't going to be an option.

Suddenly, Billy increased the pace of his movements. As Billy circled him, Gelloris wasn't quick enough to strike a blow at him, and as the fight continued Gelloris grew more and more frustrated. Finally, in an attempt to finish it, Gelloris lashed out to try to cut the legs out from under Billy.

It was just the opening that Billy had been looking for. He executed a flip over Gelloris's sword, and as he came down, he drove his dagger directly under Gelloris's chin, killing him instantly.

Billy spun away, not quite sure that he had taken care of him. Gelloris seemed to freeze in place for a couple of seconds, until he fell backward with a thud. His foot twitched a time or two, and then he didn't move again.

When they saw the queen's champion fall, the crowd let out a collective gasp, and then it was deathly quiet. No one said a word for almost twenty seconds until the queen rose from her seat and said with a quiet fury, "It's done. You're free to go; however, if I ever see you again, I'll personally cut your heads off. Be warned that I'll find a way to punish you and your people for this."

She took one last look at Gelloris lying dead in the sand, and then she turned and left the amphitheater.

The captain of the guards hurried over to them and

said, "I've never seen her that mad. You'd better follow me before the queen changes her mind and kills you anyway."

Then the captain looked at Billy in the eye and said, "I never thought anyone could defeat Gelloris, but I sure won't miss him. He killed my dad and my older brother."

The captain quickly herded them back to the shuttle, and they wasted no time taking off.

"I've got to tell you that I'm more than a little impressed," Larry said. "I know that was hard for you, but I've never seen anyone move like that."

"I can't believe I had to kill him. I just wish there had been another way."

"We've talked about this. This planet is not too dissimilar to ours, and it wasn't unusual to have to kill on Earth."

"I know, and I've had to kill before, just not that personally. I guess that takes care of trying to interact with Queen Amanirenas and her people. I can see now what King Peterovan meant when he said that it was impossible to make a real peace with them."

EVEN AS THEY were making their way back to their base, Queen Amanirenas was already plotting to destroy them.

"Gather your best scouts and send them to find out where their base is," Queen Amanirenas said. "Billy West said it was north of King Peterovan's castle, so start there. I promise you, we're going to eradicate them."

Still seething, she turned back to General Abrahams and said, "General, I want you to start preparing an army. As soon as we find out where they are, I want you take the army and kill them all. If King Peterovan tries to interfere, kill him as well."

"But we still have a truce and a trade agreement with them."

He had just gotten the words out of his mouth, when the queen struck him with a savage blow, knocking him sideways into the wall.

"Don't ever again question what I do."

"I'm sorry My Queen," General Abrahams quickly said, as he was picking himself up off the floor. "It won't happen again."

5

AFTER BILLY HAD spent several minutes telling Linda about their adventures, she interrupted to say, "I can't believe you weren't killed."

She shuddered as she pulled him to her and gave him a hug and a kiss.

"I was extremely lucky. Larry and John were right when they told me that no matter what you read, or how much you train, it's different from the real thing. I can't even explain what I felt when I had to walk out into the arena to meet the queen's champion."

"I'm just glad I wasn't there to see it. I would've been scared to death for you."

"Believe me, I was scared enough for both of us."

Not satisfied with just hearing about what had happened, she hugged him again and reached out to his mind with hers. As their minds joined, she could see and feel everything that he had experienced. It seemed like forever, but it only took a couple of minutes for her to experience everything he'd gone through, including his visit to see King Peterovan.

She shuddered as she realized how close to death he had come. Even though she was already hugging him, and their minds were fully bonded, she tried to get even closer.

After several seconds, she managed to gather her thoughts enough to tell him, "That was just awful, and I'm sorry you had to kill him, but you didn't have any choice; however, I understand now why you took the risk. I didn't realize the north was that heavily dependent on the south. Nevertheless, you've done everything you could to reach out to them, and you've verified there's no chance of an accord with Queen Amanirenas.

"Now that I've seen how your meeting with King Peterovan went, I'm worried that we're not even going to get to stay here. He didn't seem that keen on having us here."

"He's not, but I think I can win him over. Even though he may have considered it, he didn't immediately try to kill us. I've got to find a way to convince him that his people are in danger and that he needs to let us help him prepare for what's coming."

"It's times like these that make me feel like we're in the middle of a never-ending bad dream and that God must have it in for us."

"I know you don't mean that. We may have had some hard times, but you know as well as I do that God has taken a special interest in us.

"I just hope we can do whatever tasks He has in mind for us. I sure didn't do very well the last time. Most of Earth's population perished, and what's left of the human race is pretty much doomed to travel through space until they all die."

"I know you're right about God, it's just hard to remember it sometimes. But speaking of the tasks He's given us so far, you shouldn't be so hard on yourself. To hear Larry and John tell it, none of us would have survived if it hadn't been for you. So get over feeling sorry for yourself, and tell me how you intend to win over the king."

"I'm still working on it, but we may be making progress. He's throwing a feast in our honor. John said the king was ecstatic when he delivered the first shipment of the refined metals on schedule.

"Once again, Nicholas has come through for us. We're far behind schedule, and it's going to be weeks before we can finish setting up our final processing facility, but he knew how important the first shipment was, so he manually refined enough ore to deliver the king's first shipment of the gold and the silver."

THEY'D ALREADY MADE several trips to the king's castle, and on every trip, the townspeople would throw rocks and shoot arrows at the shuttle.

At first Billy thought that once the people had gotten used to the Earthlings, they would stop attacking them. Instead, the attacks seemed to be growing more violent.

There were multiple reasons why there was so much unrest, and not all of them had anything to do with their presence. The people's anger toward them was being fueled by the rumor that the king had made a pact with the devil and they were all doomed.

The biggest problem, however, had existed before they arrived: The entire kingdom was suffering from a lack of food, and the people were growing desperate.

King Peterovan was a great warrior, but he and his advisors were completely out of touch with what was going on in the kingdom. The sad reality was that if he didn't figure out how to solve his people's plight, his kingdom was doomed.

* * *

THE NIGHT BEFORE the king's feast in their honor, Billy discovered that Midgard was about to come in very close proximity to the massive meteor.

Initially, he had thought they had at least two more passes before it would be any sort of an issue; however, as he had continued to follow its progress, he saw that it would miss this time, but that the next time there would be a very high probability it would strike the planet.

When he ran the damage estimates he saw that if it made a direct hit it would cause catastrophic damage, but even if it hit with a glancing blow, the planet would still suffer tremendous damage.

The growing certainty of the impending disaster made him even more determined to get the king to let them help him prepare for it.

Just before they left for the feast, Billy programmed the *Genesis*'s computers to give them continuous updates on the meteor's progress. He wanted to make sure the king would get a good look at it as it passed by. He thought if the king saw how big it was it might convince him that he was telling the truth.

He verified he was receiving the updates, and went to find Linda.

"I want you to come with me to King Peterovan's feast," Billy said.

"I'll be happy to come along, but I thought it wasn't appropriate for me to be there."

"The king has asked that we bring our best healer with us. His only son is extremely sick, and I would like for you to take a look at him."

"No problem, I'll get my stuff."

They were accompanied by Nicholas Stavros and John Tyler. As John was bringing their shuttle in over the city, the peasants were throwing rocks and shooting arrows at them. As they neared the king's castle, there were even a few gunshots.

"It looks like some of the king's own men aren't too pleased that we're here," John said. "The only people who have guns are his men."

"They definitely don't care for us, but the really sad part is that it's not because of anything we've done," Billy said.

"At least the skies are going to be clear tonight. That should give us a great view of the meteor, and it's going to be quite impressive. Maybe seeing it will convince the king of the impending danger."

"You don't believe Midgard is going to suffer the same fate as the Earth, do you?"

"No, not to the same extent, but it's going to be pretty bad. It'll be a lot worse for King Peterovan's people, because they don't have any real reserves of food, fuel, or much of anything else. The Nubians are in much better shape to be able to survive.

"King Peterovan's people are impoverished as it is, and I'm afraid that, even if the meteor doesn't hit Midgard, they're going to eventually revolt against his rule."

THE SHUTTLE HAD just landed when the captain of the guards came rushing out to meet them. Unlike the first time they had come, he was relatively friendly.

"Welcome back," the captain said. He approached Billy and whispered, "The king has asked that I bring you to him immediately. He's with his son, and the boy isn't doing very well."

As they made their way through the castle's halls, Linda remarked, "It's amazing. This must be what the castles on Earth looked like in medieval times."

"I told you it was impressive. I haven't ever been in the upper levels of the castle, so I don't know what they're like."

When they reached the stairs that led to the king's quarters, the captain of the guards stopped and said, "I'll leave you here. Just follow the stairs to the top level. The staircase doesn't open to any of the other floors, so you can't get lost."

"You're not going to accompany us?" Billy asked.

"I've never been any farther than this. The king has a group of fifty men that provide protection for him and his family. It's every soldier's dream to be selected as one of his bodyguards. I'll be here when you return, and we'll make sure that the rest of your group has anything they need."

THE SPIRAL STAIRCASE was very steep and fairly narrow. They had been climbing for almost five minutes when Linda asked, "Do you have any idea how much further it is? It seems like we've been climbing forever."

"We've still got several more floors to go. The castle is a little over five hundred feet tall, or roughly equivalent to a fifty-story building. It's amazing that they could build all of this with no technology to speak of."

It took them almost fifteen minutes to reach King Peterovan's quarters. When they turned the last corner, they were met by two huge guards in full battle gear.

"Welcome, the king is waiting for you. Please follow me."

The guards led them to a massive door and pushed it open for them to enter. The king was sitting on his son's bed, watching the nurse bathe his forehead with a cloth.

Linda walked over to the boy's bed and said, "If you don't mind, I would like to examine your son."

"You must be Billy's wife, Linda," King Peterovan said.

She was already busy looking at the boy, so it took her a few seconds to respond. "Sorry. Yes, I'm Billy's wife. How long has your son been sick?"

"A little over two days ago he started complaining that his head hurt, and then he started running a fever."

"Has he been around any sick people?"

"Not that I'm aware of, but he was bitten by a bat a few days ago, while we were touring the lower levels of the castle. I had forgotten all about it until you asked. I don't know whether this means anything, but we've found hundreds of dead bats since then."

Linda's heart skipped a beat as she realized what it probably was. Even with their advanced medical knowledge, rabies was almost impossible to treat once the patient had symptoms.

She had brought her medical kit with her, so she spent the next fifteen minutes examining the boy. When she finished, she turned to the king and said, "I've got to get him to our ship right away. I'm almost sure he has a disease called rabies. If I don't get started treating him immediately, he's going to die."

"Thank you for looking after him."

"I'll do what I can, but I don't want to give you any false hopes. Even with me treating him, he's probably going to die anyway. Rabies is almost always fatal when the symptoms have developed."

The king paused as her words sank in. "I understand, but please do what you can. I lost his mother when he was born, and he's all that I have."

Linda turned to Billy. "I'm going to take the shuttle and leave right away. I'll send it back for you."

"Are you going back to the base, or to *Genesis*?"

"I'm going straight to *Genesis*. I don't have everything that I need on the base. I'm going to have to try something fairly radical if I want to have any chance of saving the boy's life."

The king walked over to the guard. "I want you to accompany her, and make sure that nothing gets in the way of what she wants to do."

"As you will, sire."

The guard gathered the boy up in his arms and he and Linda rushed out of the room and back down the winding staircase.

When the shuttle took off, the guard almost had a heart attack. He wasn't used to feeling fear, and he had done his best to hide it from Linda.

When she saw that the hulking guard was having a hard time handling the experience, she put her hand on his shoulder and said in her most soothing voice, "You can relax, there's nothing to fear. I know this isn't something that you've ever experienced, but I assure you that there's no danger."

As the shuttle climbed through Midgard's atmosphere and into space, he had become even more concerned. As he sat fidgeting in his chair, the *Genesis* came into view.

As they approached the enormous landing bay, he started babbling excitedly. "This has got to be the work of the devil. It's so huge, and it's just hanging there. What's holding it up, and are you sure we aren't going to fall?"

"Trust me, we're not going to fall. When we've stopped, bring the boy and follow me. We don't have any time to waste."

Linda knew that if the boy's life was going to be saved,

she would have to work quickly. She had called ahead to have William Robbins and a medical team meet her in the hospital.

"Are you sure that the boy has rabies?" William asked.

"All the symptoms point to it. I know you're going to tell me that I'm wasting my time, but it's imperative that we try. This is the king's only son, and it would go a long way toward winning him over to our side if we could save him."

"You know I would never tell you not to try. But you know as well as I do, that there have only been a few people who have ever survived once they exhibited symptoms, and that most of them had severe brain damage.

"But that's enough talk. Do you already have a course of treatment in mind?"

"I'm going to combine a couple of treatments with Dr. Willoughby's treatment protocol. First, I'm going to place him in a coma and lower his temperature as much as possible.

"Then I'm going to use a dose of the rabies immune globulin, and the normal P.E.P protocol. I think that with the combination of treatments he might have a chance.

"Can you think of anything else that we might want to try?"

"I know you know Dr. Willoughby's treatment has never been successfully duplicated. So what makes you think it'll work on the boy?"

"I've studied his notes and the paper he did afterward, and his point was that no one had followed his exact course of treatment. Besides, we've got much better technology for lowering the body temperature and inducing a coma than he did.

"Look, I know it's a long shot, but it's the only thing that gives us any chance of saving his life."

Two hours later they had Ragnar in a chemically induced coma, and had lowered his body temperature as much as possible.

All they had left to do was wait.

WHILE LINDA AND William had been working on Ragnar, Billy and the rest of the team were attending the king's celebration. When they had finished eating, Billy tried to get the king to start talking.

"That was an excellent wine you served with dinner," Billy said.

"I've got a lot more in my wine cellar, but this is one of my favorites. At one time we could grow the grapes ourselves, but now we have to import everything from Queen Amanirenas's people."

"If you've got the time, I'd like to see your wine cellar."

"I would be happy to show it to you. While we're at it, I would love to hear some more about your home."

As they descended into the bowels of the castle, Billy told the king about Earth and some more of what they had gone through before they reached Midgard.

When he finished telling the king about Earth, he took the opportunity to brief him on the approaching meteor swarm and what it might mean to Midgard.

As they toured, Billy had been in constant contact with *Genesis*. He wanted to make sure he got updates on the approaching swarm and how Linda was coming with Ragnar.

When they finished the tour, the king invited him to sample a few of his favorite wines.

They were standing around sampling different vintages when Larry called with an update: "The largest meteor is about to pass by Midgard, but several of the smaller ones are about to hit."

"Can you give me the location of the nearest one?"

"That's easy enough. One of them is going to be right on top of your current location."

Billy had just finished getting the update when the entire castle suddenly shook violently and the air filled with the dust.

"We're under attack," King Peterovan exclaimed. "I've got to get back to the upper levels to rally my men."

"I don't think it was an attack," Billy said. "I believe we'll find out that we just got hit by one of the smaller meteors we've been trying to warn you about."

"I thought you said the danger wouldn't be for several more months?"

"This was just a small taste of what's to come. The real damage will happen the next time it shows up. A relatively small one hit us; however, there have been several other areas that have also been hit."

As they made their way back to the ground floor, Linda gave Billy an update on Ragnar's condition.

"I've just gotten an update from Linda, and they've managed to stabilize your son's condition. But she said it may be several weeks before they know for sure whether he's going to recover."

The king had been so preoccupied that didn't think to ask how Billy could know all of that. When they reached the great hall, it was in shambles.

The small meteorite had punched a large hole through the outside wall when it hit, and the explosion had destroyed everything in the room.

Everywhere they looked, there was nothing but destruction. The king's massive throne had been blasted into a smoldering pile of junk. The table, where they had just finished eating, was in a thousand or more pieces, several of which were still burning.

The blast had instantly killed or wounded most of the servants in the room, and all but one of the king's guards were dead or dying.

It had been hard to see because of the smoke. The stench of burnt flesh filled the air, and they could hear the screams from the wounded.

The captain of the guards was the only soldier who hadn't been wounded. He had just stepped out into the courtyard to check on the men guarding the shuttle when the meteorite struck.

When he had rushed back inside, he had found all of his men either dead or severely wounded.

"Captain, what's happened here?" King Peterovan demanded.

"I don't know. I was in the courtyard when the explosion occurred.

"I've already checked with the men on the walls, and they said that whatever it was had come from high above, and that it was streaming fire all the way down. I didn't think Queen Amanirenas had any weapons this powerful."

"It wasn't the queen," Billy said. "This was caused by a small meteorite. I'm afraid this is just a tiny taste of what it's going to be like next time."

"I think I finally understand what you've been talking about," King Peterovan said. "What can we do to stop this from happening again?"

"There's not much we can do to stop it, but we can try to prepare for the next time. We need to prepare shelters for as many people as possible. Then we'll stockpile all the supplies we can and try and ride it out."

"How can you take shelter from something like this? The castle walls were thought to be impregnable."

"I admit it'll be very difficult, but we've got to try.

"I've got something else I need to discuss with you. I'm reluctant to bring it up at a time like this, but I don't think we can afford to wait."

"No problem, have at it."

"If you don't mind, I would rather have this discussion in private."

"Give me a minute to make sure my men know what they need to do while we're away, and then we can go back upstairs. Since Ragnar is with your wife, we'll be alone."

The king gave the captain of the guard his orders, and then they made the trek back upstairs. Even though Billy was in excellent shape, he was a little weary by the time they made the climb.

"Have a seat there by the fireplace." The king turned to Peter, his valet, and said, "Bring us some food and drink, and then you can take the rest of the night off."

"Are you sure? I don't mind waiting outside, just in case you need something."

"I'm sure. We may need to talk all night, and you have to be up early to take care of . . ." He paused as he remembered that Ragnar wasn't there.

"Never mind, go and get some rest anyway. We can take care of ourselves for the rest of the night. Send one of the guards down to let Billy's companions know that they'll be spending the night."

"Now then, what was so sensitive that we had to be alone?"

"The first thing I need to tell you is that Midgard has suffered several strikes like the one we just experienced, and several of them were more severe."

"That's terrible, but I don't know what I can do about it. We barely have enough resources to survive ourselves. So, is that it?"

"No, the next part is why I felt like we needed some privacy. I've studied your people extensively, and I've come to believe that it's imperative that you find a way to reconnect with your people. If their living conditions don't improve pretty soon, I'm afraid you're going to have a revolt on your hands."

"Impossible," the king said emphatically.

"It may have never happened before, but it's never been this bad. After studying the intelligence that we've been able to gather, I would have to say that it's not only possible, I believe it to be probable.

"Your subjects' miserable living conditions have steadily eroded their allegiance to you. Many of them have grown fearful that the kingdom could fall to Queen Amanirenas's people."

They talked and drank into the wee hours of the morning, until the king finally said, "Alright, I get it. Tell me what I need to do. I can't let my inability to deal with what's going on doom my people to slavery under the Nubian's rule."

"I've thought a lot about this, and I think that the only way you'll ever be able to understand your people's plight is to try living life as they do."

"How am I supposed to pull that off? I'm their king and they won't act normally around me."

"This is going to sound a little crazy, but for this to work, we've got to hide your true identity. If we can make the journey disguised as simple traders, we should be able to see the reality of their lives. It should also give us a chance to survey the damage from the other fragments."

"It sounds like a complete waste of time to me, but

you've convinced me I've got to do something, so I guess I'll give it a try. Are you sure you want to accompany me? It could get pretty rough out there."

"I realize that, but I feel like I should come along."

"Alright then, let's get some rest, and we'll finish our plans in the morning."

6

THE NEXT MORNING, the king was suffering a little from their late night, but they continued their discussions over breakfast.

"It's settled then. I'll be back in six days," Billy said. "Is there anything else we need to discuss?"

"I do have some concerns about you coming along. Your language skills are already good enough to fool anyone, but you're still going to stand out. No matter how you dress, you're just not big enough to be seen as one of our people."

"There's not much I can do about my size. Maybe you should say I'm your son. That might explain away some of the differences in my appearance."

ONCE THE SHUTTLE was back at the base, Billy called a strategy meeting with the entire team.

"What were you thinking?" Larry asked. "You're placing yourself in tremendous danger, and what do you hope to accomplish?"

"I hear what you're saying, but I'm convinced it's the only way King Peterovan's kingdom has any chance of surviving."

"I don't see the logic in it, but at least let us send some men along," John said.

"If we're going to be believed as traders, it needs to be just the two of us. I've already mapped out our journey. It could take several months, but once we're done you can pick us up at Novelstead."

Billy paused for a moment, as he thought about what he was going to say next, and then he turned to John. "While I'm gone, I need you to continue working on the base's defenses. I also need you to help Nicholas keep our mining operations on schedule.

"Larry, I need you to continue working with the teams on the ground to coordinate the repairs to *Genesis*."

"No problem there, but we really need to put a priority on getting some more power for the shields."

"I understand, but until then, you're just going to have to pray that you don't run into any more debris.

"Linda will stay on *Genesis* until Ragnar either gets well or he dies.

"Is there anything else we need to discuss?"

"Just so you know, our reconnaissance drones have picked up a group of Queen Amanirenas's men moving in our direction," John said. "I can't believe she's going to chance an engagement with King Peterovan's men."

"I don't know why, but the queen definitely overreacted when I killed her champion.

"I doubt she's very worried about King Peterovan's men trying to stop them. I think she knows the king doesn't have the resources to patrol this far north. You'd better keep an eye on them, because I imagine they're going to try to hit our base."

"I've already made that assumption, and I'm using the drones to try to keep tabs on them," John said. "But with the way the weather is right now, it's kind of dicey. We're relatively safe, as long as we stay inside the magnetic shields, but if it comes down to it, we're going to have a difficult time defending this position."

SIX DAYS LATER, Billy and King Peterovan were ready to get started.

As they had agreed, they were dressed as simple traders. To complete the façade, they had a couple of pack mules to carry their trade goods and a pair of stout horses to ride.

"I guess I should have asked, I just assumed you could ride a horse," King Peterovan said.

"It's a little late to be asking, but I can ride a horse. I do have to say, if I didn't already know it was you, I wouldn't have recognized you."

"Wasn't that the idea? It's been so long since I've toured my kingdom, I don't think there were ever many chances of anyone recognizing me."

"Let me send a couple of my men with you," the captain of the guards implored.

"When was the last time you saw traders with bodyguards? Besides, I can take care of myself."

As they rode out of the castle's gate, the king wondered why in the world he had agreed to make such a journey.

But, he had to admit Billy had a way with words, and if even half of what he had told him turned out to be true, the trip was an absolute necessity.

MEANWHILE, LARRY WAS desperately trying to solve the myriad of problems the *Genesis* was experiencing. It was continuing to suffer damage from space debris, and its very existence was still very much in doubt.

Nicholas was splitting his time between *Genesis* and their base camp on Midgard. So, on one of his weekly visits, Larry took the opportunity to voice his concerns about the ship:

"I'm really worried about our situation. Isn't there some way you can get the shields back online?"

"There's simply no way we can as long we have to continue maintaining the life support systems for this many people," Nicholas replied. "If you're willing to transfer some more people to the surface, I might be able to get you at least minimal shields."

"How many people are we talking about?"

"I can't give you an exact number off the top of my head, but it needs to be as many as possible. If we can get it down to two decks, I'm pretty sure that would let me get the shields back up. But, even then, they're not going stop much more than a micrometeorite."

"Only two decks? Are you sure you can handle that many people on the surface?"

"It would be really tight, but we can make it work if we have to; however, we may have bigger issues than resources. When was the last time you talked with John Tyler?"

"It's been at least three weeks. Billy's briefing was probably the last time. Why do you ask?"

"We've been tracking a group of Nubian soldiers moving in from the south, and John believes they intend to try to wipe us out. We had hoped that King Peterovan's people would try to stop them, but so far no one has even challenged them. They've already moved north of where the king's patrols are normally active, so we think we're on our own.

"We're not sure that their inaction is accidental. We knew that most of the king's people were scared to death of us, but when the meteor passed by it really aggravated their feelings toward us. To make matters even worse, we've heard that the meteorite destroyed most of their stockpiles of food, and that the Nubians have been trying to take advantage of the situation.

"They've started bringing in the emergency food they promised, but they have used the opportunity to try to incite King Peterovan's people to join them to wipe us out."

"Maybe we'll get lucky, and the king and Billy will be able to come up with a way to solve some of their problems," Larry said. "I just hope he's being careful, because we would be in a real jam if anything happened to him."

"All we can do is what Billy asked, and pray for the best."

KING PETEROVAN AND Billy had been traveling down the coast for several weeks, and they had already bypassed several smaller villages, before they stopped for the first time.

The city was fairly large, and it was one of three seaports that were being used to receive the incoming goods from the Nubians.

As they made their way into the city, they couldn't help but notice how gaunt everyone looked. There weren't any children playing in the streets, and everyone they met averted their eyes as they passed.

They decided to check out the harbor area to see what was happening. When they reached the docks, there were a large number of Nubian ships waiting in the harbor to unload their cargo.

Even before the meteorites had hit, the changes in the north's climate had forced them to import virtually all of their food.

After they had finished touring the docks, they stopped at an inn for the night. As they sat at a table eating dinner, they noticed a Nubian ship's captain come in.

The captain and his bodyguards walked straight to the large table at the back the room, where they were greeted by several of the town officials.

"WELCOME CAPTAIN MOOMBA," Mayor Zebras said. "How was your trip?"

"Rough, I lost three of my ships when whatever that was hit. I was just talking to the harbormaster, and he was telling me there were several different strikes, and that even King Peterovan's castle had been hit."

"Besides the one that hit us, I know of at least three others. From what I've heard, the one that hit the king's castle only caused minor damage. We lost three of our warehouses and almost all of our reserve food supplies. We're desperately short of food, so we're very thankful you're here.

"But how about you, did it hit anything in your country?"

"We got hit in several places, but the worst was Celebes. It was completely destroyed."

"What a shame, I've been there, and it was such a beautiful place. As big as it was, there must have been tens of thousands of people living there. Surely, they didn't all die."

"I doubt we will ever know for sure, but I heard they buried over thirty thousand people. Although I imagine that was just a guess, because from what I heard, there wasn't much left of most of them.

"But that's enough about that; let's talk about why we're here. I've got sixteen ships tied up in the harbor, and they're full of food."

"Excellent, I'll have my men begin unloading them in the morning. How long are you staying?"

"We'll be leaving as soon as you get us unloaded. I don't know what's going on, but they were very insistent that we not delay our return."

EARLY THE NEXT morning, Billy and the king went back to the docks to watch them unload the supplies. Once the food was unloaded, the longshoremen stored it in a gigantic warehouse near the docks.

It hadn't taken very long for the people to hear about the ship's arrival, and by that afternoon, there was a large crowd gathered in front of the warehouse.

The king and Billy had planned to leave after the ships were finished unloading, but when they saw the crowd gathering, they decided to stay and check it out.

"What's going on?" Billy asked the king.

"As you know, I pay the queen for the food shipments once a year. When the shipments arrive, they're stored in the warehouses. All the people have to do is show up to get whatever they need.

"Normally, they would come once or twice a month, but it has been quite a while since they could draw a full ration of food, so it's probably going to be a madhouse today."

"How much does it cost them to get the food?"

"We don't charge them anything."

"Then what are those guards taking from the people in the front of the line?"

"I don't know. Let's try to get closer so we can see."

When they got closer, they could see that the people had to pay the guards before they were being allowed to enter the warehouse.

"This just isn't right," the king exclaimed. He turned to one of the men standing in line and asked, "Sir, why are the people paying that guard?"

"What sort of a fool are you? If you don't pay, you don't get any food."

"I know for a fact that King Peterovan issued a proclamation that the food is to be given away."

"That may be, but the king doesn't ever come here, and it's been this way for years. I wish it were true, because it's all that most of us can do to pay for it. I've gotten to know some of the Nubian sailors, and they tell me that all of their food is free. I've got to tell you that sometimes I wish the Nubians would come here so we wouldn't have to worry about being able to feed our families."

They continued to mingle with the people in the crowd, and more than once they heard the same sentiments. It seemed the governor of the province had long ago begun to charge the people for their food rations.

As they moved through the crowd, they could tell that most of the citizens were half starved to death and desperate for some sort of change in their lives.

"I've known that dog of a governor since I was a child. I'm going down to his castle and straighten this out," the king said.

"I know that you're upset, but this isn't the time to deal with it. You can take care of him when we're finished. The bigger concern is that it sounds as though the Nubians are actively trying to stir up trouble."

They decided they had seen enough, and as they were

leaving, they noticed a haggard man that the guards had just beaten and tossed out of the line. When he had managed to regain his feet, he staggered over to where his wife and kids were huddled together trying to stay warm.

The children were crying, and it was easy to tell that they were all starving. As they got closer, they overheard the man say to his wife, "I'll get back in line in a little while. They're about to change guards and maybe the next ones will take pity on us."

As the man was gathering himself to try again, the king approached him and handed him a small sack of gold coins. He never said a word to the man as he turned and walked away.

The man watched, dumbfounded, as the king strolled off. When he opened the sack, he let out a choked cry of disbelief. The gold coins represented a couple of years' wages, and as Billy and the king continued to walk away from the family, they could see their tears of desperation turn to tears of joy.

Not a word was spoken as they gathered their animals and left town. They had been riding for several hours before the king finally said, "I've never been ashamed of anything in my whole life, but seeing that family starving to death, while the guards laughed at their plight, is something that I just couldn't bear.

"How could I have been so blind? My advisors never told me that this kind of evil was taking place. I pray that this was an isolated occurrence."

"I'm afraid it's not," Billy said. "These are the types of things that made me come to you in the first place. I'm afraid that we're going to find out that there are even worse things taking place."

Several weeks later they reached one of the cities that had been hit by one of the larger meteorites. The impact had wiped out the docks and warehouses that housed the entire region's food supply.

At the point of impact, all that was left was a three-hundred-foot-deep crater. The resulting fireball had incinerated a two-mile-wide circle and vaporized tens of thousands of people.

When they reached the edge of the city, they were stopped by a group of soldiers who were guarding the road.

"What business do you have here?" one of the soldiers challenged.

"We're traders, and we've come to sell our wares," King Peterovan said.

"Do you have food?" the guard asked as he stared hungrily at their mules.

"All we have are the swords and knives that we brought to trade, and we don't have any extra food."

"We haven't eaten in three days, and we'll have those animals and whatever food you have."

The six soldiers were so hungry that it almost sounded like they were growling as they moved toward them.

When he saw them move, the king yelled, "Halt, these are our animals, and you aren't going to take them."

"The devil we won't. Step aside or die."

The soldiers pulled their swords and rushed at them. The king and Billy threw back their tunics, pulled their swords, and prepared to meet their charge.

The men were all seasoned soldiers, but they had no chance against the king and Billy. As they engaged the soldiers, Billy was shocked at the sheer ferocity of the king's attack. He didn't just kill them, the savage blows from his massive sword chopped them to pieces.

In the time that it took Billy to kill two of the hapless soldiers, the king had killed all the rest. In his bloodlust, he would have killed Billy, if Billy hadn't blocked his blow.

When that happened, his murderous rage went away. "Sorry, I don't know what came over me. I'm usually fairly calculated in a fight, but when I attacked that first soldier, all I could think about was the family we helped out, and I couldn't control my rage."

By the time they reached the impact site, they realized that this city had even bigger issues than the first one. The devastation was unbelievable and there was virtually no food.

They didn't let anyone know who they were, but they had managed to plant the idea that there was food to be had on the coast. By the time they were ready to move on, there had been a steady stream of people leaving for the coast.

From there, Billy and King Peterovan had continued up the coast as they had intended. At each town they visited, however, the story had been the same.

After several more weeks, they finally reached the river Vlad. As they approached the river, they spotted a village along the river's edge.

They hadn't had a decent meal, or slept in a bed in weeks, so it hadn't taken very long for them to decide they needed a room for the night.

As they rode into the village, they were met by the village's magistrate.

"What can I do for you, strangers?"

"We need a room for the night, and we want to hire a guide to take us upriver," the king said.

"How far up do you want to go?"

"We're going all the way to the headwaters."

"That's a long journey, and it'll be expensive."

The king held up five gold coins and asked, "Would this do?"

The magistrate's eyes grew wide, "That's more money than I've seen in years. I would take you anywhere you want for that much gold. When would you like to get started?"

"As soon as possible."

"From the looks of it, you've come a long way. I also own the pub, so why don't you spend the night on me, and we'll leave at first light."

They were tired of eating their own cooking, so they decided to treat themselves to a dinner in the pub. There were only two other groups in the pub, and one of them was talking fairly loudly.

From the looks of it, they had skipped eating and were several rounds into their drinks. They were being so loud that Billy and the king couldn't help but overhear their conversation.

"I tell you that times are changing. The king isn't looking out for us, and the people that I'm talking with will make it worth our while to help them."

"You fool, your mouth is going to get us killed one of these days. You never know when one of the king's minions might overhear us."

"You worry too much. The king's men haven't been around here in years, and besides, they've got much bigger issues than us. The way it's going, the Nubians could take over at any time. We might as well get ourselves positioned to cash in when they do."

"If anyone ever finds out that were helping them, they'll have us hanged, drawn, and quartered."

"I'm willing to chance it, if it means that I don't have to starve to death. Besides, all we're doing is feeding them a little information and helping them set up their camp in the mountains."

"What do you suppose they're doing up there?"

"No idea, but they sure brought in a lot of equipment and explosives. I've never seen that many barrels of gunpowder. It looks like they are getting prepared to go after someone or something. I even asked the other day, but all they would tell me is that they're going to be moving north pretty soon."

Billy and the king sat and listened to the men until the magistrate threw them out for the night. When they got back to their room, Billy told the king, "I've got to contact the base and warn them that they're going to be attacked."

"How can you do that? Even if we had a messenger with us, it would take him weeks to reach them."

"I can contact them with this," Billy said, as he held up a satellite phone. One of the first things they had done was to ring the planet with communications satellites.

Billy placed his call to Larry on board the *Genesis*.

"They're definitely stockpiling equipment to make an attack on our base. Will you warn John for me?"

"Sure no problem, but they've already spotted them. The ones you're talking about must be reinforcements. The main body is several weeks ahead of them; however, they aren't making much progress because they're dragging a lot of equipment with them."

As they were talking, Larry took the opportunity to share some of the other challenges they were experiencing. Once they had updated each other, they agreed that Billy would call at least once a week to check in.

All during Billy's conversation, the king had been looking at him in amazement.

"If I was a superstitious man, I would think that was

witchcraft," King Peterovan said. "It sounds like they're going to be in for a fight. I would love to tell you I could help, but as you've seen, I don't have much to offer at this point."

"I'm still hoping that we can change all that. Your people still need you, probably more now than ever before, and now that you've seen what's going on, we can work together to fix it."

They met the magistrate just as the sun was coming up the next morning. As they made their way upriver, the terrain rapidly turned more rugged, and the temperature started dropping.

SEVERAL DAYS LATER, they were nearing the end of their journey and, up to that point, it had proven to be a total waste of time.

They had just rounded a bend in the river, when they caught their first glimpse of the ancient monastery. It had been built into the side of one the most rugged mountains Billy had ever seen. When they got closer, they could see a crude wooden ladder that the monks had attached to the sheer rock face of the mountainside.

"What is that up there?" Billy asked.

"It's a monastery. The monks that live there never leave once they're accepted into the order. It's been there for as long as anyone can remember, but the history of how it got started has long since been lost. This is only the second time I've ever seen it. My father brought me up here when I was just a boy.

"Put the boat to shore right here," King Peterovan told the magistrate. "You can stay with the boat. We're going to take a little walk.

"The monastery's remote location has allowed the

monks to survive several centuries of turmoil," the king added. "It's a six-thousand-foot climb up the ladder leading to the monastery, making it nearly impossible to reach them if they don't want you to."

As they were walking up the mountainside, the king told Billy, "What I'm about to show you is the only other way up there. Since my father's death, I've been the only outsider who's known where the entrance is."

They had been walking for almost twenty minutes when they came to a waterfall with a large pool beneath it.

"The entrance to the monastery is directly behind this waterfall. We won't go all the way in, because we won't have any way to warm up once we get wet; however, once you're behind the waterfall you'll find a tunnel entrance that's sealed with a locked metal door.

"The key I'm about to give you is the only other one in existence. I had it made so I could give it to Ragnar when he was old enough, but I think you may have a greater need of it. If he lives, I'll have another one made."

"What else should I expect to see if I were to go in?"

"I don't know. I've never actually been inside. My father told me that one of the monks took him all the way to the top, but he didn't get into any detail, other than that there are booby traps all through the tunnels, and if you don't know where they are, you'll never make it."

"I'm honored you've shared this with me, but to what end?"

"Just before we left, I had a dream about the monastery, and it left me with an overpowering feeling I needed to bring the key with me. I can't explain it, but when I saw the monastery, I just knew I needed to give you the key."

The king looked past Billy at the rugged mountain range behind him, and said. "We'd better be getting back. The temperature is starting to drop, and it looks like there's a big storm brewing."

When they got back to the boat, they could see the magistrate was worried.

"How much further do we need to go?" the magistrate asked. "That storm looks bad, and we don't want to get stranded up here."

"We're done," King Peterovan told him. "We can start back now."

When they got back to the village, the king paid the magistrate and gave him their animals and the supplies they had left.

They were satisfied they had seen everything they needed to, so Billy put in a call to get them picked up.

7

THE NEXT MORNING they walked out to a clearing they had scouted out. Billy turned on a homing beacon so John could find them, and they sat down to wait.

After John had picked them up, he dropped King Peterovan off at his castle, and then he took Billy to the *Genesis*.

Linda met Billy when he stepped off the shuttle, and as they stood kissing, she touched his mind to ask, *How long before you have to go back down?*

I should be able to stay for at least a few days.

I'll see if I can make it worth your while to stay with me a little longer.

She had proven to be a very persuasive influence, and two weeks later he was still there. They had hoped to spend some time on the beach, but it was one of the decks Larry had been forced to abandon. They continued to have problems with the ship's power systems, and Larry had been forced to cut the power to all but the most critical decks. Everyone who was still on board had been consolidated into the two decks, where they still had full life support. The rest of the ship still had oxygen, but it wasn't being circulated or replenished. The *Genesis* wasn't dead yet, but it had definitely seen better times.

Billy had intended to spend another three weeks on-board *Genesis*; however, Midgard had suffered several more impacts. The meteor swarm was long gone, but several meteors had been caught in Midgard's gravity, and were just now starting to hit the planet. Unfortunately, some of them were quite a bit larger than the first round, and had caused significantly more damage.

As he studied the problem, he found himself wishing they could get the *Genesis* repaired. At full power, they could have used the ship's lasers to destroy the debris. At this point, however, it wasn't possible, so he decided to stop wishing and get back to survey the damage.

It turned out several of them had fallen in the ocean surrounding both continents. The ocean strikes had generated huge tsunamis, several of which were over six hundred feet high when they reached the coastline.

The huge waves had caused massive casualties on both continents, but even worse, they had destroyed much of King Peterovan's and Queen Amanirenas's fleets.

The ones that had struck land had caused utter devastation where they had hit; however, unlike the tsunamis, the damage had been fairly localized.

After Billy had gone over the situation reports, he told Linda, "I hate to leave you, but I've got to return to the surface. We've had several more meteorites strike Midgard. The damage is horrendous, and John and Nicholas are going to need my help."

"Are you going to see King Peterovan while you're there?"

"I am sure I will at some point."

"When you do, tell him that his son is going to live, and that if he has any brain damage, it'll be minimal."

* * *

WHEN BILLY REACHED their base, he gathered everyone together so they could brief each other. He used a holographic projector to show them images he'd gathered before he left *Genesis*.

"As you can see, the tsunami damage was the most severe in the southern quadrant. Here in the north, the damage from the land strikes was much worse. I've estimated that King Peterovan may have lost a third of his population. If that wasn't bad enough, the bulk of both of their fleets has been destroyed. It's going to be almost impossible for King Peterovan's people to make it through the winter without some additional supplies from the south."

"We may have caught a little break," John said. "They had just received the bulk of their supplies for the winter, and they only lost a small portion of those. I know this is going to sound horrible, but losing a third of their population is going to help their supply problems."

"We're all going to be in for a rough winter. The first contingent of the queen's forces could be here within a few months.

"Have you discussed any of this with King Peterovan?"

"I just got back from talking with him. He asked if you would brief his governors at the castle."

THE NEXT DAY, the king was overjoyed when Billy told him that Ragnar was going to make it. When he finally finished thanking him, the king filled him in on what he wanted him to cover in the meeting.

When they reached the throne room, he saw that they had managed to repair the damage done by the comet fragment.

The governors were seated in order around a large

round table, and Billy was seated to the king's left, right after the governor of the smallest province.

The meteorite had killed several of the governors, but they had left empty chairs leaned up against the table, one for each one of them.

"Thank you for making the journey to be with me. I know that many of you were trying to deal with the difficult times we are in, so I'm going to try to keep this as brief as possible.

"The young man to my left, as many of you already know, is Billy West. He and his people are from a far-away land, and he's going to brief you on the challenges that we're all facing."

Billy stood up and spoke. "The destruction that you have experienced so far is nothing in comparison to what will happen in approximately fourteen months. I know that you all saw the meteor swarm the last time it was here, so you know what I'm talking about."

He spent over an hour detailing the likely scenarios. When he had finished his explanation, they sat in complete silence as his words sank in.

Once the shock had worn off, they started bombarding him with questions. When he had answered their questions, Billy turned the meeting back over to the king.

The King Peterovan stood and slowly turned as he made eye contact with each one of the governors.

When he finished, he took a deep breath and began to speak.

"Not too long ago, Billy West and I spent several weeks traveling across my kingdom. During that journey, I observed many things that disturbed me, but the worst was that some of you were starving your own people over money.

"I know who you are, and I'm going to give you a

choice. You can fight me, one on one, like men, or I'll have the guards take you outside and hang, draw, and quarter you.

"It's your choice, but don't make the mistake of thinking I don't know who every one of you is, or that I'm going to let this slide. Make your choices quickly, because I'm sick of looking at you."

If it had been quiet before, that was nothing. Finally, the governor seated at King Peterovan's right broke the silence. "You aren't half the man your father was, and I won't be talked to in that manner."

The governor was even larger than the king, and a warrior of some renown. When he had started speaking, the guards in the room had all taken aim with their muskets, and if he had so much as twitched, they would have cut him down.

The king walked to the center of the room, stopped, and drew his sword.

The king nodded, and the governor walked over to where he stood waiting. The governor drew his sword and the fight was on. The governor actually held his own for the first couple of minutes, but it wasn't very long before the king wounded him the first time.

As the fight progressed toward its inevitable conclusion, the king was merciless.

To his credit, the governor kept fighting, but after another couple of minutes, he was done. Bloodied and breathing heavily, he was down on one knee as he waited for the final blow.

Without hesitation, the king put a quick end to him.

Then with four more mighty blows of his sword, he cut the governor's body into quarters. He told the guards, "Take what's left of this vermin outside and place his body in the four corners of the city. I want everyone to see what happens to traitors."

The king turned to the rest of the governors and bellowed, "Alright who's next."

The remaining governors looked at each other in dread and anticipation.

After a few seconds, the three remaining traitors got up and walked over to the king.

An old man by the name of Malag was leading them. When King Peterovan's father had made him a governor, he had been the youngest ever named.

Malag looked into the king's eyes and said, "My king, I'd used up all of my funds keeping my son, Loki, out of trouble, but in the end it was in vain. We'll take our punishment at the hands of the executioners. You needn't dirty your hands killing us."

The king looked sadly at the old man and said, "I just wish you had asked me for help. We all make mistakes, but I can't give you a pass on this."

Without another word, he stabbed Malag through the heart, killing him instantly. He took one last look at the old man's body, and then he killed the other two.

"Do you want to use these three as examples as well?" the captain of the guards asked.

He glanced down at the men's bodies and said, "No, you can just bury them."

After he had used a cloth from the table to wipe the blood off of his sword, he motioned to the servants and said, "Get this mess cleaned up."

When the meeting resumed, it was much more subdued. Nevertheless, by the end of the day, they all had a good idea of the challenges that lay ahead of them.

8

WITH RAGNAR CURED, Linda decided to move to their base on Midgard to be with Billy.

"I've got to meet with one of King Peterovan's governors," Billy said. "Why don't you come with me?"

When they landed, Governor Leopold and a force of fifty heavily armed guards were there to meet them.

After Billy had introduced Linda, he asked, "Why all the soldiers?"

"We've been having a lot of trouble lately. We'd suspected some of our own people were supplying the insurgents with arms, but yesterday we captured one of their men alive and convinced him to lead us to their hideout. When we raided it, we captured three Nubian agents and seized five hundred muskets."

"If we manage to get through all of this, I'm afraid it's going to mean all-out war with the Nubians," Billy said.

"Speaking of getting through this, what did you think of our evacuation plans? I know it'll be close, but I believe we've got enough time left to build ships to evacuate our entire population."

"Don't take this the wrong way, but your plans would get you all killed. The only way anyone's going to be able to survive this is to be inland and underground, preferably high in the mountains."

"But all my people know is the sea. Many generations ago, some of our ancestors that worked in the mines, but those times are long past."

The governor's remarks sparked Billy's interest, "Do you know where the old mines were?"

"Not a clue, but the archives should have a record of them. I'd be happy to show them to you, but first, I've got a favor to ask. We've got a lot of sick children. Do you think your wife could take a look at them?"

THEY WERE USING the town hall for a hospital, and when Linda walked in, she was stunned at the number of children who were sick. Everywhere she looked, the floor was covered with children on pallets. When she examined them, she found that they all had fever, chills, and a persistent cough, and several of them were spitting up blood when they coughed. She had never actually seen an active case of TB, but the symptoms seemed to fit. She asked the woman helping her, "Can you take to me see Governor Leopold?"

They found the Governor and Billy in the archives going through the ancient records.

"Before I can begin treating the children," she said, "I'll need to take a couple of them back to *Genesis* so I can verify my initial diagnosis."

"No problem," Governor Leopold replied. "Is there anything else you need?"

"Would you mind if I take some of these records with me?" Billy asked.

"Take all you want, none of us can read them anyway."

While Linda was getting the children ready to leave, Billy had a couple of the soldiers fill several trunks with the old records.

When they were about to board the shuttle, Linda told the governor, "I've given the ladies looking after the children some medicine that should make them more comfortable. As soon as I have a firm diagnosis, I'll come back, and we'll begin treating them."

WILLIAM ROBBINS AND his team were waiting for her when they landed back on the *Genesis*.

"What is it this time?" William asked.

"I think the children have TB," Linda said. "I need your team to verify my diagnosis."

"The tests will take a little while, but we'll go ahead and start them on rifampicin just to be on the safe side. How many other children are sick?"

"There were over a hundred in the location I just left, and there may be hundreds more. How is our supply of antibiotics?"

"We should have plenty, and we can produce more if we need to. If it's TB, we'll need to vaccinate everyone who isn't already infected, including the adults. We'd better check all of our people's medical records to see who needs it."

"What do you need me to do?"

"Nothing. We can handle it from here. You can go on back with Billy."

"I've already given Larry Sheldon the coordinates where the children are located. Whenever you're ready, he'll take your team to the children, so they can begin treating them."

When they got back to base, Billy took the ancient texts and started going through them. The language turned out to be very close to Latin, so he didn't have much trouble translating them.

He had discovered the texts were a treasure trove of information. It took him a while, because they covered several centuries of history, but he finally found the section he was looking for. It had clearly described where the old mines had been located and provided a detailed rendering of layouts. The mines were made up of many miles of tunnels, and they had been in production for over six hundred years before the ore had run out.

It took him three full days, but when he was finished making his notes, he reached out to John Tyler for help.

"If your schedule will allow it, I need you and a couple of your men to take a little trip with me," Billy said.

"If it's that important, I'll make time, but what's going on?"

"There's a complex of old mines I want to check out. They've been abandoned for hundreds of years, so there's no telling what we'll find."

"To tell you the truth, I could use a break from all of this, and if anything comes up, Nicholas can handle it."

"I'm sure glad we have him, he's been invaluable."

"You should tell him. You've got no idea how much he looks up to you."

"I'll make it a point to tell him the next time I see him. But, I've got to tell you I'm more than a little flattered by that. Besides being a nice guy, he's a brilliant man."

THE NEXT MORNING they loaded their equipment on one of the shuttles and went to check out the mine.

Even though the mine had been abandoned for hundreds of years, they had no problem recognizing the ancient mine's location. They could see the miles of tailings that had been pushed down the mountainside and the remnants of the crude road that had wound around the mountain.

John moved the shuttle closer to the mountainside. They slowed until they were hovering near where the tailings began.

"Look there, could that be part of the entrance?" John asked, as he pointed to a collection of massive timbers that were sticking up out of a jumble of rocks.

"Maybe, but if it is, that would mean the tunnel's entrance has collapsed," Billy answered.

"It could be collapsed, or it could have been covered by a rock slide. I'm going to land so we can take a closer look."

John landed the shuttle as close to the site as he could, and they started walking back toward the mine's entrance.

When they got closer, they could see there had been a rock slide, and that the tunnel might still be behind the jumble of debris.

"I brought one of the mining sleds along," John said. "Give me a few minutes to unload it, and I'll try to clear away some of those rocks."

The debris from the landslide proved to be more work than he had thought. It took three hours before he could clear enough of it to see that the mine's entrance was still there.

The rest of the group rushed over to have a look. The timbers on the front of the tunnel had been torn away, but a little further back, they could see an iron gate with a large lock on it.

John took a sledgehammer and smashed the lock. He tried to pull the gate open, but the rusty hinges just squealed in protest. They all jumped in so they could help, but they couldn't budge it. Finally, John tied a chain to it and used the sled to yank it open.

"Grab some flashlights and follow me," John said to his men. He looked over at Billy and said, "Why don't you stay here until we can check it out?"

"You're as bad as Linda, I'm coming, too."

They checked the reception on their headsets and moved into the tunnel. The tunnel was a little damp, and it had a musty smell to it, but it was in amazing shape for as old as it was.

Billy had made a map from the old documents, and he was telling them what to expect as they moved further into the mine.

"This tunnel should run right into a large cavern. There should be seven tunnels that branch out from there, and on the far side of the cavern, there should be a vertical shaft that goes down to the next level."

When they reached the cavern, John shined his flashlight upward. "Wow, it must be sixty feet to the ceiling."

Their flashlights weren't strong enough to illuminate the massive cavern, so John sent one of the men to get their portable light system. When he got back, they set it up in the center of the cavern and turned it on.

The powerful floodlights bathed the cavern in light. Everywhere they looked there were tools and piles of equipment. It looked like when the Norse had closed the mine up, they had just abandoned whatever was still there and walked away.

The group spent almost an hour studying the cavern, and when they were satisfied they had seen most of it, they decided to take a look at the lower levels.

The elevator the miners had used was really no more than a crude wooden platform. They had rigged ropes to a collection of overhead pulleys to raise and lower it. The harness for the draft animals they had used to operate it was still attached to the ropes.

"Bring the sled over here, and we'll use it to operate the elevator," John said.

Once they had made sure that it was all still sound, they hooked the ropes to the sled, and John and Billy got on the platform.

"Ok, you can start lowering us, but go slow," John said.

The wooden platform creaked and groaned as they slowly lowered them to the next level, a hundred and fifty feet below.

"Alright, we're down," John said. "We'll call you when we're ready to come back up."

There were several tunnels that branched off the landing area, and in the center of the cavern was another vertical shaft that led to the next level down. They spent a couple of hours exploring the other tunnels that branched off of the cavern. When they were finished surveying the tunnels on the second level, John took a quick look at the elevator to the next level.

"The elevator looks like it's sound enough to use, but it will take longer than we have to get the sled down here, so I guess it will have to wait for another day," John said. "How many more levels are there supposed to be?"

"There should be seven more," Billy said. "Whoever did the original drawings was meticulous. So far, they seem to be completely accurate in every detail. With just a little reconstruction, these tunnels should work great for the governor's people. In fact, they look so good, that I think that I'm going to recommend that King Peterovan use this facility for any of his people who don't already have shelters."

"Are you thinking that we might want to come here as well?"

"Maybe, but it's too early to make that call."

"Even though the tunnels don't need much work, we'll

need to give the governor some help if they're going to repair them in time. When we get back, I want you to handpick a couple of your best engineers to work with his people."

"No problem there, I've got a couple of guys that should do nicely. They were engineers for the Colorado Bureau of Mines, and they live and breathe this kind of stuff."

They spent the rest of the day documenting the initial requirements for the work and taking videos so they could explain what they had in mind to Governor Leopold.

Late that afternoon, they sat down with the governor so they could brief him. The governor had never seen a video before, so it had taken him a few minutes to get over his initial shock. Once they had him convinced it wasn't magic, he listened attentively.

"I can't thank you enough for taking the time to figure this all out for me," Governor Leopold said. "When you see the king, you can tell him we would be happy to share our shelters with anyone he would care to send."

That night, over dinner, John was telling his wife, Millie, about what he had seen.

"The mines sound fascinating, but I hope that we're not going to have to spend a lot of time underground," Millie said. "Being cooped up in a mine for months or years isn't my idea of a great way to raise our son."

"We haven't made any decisions yet, and even if we do decide to go underground, it would probably be here."

As they sat talking, John was feeding Adam off of his plate and enjoying a few quiet moments with his family.

If you had been watching them, you might have thought that John Tyler was just a normal husband and father and, in many ways, he was. However, John was anything but an average man.

Even though he was an ex-Navy SEAL, at six feet tall

and two hundred pounds he wasn't a physically imposing man like Larry Sheldon. It wasn't until you looked him
in the eye that you got a glimpse of what was hiding just
beneath the surface of his quiet demeanor. Around his
family, he was a gentle caring man, but if you were in a
fight, you definitely wanted him on your side.

From the very first time Billy West had seen him in action on Linda's rooftop, he had known that John was a
man you could count on. That was about to be tested
like never before.

9

THE NEXT DAY, Billy had taken everything they had shown Governor Leopold to King Peterovan and spent most of the day updating him on what they had found.

"I'm a little surprised you got him to agree to change his plans so quickly," King Peterovan said. "He can be pretty stubborn at times. I'm going to take your advice and let everyone know that those mines are available. When will we need to begin moving people into the shelters?"

"I can't give you a firm date yet, but I'll make sure you have at least sixty days to get them moved."

When he finished briefing the king, they left to return home. As they were approaching their base, Linda asked, "Is that smoke I see coming from the base?"

"I hope they haven't had an accident," Billy replied.

They had just touched down, when they saw John Tyler running toward them. He met them as they were leaving the shuttle and yelled, "Get back in and turn on the shields. I'll come back for you after we've taken care of whoever is shooting at us."

Once they were back inside, Billy turned the shields on to the maximum setting, and called to John: "Okay we're all secure. What's going on?"

"Just stay put, and I'll explain when I get back."

A few minutes later, they saw John come running by leading three of the snipers he'd been training. They had almost reached the perimeter fence when another volley of artillery shells hit the compound.

The Nubian's artillery was extremely crude, but it was still a lot more firepower than they had at the base. The only weapons John and his men had were semiautomatic M25s and sidearms. The Nubians were too far away for those weapons to be effective, so when John's team reached the fence, he radioed the control center:

"Turn off the perimeter fence, and I'll call you when I'm ready to turn it back on."

A couple of seconds later the hum of the electric fence fell silent, and all they could hear was the whistle of the brutally cold wind through the wires.

"Okay, the fence is off. We don't have time to get to the gate, so I'm going to cut a hole in the wire."

John worked as quickly as he could, but the blowing snow and the extreme cold made it difficult. When he finished, they crawled through, and he had the control center turn the fence back on.

Other than the blowing snow that partially obscured the attackers' view, John and his men were exposed. When the Nubians spotted them moving toward their position, they tried to retrain their cannons to hit them. However, they were much too cumbersome to move, and they soon gave up and resumed firing at the camp.

Once they were within seven hundred yards of the Nubians, John called to his team. "Okay men, let's set up here. We should still be well out of the range of their muskets, so take your time, and make your shots count."

The M25s had been a favorite of the SEAL teams John

had served with, and they had an effective range of over nine hundred yards. Combined with their B&L 10x40 tactical scopes, it was like shooting fish in a barrel.

When the last Nubian fell, John sent one of his men back to get a mining sled so they could bury them. After they had searched the bodies, they buried them in the ice.

When they were finished, they blew up the Nubian weapons and went back inside.

"Do you think there's any way we can keep this from happening again?" Billy asked.

"I doubt it, there's simply too many of them. I think we should consider sending a strike force out to hit them before they reach us," John said. "If you'll let me, I'll put together some teams to take the fight to them. We won't stop them, but we can at least slow them down."

"That's a good idea, but you aren't going," Billy said as he looked John in the eye. "Before you start telling me that you have to go, it's not going to be an option. You can train the men, you can give them their orders, but I'm not going to allow you to lead the missions."

"You're really getting into this, being in command of things. That was spoken like a real commander. I'll do as you say, but at some point you may have to allow me to return to the field."

THE NEXT DAY, John Tyler contacted Larry Sheldon to talk about what he had in mind, and to get the current status of the repairs to *Genesis*.

"I heard you had some excitement yesterday," Larry said.

"A little. We had a small group of Queen Amanirenas's people shell the compound. It wasn't that big a deal, but now everyone's running a little scared. Most of our people haven't been shot at before."

"You've got to admit that it's an acquired taste," Larry said with a chuckle.

"I guess that's right. It's been so long since my first time, that I guess that I've forgotten what it was like. So how's it going with you?"

"There's no one shooting at us, but we're having our fair share of issues. Nicholas did manage to get us some more power, and it has helped, but our situation is still not good. I know your people are working as hard they can, but we need those materials as soon as possible."

There was a pause in the conversation, as Larry considered how contradictory his next statement was going to be.

"Having said all of that, I need you to help me move some more of our people."

"You know that we'll do what we can, but how many people are we talking about, and when do you want to start?"

"I want to move all but the essential positions. So it'll be around thirty thousand. I would like to do even more, but I need the rest to run the ship."

"Could you give me about three weeks? I have been afraid this might happen, so we've already framed out six more barracks, but we need some more time to make them livable."

"I think we can manage for that long, but if anything changes, I'll give you a call.

"Changing subjects on you, I heard you're putting together some strike teams to try to slow down the Nubians?"

"Billy green-lighted my plans, but he refused to let me lead one of the teams."

"Good for him. A good commander never risks what he can't afford to lose."

"That's pretty much what he said. For just a kid, he's growing up quickly."

"I know it was a long time ago, but so did we. I've followed him ever since he was born, and I can't tell you how many times he and Linda have surprised me with their abilities."

AFTER THEY WERE done talking, Larry called Ed Gutierrez to discuss their evacuation plans.

Ed was a tough combat-hardened veteran. He had graduated from West Point at the top of his class, and in other times he would have undoubtedly gone on to be a general officer.

He was extremely detail-oriented, and was the best Larry had ever seen at planning and executing an operation of any type.

"What's going on?" Ed asked.

"We need to evacuate some more of our people."

"How many are we talking about this time?"

"All but the people on this list," Larry said as he handed a list to Ed.

"I'm going to need a few days to get this laid out."

"No problem, they're not going to be ready to start receiving more people for another three weeks."

ED HAD FINISHED planning the operation several days before Larry called him.

"John Tyler called late last night, and he said they're ready to start receiving passengers."

"It's about time. I'll contact the first groups and let

them know we're ready to start moving them. With only two shuttles, it's going to take almost a month to move this many people. It would go a lot faster if we could get the *Imagination* out of landing bay three."

"I understand, but you're just going to have to make do with what you have."

Once the shuttles started moving people, they operated around the clock; however, it was going slower than John had hoped, because once people had loaded their belongings, the shuttles could only carry around thirty people at a time.

As they struggled to get the groups of people moved, the Nubians had continued to try to destroy the base.

John had finished training his first group of raiders. Once he had gotten them deployed, they were spending most of their time in the frozen wilderness harassing the Nubians.

The brutal weather conditions made the strike force's job even more difficult, but as the weeks went by, only one group of Nubians had managed to slip by them, under the cover of a massive blizzard.

Unlike the first attack, they had a team ready to respond, and the Nubians had only gotten off two cannon rounds before they were wiped out.

The latest attack had only caused one death, and a few men wounded, but the entire camp was once again bathed in fear. The rumor that was flying around the camp was that they were about to be overrun by the Nubian army.

He had been unable to quell the rumor, so Billy decided he needed to address those fears head on. In an attempt to reassure his people, he set up a series of town hall meetings. Even though he really couldn't spare the time, he spent the next couple of days updating people on what was going on.

Their parents had been in one of the last groups to arrive on the planet, and they were still getting settled in when Billy arrived at their barracks to hold his last meeting.

He was holding the meetings in the barrack's cafeteria, and there were almost thirty-five hundred people crammed into the room. They had set up a small stage with a podium on one end of the room so that more people would be able to see him.

As Billy stepped up to the microphone, he looked out into the audience, and all he saw was fear and desperation in people's faces.

"Thank you for taking the time to meet with me. I know many of you are still getting settled, so I'm going to try to keep this brief.

"I realize the latest attack has left many of you confused and scared. There's no need to panic, but I'm not going to sugarcoat the truth for you. There is a Nubian army, and they are attempting to reach us.

"At this time, they're still several hundred miles from here, and we don't believe that the main army will be able to reach our base in the near future. In order to buy us as much time as possible, we currently have two platoons of soldiers in the field. Their main duties are to harass, contain, and attempt to slow the Nubian army's progress. Other than the latest attack, our soldiers have been very successful at preventing the type of attack we just had.

"I can't stand up here and guarantee you there aren't going to be more attacks, or that we'll be successful in stopping their army. But what I can tell you is that we're going to do everything in our power to keep all of you safe.

"We'll keep you updated as things change, and now I would like to open it up for questions."

* * *

WHEN BILLY FINALLY wrapped up the meeting, he and Linda went to their parents' rooms to visit. They had just sat down, when Billy got an urgent call from John Tyler, and they had to leave.

"What's happening?" Billy asked as they walked out.

"I'm sorry I had to disturb you, but the weekly shuttle just returned with some disturbing news," John said. "King Peterovan told them he has lost control in several of his provinces, and he doesn't think he can regain control."

"I didn't think Queen Amanirenas had been able to land that many troops."

"It didn't sound like it was the queen's doing. The king told them that most of the problems were being caused by Governor Malag's son, Loki. He's formed an alliance with eleven of the surrounding provinces, and they've managed to capture or kill all the king's men in those areas."

"It looks like the king made a mistake when he didn't kill Malag's entire family like he did the governor when he challenged him. Did the king ask for our help?"

"No, he just wanted us to know he was having problems."

One of the renegade provinces was where the ancient monastery was located, and just before Billy fell asleep that night, he couldn't help but wonder what would become of the monks.

10

THE NEXT COUPLE of months seemed like a blur to all of them. In an effort to make up for lost time, they had put the teams on rotating eight-hour shifts so they could work around the clock.

Billy had decided that he needed to find the time to study the data they had gathered when the meteor swarm had passed by.

His days were filled with the day-to-day duties of keeping the teams on the tasks at hand. But late at night, when most of the camp was asleep, he would sift through the video images and tracking data, searching for some sort of answer to their problems.

He had come up with all sorts of wild schemes, but it wasn't until the eleventh night that he finally figured out what he needed to do.

He knew it was long shot, but he was determined to pursue the idea.

It didn't take him very long to realize that there was only one chance of success. In order for them to succeed, they would have to alter the meteor's path.

The problem was, once it entered the system, they wouldn't be able to change its course enough to do any good. But if they could get to it before it entered their solar system, even a relatively minor course change would be enough to save them.

As he studied the problem, he was mentally cataloging his available resources.

The *Genesis* was by far his most important resource; however, they hadn't been able to make any meaningful repairs, and in its current state it was more of a liability than an asset.

Fully engrossed in his thoughts, he lost all track of time, and before he realized it, it was morning. Since he was already up, he decided to walk over to their parents' barracks and have breakfast with them.

As he crossed the compound, all he could hear was the ice crunching under his feet, and the ever-present howl of the wind. He walked as quickly as he could, but by the time he reached the entrance to the barracks, his face and hands were numb.

When he reached the door, the guard greeted him. "Good morning, not much of a day for a walk."

"That's a bit of understatement. Is there anything going on?"

"No, sir. It was a quiet night."

When he reached the cafeteria, Linda saw him come in and waved him over to where they were sitting. It was still very early, but most of the tables were already occupied.

As he and Linda had gotten older, their senses were becoming more and more acute. As they sat talking with their parents, he felt a wave of despair and hopelessness sweep over him.

The strength of the emotions was almost overwhelming, and as he looked around the room, it struck him that many of the people had lost all hope.

Even a lot of the children in the room were sitting with their heads down, just picking at their food.

He was about to say something about it, when he felt Linda in his mind. *You're right, they're scared, unhappy, depressed, you name it. I couldn't tell you how many people I've had come to me for sedatives and antidepressants. I don't know what it would be, but we need to try and come up with something to give them some hope.*

She had just finished her thought when a cannonball pierced the windowless wall of the cafeteria and exploded.

The explosion threw people and furniture into the air and filled the room with dust and smoke. A few seconds later the lights flickered and went out, and the only light in the room was coming through the hole in the wall.

The explosion had left them all dazed, and they could already hear the screams of pain and terror throughout the room. Luckily, their table had been all the way across the room from the blast. Their ears were ringing, but none of them had been hurt.

Once Billy gathered his thoughts, he called to John on his headset. "Are we under attack?"

"Definitely, and both of my response teams are out on missions. I'm going out with a few of my trainees to take care of it. Keep everyone inside until I let you know it's safe to come out."

"It's not all that safe inside. I think we have several casualties, and we've lost power."

"Even so, you're better off inside."

After the first attack, John had had them dig strategically positioned tunnels underneath the perimeter's electric fence so they could quickly exit the compound.

IN THE TIME that it took John and the four snipers to make their way outside the perimeter, the attackers had managed to fire four more rounds into the compound.

The normally pristine white landscape of the camp was dotted with debris from the damaged buildings and the blackened craters left by the shells that had missed.

The team had only gone about a hundred yards when they were caught in a withering cross fire.

It was by far the largest group they had run up against, and the Nubian commander had done a masterful job of positioning his sharpshooters to cover their attack.

John had been on point, and he had taken several shots to the body. Luckily for him, they were all wearing advanced body armor, and all they did was knock him to the ground.

The attack had caught John's team by surprise, but when the team saw him go down, they dropped to the ground beside him and began to return fire.

The Nubians' crude weapons were no match for their semiautomatic M25s, and it was just a matter of minutes until the vicious firefight came to its inevitable conclusion.

Once they had killed everyone they could see. John took a moment to get his men organized.

As he was getting them ready to move out, he saw that Burton was dead, and Johnson's right ear had been partially blown off. He took a minute to wrap a bandage around Johnson's head, and they moved out to take care of the Nubian artillery.

As soon as they were within rifle range, they knelt down and started picking off the gun crew. John was about to kill the officer in charge, but he decided to try to take him prisoner. Instead of shooting him in the head, he put a round in both of his legs to disable him.

As soon as they had killed the rest of the gun crew, John motioned to his teams and said, "Spread out and make sure that there aren't more of them. When you're done, come back here and we'll dispose of the weapons."

John disarmed the wounded officer and made sure the rest of the Nubians were dead. When he finished, he called back to the compound. "Bring a stretcher and get out here on the double."

As they were leaving with the prisoner, he barked, "Make sure you keep him under guard at all times."

It took his team over an hour to track down the stragglers and kill them. When they finished, they went to work destroying their weapons.

While he was waiting for them to finish, John decided to give Larry Sheldon a call.

"We've just had another attack. We've taken care of them, but we managed to capture the commander. I seem to remember that you've done some interrogation work."

"It's been a while, but I've done several over the years. I'll meet you when you get back."

BY THE TIME Larry arrived, Linda had finished operating on the prisoner, and they had just gotten him to his room.

"Is the prisoner awake?" Larry asked.

"Yes, but he just got out of surgery."

"That's alright, this shouldn't take very long. Now if you don't mind, I need a little time alone with him."

"Don't you want one of the guards to stay with you?"

"That won't be necessary."

Once they had left, he locked the door, walked over to the man's bed, and said, "You need to listen up. I'm going to ask you a series of questions, and if I sense you're lying, or if you don't answer me right away, there will be repercussions.

"If you answer fully and truthfully, we can finish this quickly. Otherwise you're not going to care for the process." Then, without another word, Larry reached over and Tasered him.

While he was incapacitated, Larry strapped his hands and feet to the bed. Once he had him immobilized, he reached down and ripped off the Nubian's hospital gown.

While he was waiting for him to come around, Larry put his case on the bedside table and flipped it open.

When the Nubian had recovered enough to talk, Larry started the interrogation. At first the prisoner refused to even give his name, but a few cuts, burns, and shocks later he started to talk.

He had been answering all of the questions until Larry had started asking him some very specific questions about the Nubian army. At that point, he stopped talking. Larry used virtually every tool he had in his kit, but to no avail. By then the room was filled with the stench of the interrogation. Larry was determined to get the answers to his questions, so he used a sometimes-lethal combination of drugs to lower the prisoner's resistance.

Finally, the Nubian relented and gave Larry what he wanted. When Larry was satisfied the man didn't know anything else, he packed up his gear, untied him, and walked back into the hall.

When Larry walked out, the guard and the nurse went back into the room. When the nurse saw the naked bloody prisoner, she gasped and screamed at Larry, "What have you done to this man?"

Larry just kept on walking as he said, "What I had to."

Larry found a vacant room so he could write up his notes, and when he finished, he sent them on to John Tyler.

AFTER EVERYTHING HAD settled down, Billy and John got together with Larry to discuss what he had found out.

"How in the world did you get all of this out of him?" John asked as he was flipping through Larry's notes. "I'd tried talking to him, but he wouldn't even tell me his name."

"You wouldn't want to know, and it really doesn't matter, as long as I got what you needed."

"You did, and it's going to save a lot of lives."

As John and Larry talked, Billy was studying Larry. He was trying to get a read on what seemed to be bothering him. The last few times Billy had talked with Larry, he had noticed that he was growing more and more withdrawn. He was still carrying out his duties as well as anyone could, but Billy could tell he wasn't himself.

Billy wished he could read Larry's thoughts, but he could sense that Larry was desperately unhappy about something. He wanted to talk with Larry about what was going on with him, but he didn't want to do it in front of John.

As Larry wrapped up his briefing, Billy asked him, "Do you have a few minutes to talk with me before you go back?"

"Sure. I'm not doing much good up there right now, anyway."

After John had left, they each got a cup of coffee and sat down to talk.

"I've had the feeling that there's something bothering you," Billy said.

"You wouldn't have to be a mind reader to see that. I've spent most of my life trying to be a good soldier, but in doing so, I've had to do some truly awful things, and sometimes they're hard to live with. I don't want to burden you with the details, but even my relationship with you and Linda hasn't been what it should have been."

"I'm no psychologist, but I can listen, if you would like to talk about it."

Billy could tell he was reluctant, but once he got started, he couldn't stop.

Larry spent almost four hours just spewing out the things that he had done and seen throughout his life. Finally, completely worn down from the effort, he fell silent.

"I'd suspected there was a dark side to your career," Billy said, "and I can understand how what you've done would be hard for anyone to live with. Since you're a longtime member of the Logos, I assume you believe in God. Have you ever asked him to forgive you?"

It was a straightforward question, but Larry thought for several seconds before he answered.

"Pastor Williams once asked me the same thing. At the time, I told him yes, because that's what he wanted to hear; however, I'm not sure I've ever been ready to forgive myself, let alone allow God to forgive me. I'm afraid it's something I've got to work out in my own way, but thanks for listening.

"I do want to make you this offer. When the time is right, I would like to sit down and tell you and Linda the full story of why you are the way you are."

"I'll take you up on that, whenever you think the time is right."

* * *

JOHN USED LARRY'S information in order to realign his field teams and warn King Peterovan that several of his people were defecting to the other side.

Billy continued working on his plan, and two weeks later, he called a meeting with John Tyler, Nicholas Stavros, and Larry Sheldon to talk about it.

"Thanks for coming, and what I'm about to show you is the first version of my plan to change the meteor's path."

"How can you hope to affect something that large?" John asked.

"The critical aspect of the plan is that we have to intercept it before it enters the solar system. That way we won't have to change its course by more than a couple of degrees. If we can't, then there's no chance of success."

Billy turned on the holographic projector so he could show them what he was proposing.

"Once we've repaired the *Genesis,* we'll intercept the largest meteor at this location.

"At full power, the ship's magnetic projectors should be powerful enough to alter the meteor's course by two degrees. At that distance, the two degree shift will cause it to miss by a wide margin."

"That's great, but we haven't been able to fix the ship yet," Nicholas said. "In fact, I'm worried we aren't going to be able to fix it."

Billy paused as he considered what Nicholas had said.

"That's the first time you've come out and admitted we may not be able to repair the ship. What's changed?"

"There's no doubt we could repair it if we had more time, but the quality of the materials we've been getting aren't up to spec, and in the best case, we're not going to get started for several more months."

Billy didn't say anything for a few seconds as he considered what to say next. "I'll see if I can help you get us back on schedule, but do you think my plan would work if we can repair the ship?"

"Probably, but it's still a long shot on getting the ship fixed."

11

Now that Billy had floated his idea on deflecting the meteor to the rest of his team, he decided to make another trip to see King Peterovan.

"It's good to see you again, my young friend," King Peterovan bellowed. He slapped Billy on the back.

The slap almost knocked him down, but Billy laughed and said, "It's good to see you too, but I'm glad you were happy to see me. I wouldn't want to see you mad."

"So, what brings you all the way out here?"

"I wanted to see how you were doing and brief you on a plan I've been working on."

"If you don't count the fact that my people are starving, I've lost control of almost half my kingdom, or that we may all be killed by the meteor, then I guess I'm fine."

Billy chuckled and said, "I guess when you put it that way it's pretty depressing, and we've been having our problems as well. I know John briefed you on what we found out from the Nubian we captured. Do you really believe they're being successful recruiting your people?"

"If you'll remember back to our trip, we saw and heard instances of it even then. With the way things have gone since then, I'm not sure I can even blame them. So tell me about this plan you're working on."

"I've put together a plan to divert the meteor before it gets here."

Before the king even had a chance to respond, Bill shook his head and said, "I don't know why I even brought it up, because it doesn't look like we'll ever get a chance to try it."

"What's to stop you?"

"We've got to have the *Genesis* available to do the job, and it doesn't look like we're going to be able to repair it in time."

"That's horrible news, how will you ever get back to the rest of your people?"

"If Nicholas is right, you may have to put up with us for a lot longer than we had intended."

"That wouldn't be a problem, but I'm not sure it's going to be much of a place to live if that infernal meteor hits us."

They talked for most of the morning, and when lunchtime came, the king offered to feed them before they left.

When lunch arrived, the pan slipped out of the server's hand and hot grease covered Billy's right arm and hand. The hot grease horribly blistered him before they could wipe it off.

The king was about to kill the man out of hand, before Billy said, "There's no need to kill him, it was just an accident."

"But I've seen people die from lesser wounds."

"Only if it gets infected, and that shouldn't be a problem. When I get back, I'll have Linda take a look at it."

Most people would have been screaming in pain, but Billy had managed to block most of it out.

They spent an hour or so over lunch, and then they walked down to the shuttle.

"I'll try and see you again in a month or so," Billy

said. "By then I should know whether we can save the ship, and if we need to use some of your shelters. Thanks for loaning us the hundred men. John will do a great job training them, and when you get them back they'll be the best soldiers you've ever had."

Not thinking, the king reached out to shake Billy's hand.

When Billy responded, the king gasped and said, "It's magic, your arm has already healed."

Billy laughed, "No, not magic, but Linda and I do heal very quickly. I know it seems odd, and this is one thing that I really can't explain to you, because we don't understand it ourselves. All I can tell you is that we've both been this way from birth."

They said their goodbyes and when the shuttle had disappeared into the distance, the king shook his head in bewilderment as he walked back inside.

As soon as John had found out that he was getting a hundred battle-hardened veterans, he rushed off to start putting together their training schedule.

Shortly after John had left, Billy got an urgent call from Larry.

"I think you'd better get up here. I'm afraid we're about to lose the ship. We've had a major malfunction with one of the containment fields on the auxiliary reactor. We managed to get it stabilized, but I don't know how much longer it's going to last."

Billy called Nicholas and called John back in so that they could help decide on a course of action. It didn't take very long for them do their initial assessments of the situation.

"I've just finished talking to the reactor team, and it's

bad," Nicholas said. "We'll be lucky if the reactor lasts another week. We need to go ahead and salvage what we can, because, when it fails, it's going to take out the entire ship."

"Isn't there anything else we can try?" John asked.

"I don't think so, but if someone else has any ideas, now would be the time to speak up."

Nicholas paused to see if anyone had something to add.

After several seconds of complete silence, Billy looked at Nicholas and said, "I do have an idea that'll let us get the *Imagination* free. Do you think you could mount one of the Petawatt lasers on a sled?"

"Sure, but unless we have some other source of power it won't last more than a couple of seconds."

"What if we tapped into the main power feed on *Genesis*? We've been afraid to try it before because of the power drain, but it doesn't much matter at this point."

Nicholas thought about it for a few seconds and said, "Sure, it'll work. But if we do it, we'll need to be ready to leave the ship immediately. I think there's a very good chance that it'll drive the reactor critical."

They spent several hours making a list of the things they wanted to salvage.

Their first task had been to make sure they didn't lose any of the data stored in *Genesis*'s computer systems.

When they had first built the base, they had wanted to ensure they had a robust computer system on the planet. Since the ship's systems were fully redundant, all they had to do was turn off the fail-over between the two systems and move half of it to the base.

At the time, the data had been mirrored between the two systems, so all they had left to do was move any new data that they had collected after the split. While the computer team was moving the data, the rest of them got started moving the men and materials.

It had taken them five more days to get everything moved. When they were getting close to being finished, they got back together to try and free the *Imagination*.

When the reactor had overloaded, it had fused the doors shut to the hanger where the *Imagination* was stored. To get it out, they were going to have to cut through the two twelve-inch-thick, hardened steel doors.

When Billy was sure that everyone understood their part of the plan, they took a shuttle back to *Genesis*.

As they were landing, they passed the other shuttle as it was leaving with the final group of people.

The massive ship had been their salvation and their home, and they all knew that when it was gone, they no longer had a realistic chance of ever rejoining the rest of the Earth's fleet.

While the rest of the team was wiring the laser sled into the ship's power, Billy took one last quick tour of the ship. His last stop was the beach deck where he and Linda had spent so many special hours. He had turned the emergency lighting on so he could see a little, but it just wasn't the same.

A little disappointed, and more than a little sad, Billy took one last look, turned off the lights, and returned to the hanger deck.

As he walked onto the hanger deck, he saw a brilliant arc of fire from the wall beside one of the elevators. Startled, he jumped back and called to the team. "Was that something you did, or is the ship already falling apart?"

"It wasn't us," Nicholas said. "The power is starting to surge, and the weak points in the system are failing. We'd better hurry up, or we may not get a chance to try this."

When Billy got to them, he told Nicholas and Larry, "As soon as we get it free I want you two to take the shuttle and leave. If everything goes as planned, John and I will be right behind you."

"What are the odds of anything going as planned?" Larry asked.

"Don't you think we're way overdue for a little good luck? But let's quit talking about it and go do it."

Nicholas mounted the sled and triggered the laser. He'd already programmed it, so all he had to do was move it to the next doorway when he finished the first cut.

It only took three minutes for the powerful laser to cut the opening. Nicholas used the sled's magnetic beam to pull the huge metal door out of the way.

As soon the metal disc hit the deck with a thunderous clang, he moved into position and started making the second cut. He had just gotten started when the ship's power surged and the laser lost its focus.

For a moment or two Nicholas was afraid the surge had damaged the laser. But as soon as the power stabilized it regained its focus, and he could continue. Once the second doorway was cut and moved out of the way, he loaded the sled in the shuttle, and called to Larry, "Let's go, they'll follow us as soon as they can."

They quickly boarded the shuttle and left. They didn't stop until they were far enough away so that they wouldn't be in any danger if the ship exploded.

Billy and John had memorized the preflight checklist, and a minute or so later the ship was almost ready to launch.

Suddenly, Billy looked at John and said, "I'll be right back."

"Where do you think you're going?" John asked. "We've got to get out of here. The ship could go up any minute."

"I've got to make sure the ship doesn't fall back into the atmosphere."

John started to protest, but Billy was already gone.

Billy went straight to a computer panel and started rerouting all the power to the propulsion system.

Then he programmed a course to take the ship away from Midgard. When he finished, he hit execute and took off at a dead run for the *Imagination*.

John saw him coming on the monitor, so as soon as he had reached the top of the ramp, he closed it and turned on the power to the hull plates.

Billy came running onto the bridge. "Sorry about that, but I got worried at the last moment."

"It's not a problem, unless we get killed before we can get out of here."

Billy carefully guided the *Imagination* through the holes that Nicholas had cut. There was no margin for error, but they made it through with no problems.

Once they were free, he accelerated toward the opening at the end of the massive hanger deck.

As they rushed toward the opening, there were several brilliant flashes of electricity as it arced along the hanger's walls.

Larry saw the *Imagination* when it came shooting out of the hanger like a bullet, and he yelled, "They made it, I thought they were goners."

As the *Imagination* was speeding toward the shuttle, the *Genesis* was beginning to move away from the planet.

By the time Billy slowed to a stop beside the shuttle, the *Genesis* was already several hundred miles away and was still accelerating.

They had been watching it for a couple of minutes when they began to see electricity arcing all around the edges of the *Genesis*'s hull. The bolts of electricity grew in frequency and strength until it looked like the biggest summertime lightning storm they had ever seen.

Just when they thought that it couldn't get any more violent, the *Genesis* exploded in a tremendous blast of light.

The force of the explosion tore the massive ship into millions of tiny fragments.

"That was some light show," Larry said.

"I can't believe it's gone," Nicholas said. "It looks as though we just postponed our deaths when we escaped from Earth."

"I wouldn't write us off just yet," Billy replied.

12

WITH THE *GENESIS* destroyed, Billy no longer had any chance of implementing his original plan. He and Nicholas had been meeting every day to discuss their options, but they hadn't come up with anything yet.

Several nights later, Billy had a nightmare. He dreamed of a strange ship, and that it was flying straight into the side of the meteor. He had the same nightmare for three straight nights before he finally mentioned it to Linda over breakfast.

"I've been having a recurrent nightmare. I've been dreaming that I'm on a strange ship, and it's flying directly into the side of the onrushing meteor. The meteor keeps getting closer and closer, until that's all I can see, and then I wake up."

"I've been having the same dream. Do you think that it's God's way of saying he has a mission for us?"

"I hope not, because it seemed like a one-way mission to me. Nevertheless, I'm going to discuss the feasibility of that type of mission with Nicholas."

They spent several days running different simulations, but none of their ships, including the *Imagination,* had had enough mass to deflect the meteor's path.

"I know that you believe God is giving you a message, but this just won't work," Nicholas said.

"What if we packed the *Imagination* full of explosives and rigged it to explode upon impact?"

Nicholas ran the numbers and said, "Closer, but it's still not nearly enough."

"Drat, I just knew that wouldn't work. Let's keep working on it, there's got to be some way of getting it done.

"Oh before I forget, I'm going to tell King Peterovan that we're going to use the tunnels that we've built as our shelters. Also, since we don't have anything left to rebuild, you can stop the mining operation. That way the miners can get started preparing the tunnels to be used as shelters."

"It's a shame. We were close to having enough materials to rebuild the *Genesis*."

Billy thought for a moment before he asked, "Do you have enough materials to build a couple of small reactors?"

"Sure, but what are you thinking now?"

"Since we don't have a big enough ship to fill with explosives, what if we build another ship and turn the entire ship into a bomb? If we build it to act like a shaped charge, we should be able to maximize the explosion's effect."

Nicholas thought for a moment. "That just might work, and we already have most of the materials we'll need. The only thing we're short of is plutonium. The uranium ore we've been getting out of our mine isn't pure enough to make weapons-grade plutonium."

"Go ahead and get started building the reactors to process it, and I'll take care of getting the uranium. I just happen to know where there's an old abandoned Nubian quarry that contains some really high-grade uranium ore."

"You're going to mine the ore in Queen Amanirenas's territory?"

"I am, but I'm sure not going to ask her permission.

The old quarry is located in a remote section of her territory, so I doubt we'll be noticed. But even if we are, it doesn't matter. We need the ore, so I'm not going to let her stop us."

THE NEXT MORNING, Billy sat down with John and told him about the mission.

"Let me make sure I understand," John said, "You want my men to provide security so that a team of Nicholas's men can mine for uranium in the queen's territory."

"You've got it. When can you have a team ready?"

"I've got just the team for this. We've just finished training the first fifty of King Peterovan's men. They're all crack shots, and there's no doubt that they'll kill without hesitation. That being said, I want to go on record as saying that this is a really bad idea."

"I understand your concerns, but it's the only way I can get enough tons of Pu-239 in time for the mission."

John let out a whistle and asked, "What in the world are you going to do with that much plutonium?"

"I've come up with another plan to deflect the meteor. I'd be happy to explain it, if you would like to hear about it."

"Nope, not necessary. If you say it'll work, that's all I need to know. I'll have the men ready to go by oh-six-hundred tomorrow."

THE NEXT MORNING, they all met outside by the shuttles. "I'm coming along with you to help them get set up," John said.

"No problem, that's why I'm going, and when we're finished, we can ride back together," Billy replied.

To make sure they weren't spotted, they stayed at a high altitude until they reached the quarry. When they got low enough, they could see the massive hole the Nubians had dug in the rugged foothills. The quarry had once produced much of the stone they had used to build the capital's pyramids.

When it had been in production, they had used the dried-up river, which ran right next to the quarry, to transport the blocks of stone to the ocean.

Before the river had dried up, the whole area had been one of the most fertile parts of the country, but now it was little more than an arid wasteland. Most of the ancient settlements had been covered by the seemingly ever-present sandstorms; however, in a few places you could still see small sections of the buildings that lay buried beneath the sand.

"This thing is huge," John said.

"It ought to be; they worked at this location for over a thousand years before the river ran dry and they abandoned it."

Billy pointed to the western side of the quarry and said, "The best uranium deposits are located right there. If I'm right, we shouldn't even have to dig it up. I believe that large mound of crushed rock over there contains all the ore we're going to need."

While they were unloading the equipment, John showed Lieutenant Sharp where to position his men. When they were sure that everyone understood what they needed to do, he and Billy took one of the shuttles and returned to their base.

IT TURNED OUT that Billy had been right, and all they had to do was to sift through the rock pile for the uranium. Since they didn't have to dig, it only took them a couple of days to start delivering the uranium ore for processing. They worked day and night and by the end of the third week they had plenty of ore.

"I think we've got more than enough uranium ore," Nicholas said.

"Great, I'm going to go ahead and pull our men out of there," John said. "I've been worried the Nubians would find them."

The next morning, John took the two shuttles to retrieve their teams. He was piloting one of the shuttles, and as they were coming in for a landing, he spotted a contingent of the queen's men who were poised to attack the quarry.

He hurriedly called to Lieutenant Sharp, "Heads up, you've got an enemy force on your left flank, and it looks like they're about to attack."

THE ENEMY FORCE was a group of a hundred and twenty commandos who had been on a survival training mission when they stumbled across the mining operation.

Their commander was an aging general who had fallen out of favor and had been relegated to leading training missions. As the general had assessed the situation, he had dreamed of his long lost glory days. Seeing this as an opportunity for one last moment in the sun, he had decided to attack.

The general turned to give his men the order to attack, and as he did, he took a moment to survey the faces of the young commandos.

As he did, he thought back to his first battle and the thrill of anticipation that he had felt. Then he remembered the reality of combat, and how it hadn't been what he had expected.

Had he properly surveyed the situation, he would have realized that they had already been seen, and that they weren't going to have the element of surprise.

As he gave the order to attack, he wondered if the queen would hold another parade in his honor.

"WE'VE ALREADY SEEN them and we're ready. As soon as they clear that ridge, we'll engage," said Lieutenant Sharp.

As the Nubian commandos charged around the ridge, Lieutenant Sharp gave the order to fire. His men were all carrying M16s, and they laid down a withering barrage as the Nubians charged their position.

The young commandos had never faced that sort of firepower before. The only guns that they had ever encountered were the crude muskets that King Peterovan's people had.

Stunned by the ferocious defensive fire, they stopped and started to retreat; however, it was much too late, and they were quickly cut down by the automatic weapons.

The old general had been one of the last to fall, and as he died, he had one final silly thought: "Well there goes my parade."

"WELL DONE, LIEUTENANT," John said.

"There wasn't much to it. I don't know what they were thinking, charging straight into us like that."

"There was no way they could have anticipated the

kind of firepower you threw at them. Get your men ready, we're getting out of here."

"Good deal, I'm tired of all this sand. We'll get started loading the equipment. It shouldn't take more than a couple of hours."

"Just leave it. We may need to come back for some more ore, and besides, we don't really need it right now."

It only took them thirty minutes to load the men and what little equipment they did take with them. As the shuttles were climbing away from the quarry, they could see a massive sandstorm headed their way.

"That sure looks bad," Lieutenant Sharp said.

"It does, at that. I can't believe how screwed up the weather is right now. On the way down here we spotted three huge tornados along the coastline. I can't decide what's worse—the weather, the earthquakes, or that the Nubians are always trying to wipe us out. Most of the time it feels like the whole planet's trying to kill us."

THAT AFTERNOON BILLY and Nicholas got together for a status meeting.

"How much plutonium have you produced so far?" Billy asked.

"We've only processed just over a hundred pounds," Nicholas replied. "We had some problems at first, but I think we've finally got it figured out. We should be able to finish the rest of it in plenty of time."

"I can't tell you how much I appreciate all of your hard work, and I don't know what we would have done without you," Billy told him, as he reached out to shake his hand.

"It's been a pleasure working with you as well."

"From your accent, I would guess you're Russian."

"I am, but I spent most of my life in the States. My father sent me to MIT when I was just ten years old, and I never went back."

"I'm a little reluctant to ask, but did your father make it on board one of the other ships?"

"No, I'm afraid that he's been dead for several years."

"I'm sorry. He must have died pretty young."

"Yes, he did, and I'm afraid that I'm still bitter about it. He'd made his fortune in oil, but when the government nationalized the oil fields, they trumped up some charges so they could imprison him for tax evasion.

"He was killed in prison a short time later, and I've always believed that they had him killed; however, I don't suppose it matters much anymore," he said sadly.

Billy couldn't think of anything else to say, so he thanked God that he and Linda Lou still had their parents.

BILLY AND NICHOLAS had been able to finish the plans for their new ship, but the work crews were struggling to get it finished.

At the time, the Nubian attack hadn't seemed like a big deal. Unlike their previous attacks, they had used a lightly armed force so that they could move quickly enough to evade the containment teams.

The strike force hadn't brought any heavy weapons with them at all. Instead they were each carrying a crossbow and a quiver of explosive arrows. When they launched their attack, they had managed to shoot almost all of their arrows before one of John's response teams had wiped them out.

At first it had seemed that all they had done was to cause a lot of noise, and there were almost no casualties. Unfortunately, it turned out that they had gotten lucky and destroyed a significant portion of the food supplies.

Too late to be of any help, the remainder of the supplies were moved inside the magnetic barrier for safekeeping. The loss of the supplies had forced the base to start severely rationing food.

As their situation became more desperate by the day, Billy decided they needed to meet and talk about their options.

"I don't think we have any choice," Larry said. "We've got to get some more food."

"How do you propose to do that?" Billy asked.

"I want to put together a small team and take what we need from the Nubians."

"I really hate it, but I guess that it's come to that," Billy said. "I would ask King Peterovan for help, but I know he's not in any better shape than we are. In fact, we might as well get them some food while we're at it."

"I'll come with you," John said.

"Not gonna happen, I need you here," Billy replied. "How many men are you going to need?"

"The team doesn't need to be very big. A squad of soldiers, and thirty or so people to load the supplies, should be all we need. It would help if we could get several of the magnetic sleds to help us load the supplies."

"I'll get you whatever you need," Nicholas said.

"Lieutenant Sharp's squad is ready to go, if that'll work for you," John said.

"After hearing about their last mission, I believe they should do fine. Also, I would like to use the *Imagination* to move the supplies, if that's alright."

"You can have whatever resources we have left," Billy said. "If I hadn't messed up so badly, we might have been able to get Queen Amanirenas to help us out."

"Like I told you before, you didn't mess up. There was no way she was going to help us. If you'll remember, once she found out you had helped King Peterovan, we were lucky we got out alive."

"I guess you're right. When do you want to start?"

"ASAP," Larry said. He looked over at John and asked, "Have you identified any suitable locations for us?"

"Several, but I thought you should start with the most remote ones, and I think I've found one that's perfect. It's right on the coast, and it's over twenty-five hundred miles from the capital. It's a regional center, but so far as I can tell, there are only about fifty guards."

"Sounds perfect, we'll have a go at it tomorrow night."

THEY TOOK ONE of the shuttles and the *Imagination* on the mission. They landed just after dark, and they spent several hours doing reconnaissance before they were ready to make their move.

"There are only five guards on duty," Larry told Lieutenant Sharp. "When I give the signal, have your snipers take them out, and be sure and use the silencers, so we don't wake the rest of the garrison.

"Once they're out of the way, we'll land the shuttle in the town square and take out the rest of the guards. We'll signal you when you can bring the *Imagination* in."

At just past midnight, they launched their attack. The snipers fired simultaneously, and the guards on the walls dropped in their tracks. Once they were out of the way, Larry landed the shuttle and led the rest of the team down the ramp to attack the rest of the guards.

Moving quickly and quietly, they ran across the court-yard to the barracks. They kicked in the door and rushed inside. The attack caught the sleeping guards completely by surprise, and they were captured without a fight. They were herded into a windowless room and the door was locked. Larry stationed a couple of his men by the door and said, "Make sure they don't escape, and if they try anything, kill them."

Larry signaled the *Imagination* to land, and they went to work emptying the warehouse. They worked as quickly as possible, but as the *Imagination* and the shuttle were leaving, they could see the sun just starting to rise on the horizon.

"That wasn't too bad," Lieutenant Sharp said.

"We were lucky," Larry said. "They weren't expecting an attack, and we managed to catch them by surprise. Now that we have gotten started, we need to move quickly. If they manage to contact the other facilities before we can hit them, it's going to get a lot harder."

When they got back to base, they lay down to get some rest while Nicholas's people unloaded the ships.

The next night they hit the next installation on their list. They had moved a couple of hundred miles away from their first target, so they could maintain the element of surprise. As long as they moved further away than a day's ride, they knew that the Nubians wouldn't be able to get a warning out before they attacked.

They had a little more trouble with the next location, but they were once again able to load their ships with supplies.

They went out every night for almost six weeks, as they worked their way across the countryside.

When they got near the capital city, they skipped over it and went on to the next location on the list.

They were able to stockpile enough supplies to feed their people for quite a while. They didn't have to worry about any of it spoiling, because the extreme cold made it easy for them to store the food in vaults in the ice.

Their efforts had been so successful, that they had even managed to gather enough supplies to share some with King Peterovan's people.

AFTER SEVERAL DAYS of well-deserved rest, Billy got his team together to discuss where they were and what they needed to do next.

"If we're careful, I think we have enough supplies to last us for a couple of years," Larry said. "How are we coming with the new ship?"

"It's going to be really close, but I think we can still make the deadline," Nicholas said. "We're going to have to keep working twenty-four hours a day, but now that we have plenty of people trained, it's not as big of a strain as it was."

Billy was about to speak to the group when Lieutenant Sharp came running in, and pulled John Tyler aside to share some urgent information with him.

When they finished talking, John told the group, "We've just gotten word that there's been a large-scale outbreak of TB in one of the eastern provinces. King Peterovan has asked us to send a medical team to treat them."

"I can go," Linda said.

"Lieutenant Sharp, you go with her," John ordered.

"Yes, sir." He turned to Linda and asked, "When would you like to leave?"

"Give me about an hour to gather some supplies." She turned to Billy. "I shouldn't be gone very long."

"You be careful, it's very dangerous out there. If Lieutenant Sharp asks you to do something, you do it. He's there to take care of you."

"Don't worry, I'll be careful, and I'll do what Lieutenant Sharp asks."

Linda gave him a kiss and left to get ready.

"Lieutenant, I expect you to take very good care of her," Billy said.

"You can depend on me. I'll guard her with my life."

After they had left, Billy returned to the briefing.

"The plan's pretty involved, so I'm only going to give you an overview." He turned on the holographic projector, and a map of the solar system appeared before them.

"The ship will need to leave here no later than December tenth. This will be the course it will follow to the edge of the solar system." He highlighted the ship's projected path. "If everything goes as planned, three months later it will reach this position at the edge of the solar system. From there it will make a sixty degree turn and make its attempt to divert the meteor."

"Divert it? I figured the ship would try to destroy it," John said.

"It's much too large for that. My current calculations show that, at best, the impact will result in a two degree course change."

"That doesn't sound like very much," John said.

"I know it doesn't, but that'll be more than enough to ensure that it won't threaten Midgard ever again."

"When you say an impact, you don't mean that the ship's going to have to ram the meteor, do you?" Larry asked.

You could have heard a pin drop as they waited for Billy's reply. Billy's brow furrowed as he looked Larry in the eye and said, "I'm afraid that's exactly what I mean."

"What are you going to do about a crew?"

"I'll be piloting the ship, but I am going to need a few volunteers."

There was a moment or two of stunned silence, and then the room erupted as everyone tried to talk at once. Finally, Billy held up his hands and said, "If everyone will calm down, I'll take whatever questions or comments you have."

"Can't you just program the ship to intercept the meteor?" John asked.

"Normally I would say yes; however, there's simply too many smaller meteors surrounding the big one. I can't be sure the ship would reach it without multiple course corrections, and we can't chance a failure. Believe me, I've thought long and hard about the options, but I just don't see any other way."

"Then you need to let one of us take care of it," Larry said. "You're way too important to the survival of our people."

They grilled Billy for over an hour before they finally gave up, for the time being, and the meeting broke up.

MEANWHILE, IT HAD only taken Lieutenant Sharp and Linda an hour and a half to reach the province that needed their help.

When they landed, they were met by Governor Swenson and twenty armed soldiers. By this time, they were getting used to these security precautions, and it actually made Lieutenant Sharp feel a little better about their situation.

"Let me carry those cases for you," Lieutenant Sharp said.

"Okay, but they aren't that heavy," Linda replied as he took them.

As they walked toward the waiting carriage, Lieutenant Sharp heard a noise behind them.

It probably wouldn't have mattered, but with both hands full, he never even had a chance to pull his pistol.

As the sword's blade penetrated his back, it pierced his heart, killing him almost instantly. He dropped the cases, and as he stumbled forward he was spitting up blood. It startled Linda, but she lunged to try to catch him as he fell.

Before she could reach him, one of the soldiers grabbed her from behind, pinning her arms to her sides. The soldier that held her was twice her size and tremendously strong.

Unable to move, she screamed, "Let me go! Someone needs to help Lieutenant Sharp!"

As she struggled to free herself, she saw what looked like a military officer step forward. He took a moment to check on Lieutenant Sharp, and then he told Linda, "I can assure you that Lieutenant Sharp doesn't need anything, he's quite dead. What you need to do right now is to calm down and listen very carefully to what I'm about to tell you. You're a prisoner of the Nubian Empire, and you need to follow my instructions without hesitation. Any resistance on your part will result in punishment."

"Who are you, and what do you want from me?"

"My name is Admiral Massawa, and I'm Queen Amanirenas's representative. I don't require anything from you; however, I do need your husband to be reasonable. One of my men is going to give the crew of your vessel a document that spells out our demands. If your husband meets them, we will return you unharmed—otherwise I'm afraid it's not going to end any better for you than it did for the lieutenant."

"I don't know what you expect to get from Billy, but he won't endanger our people just to save me."

"For your sake, you'd better hope that doesn't prove to be true."

The admiral motioned to his men, and they blind-folded her. They led her over to a waiting carriage, and after they had bound her hands and feet, they threw her in the back.

She felt Billy in her mind as he frantically asked, *What's going on?*

Governor Swenson's men have killed Lieutenant Sharp, and they have taken me captive. They've tied me up and put me in the back of his carriage. A Nubian admiral, by the name of Massawa, said that they were sending their demands back with the shuttle crew. But I don't have any idea what they're going to ask for.

I'll deal with that later. Are you alright, have they hurt you?

Only my pride; I didn't even manage to put up a fight.

It's just as well. You would have only gotten hurt. You do whatever they ask. I promise I'm going to get you back. If anything changes, or you just need to talk, just reach out.

Linda's captors had no idea she could talk to Billy any-time she wanted, or they would have knocked her out.

WHEN BILLY FOUND John, he told him, "They've ab-ducted Linda."

"Who abducted her? I haven't heard anything about it from Lieutenant Sharp."

"Lieutenant Sharp is dead. Linda said he never had a chance. Shortly after they arrived, one of the governor's soldiers stabbed him in the back with a sword. It sounds like the whole medical emergency thing was a hoax."

John motioned for Billy to be quiet, as he received a call on his headset.

"The shuttle just radioed in with the same story. They should be landing in about twenty minutes."

"Did they say what they're demanding?"

"They haven't read the document."

When the shuttle landed, they ran out to meet it. The pilot handed the parchment to John and said, "There wasn't anything we could do. The cowards killed Lieutenant Sharp before we even knew there was trouble."

John handed the parchment to Billy, and said, "Don't worry, we're going to get her back."

Nobody said a word as Billy read the admiral's demands. As he was reading, they saw the veins in his neck pulsating as his anger grew. When he finished, he threw the parchment on the table and said, "They want us to surrender the base and all of our technology. We're supposed to deliver the weapons and ships to Queen Amanirenas's palace in no more than a hundred and twenty days. If we don't surrender by then, they're going to kill Linda."

"It's not surprising that the queen is behind all of this," John said.

"I promise you that I'm going to get her back, and after I do, I'm going to make them pay dearly for this treachery," Billy said, as he struggled to control his rage.

They could see that Billy was beside himself.

Larry had seen him in action, and he knew that given the right set of circumstances, he could probably be as brutal as either one of them.

"I'll launch some additional drones. It shouldn't take us very long to find her," John said.

* * *

THE ADMIRAL WAS brighter than they had given him credit for, and they had already abandoned the carriage, and were now on horseback.

The admiral had known they could track him from the air, so they were traveling under the cover of the heavy forests found in the region.

Billy's men had finally given up on finding Linda around midnight. Billy had just managed to fall into an exhausted sleep when he was awakened by Linda's mind in his.

Are you alright? Billy asked.

They've still got me tied up like a Christmas turkey, but other than that I'm fine. They abandoned the carriage several hours ago, and we've been traveling by horseback ever since. They've got teams of men waiting for them all along the way, and about every two hours, they change riders.

WE'VE JUST STOPPED again, but this time they have put me on board some sort of boat.

A boat, are you at sea?

I don't think so. I'm pretty sure that we're on a river.

I'm coming to get you as soon as I can figure out where you're at. Until then, don't do anything to antagonize them, and I think you'll be alright.

Queen Amanirenas has given me a hundred and twenty days to turn the base and all of our technology over to her. If I don't, they're going to kill you.

I won't do anything to stir them up, but don't you give them anything. Without the ships and our technology, we wouldn't last very long anyway. If I have to die to save the rest of our people, then so be it.

You're not going to die. I'm going to get you back, no matter what I have to do.

As scared as she was, Linda was even more scared of the burning rage she had felt in Billy's mind. She knew he meant it when he said he would do whatever it took.

HE AND THE rest of the team needed sleep badly and he only slept for a couple hours before he got back up.

"I've talked with Linda again. She said they had abandoned the carriage, and they've been using teams of riders to move her. They had just put her on board a boat of some sort, and she thought they were on a river."

"Even though they were using teams of riders, the only river they could've reached is the Vlad," John said. "But I don't know why they would be headed up there, because there's nothing there."

"That's not entirely accurate. There's an ancient monastery up there, and that's got be where they're taking her."

"If you'll let me put a team together we can be there in a couple of hours," Larry said.

"That's not going to work. If they even see a shuttle, they'll kill her," Billy said. "I'll take a shuttle to the coast, and then I'll take a boat upriver until I reach the monastery."

"I can only imagine how I would react if they had Millie. But rushing out to get yourself killed isn't the answer," John said. "Give me a few hours, and I'll try to map out a plan of attack."

They could see that Billy's emotions were about to overcome him, but he finally drew a deep breath and said, "Alright, but make it quick."

13

IT HAD TURNED out to be easier said than done; it had taken John Tyler several hours to work out a plan to rescue Linda. When he finished, he called them all back so he could go over it with them.

"I just got through analyzing the surveillance video," John said as he turned on the holographic projector. He used his laser pointer to highlight the area he was talking about. "If you'll look right here, you can see that the queen's men have taken over the entire area where the monastery is located. They've got patrols all up and down the river, so using it is out of the question. I've considered several other options, but it looks like the only viable way to reach her is by going overland."

"When can we get going?" Billy asked.

"I know you're not going to want to hear this, but I think it's better if I go alone."

Larry Sheldon could see the desperation in Billy's face. "I know how badly you want to help, but I honestly believe that there's a better chance of success if you let him handle it."

Billy didn't say a word for several seconds as he tried to digest what they had told him. "Alright," he said, "I get it, but I don't have to like it."

"It's settled then. I'll get my gear ready, and then I'll

have the shuttle drop me off at the river after it gets dark tonight."

In all the confusion, Billy hadn't thought to mention what the king had told him about the monastery. "Before we drop you off, we need to stop and talk with King Peterovan."

EVEN THOUGH IT seemed like an eternity to Billy, it was only a couple of hours before they met with the king.

"I was duped into helping them, but I still feel responsible," King Peterovan said. "Is there anything I can do to help?"

"We think they've taken Linda to the monastery we saw on our trip. Would it be alright if I give John Tyler my key to the tunnel?"

"Of course, but if he's going to try to use the tunnel, there're a couple of things I'm going to need to tell him. The first thing you need to know is that you're going to need a guide to make it through the tunnels."

"Where am I supposed to find a guide?" John quickly asked.

"I'm getting to that. Every day at sunrise, one of the monks will make a visit to the waterfall. When he approaches you, you must hold out the key and say, "I come in peace and seek your guidance, so that I may reach enlightenment."

"What's that supposed to mean?"

"I have no idea. My father never told me, if he even knew. All I know is that if you say it just that way, the monk is supposed to lead you through the tunnels to the monastery."

"That sounds easy enough," John said. "Is that all there is to it?"

"There is one other thing. You've got to be alone. If the monk sees anyone else he won't help you. That's everything that I know, but I do have one question for you. How are you planning to get to the monastery?"

"The Nubians are patroling the river, so I'm going to have the shuttle drop me off near the mouth of the river, and then I'll continue on horseback."

"You're in for a rough trip. But if you're going by horseback, I would like to give you one of my horses."

Later that night, the shuttle dropped John Tyler off. The area was heavily forested, but after a short search, they found a small clearing to land in. As soon as they were down, John led his horse and a pack mule down the ramp into the clearing.

"Is there anything else you need?" Billy asked.

"No, I think I've got everything, besides, I don't think the mule could carry anything else. I'm only going to travel at night, and I'll check in every morning when I stop for the day."

"Good luck, and please bring her back to me," Billy pleaded.

"I won't come back without her," John said as he shook Billy's hand.

He slipped on his night-vision goggles, mounted his horse, and rode away into the night.

IT HAD ALREADY been two weeks since they abducted Linda, and she had talked with Billy every day, and even though she tried to hide it, she was scared and lonely. But the very next morning he sensed a change in her.

I know this is going to sound ridiculous, but it's breath-taking here, Linda said. *If it weren't for the circumstances,*

I would have to say it's the most beautiful and peaceful place I've ever seen.

That's quite a change from yesterday. Do they still have you locked up in the basement?

No, yesterday afternoon they moved me to a room on the top level of the monastery, and it's got a small balcony where I can sit out and enjoy the view. It's got to be over seven thousand feet straight down, and it took me a couple of tries to get over being scared when I go out there. But I'm glad I kept trying, because watching the sun set behind the mountains was incredible. I enjoyed it so much that I got up early so I could watch the sunrise this morning.

I'm glad they've made you more comfortable. I'm going to talk with John Tyler in the morning; have you noticed anything we should warn him about?

It may not mean anything, but there was an unusual amount of activity this week. They've brought in hundreds of barrels of something. But when I asked the monks about it, none of them knew what was in them.

Keep trying to find out what's going on, but it doesn't sound like anything that should affect John's mission.

JOHN TYLER HAD been on the trail for a couple of weeks, and as King Peterovan had warned him, his trip had been difficult. There weren't any established routes through the rugged terrain, so he had to forge his own trail.

He had just gotten started for the night when a late winter blizzard swept down the river valley. When the snow had first started, he wasn't that worried since he had already made it through a couple of snowstorms. He kept going, but as the wind had picked up, and the snowfall got heavier, travel had gotten steadily more difficult. Finally, he decided that he needed to find some sort of shelter.

As he struggled through the growing snowdrifts, he chanced upon a small cave. After he'd checked it for wild animals, he went inside to get out of the weather.

The wind was whipping snow into the cave, so he took a plastic tarp and secured it across the cave's opening. Once he had the cave secured, he lit his small stove and melted some snow for water. After he'd eaten and taken care of the animals, he crawled into his sleeping bag to try and warm up.

As he watched the shadows of the horse and mule on the cave wall, he started thinking about his mission and how little chance he had of saving Linda West, or even surviving.

He'd only intended to stay until the storm passed, but it took three days to let up. Finally, on the fourth night, the storm passed, and he could get going again.

The storm had left monstrous snowdrifts everywhere, and there were several times that night that he had to dismount and lead the horse and mule through the drifts.

By dawn he was wet, cold, and exhausted. By the time he stopped for the day, he was so tired that he didn't bother to check in.

The sun was just setting when he was awakened by a call on his headset.

"John, are you there?" Billy asked. "Come in if you can hear this."

"I'm here. What's up?"

"When you didn't check in this morning, we started to worry. We waited all day, and when you still hadn't checked in, we finally decided to try to call you."

"I'm fine. I was just exhausted from busting through snowdrifts all night."

"How much is the weather going to slow you down?"

"It's hard to say, but I would guess at least a week. Do you think she can hold out that long?"

"That shouldn't be a problem. Other than that she's a prisoner, she's actually fairly comfortable at this point."

When they finished talking, John broke camp and got back on the trail. The snowdrifts had been a problem at first, but he finally reached an area where the drifting snow had left him a clear path.

He was making such good progress that he continued on longer than usual. The first glimmer of light was showing over the mountains when he heard a rustle in the undergrowth behind him.

He glanced back over his right shoulder, and as he did, he saw a large gray wolf step out of the brush, its eyes glowing in the early morning light. Following close behind it were six more wolves.

The snowstorm had kept them from finding food for a couple of days, and they were hungry.

When the leader of the pack started toward the mule, it panicked. John had the mule's lead rope wound around his horse's saddle horn, and it almost pulled him over when it tried to bolt.

After he had managed to steady his horse, he threw his leg over the saddle and slid to the ground. As soon as he hit the ground, he drew his pistol and quickly sized up the situation.

The silenced SIG Sauer P226's forty-caliber S&W slugs were perfect for the task. John's first shot dropped the lead wolf in his tracks, and the rest of the pack hesitated for a second. He knew that he couldn't chance just wounding any of them, because their cries might draw attention that he didn't need.

He took his time to ensure each shot was a clean kill. It was just a matter of seconds before he killed two more, and the rest of them turned and ran off. The blood from the wolves was starting to stain the snow red, but he didn't pay any attention to them.

He looked over to where his horse had stopped in its tracks when he dismounted, and he was thankful the king had provided him a well-trained mount.

Once he had calmed the mule down, he decided to put a little distance between himself and the remainder of the pack. So even though it was now full daylight, he decided to press on for a little while longer.

He had only gone about a mile when he heard the sound of voices approaching. He dismounted and led his animals into some evergreens for cover. He tied them up and crept through the trees to try and see who was coming.

It took him a couple of minutes to locate them, but it turned out to be a small group of Nubian soldiers who had decided to go hunting for some fresh meat. They hadn't gotten used to the weather yet, and they were whining about how cold it was.

John could have easily killed the three men before they even knew he was there, but he didn't want the rest of the Nubians out hunting for them.

As he let them pass, he was glad he wasn't depending on them for food; they had been making so much noise that every animal for miles could hear them coming.

It was the first time he had encountered any Nubians, and he realized he might have gotten too close to the river. Once they were gone, he rode another mile into the forest before he stopped for the day.

After his encounter with the Nubians, he didn't want to chance lighting a fire, so he sat down to eat some cold field rations. When he finished, he pitched his small tent and crawled inside with his sleeping bag. As he was lying there trying to warm up, he replayed the day's events in his mind.

It had been an eventful day. Everything had worked out, but he knew he'd gotten lucky, and that either encounter could have ended badly. He couldn't afford to lose any of his animals, and he sure didn't need the Nubians hunting him.

As he was falling asleep, he yearned for the support structure that he had been used to, and he realized how terribly alone he was. Just before he dropped off to sleep, he said a prayer for Millie and Adam, and for the strength to fulfill his promise to Billy.

14

"THE OPERATION WENT just as I planned," Admiral Massawa boasted. "And I captured Linda West without a fight."

"Captured, you were supposed to kill her, not capture her," Queen Amanirenas said, clearly unhappy. "I hope, for your sake, that you executed her before you left?"

Too arrogant to realize how much trouble he was in, the admiral continued boasting. "I did much better than that. I sent them a ransom note demanding that they surrender their base and all of their technology. I gave them a deadline of no more than a hundred and twenty days, or I would execute her."

Livid with anger, the queen was about to draw her sword and behead the admiral. Then she paused to consider what he had done, and their current situation. She had just read the assessment of the raids on their supply depots. In just weeks, the strangers had managed to raid over a hundred Nubian depots. They had taken tons of their supplies, but her men hadn't managed to kill even one of the attackers. Since it wouldn't cost her anything to wait, she decided to wait and see how his plan played out.

"What's to stop them from just taking her back?" she asked.

"I've already had her moved to the monastery I told you about, and I let the strangers know that if we even saw one of their people, we would immediately kill her. I do have to admit that, after I had her moved, I became worried they might try and rescue her anyway, so I had the basement of the monastery filled with gunpowder. If they make any attempt to rescue her, the guards will blow up the whole place."

"I guess what's done is done. How are the rest of our plans coming along?"

"Several of King Peterovan's provinces have already come over to our side, and I expect several more to follow shortly. I'm afraid the remainder of my report isn't nearly as positive. General Abrahams's army is still advancing, but they're making very slow progress."

"What's his problem now?"

"It's a combination of things. The weather is brutal, and Billy West's people are carrying out a highly effective delaying strategy. Between the weather and the enemy, the general has already lost over seven hundred men."

"I'm going to think about this tonight. Come for breakfast in the morning, and I'll let you know what I want you to do next."

THE ADMIRAL DIDN'T sleep well that night as he worried about what the queen might have in store for him.

He was back to see the queen early the next morning.

"How long will it take you to get back to the monastery?" Queen Amanirenas asked.

"If I have favorable winds, it'll take me about two and a half weeks."

"Good, then this is what I want you to do. I want you to get Linda West and join up with General Abrahams's army. Once the army reaches the base, I want you to handle all the negotiations."

"Do you have a list of demands?"

"I was getting to that. You're to demand their immediate surrender, or you'll kill her, and don't accept anything less than unconditional surrender."

"What do you want me to do with her once they surrender?"

"I want you to make sure that you've captured Billy West. Once you have him, I want you to kill her in front of him, and then I want you to kill him."

He almost asked why, but luckily for him, he thought better of it.

"I understand, and I'll leave right after breakfast."

"You're not eating. You need to prepare your ships for the trip, but don't leave until General Staneus gets there. He's going to assume command of the army when he gets there."

AFTER THE ADMIRAL left, the queen called General Staneus in.

"I want you to accompany Admiral Massawa on his mission. I've already given him his orders, so you don't have to worry about what he's up to. I just want you to observe until he has killed Billy and Linda West. After he finishes with them, I want you to kill him. But don't do it quickly. I want you to make him suffer. Once you're finished with him, I want you assume command of the army."

"No problem, but what about General Abrahams?"

"Kill him as well. He's turned out to be a real disappointment to me. He should have captured their base months ago."

General Staneus managed to hide his emotions, but

he was shocked that he was being asked to execute General Abrahams. General Abrahams was a legend with the troops, and he was easily the best general they had.

When General Staneus left the palace, he saw the queen had a carriage waiting outside to take him to the dock. He wasn't prepared for a new assignment, so he had it go by his villa, so he could get packed for the trip.

On the way to his villa, he sat wondering when the queen would turn on him. He knew it was just a matter of time, but maybe he could find a way to disappear while he was away.

When the carriage got to the general's villa, he had the driver wait for him. He hurried inside, where he found his wife and two young sons eating breakfast in the garden. When he saw them sitting there, he made a fateful decision. "Pack some clothes for all of us, we're leaving."

His wife, Tara, didn't even ask why. She just turned to the servants and said, "You heard the general, help me get packed."

When the general came out with his entire family, the driver thought it was rather odd, but he wasn't about to ask any questions.

Admiral Massawa met them as they were boarding the ship.

"I wasn't expecting you to bring your family along. Give me a few minutes to move my stuff, and you and your family can have my quarters. In fact, I'm going to move to the other ship. I'm just along for the ride, so it doesn't matter which one I'm on."

THEY HAD FAVORABLE winds all the way, and they made the voyage in only thirteen days.

As they were approaching the rugged coastline, they

ran into a massive storm system. It wasn't supposed to be the stormy time of year, but Midgard's weather patterns had become extremely unpredictable.

In a matter of minutes, the wind-driven waves were already running at over eleven feet high, and the weather was deteriorating quickly as the storm swept toward them.

Admiral Massawa turned to Captain Zapata and asked, "Don't you think we should turn back out to sea and try to ride this out?"

"Nonsense, I've been making this run for years, and these storms never amount to anything much at this time of the year."

That had been true before, but the impact from the meteorites had rerouted the jet streams, and that had permanently altered the weather patterns.

As the ships made the turn to enter the harbor, the full fury of the storm hit them. The waves were now over thirty feet high as the wind-driven storm surge reached the shallow water of the coastline. General Staneus's ship was being tossed about by the storm's wind and waves.

"I wish I'd have never come along," Tara whimpered.

The general knew she was terrified of water, but he had to admit he was becoming concerned himself. "I'm sure that there's nothing to worry about. We're getting close to the coastline, and we should be there by nightfall."

He took her in his arms to comfort her, and as he did, his two young sons rushed over and joined them.

As the storm's full fury struck their ship, it was pitching and rolling wildly. Their gear was being flung all over the cabin, and they could hear the ship's rigging being torn away by the wind.

Suddenly, they were all thrown across the cabin as the ship was impaled on the rocks that guarded the entrance to the harbor.

The ship listed violently to starboard as the next waves hit it, and they were thrown back across the cabin into the other wall.

Bloodied and dazed by the impact, the general tried to regain his footing so he could help his family, but by then the ship was beginning to break up, and its death throes were bouncing them around like Ping-Pong balls. Badly injured, he was forced to look on helplessly as his wife and children screamed in pain and terror.

The rocks had torn the bottom out of their ship, and the monstrous waves smashed the rest of it into kindling.

As the general and his family died, he thought, "At least we've died together, and not at the hands of the queen."

The ship carrying Admiral Massawa had suffered a great deal of damage, but it managed to skirt the rocks. As they passed into relative calm of the harbor, they saw the general's ship being ripped apart.

"We've got to try and help them," Admiral Massawa said.

"No way. We'll be lucky to survive ourselves," Captain Zapata replied. "Besides there's nothing anyone can do for them now."

Behind them, there was nothing left of the general's ill-fated ship except the shattered pieces that were being driven ashore by the waves.

Admiral Massawa would never know that the unfortunate demise of General Staneus and his family had saved his, and General Abrahams's, lives.

Shaken by the experience, the admiral spent the night at the governor's residence. The next morning the governor gave him a couple of boats, a contingent of soldiers, and sent him on his way.

* * *

MEANWHILE, JOHN TYLER continued his struggle to reach the monastery. After his chance encounter with the Nubians, he had adjusted his route in order to keep a safe distance from their patrols.

He thought it was going to slow his progress; however, it had turned out that by moving further away from the river, he had actually had an easier time of it.

By the time Admiral Massawa had left for the monastery, John had just arrived at the waterfall. It was getting light out, and he considered trying to make contact immediately. But it had already been a long night, so he decided to get some rest before he tried to meet up with the monk.

He pitched his tent far enough away from the waterfall so he wouldn't be seen, and he went to sleep. It had been a brutal trip, but for the first time in weeks, he allowed himself a glimmer of hope that he might succeed.

The next morning he was up well before dawn. At first he couldn't decide what to do with his animals, but finally he unloaded his supplies, fed them, and turned them loose.

It wasn't that far, but by the time he reached the waterfall, he was struggling under the weight of his pack and weapons. As he sat down beside the waterfall to rest for a moment, he wondered how it was all going to end.

15

Nicholas Stavros was getting worried. His teams had been working around the clock, but as he sat going over the production schedule, he could see they weren't going to make it.

He had used Andre Dubois, one of his best engineers, to put together the construction calendar, but when he dug into the schedule for the next phase, he realized that Andre had used one of their original scheduling templates.

He understood why he had used it, but the template had been built to provide ships with an entirely different purpose. Their new ship was going to be almost fifty percent larger than the *Imagination*, but it didn't need any of the amenities that a regular ship would.

Since they had built the ship's frame around its reactor, they were much further along than the production schedule showed. All they had left to do was to add some bulkheads for the minimal crew quarters and to pack the rest of the interior with the enriched Pu-239.

When he had rebuilt the construction schedule, he was elated to see how much time they were going to save. He had just finished his final tweaks to the schedule when he noticed that Billy had uploaded a design change request to the server.

Billy had just made a last minute design change that called for the crew quarters to be mounted on the outside of the ship's hull.

After he had sent them over, Billy gave Nicholas a couple of hours to go over the changes, and then he went to discuss them.

"The changes shouldn't set us back more than a couple of days," Nicholas said. "We're going to fill the old crew area with Pu-239, but do you really think it's going to take that big of an explosion?"

"It can't hurt, but that wasn't the reason for the changes. When I shared the estimated radiation exposure with her, Linda became concerned that we wouldn't survive long enough to complete the mission. I'm hoping that by mounting the crew module outside the ship and adding some additional shielding, it will give us a better level of protection."

Nicholas considered saying what they were both thinking. That as long as they survived until they reached the meteor, it didn't really matter, because it was definitely a one-way trip.

Trying to change the subject, Billy asked, "How's the uranium processing coming?"

"We're doing alright. The quality of the ore isn't as good as it might be, but we're getting there. Unless the queen's people cause us more problems, we should even finish a little ahead of schedule."

JOHN TYLER HAD made sure he was in the proper position, with time to spare. As he sat waiting for the monk to arrive, he thought of Millie and Adam, and hoped he would see them again.

He was lost in his thoughts until he heard a quiet cough,

as the monk let him know he was standing right beside him.

The monk, like most of King Peterovan's people, was a very large man by Earth standards. He stood seven feet, three inches tall, and weighed over three hundred and fifty pounds.

As he stared at the mountain of a man standing beside him, John was more than a little surprised that the monk had been able to sneak up on him.

John had always been calm under pressure, but as he hurried to get the key out of his pocket, his fingers didn't seem to work right. Finally, it came free, and he held it out, and spoke the words he'd memorized: "I come in peace and seek your guidance, so that I may reach enlightenment."

The monk took the key from his hand and responded, "I welcome you in peace, and enlightenment shall be yours."

Then the monk chuckled and said, "I've spent most of my life waiting to say those words. Welcome, my name is Brother Dalmatius, and I'll make sure that you reach the monastery. I would ask why you're here, but I imagine it's to try to rescue Linda West."

"I'm John Tyler, and that's precisely why I'm here. Is she alright?"

"She's doing fine, considering the circumstances. In fact, the Nubians pretty much ignore her, and my fellow monks and I have been looking after her."

"How long will it take to reach the monastery?"

"I can't say, since none of us have ever made the journey. We've all memorized the instructions, but we're forbidden from even entering the tunnels."

John thought to himself, *Great, the blind leading the blind.*

"Can we get started, or do you have to let them know I'm here?"

"We can get going. When I don't return, they'll assume someone has arrived. You sure got a lot of gear. Give me some of it, and I'll help you carry it. How did you manage to carry all that?"

"I didn't have to carry it. I had a horse and a pack mule."

"Where did you leave them?"

"I was afraid I might not make it back, so I turned them loose."

"I'll leave a note, and the brother who comes in the morning will find them and make sure they're cared for.

"We'd better get going. You never know when those accursed Nubians will wander by."

Brother Dalmatius used John's key to unlock the gate, but it took both of them to open it.

As they made their way into the pitch black tunnel, they couldn't see a thing. Brother Dalmatius had to feel his way along the wall until he bumped into the pile of torches he had been looking for.

He was about to light one when John switched on his flashlight.

The monk was startled by the light and asked, "What manner of magic is this? Where's the flame?"

"It's not magic. It's what we call a flashlight."

"Well, it looks like magic to me. But no matter, it's none of my business. My only job is to get you to the monastery alive."

"Why would that be a problem? It doesn't look like there's been anyone in these tunnels for a long time."

"I'll do my best to get you through safely, but I've got

to warn you that we may run into dangers that I'm not aware of."

"I appreciate your honesty, but Linda West is well worth the risk."

"I agree. The other brothers and I have been trying to come up with a way to set her free, but I'm afraid we're ill-equipped for that sort of thing."

"Don't worry about it, that's why I'm here. Which way do we go?"

"We'll take the tunnel on the left."

At that point, the tunnel was only about seven feet high and no more than five feet wide, so the flashlight clearly illuminated it.

The brother had to stoop a little as they walked, but by three hundred feet in, the tunnel had grown big enough so that the flashlight no longer illuminated both sides.

John decided to conserve the batteries, so they stopped to light their torches.

"I can't believe how big the tunnel has gotten. It must have taken them years to dig."

"If our lessons are accurate, this is just the start of the tunnels. They're supposed to honeycomb the entire mountain."

"Your people dug all of this?"

"I believe that my ancestors did."

"What in the world for? Were they mining for something?"

"None of us know their purpose."

As they continued down the tunnel, they started to notice small rooms that had been carved into the sides of the tunnel.

Finally, their curiosity got the better of them, and they paused to look inside of one of the larger ones.

John stuck his torch inside the room, and they saw there was a fireplace, stone benches, and a table. The details were hard to make out because there were several inches of dust covering everything.

"It must have been a very long time ago, but it looks like people lived in here at one time," John said.

"It does at that, but nothing I've been taught ever mentioned anything about it."

They had just gotten started again, when they reached their first decision point. There were three tunnels that branched out in front of them.

"Which one?" John asked.

"I believe it's the one in the center."

"You believe? Don't you know?"

"Not exactly. Our teachers told us to bear to the left, but none of them ever mentioned having three choices."

"That's good enough for me, straight it is."

They hadn't gone very far when Brother Dalmatius came to an abrupt halt. "Stop. Do you see that shiny spot on the wall?"

"You mean that small spot of mica?"

"If that's what you call it. It's supposed to mark a trap."

"Let me take a quick look. I'm pretty good at spotting that sort of thing."

The monk had no way of knowing how much of an understatement that was. John Tyler had spent several years training men to set all sorts of booby traps.

It took him several seconds to spot the tiny seam in the cave's floor and brush the dust off of it. He didn't see any trip wires, so he took one of their spare torches and swung it at the floor like an axe.

The stone he hit was set to act as a pressure switch, and when he struck it, thirty metal darts shot out of the wall. They were expelled with so much velocity that several of them stuck in the solid rock wall on the other side.

The monk let out a yelp and jumped back.

"It's alright, they missed us, but that was pretty nasty. If we had walked into that we wouldn't have lived to tell about it. I guess your lessons are right on so far. Do we continue down this tunnel or not?"

"I'm afraid I was wrong. We need to go back and take the tunnel on the far left."

They retraced their steps and went down the tunnel on the left. The monk was still a little scared, so he was definitely taking more time than before, and they gingerly inched their way through the tunnel.

They had been walking for a couple of hours when Brother Dalmatius remarked, "I think it's getting cooler."

"I've been thinking the same thing for a while now. I think there's even a little breeze. Surely, we haven't reached the end of the tunnel already."

As they rounded a sharp bend, John said, "That sounds like water. Did your teachings mention water?"

"I'm afraid not. It looks like we've forgotten more details than I thought."

Dalmatius was still being very cautious, so it took them almost an hour to reach the source of the sound. When they stepped out of the tunnel, into a gigantic cavern, they could see where the sound was coming from.

There was a large waterfall that was entering the cavern from an opening that was at least seventy feet up. The rapidly flowing stream was cascading into a pool of water that stretched further than they could see.

They had been walking for quite a while, so John walked over to the pool, dipped his hand into the water, and took a sip.

The cold clear water tasted good to him, so he turned to Brother Dalmatius and said, "The water is alright to drink. In fact, it's really good. Get yourself a drink, and then let's see if we can find a way around this. Otherwise, I guess we'll have to backtrack and try the other tunnel."

Dalmatius had a drink, and then walked over to where John was sitting. "I'm concerned that my lessons have left out a great deal of information. The room, the lake, none of it was ever mentioned."

"Stop worrying, we'll get through whatever we find," John said, trying to reassure him.

They attempted to work their way around the lake, but after they had walked for almost forty minutes, they came to a dead end. They had hoped to find a way out of the cavern, but the water extended right up to the wall. As they were searching for any sign of an opening, they spotted a small rowboat that was tied off to the cavern's wall.

"That's interesting," John said. "There must be something on the other side of the lake. Are you game to give it a try?"

"Sure, but I should already know what we'll find."

"Stop worrying about it. Heck, they may not have known themselves. How long has it been since anyone was down here?"

"It's been at least several centuries."

"Well, there you go. You can tell them all about it when we get there."

They lit the torches that were on both ends of the boat and started across the lake. They rowed for almost an hour before they reached the other side.

As they approached the shoreline their torches illuminated a large building. They tied their boat up at a small dock and walked toward it.

"That looks like a church to me," John remarked.

"It does at that. Would it be alright to take a few minutes to look inside?"

"We might as well go ahead and stop for the night. After we've eaten, we'll look around a little while."

Once they had eaten, they started searching to see if they could find out anything about the caverns. There wasn't much left to look at, but they finally spotted what looked like inscriptions on the wall behind an altar.

"Can you read any of this?" John asked.

"We all had to study the ancient dialects, so I should be able to. Nevertheless, it's been quite a while, so you're going to have to give me a few minutes."

After almost twenty minutes, John asked impatiently, "Well, what does it say?"

"The inscriptions detail the story of a great prophet who foretold of a large light in the sky and that it was going to threaten their very existence. It goes on to detail how my ancestors took refuge in these tunnels in an attempt to survive. It took them an entire generation to build what's contained in the tunnels. They spent, if I've got the time right, almost ten years in here before they attempted to go outside again."

"They lived in here for ten years? I don't see how they could have survived in here for that long. The tunnels are big, but I didn't think they were that large. Does it say how many people came down here?"

"No, all it says is that the ones who didn't all died."

John decided to look around on his own while Brother Dalmatius continued reading. He had made it about halfway through the room when he saw something on the far wall that caught his eye.

When he got closer, he could see it was a map of the tunnels. He had spent several minutes studying the map when he realized that the tunnels were much far more extensive than he had first thought.

It took him a few minutes to figure out where they were at on the map. Once he had it pinpointed, he traced the path that they had followed. When he figured out the scale of the map, he developed an estimate of the scope of the tunnels. He found it hard to believe, but it looked like the network of tunnels could easily cover over a hundred miles. Once he had deciphered the symbols on the map, he determined that there were many more caverns, and that a couple of them were even more massive than the ones they had encountered.

The map was far too elaborate to copy by hand. He tried to take a picture of it with the camera in his satellite phone, but when he checked the picture, it wasn't readable.

It took him several tries to get the distance right, but he finally managed to photograph the map in sections. Once he'd made sure they were readable, he went back to see how Brother Dalmatius was doing.

"How are you coming?"

"Fine, but if you'll allow me the time, I would like to read the rest of this."

John could understand his excitement, but he was anxious to get Linda and be on his way.

"Maybe you can come back when we're done, but right now we'd better try to get some rest. There's no telling what we're going to run into tomorrow."

LARRY SHELDON WAS jarred out of a sound sleep by Billy's urgent call. "I'm sorry to call you in the middle of the night, but we've got big trouble, and I need your help."

"Ok, calm down. Give me a couple of minutes to get dressed, and I'll be right over."

When Larry got to the main building, Billy was hunched over his computer terminal studying some photographs.

"What's going on?" Larry asked.

"Somehow the Nubians have managed to get a large detachment of men within four hundred miles of us. I need you to take a look at these reconnaissance photos and tell me if we can stop them."

"How could we have missed them?"

"We were supposed to have a team shadowing them. When I asked about their status, I discovered that they hadn't checked in for thirteen days."

"It's my fault. With John Tyler gone, I should have paid more attention to what's been going on. Give me a few minutes to look at the photos, and then I'll let you know what I think."

Almost twenty minutes later, Larry said, "Alright, I know as much as I'm going to. This looks pretty bad. We can assume the team that was shadowing them has been wiped out."

"That only leaves us with ninety trained men, and that's not enough to try and stop a force of ten thousand men."

"Even if we had the other team, it wouldn't make much difference. I'm afraid we're going to have to resort to more desperate measures. We're going to need Nicholas's teams to help out, but I think I've got a plan that might work."

Billy woke up Nicholas Stavros and asked him to come over.

After Larry had briefed him, Nicholas sat quietly for a few moments, before he said, "It sounds like we're in a jam, what can I do to help?"

"Can you install a couple of Petawatt lasers on the shuttles?"

"Sure, but you're not going to be able to run multiple lasers and keep the shields up. What else are you going to need?"

"I need you to upgrade every snowmobile that you can with a seven-point-six-two-millimeter Minigun. I know they're small, but I need them to carry as many rounds of ammo as you can pack into them."

As they continued talking, Larry thought about how lucky they were to have the Miniguns.

General Medley had been killed before they left Earth, but he had made sure the *Genesis* had been well stocked with arms. Nicholas Stavros had been right when he had said that the general was a little obsessed about it, because they had found a very interesting cross section of weapons.

When they were finished talking, Nicholas pulled in every man he could to work on Larry's project. The snowmobiles were quite a task, but it didn't take very long to install the additional lasers on the shuttles. When they were finished, they got together to try them out.

When they were all on board, Larry guided the shuttle away from the base so they could test-fire the lasers. When they reached a safe distance, he raised the shields and triggered the twin lasers.

The lasers worked, but they all heard the shields drop as they lost power.

"It's like I warned you, there isn't enough power to run the lasers and the shields at the same time," Nicholas said.

"We'll just have to make do," Larry replied. "How are you coming with the Miniguns?"

"We don't have enough time to convert all the snow-mobiles, but we should finish up by tomorrow night."

THE DAY AFTER they finished, they sent out thirty-six armed snowmobiles and another fifty that were carrying extra ammunition and gasoline.

For the first two days, they had to endure gale-force winds and almost whiteout conditions as they sped toward the advancing Nubian column.

They couldn't have continued if Nicholas's teams hadn't added fairings to deflect the wind and snow as they were speeding across the frozen wasteland. They rode day and night, only stopping to catch a few hours rest when exhaustion set in.

Seen from the air, the frozen landscape looked smooth. In reality, it was extremely rough, and the constant pounding made for a very taxing journey.

It took five days and four nights to reach the Nubian army's location. When they were within a couple of miles of the Nubians, they stopped so they could set up their base camp and give everyone a little rest before they engaged for the first time. Once they were started, Larry's strategy called for them to keep constant pressure on the Nubians.

When everything was ready, they split the armed snow-mobiles into two teams so they could take turns stopping to refuel and rearm.

When everyone was in position, the shuttles took off. They would provide air support, and command and control for the attack. Larry Sheldon was in the lead shuttle to keep the attack properly coordinated.

The Nubian column stretched out for over three miles,

and it was made up of ten thousand men, five hundred horse-drawn cannons, and a hundred wagons full of supplies.

The first team launched their attack when they reached the main column. The roar of their engines and the distinctive sound of the Miniguns filled the air as they came rushing in. Each gun could fire up to three thousand rounds a minute, and their combined firepower was devastating. As they made their first pass at the Nubians, the shuttles swooped down with their lasers blazing.

Every time the snowmobiles made a pass at the Nubians, their Miniguns cut a swath of death through their ranks. They were attacking from all directions, trying to keep the Nubians off balance.

The initial attacks had caught the Nubians by surprise, but they were battle-hardened veterans, and their officers soon steadied them. The snowmobiles were staying well out of the range of the Nubian muskets, but their artillery had started to return fire.

They weren't terribly accurate, but there were a lot of them. Most of the rounds missed, but some didn't, and Larry's soldiers began to lose snowmobiles.

"We've got to take out those cannons," Larry said. He called to the other shuttle. "We need to concentrate our fire on their artillery."

The shuttles turned and went directly at the massed artillery. When the Nubians saw the shuttles turn toward them, they hurriedly elevated their cannons to try to hit them.

During the next forty minutes, the shuttles made seven passes, and their lasers took a terrible toll on the Nubian artillery. The Nubian artillery commander was killed in the first pass, and the gun crews were now firing wildly into the sky.

When their commanding officer, Colonel Zacharias, realized what was happening, he stepped in and took control of the gun crews.

"Set your guns at the maximum elevation, and hold your fire until they come around again. Don't fire until I give the order."

When the shuttles came around again, he waited until they were within range before he ordered the gun crews to fire.

They still had over two hundred guns left, and when they fired, they threw up a curtain of shells, hitting both shuttles.

The two shells that hit Larry's shuttle knocked it off course, but it managed to stay in the air.

The other shuttle took several direct hits and exploded. The explosion was so violent that the Nubians momentarily stopped firing.

The pilot of Larry's shuttle said, "We're losing power, and I'm not sure how much longer I can keep it in the air."

Larry made a quick assessment of their situation and said, "Okay, let's get back to base."

Before they left, he called to the commander of the snowmobiles. "We've been hit, and we're returning to base. You're on your own, but keep pressing the attack as long as you can."

The men they had chosen for the mission were absolutely fearless, and even as their numbers dwindled, they continued to drive home their attacks. The only time they stopped was when they needed ammunition or gas.

The sun was starting to set when what remained of the Nubian column abandoned their equipment and ran.

Of the thirty-six snowmobiles they had started with, only two had survived.

Billy had been monitoring the battle with their drones,

but after they lost the shuttles, there had been little else they could do.

The surviving snowmobiles had taken off after the retreating Nubians, but when Billy realized what was happening, he called them back. Once he was sure they were headed back, he met with the rest of the team to try and figure out what assets they had left.

"How bad is the shuttle damaged?" Billy asked.

"It'll still fly, but not for very long," Nicholas said. "The power system is pretty well shot. It's got maybe three hours of flight time before it's completely dead."

"How did we do against the Nubians?" Larry asked.

"We're still analyzing the video, but it looks like we managed to destroy most of their artillery and all but a few hundred of their troops. The survivors abandoned their equipment and were running for home when I called off the attack."

"Good, maybe we bought a little more time."

"We did, but I'm afraid that we've paid a heavy price for it."

16

WHEN JOHN TYLER woke up, Brother Dalmatius was missing. As he had suspected, he found him busy reading the passages on the church's wall.

"You're up early," John said.

"I was having a hard time sleeping. So I decided to try and finish reading about my ancestors, and I'm glad I did. The final section was added several years after they had left the tunnels."

"Is there anything that'll help us out?"

"Not really, but it details the terrible destruction they found when they returned to the surface, and the struggles they experienced."

"That's all very interesting," John said impatiently. "But we really need to get going."

"You're the boss. I just wish we could stay here a little longer."

"You can always come back, once I've rescued Linda."

"I'm afraid the elders would never allow it, but I guess I could ask."

After they ate breakfast, John told Brother Dalmatius, "We need to follow the shoreline for about two miles in that direction."

As they neared the far side of the cavern, the sound of the waterfall faded away, and all they could hear was the crunch of the sand under their feet and the rhythmic sound of the waves hitting the shoreline.

When they reached the other side, there was only one tunnel.

"It looks like this is going to be little easier," John said.

He called up the pictures of the map and said, "That's funny, the map shows two tunnels, and this one looks like it should be the one on the right."

"Let me take a look at it before we go in," Brother Dalmatius said.

As he carefully inspected the tunnel's entrance, John asked impatiently, "What are you looking for? We need to pick up the pace."

"I don't know where the other one is, but this isn't the right one."

After John had studied the map for a few seconds, he said, "What if the water level has changed over the years and the other cave is under water?"

"If that's the case, I guess we're finished. We might as well turn around and go back. Maybe I can think of a way to sneak you into the monastery."

"There's no way that's going to work. Let me think about this for a minute."

They sat down beside the lake and they considered their options.

After he'd thought about it for a few minutes, John came to a decision. He didn't say a word as unloaded the gear he was carrying, and removed his boots and socks.

"What are you doing?"

"I'm going to see if the other tunnel is underwater."

"What good would that do? If it's underwater we won't be able to use it."

"Look at the other tunnel. It looks like it's starting to

angle upward. If the other one does as well, the water shouldn't go in very far."

"Okay, but I've got to tell you that I can't swim."

"That could be a problem, but we'll deal with that if we need to."

John waded out until the water was over his head. He treaded water for a few seconds, took a deep breath, and dove out of sight.

He had been gone for over ten minutes, and Brother Dalmatius was getting worried. He was trying to decide what to do when John popped up and swam ashore.

"I was afraid you'd drowned."

"Sorry, I stayed longer than I intended. But I've got good news. I found the second tunnel, and the water only goes back for about ten feet. Past that point, it's bone dry."

Brother Dalmatius shivered as he considered what that meant. "I'm sorry, but I just can't do it. I'm deathly afraid of water."

"Don't worry about it. It'll take me a couple of trips to move our equipment, and then I'll take you."

When John finished moving the equipment, he sat down on the beach to rest for a few minutes.

When John looked over at Brother Dalmatius, he could tell he was almost beside himself with fear. He had seen fear before, but this was about as bad as he had ever seen. He knew that once they were in the water, it was going to get even worse, and the brother was a very large man.

John moved over beside him and said, "Look, I know that you're scared, but I'm going to show you a little trick that I've learned. Close your eyes and count backward from ten."

"What good will that do?"

"Trust me, just try it."

Brother Dalmatius closed his eyes and started counting, "Ten, nine, eight . . ."

John stood up and knocked him out cold.

He had a hard time dragging the monk's unconscious body across the sand. When he got him to the water's edge, he put a large plastic bag over his head. Just before he sealed it, he made sure there was enough air trapped inside so the man could breathe.

Once he had him in the water, John didn't have any trouble getting him into the underwater cave. A couple of minutes later Brother Dalmatius woke up and asked, "How did I get in here, and why does my jaw hurt so much?"

"I'm sorry. I had to knock you out. But I had to get you in here, and it seemed like the easiest way to do it."

The monk thought about it and said, "You're probably right. It could've gotten ugly if you had tried to force me into the water."

Once Dalmatius was up to it, they lit another set of torches and started up the tunnel.

They made good progress, since they were relatively sure the tunnel wasn't going to be booby trapped. A couple of hours later they reached the next cavern.

"From what I can tell by looking at the map, this is the largest cavern," John said.

The cavern stretched far out of the range of their torches. John switched on his flashlight so he could gain a perspective on how big it was.

As he swept his flashlight around the cavern, they could see that, unlike the others, this one had several levels of living areas.

"Wow, this is big," John said. "I've already counted fifteen levels in here."

He continued sweeping the light around for a couple

of minutes, then he turned it off to conserve the batteries. When he did, he noticed there was a faint light at the top of the cavern.

"I wonder where the light is coming from," John said.

"It's hard to say, but I don't think it was there a few minutes ago."

As they moved across the cavern, it continued to get brighter. By the time they had reached the center, it was as bright as a summer day.

"This is really weird. I know we're probably several thousand feet underground, but this is like being outside," John remarked.

He raised his M-25 rifle to his shoulder and used its scope to get a closer look at the top of the cavern.

It took him a few seconds to locate them, but he saw that the light was being reflected off of a series of mirrors that had been placed all along the top edges of the cavern. Light was coming out of four vertical shafts, then reflecting off the mirrors below. He realized there must be a solar collection system that was being used to focus sunlight down the shafts to the mirrors below.

He was amazed that the light was intense enough to feel like direct sunlight.

"I was wondering how they managed to live down here for that many years with nothing but torchlight," John said. "That's ingenious, and it also explains how they got air, and where the smoke from the fires went.

"Let's keep moving. I would like to get there today, if we can."

"We should be getting close," Dalmatius said. "Does the map show what's coming up next?"

John studied it for a moment, and said, "We should be coming up on three tunnels. It looks like they all end at the vertical shaft that leads to the monastery's basement."

"That sounds right, but two of them will contain traps."

"THAT'S NOT GOOD," John exclaimed when he saw that the tunnel they needed to use had collapsed. "Now what are we supposed to do?"

"I guess we'll have to try to make it through one of the other tunnels."

"I thought you said they would both be booby trapped?"

"I'm sure they are, but it's the only way, unless the map shows some other route."

John studied the map for several minutes, and he said, "Nope that's all there is. Do you want me to go first?"

"I'll do it. After all, I've spent most of my life preparing for this moment."

The tunnel next to the cave-in looked shaky, so they took the other one.

They had only gone for a couple hundred feet when Dalmatius stopped and said, "Here's one, and it should be just like the others."

John used one of their torches to trigger the trap, and once again the darts came flying out. "So far so good, let's keep going."

Their progress was painfully slow as they made their way through the tunnel. Their caution was justified, however, because over the next hour and half, they had to stop and disarm three more dart traps.

Brother Dalmatius had been inching along the tunnel's wall when his left foot broke through the floor. Off balance, he started to fall forward, but John grabbed him by his shirt collar and yanked him backward so hard that they both fell to the ground.

Dalmatius picked up his torch and held it over the hole in the tunnel's floor. The wind from the shaft below made the flame of his torch dance.

His voice quavered when he told John, "Thanks, that was close. Once again, there seems to be a minor gap in my lessons."

"I'm just glad I managed to grab you," John said as he looked down at the gaping hole in the floor.

Still lying down, John took one their spare torches and smashed the floor on the other side of the hole. It took him five tries before he was satisfied he'd reached solid footing again. When he was finished, the hole was almost four feet wide.

Once he had Brother Dalmatius calmed down, they jumped over the hole and continued down the tunnel.

As they rounded a bend, they saw a small cavern at the end of the tunnel. On the far wall, they could see the wooden ladder that would lead them to the monastery.

"Look there it is," Dalmatius said excitedly. "That ladder should lead straight to the monastery's basement."

Before John could stop him, he took off running toward the ladder.

As he came rushing out of the tunnel, he tripped the last of the booby traps. Most of the darts missed him, but two struck him with such force that they lifted him off of the floor and slammed him against the wall.

By the time John reached him, he was almost dead. When he tried to raise his head up to speak, blood bubbled out of his nose and mouth.

He was trying to tell John something, so John bent down to try to hear what he was saying.

"I'm so sorry that I've failed you. The ladder should lead to the basement. Don't forget, Linda is on the very top level of the monastery." He paused, as he tried to clear his lungs, and every time he coughed, a spray of blood speckled the sand. It took several tries, but he was finally able to continue. "When you reach the ground floor, take the stairs on your left. They'll take you to the top floor. May God speed, but I don't know how you're going to make it, because every floor has soldiers guarding it."

"You don't need to worry about that, I'll be fine. Now, let me see if I can get the bleeding stopped."

"Don't waste your time on me, because I'm going to see God, and that's all that any man could ask for."

John started to answer, but Brother Dalmatius was already gone. He took a moment to ask God to receive Dalmatius's soul and to grant him the strength to save Linda.

After he finished his prayer, he took a few minutes to sort through his equipment. He knew he was going to have to move fast, so he abandoned everything but the essentials.

He clipped his flashlight onto his shoulder, took a deep breath, and started up the ancient wooden ladder. The ladder creaked and groaned with every step, but he made it safely to the top.

When he stepped off the ladder, into the tiny room at the top, the only thing he saw was a small wooden door with an iron bar holding it shut. He lifted the bar out of the way and pushed on the door. It didn't give at first, so he braced his feet against the other wall and pushed with all of his strength.

When he had it open far enough, he slipped through into the basement.

As he shined his flashlight around the room, he saw why the door had been so difficult to open. The basement was packed with barrels, and one of them had gotten wedged against the door. Curious, he took his knife out and pried up the lid on one of them.

When he saw that the barrel was filled with gunpowder, he was very glad he wasn't holding a torch.

Once he found the stairway, he paused to make one last check of his weapons. He knew he was vastly outnumbered, but he hoped his vastly superior weapons and training would give him at least an outside chance of success.

When he was ready, he started jogging up the stairs. He managed to get by the first floor without being spotted, but when he reached the second floor, he ran into two armed guards.

They had been startled to see him, which gave him just enough time to shoot them both in the head with his silenced pistol.

He paused just long enough to hide their bodies on the staircase before he moved on.

The next floor only had one guard, and he had his back to the stairway. He never knew John was there, as he crept up behind him and slit his throat. John wiped his knife off on the man's shirt and hid his body in the stairway.

As he continued up the stairs, it was much the same on the other floors. He had to kill seven more guards on the way up, but none of them even managed to fire a shot.

When he reached the door to the top floor, he paused for several seconds to catch his breath. He was a little surprised that he was still alive, but he knew the hard part was coming up.

When he was ready, he moved through the doorway into the hallway. Unluckily for all concerned, they were in the process of changing the guards.

Even though he was badly outnumbered, he never hesitated; he drew his pistol and started moving toward the guards. His years of combat experience were paying off, as he calmly emptied his pistol into the group. When the pistol was empty he holstered it and unlimbered his rifle. He didn't have a silencer on his rifle and the rapid boom reverberated throughout the normally quiet hall.

As he moved down the hallway toward Linda's room, he cut down three more heavily armed guards who came rushing down the hall to intercept him.

John had just killed the two guards standing in front of Linda's door when he was hit by a volley of bullets.

The first one shattered his flashlight, and several more shredded his backpack. His body armor saved him from any serious injury, but the impacts knocked him off balance.

He steadied himself against the wall and put several rounds into the group firing at him.

When he turned back to the door, Linda jerked it open and said, "I've never been so happy to see anyone in my whole life."

"Same here, but we need to get going. Do you know of any other way out of here?"

"The stairs are the only way up here."

When he looked back at the stairs, he could see that the guards were getting organized to make another charge at him. He put several rounds into them to slow them down and pushed Linda back inside the room.

He saw that the door had a place for a bar, so he picked up a dead soldier's sword. After he had closed the heavy oak door, he used the sword to bar the door.

He quickly surveyed the room and said, "What's outside that window?"

"Not much: a small patio and a sheer drop of several thousand feet."

He wanted to buy them some time, so he told her, "Let's push some of this furniture up against the door. It might slow them down a little."

After they had barricaded the door as best they could, John took off his pack so he could get at the two parachutes he had brought along. The top one had several holes in it where the musket fire had hit him. After he had checked it out, he decided it wasn't safe to use. As he was inspecting their remaining chute for damage, he heard soldiers trying to force their way through the door.

WHILE THE REST of the guards were trying to break down the door, one of the soldiers went to get help. When the soldier told his lieutenant that someone was attempting to free Linda West, it sent a cold chill down the officer's back.

Even though he knew it was pointless, he sent the remainder of his men up the stairs to reinforce the guards. Once they had left, he went directly to the basement to carry out his orders.

The lieutenant was only thirty years old, and as he lit the fuse, he thought of his young family. He knew that if he failed to carry out his orders, the queen would have them all killed. Knowing that there was no way for him to reach safety, he sat down on the stairs to wait as the fuse blazed up its path toward the gunpowder.

JOHN PUT THE chute on and rushed out onto the balcony. He moved a stone bench over to the railing and climbed up on it.

When he looked over at Linda, she asked nervously, "We're going to have to jump, aren't we?"

"Yes, we are. Climb up here and I'll strap this harness around you."

Once he had her strapped to him, he took a deep breath and launched out over the railing. As they hurtled down the face of the cliff, it took him a couple of seconds to get oriented correctly, and then he pulled the rip cord.

They descended for several seconds as he guided the chute away from the mountainside as quickly as he could; they were just about to cross over the river when the fuse reached the gunpowder.

The explosion ripped through the multiple floors of the monastery, killing everyone inside. Shortly after, the entire mountainside exploded in a shower of fire and shattered rock.

The tremendous shockwave from the explosion pushed their chute past the river and out over the forest. John desperately searched for an opening in the thick canopy of trees, but he couldn't see any. As the ground rushed up at them, he gave up on finding an opening. When he saw a section of trees that looked a little thinner than the rest, he guided their chute toward them.

He called to Linda, "Cover your face with your arms."

As they crashed through the tree limbs, one of them smashed against John's head. Knocked cold, he went limp just before they crashed into the ground.

Even though she had tried to cover it, Linda's face was pretty cut up from the tree branches. The landing knocked the wind out of her, but otherwise she was alright.

Their chute was still billowing in the breeze, and it was slowly dragging them through the trees.

Linda struggled to regain her breath, and when she had, she asked John, "Can you believe we made it?"

When there was no answer she asked, "John, are you alright?"

She was worried that he might be badly injured. It was a bit of a struggle, but she finally found his knife and cut the chute loose. Then she used it to cut herself out of the harness.

When she stood up, she felt something running down her cheek, and when she wiped it off, she saw it was blood.

She felt Billy in her mind as he asked, *Are you alright. You seemed terrified a few moments ago.*

Instead of answering him, she simply showed him what had just happened.

Wow that was intense. How badly are you and John hurt?

I've got several cuts on my face, but other than that, I'm not hurt.

Even as she was telling Billy about it, the blood had already stopped, and the cuts were almost healed.

She took a quick look at John and said, *He's out cold, so it's going to be hard to tell for sure. The wound on his head doesn't look that bad, but I won't know much more until he wakes up. Right now my biggest worry is that the Nubians will find us.*

Give us a couple of minutes to move some drones over your position, and I'll try to find out what you're up against. Meanwhile, just stay where you're at. If they do find you, just surrender, don't put up a fight.

IT TOOK BILLY only a few minutes to gather the team so they could start figuring out what was going on.

"What have you found so far?" Billy asked.

"It looks like the entire mountain blew up," Larry replied. He pointed to the screen where he was reviewing the high-resolution photos from the drone. "If you'll look right here, you can see where the bottom portion of the monastery blew straight out toward the river. It looks like the rest of it slid straight down as it collapsed. There's no way that anyone who was inside survived."

"Have you been able to spot them yet?"

"We have, but it's a little hard to see because of the trees. But if you'll look closely, you can just see their chute. We had to use infrared to find their heat signatures, but they're lying on the ground about thirty meters to the left of it. The Nubians must think that they're dead, because it doesn't look like they're even looking for them."

"What are the chances of us getting in there with the shuttle?"

"The shuttle's got less than three hours of flight time left, so we're only going to get one chance. Given the terrain, and all the activity going on around them, I think that we should let them make their way back downriver before we try."

After Billy and Larry had finished discussing their options, Billy contacted Linda again.

As disorganized as the Nubians seem to be, we think that you'll be alright where you're at, Billy said. *Larry's going to keep a drone over your position so that we can keep an eye on you until we can figure out how to come and get you.*

When do you think that will be?

Larry and I think that it would be best if you moved downriver before we try to pick you up.

I'm not sure when we'll be able to do that. It'll depend on what sort of shape John's in when he wakes up.

I understand. I hate it, but I'm afraid that means that you're going to have to spend the night out there.

Okay, I need to get busy and see if I can find something to help us stay warm during the night. It might not hurt to try to camouflage our location a little.

WHEN THEY FINISHED talking, she took another look at John's wounds. When she was satisfied that she had done what she could for him, she went to work on getting them set for the night.

She knew they were going to need water, but when she found John's canteen, it was empty. She could hear the faint sounds of a stream, so she crept through the forest to get some water.

She had always loved the smell of a campfire on a crisp autumn night, but the smoke from the monastery smelled more like a burning garbage dump.

She could still hear a lot of activity in the distance, but as night fell, a hush settled over the valley. She shivered a little as the temperature started to drop. They were both dressed warmly, but the nights in that part of Midgard were always cold.

She was hungry, so she rummaged through John's pack, but he had abandoned all of his food.

Cold, hungry, and more than a little scared, she crawled into the shelter she'd built and snuggled up against John to try and keep him warm.

She had a difficult time sleeping, but when she did, she kept having horrendous nightmares.

In her dreams, she and Billy were in a strange spaceship,

and it was on a collision path with the meteor. In each of her dreams, the meteor would get closer and closer until it was the only thing they could see, and then she would wake up in a cold sweat.

JUST AS THE sun was starting to rise over the mountains, she felt Billy in her mind.

Hey you, how was your night?

Terrible. I'm cold, hungry, and I kept having the worst nightmares.

I did, too, but how's John doing?

I'll check him again when I can see a little better. But he's still breathing, and that's a good start.

I just realized that you're snuggled up to him. I'm jealous.

You are not. I know you can tell that I'm just doing it for warmth.

Of course I can, but I love pulling your chain once in a while. Contact me when you know how John is doing. Millie keeps calling me to ask, and I would love to be able to tell her that he's alright.

When it was light enough to see, Linda decided to take a look a John's head wound. The wound had bled through the bandage, so it pulled a little when she removed it.

"Hey, that hurts."

"Good, you're awake. How do you feel?"

He took a moment to answer, lifting himself up on one elbow.

"Okay I guess. Other than that my head really hurts, and I feel like someone beat me. How long have I been out?"

"You've been unconscious ever since we jumped yesterday. I was beginning to worry that you were hurt worse than I thought."

Fully awake, John glanced around the crude lean-to and said, "You did a good job. Have you had any trouble with the Nubians?"

"Not yet. Larry has a drone over us, and he didn't think they were even looking for us."

"Are you sure you're alright?" John asked. "There's blood all over your shirt, but I don't see any marks on you."

"I had some cuts from the tree limbs, but I'm better now."

"I'd heard rumors about how fast you and Billy could heal."

"As you can see, it's not a rumor."

"I tell you what. Let's get out of here. I'll give them a call and get them to come and pick us up."

When he pulled his satellite phone out of his pocket, he looked at it and said, "This thing is a complete mess. How in the world did you get it to work?"

"I didn't use the phone."

He started to ask how she had talked to Billy, when he remembered that they were telepathic.

"You've told me before, but I don't think I've ever really believed it. Would you mind trying to contact him?"

WHAT'S GOING ON, are you in trouble? Billy asked.

Not at all. John just wanted me to try to reach you.

That's sounds promising. Does that mean he's going to be alright?

He seems fine, but he wants to know what you're seeing of the Nubians, and when you can come and get us.

They're still disorganized. You may have a problem, however, because it looks like they have reinforcements on the way. We've had issues since John left, and we're down to one shuttle, and it only has an enough power for one more trip. There's still too much activity in your area for us to be sure that we can get in and out. If you're up to it, we would like you to move down the river a few miles.

After John and Linda had discussed it, she told Billy, *We'll leave tonight after it gets dark, and we'll be following the river, because John had to abandon his night-vision gear. I'll let you know when we leave.*

When they finished talking, Linda asked John, "I'm starving, can you tell me how to find us something to eat?"

"You should be able to find some nuts in the woods, but I'm afraid there won't be much else."

"There's a stream about seventy yards from here. Do you think I could catch some fish?"

"I've got a hook and a piece of a line in my kit. I'll give it a try while you gather some nuts."

It had taken most of the day, but John managed to catch two nice-sized fish, and Linda had gathered a couple of pounds of nuts. They couldn't chance lighting a fire, so they had to eat the fish raw.

When it got dark, they started downriver. John had a terrific headache, and was still a little weak, so they split up their meager possessions to lighten the load on him.

They were staying as close to the river as possible, which meant they were visible from the water. The river was heavily patrolled, and every time a patrol boat would pass by, they had to hide in the brush.

The darkness and the terrain had made it tough going, but they managed to cover about five miles by the time the sun started to come up.

It was too dangerous travel in the daylight, and John could see that Linda was getting tired.

"We need to find some place to hole up. Keep your eye out for a cave or a heavy stand of brush."

"Isn't that a cave over there?"

"It sure is, but let me check it out before you get too close."

He slowly made his way to the mouth of the cave and flipped his lighter open so he could look inside. He wasn't pleased when he saw the flame reflecting in the eyes of the biggest bear he had ever seen.

John wasn't prone to panicking, but as the bear roared and charged him, he knew that he was in real trouble.

Linda was carrying his rifle, so all he had was his pistol. He took a couple of steps backward, and yelled, "Run, run for your life, and I'll try to slow it up."

He whipped his pistol out and started shooting. He emptied a full magazine of the SIG Sauer's forty-caliber slugs into the bear, but all he managed to do was slow it down.

Linda had grown up around guns, so instead of running, she dropped to one knee and took aim. The rifle didn't fire the first time because she forgot to flip the safety off.

After John had burned through the clip in his pistol, he pulled his knife and tried to brace himself for the bear's charge. When the bear reached him, it reared up on its hind legs and swatted him in the chest with its massive paw. The vicious blow launched him through the air into a large pile of brush. It momentarily stunned him, but his body armor had absorbed most of the blow.

As his mind raced through his limited options, he was surprised to hear Linda start shooting.

She had flinched a little from the recoil of the first shot, but she quickly recovered and resumed firing.

Even though the M-25 was more than capable of killing the bear, she had to put eight more rounds into it before it dropped dead in front of her.

As John scrambled to his feet, he told her, "We'd better get moving. I imagine that someone heard the shots, and they'll be sending someone to check it out."

"THAT WAS GUNFIRE," Admiral Massawa said. "It sounded like it came from over there. Send a couple of the boats over to check it out."

AS JOHN WAS retrieving his knife and pistol, he asked, "Can you handle a pistol?"

"Better than a rifle."

He slipped another clip in the pistol, and said, "Let's trade, then. I'm afraid that we may be in for a fight. But who knows, maybe we'll get lucky and no one heard the shots."

As they stepped out of the brush beside the river, they ran right into the two boats that Admiral Massawa had just dispatched.

The boats were only a couple hundred yards away, so John immediately opened fire.

At that range, they had no chance against his rifle. In a matter of seconds, he had killed the crew of the lead boat, and the second one turned tail and ran.

THE ADMIRAL WAS using the captain's spyglass, so he could see that there were only two of them, and that one of them was a girl.

Even though only one of them was shooting, he quickly realized that his men were outgunned.

When he saw the second boat turn around, he yelled to his boat's captain, "Get us out of here."

"What about the other boat?"

"Leave it. I'm not going to get killed over one lousy boat."

They didn't even wait for the remaining boat to rejoin them as they turned and resumed their course upriver.

WITH NOBODY LEFT alive to steer it, the lead boat continued on its course until it ran aground just down from John and Linda Lou.

"They know we're here, so we might as well take a chance and use their boat," John said. "There's no need for you to see this, so give me a few minutes to dispose of the bodies."

"I've seen worse, and it'll go quicker if I help."

Working together, it didn't take very long to throw the bodies overboard. When they finished, Linda held the tiller while John pushed the boat off the bank and back into the river channel.

They met a few boats as they raced down the river, but the Nubians didn't pay any attention to them.

By noon they had reached the point where the river intersected with another even larger river. The other river had been dammed up, so the flow of water had been reduced to a gentle current.

"That sure is a big dam," Linda remarked.

"It sure is. I've been amazed at what they've managed accomplish with little or no technology."

As they passed by the dock at the mouth the river, there

were a group of Nubian sailors who were about to un-load a string of barges.

They were close enough for the sailors to see them, and when the Nubians realized that strangers had one of their boats, several of them started to pile into one of the boats to give chase.

When John saw what they were doing, he shot a couple of the sailors to discourage them. When they saw their men go down, the rest of them dived for cover, and by the time they regained their courage, John's boat was out of sight.

ABOUT AN HOUR after Admiral Massawa had turned tail and ran, he came to the realization that the queen wasn't going to look favorably on his lack of courage. As he pondered what he should do, he saw one of their boats racing down the river toward them.

When they stopped it to find out what was going on, the young sergeant told him, "They've attacked the monastery, and it's been blown to rubble."

The admiral knew immediately what had happened. They had carried out his orders to destroy the monastery in the event of a rescue attempt. Seconds later, it hit him that the girl on the riverbank could have been Linda West.

His blood ran cold as he realized that if it had been Linda West, he and everyone in his entire family would be put to a terrible death.

He told the sergeant, "You're coming with us." He turned to the boat captain and said, "We're turning around, we've got to find those people again."

* * *

IT HAD BEEN so crazy that Linda hadn't reached out to Billy until they had passed the dam.

When she finished sharing what had happened to them, he told her, *Stay on your current heading, and we'll be there as soon as we can.*

Billy met Larry at the shuttle. "They're on a captured Nubian boat, and Linda said that they just passed a large dam," Billy said as they took off.

WHEN ADMIRAL MASSAWA reached the dam, the group that John Tyler had just shot up was still milling about discussing what had happened.

"Have any of you seen a boat go by here in the last couple of hours?" Admiral Massawa asked.

"Yes, sir, they went by here about an hour ago. They killed two of our men when we tried to stop them."

As the admiral contemplated what he should do, he was growing more desperate by the minute. He knew that they probably couldn't catch them, but he had to do something.

As he looked around frantically, he noticed the barges full of gunpowder barrels and the massive dam, and thought to himself, "It might work, and besides, I can't think of anything else to try."

He knew that what he was contemplating was an act of desperation, but he didn't care.

"I want you to take all of those barrels of gunpowder and put them at the base of the dam," Admiral Massawa ordered.

"Why would you want to do that?" The commander asked. "They might accidentally explode and destroy the dam."

"You fool, I intend to blow it up. I've got to stop the

people that shot up your men. If I don't manage to kill them, the queen will kill my entire family."

After he had said it, he didn't have any idea why he had told him that.

Spurred on by the admiral, the men worked frantically, and in less than an hour they had the gunpowder in place.

"Are you sure that you want to do this?" the commander asked. "It's going to flood every settlement from here to the ocean."

"Shut up and light the fuse."

The explosion ripped the center out of the dam, and in seconds there was a hundred-foot-tall wall of water racing down the valley.

The admiral knew that he was killing thousands of people, but he didn't care as long as it saved his family.

WHEN THE VIDEO from the drones had first come in Larry exclaimed, "Unbelievable, the maniacs have blown the dam. There's a wall of water headed straight for Linda and John."

The shuttle was already at its maximum speed, so there wasn't anything else they could do.

"We'll be there in a few minutes, but it's going to be close," Larry Sheldon said.

Billy let Linda know that they were going to take them directly off the boat.

John tied the boat's tiller in place, and they moved to the bow of the boat.

As soon as the bulk of the water had gone down the river, the admiral took his men and followed. He knew that he needed to make absolutely sure that Linda West was dead.

"There they are," Larry said. "When I lower the ramp, tie off a couple of ropes and throw them down the ramp. That way they'll have something to hold on to."

Larry brought the shuttle down quickly and matched its speed to the boat. When he lowered the ramp, all they could hear was the roar of the water as it approached.

When the ramp was within three feet of the boat's deck, Linda and John jumped onto the ramp and grabbed the ropes.

As soon as he saw them grab the ropes, Larry screamed to them over the ship's loudspeaker, "Hold on tight, the water's on top of us and I've got to climb."

Larry put the shuttle into a steep climb, and they were thrown off their feet.

As they both struggled to keep their grip on the ropes, Billy touched Linda's mind. *Please hold on. It'll only be a few more seconds until he can level out.*

It seemed like forever, but it was less than six seconds before Larry leveled the ship out. As soon as it started to level off, several of the crew rushed down the ramp to help them.

When Billy reached Linda, he picked her up in his arms and said, "You're safe, you can let go of the rope."

"I'd given up ever being safe again."

Once they were safely on board, Larry closed the ramp and they all walked up to the bridge.

Larry was circling over the torrent of water below them when they got to the shuttle's bridge.

"What madman would kill all those people in an attempt to murder you?" Larry asked.

"I imagine it was Admiral Massawa," Linda said. "He was the one that carried out the scheme to kidnap me. He was also the one that had them stuff the monastery full of explosives."

"Do you think you would recognize him if you saw him again?" Larry asked.

"Without a doubt," Linda said. "I only saw him once, but I'll never forget his face."

Larry focused the forward camera in on the Nubian boats below them. "Is he in that group of men?"

She studied the screen for a couple of seconds and said, "Yes, he's the one standing off by himself."

Larry didn't say a word. He lowered the ramp again and put the shuttle on autopilot. When he got to the rear of the ship, he took one of the sniper M-25s and walked over to the opening.

He braced himself against the edge of the doorway, and then he put one shot right between the admiral's eyes.

When he got back to the bridge, he looked at Linda and said, "He won't be bothering you again."

17

It wasn't that anyone had a problem with what Larry Sheldon had done, but no one said anything for the first ten minutes of their flight back to the base.

They were still several hundred miles away from their base when they caught sight of the main Nubian army. They were too high for the Nubians to be able to see them, but Larry had turned on the holographic projectors so the shuttle crew had a great view of the column.

It was strung out over five miles, and it was the largest single army the Nubians had ever fielded. It was made up of almost a hundred thousand infantry, fifteen thousand cavalry, a thousand cannons, and seven hundred supply wagons.

At one time it had been the crown jewel of Queen Amanirenas's military, but the journey from the coast had taken its toll on them. They had done their best to outfit the army for the bitter cold, but there was simply no way to prepare them for the conditions they had encountered. The persistent attacks by John Tyler's raiders and the horrible weather conditions had caused their morale to fall to a dangerous level; however, their latest debacle was threatening to destroy it altogether.

General Abrahams had personally developed their latest plan to attack the Earth settlement. He could have sent a larger force, but he had been confident that ten thousand seasoned warriors would be more than enough to get the job done.

When the first survivor came straggling in, the general dismissed his story as a coward's attempt to cover his desertion under fire. The general had decided to make an example of him and had him executed the next morning.

A couple of days later, the rest of the survivors started to show up, and he realized the soldier had been telling the truth. In an attempt to limit the damage to the army's morale, he spent almost two weeks personally interrogating them before he felt like he had the whole story.

By the time he'd finished going over his notes, he had come to the conclusion that their entire mission was at risk.

He had gone ahead and executed the rest of the survivors in a vain attempt to keep the group's fate a secret. He'd been much too late, however, because the survivors had already shared their stories with the guards.

The queen had been very specific, so General Abrahams already knew what the price of failure would be, and he was determined to try to complete his mission.

LARRY HAD SLOWED the shuttle to a hover over the Nubian column, and as they watched in awe, they had no way of knowing how desperate the Nubian army's situation had become.

They were running out of time, but they took a few more minutes to take some video of the enemy column before they left.

The shuttle had already started to descend when they reached the scene of the latest battle with the Nubians. The remnants from the battle were spread out over almost four miles. The wind-driven snow had already begun to cover the scars of the battle, but it was still readily apparent that a battle had taken place.

"They didn't even bother to bury their dead," John remarked in disgust.

"We didn't either," Larry replied.

It wasn't hard to tell the difference, since the blasted remnants of their snowmobiles encircled the mass of destruction that had been the Nubian strike force.

John glared at Larry and said, "We need to land, right now, and bury those men."

"I wish that I could. But we're almost out of power, and we'll be lucky to make it back as it is. I'll tell you what I will do. When we get back, I'll come back out here with some men and make sure that they all get a proper burial."

When they landed, Linda told Billy, "I'm going to take John to the infirmary and get him checked out. Then I'm going to take a nice hot bath and get some sleep."

As they were about to leave, Billy pulled John aside. "Linda is going to get you checked out at the infirmary, and when she's done with you, I want you to take some time off. I don't want you to worry about anything for a while, other than spending some time with your family. I don't know that I can ever repay what you've done for me, but if you ever need anything, anything at all, all you have to do is ask."

"Thanks, and I'll take you up on your offer of the time off, but it was my honor to do it."

After everyone else had gone, Larry and Billy stayed on the shuttle to discuss what to do about the Nubian army. Finally, Larry told him, "Let's go and kick this around with Nicholas."

* * *

"DIDN'T YOU JUST make a couple of mortars for one of John's teams?" Larry asked Nicholas.

"Yes, we did. We patterned them after the ones we found in the weapons locker. They're a hundred and twenty millimeter, and with the rocket assist package we added, we've gotten the range up to twelve kilometers."

"Great, how many can you make me?"

"I hadn't thought about mass production, but it's a pretty simple manufacturing process. Give me just a moment.

"Using our current processes, we should be able to make about twenty a day. How many do you think you're going to want?"

"We'll need at least five hundred for total coverage, but fifty would get me started."

"What type of rounds do you want?"

"I'll need all the high explosive rounds you can make. Wait, on second thought, could you do half HE, and half as cluster rounds using the ADAM technology?"

"I'm afraid I don't know what that is."

"It stands for Area Denial Artillery Munitions. When the round explodes it spreads small mines that are attached to trip wires."

"I'll have to do some research on that, but it sounds doable. While I'm at it, I'll have them double-check the stuff we got out of the *Genesis*'s weapons locker to see if there are any more mortars."

After Nicholas left, Billy asked, "It sounds like you've got a plan. Care to let me in on it?"

"There's simply too many of them to attack directly, so I'm going to mount the first fifty mortars on snowmobiles and use them to try to keep a mine field in front the Nubians. If I can, it should slow them down quite a bit.

"When we have enough mortars, I'm going to ring the

camp with mortar positions. Each position will have a fifty-caliber machine gun, half a dozen snipers, and a mortar crew. Once we get them in place, they should allow us some measure of protection from their raiding parties."

Billy stayed for a couple of hours to help Nicholas lay out his plans.

"I think that should do it," Billy said. "If you can do without me for a few days, I'm going to try to spend some time with Linda. Call me if you need anything."

LINDA SLEPT FOR the rest of the day and all through the night, but the next morning she was rested and ready to go. *We're supposed to eat breakfast with our parents this morning*, she said in her mind to Billy.

She felt Billy's answer in her mind: *Why don't you give them a call and tell them we'll have lunch with them?*

When she saw what else he had in mind, she smiled and said, *Oh, that's a much better idea. Hold that thought, and I'll be right there.*

"YOU LOOK LIKE you weathered your ordeal pretty well," Beth, her mom, said. "In fact, you have a glow about you."

Linda blushed and said, "I'm just glad to see you guys."

"It looks more like you were glad to see Billy," Rob said.

"Okay, Daddy, you be nice."

"I was being nice, and besides, you're married."

Quickly changing the subject, Linda asked, "So how are you guys doing?"

"I guess we're all doing okay, but tell us about what happened to you," Rob said.

Linda spent the next hour and a half telling them all about her ordeal.

"What kind of monsters would kill all those people in cold blood?" Beth asked.

"I admit that what the admiral did was awful, but not all of the Nubians are evil," Linda replied.

After an hour or so, the conversation turned to the meteor. "Have you come up with a plan to blow up the meteor?" Rob asked.

"No, but I'm working on a plan to try to deflect it," Billy replied.

"How in the world do you deflect a meteor?" his father asked.

"Very carefully," Billy said jokingly. "I'd intended to use the *Genesis*, but since that's out, we've started building another ship."

"That sounds dangerous," Ben said. "Who's going to pilot it?"

"That would be me."

His comments set off a heated discussion as they tried to talk him out of it.

"I'm sorry, but we've got to get going," Billy finally said. "We both have meetings, and we've got to leave or we're going to be late."

We don't have any meetings, Linda said in her mind.

I know, but letting them vent some more wasn't going to change a thing. I understand why they're upset, but that doesn't change the fact that this is something that God has called on me to do.

She shuddered at the thought, but she didn't say anything more about it.

* * *

THAT NIGHT BOTH had the same recurring dream all night long, but this time they were holding each other as they watched the meteor grow ever closer in the holographic viewer.

The next morning they were both exhausted.

"Now I understand the task that God has set out for us," Linda said.

"I know you were there this time, but there's no way you're coming."

"Listen you—if you're going, I'm going."

"We'll talk about this later, but right now, let's go see how they're coming with the ship."

William Robbins called just as they were about to walk out. "I wanted to let you know that we had to rush John Tyler to the hospital last night."

"What happened?" Linda asked.

"He suffered a severe pulmonary embolism in his right lung."

"He seemed fine when I examined him. Have you been able to determine the cause?"

"I'm almost certain it came from one of the bruises on his legs."

"Is he going to be alright?" Billy asked.

"It was touch-and-go for a while, but he should make a full recovery."

When they finished talking with William, they went to see Nicholas.

"How's it going?" Billy asked.

"Not too bad, but we need some more palladium so we can finish the fuel cells," Nicholas replied.

"I'll see if Larry can get you some more. Is there anything else you need?"

"Nothing but time. I guess I should tell you that I've changed the schedule again. We're worried about the possibility of radiation buildup, so we're not going to mount the crew module until the very last minute."

"Do you think we've got enough shielding to keep us alive until we can deal with the meteor?"

"We think so, but what do you mean by 'keep you alive'? You're not going."

"Not you, too. I'm going to be piloting the ship."

"That's sheer lunacy. Has Larry already signed off on this?"

"I haven't talked to Larry yet, and I would appreciate it if you didn't either."

"Okay, I won't, but we're all going to need to sit down and discuss this before you go through with it. Next you'll be telling me that Linda is going along as well."

"Good guess," Linda said.

"Oh Lord, please save us, you've both gone daft."

When they were done with Nicholas, they went over to see Larry.

"We were just talking with Nicholas, and he told me that he's going to need some more palladium. Do you think you can locate some more?"

"I already know where the Nubians have some stored. When do you need it?"

"ASAP, as always."

"That figures. Let me know how much you need, and give me a couple of days to put together a team, and I'll go get it for you."

TWO DAYS LATER, Larry and a team of John's newly trained commandos were making their final preparations to leave.

"Lieutenant, get one of the mortars out of the weapons locker and meet me at the *Imagination* in an hour."

"Yes, sir. How many rounds do you want?"

"I think ten HE should be enough."

When the lieutenant got to the weapons locker, he told the guard on duty, "I need a mortar and ten high explosive rounds."

"The third door on your right for the mortar, and the HE rounds should be in the room right across the hall."

The lieutenant could only find nine rounds, but he was determined to get what Larry wanted. He was on his way back to check with the guard when he noticed that the storeroom next door was open.

When he looked in, he saw a couple of rounds sitting on the floor, so he took one and went on his way.

"Did you get everything?" Larry asked.

"We did, and the men are already on board."

It was a little before midnight when the *Imagination* landed, undetected, on the outskirts of the village.

The village was surrounded by a twenty-foot-tall wall, and there were sentries stationed all the way around. As Larry was pointing them out to the snipers, the light from the torches made the sentries look like wraiths as they walked their posts.

Once he had given the snipers their assignments, he turned to the men he was leaving behind to guard the shuttle. "Set up the mortar and the machine gun right here, but don't fire unless I tell you to."

At precisely 1:00 AM they launched their attack.

The snipers all had silenced M-25s with night vision, so the sentries never knew what hit them. After they had killed the sentries, one of commandos scaled the wall and opened the main gate.

Once they were inside, they crept silently through the narrow streets to the small warehouse where the palladium was stored. Since they only needed a few hundred pounds of palladium, they were in and out in a matter of minutes.

They managed to get out of the village without being discovered, but their luck ran out when the Nubians discovered the dead guards and started shooting their artillery.

The first rounds fell short, but they were quickly starting to get in range. As the rounds neared the shuttle, Larry gave the order to fire.

"Put a couple of mortar rounds on those cannons."

The Commandos had made it to within a hundred and fifty feet of their ship when the mortar round hit. One minute they were running through the black of the night, and the next it was broad daylight.

A second or two later, the fiery shockwave knocked Larry and his men to the ground.

"Oh my God, I think that was a nuclear explosion," Larry thought to himself.

Once his head had cleared a little, he jumped up and yelled to his team, "Get on board, we've got to get out of here."

They had all suffered burns, and they sat in quiet agony on the flight back to base. Any area of exposed skin had at least second-degree burns, and one of commandos had been blinded by the blast. None of the men knew what had happened, but Larry did.

As they neared the base, Larry got on the radio. "I need a medical team meet us when we land. We've all suffered burns and some level of radiation exposure. Also, tell Nicholas Stavros to get a team ready to try to decontaminate the *Imagination*."

"WE JUST HEARD from Larry, and it seems that they've all suffered radiation exposure and burns," Billy said.

"How badly are they hurt?" Linda asked.

"That's all I know, but they'll be here in a couple of minutes."

As Larry walked off the ship, Billy asked, "What happened?"

"We fired a mortar round to cover our escape, and they must have gotten one of the nukes by mistake, because we wiped out the whole village. We were far enough away that it didn't kill us, at least not right away."

"Don't worry about that," Linda said. "We've had plenty of experience with radiation exposure, and we're going to take good care of you."

THE NEXT DAY, Nicholas was bringing Billy up to speed on their current status.

"I knew we should have left those rounds on *Genesis*," Nicholas said. "I don't know why the general even had them on board. The whole premise was flawed from the beginning. It's a little late, but I've had the other one destroyed so this doesn't happen again.

"I do have some good news for you. Larry got us more than enough palladium to finish the fuel cells, and the ship's construction seems to be back on schedule."

"That's good, but speaking of schedules, I wish we had a way to get some current tracking data on the meteor."

"Why don't you use the *Imagination*? We should be finished decontaminating it in a couple of weeks."

"It'll take too long to get close enough to take the readings."

"I think that I can solve that for you. I can install some of the sensor arrays that I salvaged from the *Genesis,* and they should give you plenty of range."

Three weeks later, Nicholas had finished installing the

sensors, and Billy was about to leave to gather his tracking data.

Larry was still in the infirmary, so Billy decided to go see him before he left.

"How are you feeling?"

"I'm better, but I can't stop thinking about what happened to all those people. But you don't need to be hearing about my problems. What do you need?"

"I'm going to take the *Imagination* and gather some better tracking data on the meteor. While I'm gone, I need you to take command of John's raiders."

"I can do that. Do you have any idea where they're at on the defense perimeter?"

"They've laid the outer bands of the minefields, and they've started installing the mortar positions. But there are still far too many gaps for them to be effective."

Once Billy was convinced that Larry felt well enough to take on the job, he left so he could get ready for his journey.

LARRY HAD BEEN glad to be back to work, but it didn't take very long for him to decide that he wanted to experience firsthand what was happening.

There was a strike force that was leaving a couple of days later to harass the Nubians. The team consisted of fifty mobile mortars, fifty snowmobiles outfitted with Miniguns, and a support team of ten snowcats with supply trailers. This would be the first time they had attempted a dual mission, and Larry wanted to make sure it went well.

The mobile mortars would stay just ahead of the advancing Nubians, and they would lay ADAMs to try and slow their advance. Simultaneously, the Minigun-armed snowmobiles would be responsible for making sure that the Nubians didn't sneak any more raiding parties out.

Nicholas had come to see him off, and to take care of any last-minute requests.

"We'll resupply you as often as we can turn the snow-cats around," Nicholas said. "Are you going to stay with them, or are you coming back?"

"I'll stay until I'm satisfied that they understand their mission," Larry replied. "I'll give you a call when we make contact with the main body."

18

Captain Zapata had never been inside the queen's palace; however, today he was not only going inside, he was going to have to make his report directly to the queen.

He had heard all the horror stories over the years, so he had no idea whether he would leave alive. It was rumored that she often killed the bearers of bad news, and that was exactly what he had for her.

When Captain Zapata entered, Queen Amanirenas looked up from the report she had been reading. "Come in and take a seat, and I'll be right with you."

When she was finished reading the report, she told him, "I've read the action reports, so I already know what you're going to tell me. From the looks of it, Billy West's people are continuing to cause us problems.

I should have killed him when I had the chance, she thought to herself.

"There wasn't a lot of detail in the report about how the admiral died. Do you have anything that you can add?"

"I wasn't there, but I did talk with the commander of the group he was traveling with. He told me that the admiral had been acting very strangely before he was killed. He said the admiral had made them blow up the dam to try to kill a man and a woman who had passed by earlier. The commander said that he wasn't making much sense, but the admiral had said something about the queen killing his entire family if he didn't kill the woman."

He paused when he realized what he had just said, but the queen motioned at him to continue.

"He said they didn't see who shot the admiral, but they assumed it had something to do with the people he was trying to kill."

The queen didn't say anything, but she knew the admiral had been trying to cover up his mistake of not killing Linda West when he was supposed to.

"Can you tell me anything about the status of General Abrahams's army?"

"The story that I heard was that General Abrahams had sent out a ten-thousand-man strike force to try and take out the enemy base and that the mission had failed."

"Did you hear how the general handled a setback like that?"

"From what I've heard, the general executed the survivors to try to keep it quiet. But it didn't work, because that's all anyone wanted to talk about. The men that I talked with said that the morale was horrible and getting worse."

"I was afraid of that. General Staneus was supposed to relieve him, but he was killed on the way."

She picked up a sealed dispatch pouch and handed it to him. "I need you to take this back to the general."

When the captain had gone, the queen told one of her aides, "Have Admiral Gupta get my ship ready to travel. I'm going to take charge of this debacle. Tell the admiral that I want every ship that we have left to accompany me."

Two days later, the queen went to the harbor to board her ship. At one time her battle fleet had numbered hundreds of ships, but all that was left was her flagship and six others. Virtually everything else had been destroyed, except for a handful of cargo vessels.

"Where's the rest of my fleet?" the queen demanded.

"I'm afraid that the storms have taken a heavy toll, and this is all that's left," Admiral Gupta said.

They were about to weigh anchor when a savage storm struck the harbor. Even in the supposed safety of the harbor, the ninety-mile-per-hour winds drove the waves to over ten feet.

The ships were still moored, but the ferocity of the storm ripped the lines free on one of them and drove it into the dock pilings. The impact crushed its side in, and it started to sink.

The crew scrambled to escape before it sank, but almost a hundred of them never made it topside.

When the storm had passed, the entire harbor was covered with debris. The water was shallow enough that they could still see the upper portions of the sunken ship's masts.

"I see what you meant about the storms," Queen Amanirenas said. "I've never seen anything like that."

"That was nothing. We ran into two different storms on the way back that were much worse than that."

As the remaining ships left the harbor, there was a small break in the clouds, and the rays of the sun seemed to shine only on the queen's ship.

As the sun warmed her face, the queen hoped that it was a sign of good things to come.

A couple of days later, the queen was sitting in her cabin thinking about what was at risk. She was down to the last of her ships, and she had already committed the bulk of her army to the conflict. King Peterovan had far fewer resources, but she knew that the weather and the terrain favored the defender more than the attacker. She wasn't sure what she hoped to accomplish by coming, but she had to do something.

The night before they reached the coast, the queen was sitting in her cabin eating dinner. As she was eating, she thought back to Billy's visit. At the time, she had thought he was deranged. However, the events that had transpired since then had removed any doubt about what he'd said.

She had never concerned herself with regrets, so she finished her dinner and turned in for the night.

As she was about to fall asleep, she thought to herself, *I'm still going to get my revenge on Billy West. If only that fool of an admiral had followed his orders, none of this would've been necessary.*

When she landed, the governor met her at the docks. "What have you heard from General Abrahams?" Queen Amanirenas asked.

"It's been over a week, but the last we heard, he had stopped and was trying to figure out how to proceed. The story I got was that they had lost a raiding party of more than ten thousand men."

"I've already heard about that. How long will it take us to reach them?"

"It's about a three-week trip. But are you sure you want to go out there? The conditions are unbelievably bad where they are."

"It doesn't matter. It's something that I've got to do. Can we be ready to leave in the morning?"

"I'll make the arrangements."

The queen had been quick to condemn General Abrahams's actions, but the reality was that he was the most able officer she had. Anyone who had ever dealt with him had the utmost respect for him; however, the queen never allowed herself to give anyone any real respect or backing.

19

WHEN LARRY'S MEN got within a couple of miles of the Nubians, they stopped so they could make their final preparations.

Larry spent the evening briefing the teams who were assigned to ensure the Nubian raiding parties didn't reach their base.

When he was finished, the first group went out to keep an eye on the Nubians.

They were split into five groups of ten. Each group would circle the Nubians at least once a day to make sure they didn't sneak out to attack the base.

The next morning, Larry supervised as they laid the first minefield in front of the advancing Nubian column.

The Nubians had never seen anything like the ADAM munitions, so they marched straight into the minefield.

When they started to trip the mines, they panicked, and even though they didn't have any targets, they started shooting wildly in all directions.

"What idiots, there's nobody out there," General Abrahams bellowed. "Get out there and tell them to stop shooting."

The explosions had ripped the lead riders to shreds.

The sprays of blood had stained the area red, and the cries of dying men and animals filled the air.

After he had gotten them to stop shooting, the general left his wagon and rode up to the front of the column to see what was happening.

"Alright, colonel, tell me what's going on," General Abrahams ordered.

"Earlier this morning, we heard several explosions, but none of them were close to us, so we didn't worry about it. Then one minute we were riding along, and the next thing we knew, there were explosions all around us. We thought someone was shooting at us, but we haven't been able to find anyone yet."

"You're not making any sense. I don't see how there can be explosions without someone causing them." General Abrahams walked past the colonel. "What are those things scattered all over the ground? Send one of your men out there and bring one back here so we can take a look at it."

The soldier picked his way through the bloody debris until he reached one of the unexploded mines. When he tried to pick it up, it exploded, blasting him into little bloody pieces.

"Well that answers the question of what was causing the explosions," General Abrahams said. "We'll need to find some way of clearing those things out of our way." As he was mounting his horse, he told the colonel, "I'll send Colonel Harish up here to look it over. He's good at figuring out this sort of thing."

Over the next week, Colonel Harish tried several techniques for clearing the mines out of the way. He tried cannons, muskets, archers, and even tried throwing chunks of ice at the mines.

None of their efforts were entirely successful, but he finally decided to use a combination of cannons and sharpshooters. It had been slow going, but they managed to clear a path through the mines in five days.

"We're through the explosives," Colonel Harish said. "We've lost fifteen more men, but we have a clear path at this point. I've got a good handle on what it takes to clear them out, so it's not going to take that long the next time."

"Good work, but I hope there won't be a next time," General Abrahams said.

"I'm afraid that's wishful thinking, because we've already heard more explosions in the distance, so I expect that we'll find more of the same."

"THE NUBIANS HAVE managed to clear a path through the first minefield we laid, but it took them almost a week to do it," Larry said.

"That's good news, isn't it?" Billy asked.

"I suppose it is, but if we don't find some way to break their resolve, it's just a matter of time until they reach us."

Larry paused, as he considered how to broach the next subject.

"I know I said that we shouldn't try to attack them directly, but it doesn't look like the mines are going to cut it. Their scouts are working out pretty far from the main column, so I'm going to use the snipers to hit them when we have the opportunity. We may not kill very many, but we might be able to demoralize them."

"Do whatever you think is necessary. Just let me know if I can help."

* * *

EARLY THE NEXT morning, when the Nubians had just started moving for the day, the snipers hit them.

They had ten men on point, and the snipers killed or wounded all of them with their first volleys.

When the Nubians saw them go down, they immediately sent reinforcements, but the snipers cut them down as well.

It had gone back and forth all morning, and by noon, the snipers had killed or wounded over fifty of their men.

Frustrated at their inability to move, General Abrahams decided to call a halt for the day while he tried to come up with some different tactics.

The general might not have had the advanced technology that his enemy had, but he was a seasoned warrior, and he wasn't about to give up on his mission.

As the Nubian column prepared move out the next morning, the scouts were in the lead again.

The snipers had moved back into position before dawn, so when the column stared to move, their deadly accurate fire cut the scouts down in seconds.

The snipers had expected the same back and forth tactics as the day before, but the general had repositioned his artillery during the night, and he quickly brought the snipers under heavy cannon fire.

Outgunned, the snipers decided to retreat. They had just started to move when they were attacked by over a hundred men that had snuck out of camp under the cover of darkness.

Only one of the snipers managed to escape, but worse yet, the Nubians captured all of their gear, including their sniper rifles.

Once they had wiped out the snipers, they stopped so they could study the weapons they had captured. It didn't take them very long to figure out the rifles, and once they did, they gave them to their best sharpshooters and spread them throughout the column.

The next morning the Nubians moved out at first light. They had only been traveling for a short time when the snowmobiles started making their daily passage around the column.

They had always made a point of staying out of the range of the Nubian weapons, but they didn't know that they had gotten their hands on the M-25s.

The Nubian sharpshooters had killed four of the snowmobile riders before they realized what was happening and quickly retreated to regroup.

"WE'VE RUN INTO some trouble," Sergeant Marshal said. "We've lost four of the armed snowmobiles."

"I told you to stay out of their range," Larry barked.

"We were well outside the range of their weapons, but it looks like they've captured several M-25s."

"That's the first I've heard of it."

"Obviously we didn't know, either; however, as we were retreating, we picked up the sole survivor from the sniper team. The Nubians jumped them this morning, and they've got all ten M-25s and several thousand rounds of ammo."

"The rifles have an effective range of just under a thousand yards, so if you'll stay at least eleven hundred yards away, you should be fine. Were you able to salvage the snowmobiles?"

"Not yet, but we're going back out in a couple of hours. If they'll still run we'll drive them back, otherwise we'll drag them. I just wanted to let you know what happened."

"I'll give you a call tomorrow morning with further

orders. Until then, you can continue laying minefields, but don't do anything else until you hear from me."

When Larry had made sure the sergeant understood his orders, he walked over to talk with John.

"We've got trouble," Larry said. "We've lost thirteen men, and they've captured ten M-25s."

"I thought I trained them better than that."

"They followed their orders, but the Nubians outsmarted us. They snuck out a large group of men and waited for us to make our attack. Their weapons may be primitive, but they're not bad tacticians. We got overconfident and men lost their lives."

"I'm ready to get back to work," John said anxiously. "What can I help with?"

"If Linda will release you, I'll put you to work. We're in desperate need of some more trained men. But don't think you're going to do anything else. Billy has already given strict orders that you're not to go back into the field."

"There he goes again, thinking that he's in command," John said with a chuckle.

20

As the queen's convoy made its way upriver, they stopped at the monastery for the night.

They pitched their camp across the river from it, and as the queen sat by her campfire, she could see what was left of the building. They had already seen the devastation that had been caused by the admiral blowing up the dam, and now they were confronted by this.

As she studied what was left of the monastery, she thought to herself, "What an idiot. He caused all this destruction, and he still didn't carry out his mission."

It wasn't that she disagreed with his methods; she was quite capable of immense brutality herself. The big difference was that she usually achieved her goals.

As the sun set behind the mountains, the air had begun to turn even colder. As she moved closer to the fire, she was dreading having to go out into the frozen wilderness, but there didn't seem to be any other choice. She had fully committed what was left of her armies, and they had to succeed this time.

When the queen's party reached the river's headwaters, they were met by a detachment of soldiers that General Abrahams had sent to escort her.

He knew that she had never experienced cold like

they'd found here, so he sent a specially prepared covered wagon for her to ride in.

Nevertheless, when she saw it, her pride wouldn't let her use it. "I'll not ride in that. Bring me a horse," she said.

After only three hours on the trail, she had already started to regret her decision. Even though she had dressed as warmly she knew how, she was already freezing.

As she watched the soldiers that were riding with her, she marveled that they had been able to withstand the cold for so long. Most of them had been out here for several months, but somehow they had managed to adapt to cold fairly well.

She was determined not to show weakness in front of her men, so she rode on for another hour before she told the captain leading the detachment, "I've seen enough, bring my wagon up here." She blustered, "I've got some work to do. Let me know if you see anything, otherwise don't disturb me."

As she sat in the wagon trying to warm up, she was beginning to wonder if she had made a mistake by coming out there.

It took them almost three weeks to reach the main column. When they were within a couple of days of reaching them, the captain sent a rider on ahead to warn General Abrahams.

As they approached General Abrahams's army, the queen opened a flap in the side of the wagon so she could observe the men in the column as they passed by.

She remembered watching them march off to the docks at the beginning of the campaign. They had marched with pride and determination. They had never been defeated or even seriously challenged at that point, but now she could see that they were just about finished.

As she watched the cavalry file by, she saw that they all had their heads down. At first she had thought it was because of the bitterly cold wind; however, when she had gotten close enough to see their faces, she knew that it was because they had given up.

"I've never seen a sorrier lot of men in my whole life," Queen Amanirenas said. "And what were those explosions I heard as we rode up?"

"We're clearing the explosives they've spread in front of us," General Abrahams said.

"Take me up there. I want to see for myself."

When they reached the front of the column, the queen climbed down from the wagon and walked out to where the sharpshooters were clearing the last of the mines.

"You mean to tell me that those little things are what this is about," the queen chided General Abrahams. "They don't seem very dangerous to me." She turned to one of the soldiers and said, "Go out there and get me one of those so I can have a look at it."

The man looked at her in disbelief.

"I won't ask again," she said, as she placed her hand on her sword.

The terrified soldier did as he was told, and when he picked up the mine, it detonated, blowing him into a thousand bloody pieces.

"Very impressive," said the queen.

"You got that man killed just so you could see how they worked?" General Abrahams asked.

"Of course. How else was I going to see one in action? Now I understand why you're being so cautious, but why don't you just go around them?"

"We've tried, but every time we do, they simply lay down another band of explosives. But, believe it or not, we've gotten quite adept at clearing them out of our way.

"Now, if we're done discussing the mines, let me show you one of their weapons that we've managed to capture."

The general had one of the snipers come forward with an M-25. Then he had one of his men ride out with a clay pot filled with red wine. When he was several hundred yards away, the general fired a shot to let him know to put the pot down.

Once he was clear, the general had a sniper put a round through the pot. When the bullet struck, it exploded, showering the snow with a mist of red wine.

"Very impressive. Our muskets can't reach even a third that far. How in the world did you get ahold of it?"

The general recounted their ambush and said, "We have ten of the weapons, and several thousand rounds of ammunition. With these, we've managed to keep them from attacking us with the roaring beasts that they ride."

"You've done well, but how much longer until you reach their base?"

"If we could march without all of these interruptions, it would only take about ten weeks. As it is right now, I'm not sure that we'll ever reach them. The men are pretty well spent, and I've had to shoot a deserter almost every day."

"We've never had that problem before. Is it really that bad?"

"Between this accursed weather and the enemy, it's very bad. We'll keep going, if that's what you want, but I have to say that our chances of success dwindle by the day."

"Let me think about it for a couple of days. I'm going to observe a little longer before I make my decision."

The queen rode near the front of the column for the next two days. The weather had moderated a little, so it wasn't nearly as bad as what they had been experiencing.

Even the men's morale improved, seeing their queen riding with them.

Then, on the third day, the weather turned for the worse. The snowmobiles hadn't attempted a direct assault in quite a while, but they decided to risk it when the storm hit.

The snow was being driven by a sixty-five-mile-an-hour wind, which made it almost impossible to see.

The snowmobiles made their attack at noon, and the Nubians didn't seen them until they opened fire.

The roar of the snowmobile engines and the clamor of the Miniguns spooked the queen's horse. She was an accomplished rider, so she quickly dismounted and pulled the horse to the ground for cover.

When the Minigun fire swept over them, it killed her horse and everyone around her. Once the snowmobiles were gone, she got up to assess the damage.

It was still very difficult to see because of the snow, but as she looked around, she could see that all the men and horses around her had been slaughtered.

As she stared at the carnage, she realized that she was lucky to be alive.

When she had seen enough, she started walking back toward where the general was, but he met her about halfway.

"Are you alright?" General Abrahams asked.

"I'm fine, but what just happened?"

"They attacked us with the roaring beasts that I was telling you about."

The queen didn't respond, but she knew at that moment that their mission to destroy Billy West's people was doomed to failure. This was her last effective fighting force, and she needed them to maintain control of her own territory. As much as she hated to admit it, she had acted rashly when she had decided to punish Billy West for killing her future mate.

She tried to walk with the general as he surveyed the damage to the column, but she had to give up. It was simply too cold for her.

As she sat in her wagon trying to get warm, she decided to cut her losses and leave King Peterovan's kingdom. Seeing no reason to delay the inevitable, she sent one of her guards to find the general.

"Come in and warm up," Queen Amanirenas said, as she watched him break the ice off of the wrappings on his face. She handed him a cup full of hot spiced rum and motioned for him to sit down.

"I've seen enough. Prepare your men to move. I've decided that we're leaving in the morning."

"Where to this time?"

"We're going back home, and we need to get started as soon as possible."

"I'm obviously pleased that we're leaving, but what's the rush?"

"As I was sitting here thinking, I remembered that Billy West's prophecy is due to happen a few months from now. I didn't believe him before, but now I do, and we need to return home and make our preparations."

The general didn't respond for a few seconds, but the queen could see the stress begin to flow out of his face.

"I'll get right on it," the general said, clearly relieved to be leaving the frozen wasteland.

The next morning the column turned around and began the retreat back to the coast.

"I'm going on ahead of you," the queen told General Abrahams. "I can fit a few thousand men on the ships, so I'll take them with me. As soon as we land, I'll send the ships back for you."

* * *

THE NEXT AFTERNOON, a soldier came running into the room where Billy and his team were meeting to discuss their next moves. He handed Billy a copy of the message from the field team. When Billy finished reading it, he stood up and said with a grin on his face, "The Nubians are retreating. They've pulled in all of their raiding parties and have turned their main column back toward the coast."

The meeting had been rather somber, but it was like a dark cloud had lifted, and everyone started cheering and congratulating each other.

However, when the celebration started to quiet down, Larry told them, "I agree that this is great news, but while we have the chance, we should hit them with everything we've got."

Billy knew that he was deadly serious, and on some level he even agreed with him, but he knew that this might be their only chance for peace.

"No, we're going to let them go. There's no need to shed any more blood. If any of us survives the meteor, we'll deal with them then."

The conversation became quite heated as Larry spent several minutes trying to convince Billy to hit them with everything they had left. Finally, he came to the conclusion that he wasn't going to change Billy's mind.

"I think you're making a terrible mistake, but you're the boss."

THE NUBIANS HAD abandoned most of their equipment when they started retreating, so it only took the queen's party seven weeks to reach the coast. Worn out from the trip, the queen stopped at the governor's castle to rest up before she left.

"You mean that you're just leaving?" Governor Swenson asked in desperation.

"Yes, and we're taking all of our men with us," Queen Amanirenas said.

"Take me with you," the governor pleaded.

"Why would I want to take a cowardly traitor like you with me? I should probably have you killed before I leave, but I think that I'll leave that pleasure to King Peterovan."

The next morning, the queen was just boarding her ship to leave, when one of the governor's men came running up to her. Fearing an attack, her guards grabbed him and threw him to the ground. Once they had disarmed him, they dragged him over to where the queen was standing.

"What's your business here?" Queen Amanirenas asked.

"The governor is dead. He shot himself in the head last night."

"Good riddance," the queen said. "He took the coward's way out, but that doesn't surprise me."

21

WITH ONLY SIX ships, it had taken the Nubians almost five months to move their people back home.

They weren't supposed to bring any of King Peterovan's people back with them; however, several of the soldiers had intermarried with the locals, and they had been unwilling to abandon their new families.

Several of the children had gotten sick on the voyage back, but it had taken a few weeks for the news to reach the attention of the queen, and by then it was an epidemic.

"We have over a thousand people who are sick, and it's spreading like wildfire," General Abrahams said. "It seems that several of our people brought back their families from the campaign, and some of the children were sick."

"Simple enough to handle," Queen Amanirenas said. "Just have them executed."

Her casual manner about having women and children killed didn't shock him. He had seen her do many despicable things in the time he had served her.

"I can do that, but it's not going to do any good. The outbreak has already spread far beyond the small groups that were brought back. From the reports I've received so far, I'm afraid that it's already spread throughout the country.

"There is one bit of good news. When I talked with one of the healers, they said that several of them told stories of Billy West's wife, Linda, curing several of their people."

"Am I never going to be free of these strangers? I guess that's good news, but they're not going to help us out. Tell the healers to do the best they can.

"Do you have the inventory reports I asked for?"

"Here they are, but you're not going to like what we found. We're short of almost everything. We lost a lot of our supplies when we left in such a hurry, and with most of our fishing fleets destroyed, it's going to be a very difficult year."

"I'll read them tonight, and then I'll let you know what I want you to do next."

When the general had left, the queen had them bring in her priestess.

"You were with me when Billy West was here," Queen Amanirenas said. "Do you remember when he was warning us of the coming disaster? What did he call it?"

"He called it a meteor," Priestess Ghia said.

"Yes that was it. Do you remember when he said it was going to hit us?"

She thought for few seconds. "I believe it was supposed to be a few months from now. But you don't believe what he said, do you? Besides, none of us have had any visions about this."

"Oh, give me a break; you don't really believe your own crap do you?"

The priestess looked at her quizzically for a second or two, then said, "No, but I thought that you did. I've known you since we were both children, and I never guessed that you had seen through all the charades."

"From as early as I can remember, my mother drilled it into me that I had to pretend that I believed. She said that it was one of the things that had allowed our family to maintain our hold on the country.

"But enough of this, can you think of anything that we can do to get ready for this meteor thing?"

"After Billy West told you his story, I did some research in our archives. I really didn't think I would find anything, but I did. There was a fairly complete account of the last time Midgard encountered the meteor."

"Did you find anything that we could use?"

"There may be. The records said that the only people who survived went underground. There was even a map that was supposed to show the location of the shelter they used."

"Is it still there?"

"I'm not sure. I did send out a group to try to find it. It's supposed to be located in one of the remotest areas of the country, and they weren't able to find it before a terrible sandstorm forced them to turn back.

"At the time, I didn't really believe the threat was real, so I never bothered to send them back."

"I'm convinced that if we're going to survive, we're going to have to find something to use for shelters."

THE NEXT DAY the queen had General Abrahams put together an expedition to search for the shelter.

When he was finished, the general decided to take a little time off to visit his family.

His home was located in the mountains, almost eleven days hard ride from the capital. He had been anxious to see them again, but every time he had mentioned it, the queen would give him another urgent project.

Once the queen had left, he rode almost day and night as he hurried home.

He arrived just before noon, and as he rode up the tree-lined road to his villa, he became concerned when he didn't see the guards at the entrance.

He spurred his horse forward, and his bodyguards had to scramble to keep up. When he reached the gate to the house, he saw that it had been ripped off its hinges and was lying beside the wall.

He was terrified that he already knew what he would find, but he rushed through the opening into the walled garden that surrounded the main house.

He had smelled death many times in his life and when that familiar smell hit him, he stopped.

He stood frozen in place for almost thirty seconds before the captain of his guards asked, "Sir, would you like me to check it out before you go in?"

"Do not enter under any circumstances; I've got to do this myself." He placed a rag over his face to lessen the stench and walked through the shattered door to his villa.

The first bodies he found were the family's bodyguards. He had handpicked them himself, and judging by the number of bodies he saw, they hadn't died easily.

He found the servants next, and from what he could tell, they had been bound, hands and feet, before they had been hacked to death.

The general was not a fainthearted man, but he feared what he was likely to find next. Almost beside himself with dread, he took a deep breath and slowly moved through the house until he reached the great room at the center of the villa.

Nothing could have prepared him for what he found.

When he first saw the piles of bodies, he had a hard time grasping the enormity of what he was looking at. The queen hadn't just killed his family, she had rounded up all one hundred and fifty-three of his relatives and had them brought to the villa. They had been herded into the great room and slaughtered.

Their bodies were so decomposed that it was hard to tell who was who. He had to stop and throw up a few times as he searched through the bodies for his wife and kids.

He would have never recognized his wife if she hadn't been wearing her favorite dress when they killed her. From what he could tell, their children had been clinging to her when they had been killed, because all of their bodies were still lying together in a heap.

Seeing them like that was too much for him, and he fell to his knees and cried out in agony.

The guards had wanted to rush in when they heard his cry of anguish, but they knew better than to disobey his orders.

It was several minutes before the general managed to regain enough composure to carry on. Unlike the majority of the Nubian upper class, the general believed in one God. He knew in his heart that they were already with God. As he knelt beside their bodies, he asked God to look after them until they were reunited.

When he rejoined his men, they started the unpleasant task of burying the bodies.

It was dusk by the time they had finished burying everyone. As they were about to leave, the general set fire to the villa.

As they rode away, he turned back and saw the sparks from the fire drifting up into the night sky. As he watched, he imagined that the sparks were his family's souls, and he once again asked God to take care of them.

As the general rode, his mind was filled with rage and thoughts of how he might be able to carry out his revenge on the queen.

By the time they had reached the capital city, though, he had calmed down enough to know that he needed to bide his time. He decided that he would look for the right opportunity, and then he would extract his revenge.

MEANWHILE, IT HAD taken the queen's expedition six weeks to reach the area where the shelter was supposed to be. It turned out that the shelter was located just to the north of the quarry where Billy's group had mined the uranium ore.

As they moved around the old quarry, they ran across the remnants of the training group that had been wiped out when they had attacked Billy's miners.

"We've found the group of commandos that went missing several months ago," Priestess Ghia said. "It looks like they were in a battle, and they're all dead."

"No doubt it has something to do with Billy West's people, but I don't suppose that it matters much anymore. How far are we from this shelter of yours?"

"It's supposed to be in a small valley just east of our current position."

When they got there, however, all they found was more sand. Frustrated by Priestess Ghia's inability to find it, the queen sent virtually everyone out to try to find the valley.

Several days later, Priestess Ghia told the queen, "They've found what looks like the top of the pyramid depicted on the map. Would you like to come and take a look?"

"No, I would rather sit here in my tent and sweat," she said sarcastically.

Once the queen got a look at the pyramid, she had them start digging it out of the sand. The shifting sand made digging very difficult, but after four days they had uncovered what looked like a window shutter.

When the queen came to check it out, she had them pry it open, and said, "Ghia, you and I are going to take a look at what's inside. Have the men set up a perimeter to make sure that we're not disturbed."

"Don't you want to send the soldiers in first?"

She saw the flash of anger in the queen's eyes and decided to drop the subject. One of the soldiers lit a couple of torches for them, and they climbed through the window.

The room wasn't very big, but from the way it was furnished, they could tell it was once occupied by someone of fairly high rank. As they looked around they discovered a crib and a couple of children's beds.

"This looks like it might have been a nursery," Priestess Ghia said.

"It does at that, and that's my family's crest on the crib."

They spent a few more minutes looking around before they opened the only door in the room and moved into the hall outside.

There was only one other room on the floor they were on, and it looked like it might have been where the children's nanny had stayed. When they reached the end of the hallway, they found a staircase that led downward.

They spent the next three hours making their way from floor to floor. On every floor that they searched, the rooms had all looked like they had been used as living quarters, and after a while they had started moving through them pretty quickly.

They had been growing frustrated at what they were finding, when the stairs abruptly ended on a small stone landing.

It was too dark to see anything below them, so Priestess Ghia held her torch out over the edge. She still couldn't see a thing. She leaned out over the void as much as she dared, but it was too far down.

"I still can't see anything, but there's got to be something down there because there's a ladder on the wall over there," Priestess Ghia said.

The queen held her torch a little higher so she could get a better look at the crude wooden ladder. "We've come this far, we might as well see where it leads. I just hope that we find something that we can use."

It turned out that the ladder went down a little over three hundred feet. By the time they reached the bottom, they were getting tired, and their torches were just about used up.

There were torches all along the wall, so they grabbed a couple and lit them off the old ones.

Each level of the structure had been getting progressively larger, but this one seemed to be gigantic. As they started to explore further, they could hear the sounds of their voices echoing throughout the room.

"This level must be huge," Queen Amanirenas said. "Let's light some more of these torches so that we can see a little better."

As they continued to move along the wall, they kept lighting torches as they went.

They didn't find anything of interest until they reached a series of large metal levers.

The priestess counted them and said, "There're sixty-five levers here. But I don't have any idea what they're for."

"Pull one and see what happens."

The lever didn't move when Ghia tried to pull it down, so she grabbed it with both arms and threw her entire weight on it.

They could hear something moving far above them, but they couldn't make out what it was. When the lever reached the bottom, there was a loud clunking sound that reverberated throughout the darkness.

A few seconds later the queen said, "I think that it's lighter in here. Go ahead and pull another one of those levers."

The queen hadn't offered to help, so it took Ghia almost an hour to pull the rest of the levers. By the time she was finished, it was as bright as the noonday sun.

The massive cavern stretched out farther than they could see. As they tried to get a sense of what they were looking at, it struck them that it didn't look much like a room. Instead, it looked more like one of the villages in the ancient paintings that adorned the palace walls.

As they walked through the village's streets, they almost expected someone to step out of one of the buildings and greet them. They had been walking for several minutes when they reached what looked like the town square.

"That looks like the library in Ichris," the queen said.

The massive brass door was fifteen feet high and seven feet wide. It took both of them to pull it open, and the hinges squealed in protest.

When they walked in they saw a gigantic altar with a forty-foot-high cross behind it.

The only thing on the altar was a very large book. As they walked toward the altar they left footprints in the several inches of dust that covered everything in the room.

The queen stopped, dusted off the book, and opened it. She stood reading for over twenty minutes before Ghia asked, "What sort of a book is it?"

"I believe that it's a journal. It looks like they documented everything that they went through to survive. It took them over fifty years to build the pyramid. The levers that you pulled are how they let sunlight in. A series of mirrors collects the sunlight and directs it down into this level."

"Does it say why they built it?"

"It said that they built it after God gave the priest a vision of a danger that would come out of the sky."

"You mean priestess don't you?"

"No, it distinctly says priest, and there's even a portrait of him. It also clearly speaks of the one god that they worshiped. There's no mention of multiple gods or even Isis."

"That would be more like the god that King Peterovan's people worship."

They spent a little time discussing the implications of what she had read so far. Since it was getting late, they decided to return to the surface.

The queen wanted to bring the book with them, but when they reached the ladder, they decided to send a couple of soldiers back with a rope to retrieve it.

Once they had it on the surface, the queen took it to her tent and spent the next six days reading it. When she was finished, she sat down with Priestess Ghia to discuss what she had found.

"I'm afraid that what Billy West was trying to tell us is true, and it looks like it has all happened before. The pyramid was constructed in an attempt to help our ancestors survive one of its previous visits. They spent almost fifteen years down there before they could return to the surface.

"I was a little shocked to find out that there's one way

in and out. If the drawings are accurate, the only real entrance is about fifteen feet below the window where we entered."

"I thought the whole thing had been covered by the sandstorms over the centuries," Priestess Ghia said.

"I did, too, but when they finished building the pyramid, they spent another five years covering it with sand for extra protection. The drifting sand did cover the top twenty-five feet of it, but the rest they did themselves.

"We're going to need to check out the entire facility to see if we can use it for shelter this time. From what I've read, it looks like it can house around twenty-five thousand people."

"But that's only a tiny fraction of our people."

"True, but it's a start. I want you to get our brightest minds down here and put together a plan to replicate what they did. There are miles of natural caverns in the eastern mountains, and we might be able to get them ready in time."

By the time they got back to the capital, it was in complete turmoil. As the general had warned, the epidemic had spread like wildfire, and since the Nubians had no natural resistance to the disease, it was proving to be fatal in most cases.

General Abrahams had been back for several weeks, so he had already prepared a complete status report for the queen.

"There has been a complete breakdown in communications, but as far as we can tell, there are tens of thousands of people who are sick, and several thousand more that have already died. If we don't find some way of controlling it, I fear it's going to wipe us out."

"What would you have me do?" Queen Amanirenas asked.

"That's up to you, but if it was me, I would try to talk Billy West's wife into helping us out."

"I seriously doubt that she would chance trying to help us again, after what we pulled the last time."

"You're probably right, but if you would allow me, I would at least like to ask."

"Go ahead, it's your funeral. But, I think that they're just as likely to execute you as they are to help us."

The general thought to himself, *Yeah that's what you would do, but I've sensed that they are different.*

EVEN THOUGH HE knew he was probably going to his death, General Abrahams took the queen's ship and made the treacherous journey back to King Peterovan's territory.

When he landed, he made the journey to see Governor Leopold. He knew that the governor was well thought of, and that if he could convince him they were sincere, he might reach out to King Peterovan to plead their case.

"I only agreed to meet with you because I couldn't believe that you had the audacity to come here," Governor Leopold said. "What's to stop me from just killing you?"

"Not a thing, but I hope that you'll at least hear me out before you do. Tens of thousands of my people are sick, and thousands more have already died. I think it may be the same disease that struck your people. We've heard that Linda West helped cure your people, and I've come to beg you to get her to help us."

"It's true that she and her team did cure my people. But, why would you think that she would agree to help you out? Your people just got done trying to kill her."

"I realize that, and I'm not going to try to make excuses

for it, or even try to convince you that the queen wouldn't try it again."

"Then why did you bother to come, if you can't guarantee her safety?"

"I didn't say that I couldn't guarantee her safety, I said that I couldn't guarantee that the queen wouldn't do it again. What if the queen wasn't a factor?"

"Then I would be willing to talk to the king on your behalf. But, how can you speak for the queen?"

"I'm not prepared to talk about that. I just need to know that you'll try to help us if I can guarantee her safety."

"You have my word on it, but you're going to have to prove that you're being truthful."

When they were finished talking, the general returned to the ship and started back home.

However, when they reached the Nubian coastline, he didn't return to the capital. He had the ship detour to a small coastal city not too far from the capital.

As soon as he landed, he sent for the sharpshooters he had trained to use the M-25s that they had captured. Every one of them was completely loyal to him, and when they arrived, he spent the next two days detailing his plans for them.

When he was sure they understood their orders, he sent them on ahead. Two days later he returned to the ship and went on to meet with the queen.

The general knew that Queen Amanirenas would hold her meeting with him on the balcony of her quarters. It was near the top of the palace, and she considered it to be secure enough to hold meetings.

The queen had always been very self-assured, but she had been growing more and more paranoid as their situation had deteriorated. Ever since she had returned from their abortive campaign, she had started having her guards disarm her own military leaders before they would be allowed into her presence.

"So general, what sort of a deal did you get worked out?" Queen Amanirenas asked mockingly, as she sat down at the table on the balcony.

"I've convinced Governor Leopold to speak on our behalf."

"I can't believe he would trust me enough to do that," the queen said in disbelief.

The general looked at her with disdain. "He doesn't, but he told me he would trust my word, if I could prove that I was being honest with him."

The queen's eyes flashed with anger, and as she stood to draw her sword, she screamed, "You've overstepped your boundaries for the last time." She growled, "I should have done this a long time ago."

She had just managed to pull her sword when the first bullet hit her. She got a look of utter disbelief on her face, and as she tried to speak, a volley of bullets pierced her body.

The impact from the bullets spun her around, and then she collapsed at the general's feet. He drew the dagger he had hidden in his tunic to finish her off, but she had been dead before she hit the floor.

As General Abrahams stood over her lifeless body, his mind was flooded with all sorts of emotions. Her death could never make up for her killing his entire family, but at least no one else would ever have to suffer like he had.

He sat down to gather his thoughts before he went downstairs to take the next step in his plan.

He was absolutely sure that what remained of the army would follow him, but he wasn't sure how the nobles and the rest of the people were going to react to the news.

He helped himself to some of the queen's wine, and after he finished it, he thought to himself, "Well, I might as well find out how this is going to go."

When he reached the throne room, he took the captain of the guards aside and told him, "The queen is dead, and I'm taking control."

The captain hesitated for a couple of seconds as his mind processed the general's statement.

The general was starting to get worried, but then he saw a slight smile crease the captain's face.

The captain turned back to the crowded room, snapped to attention, and called at the top of his voice, "The queen is dead, long live King Abrahams."

After a short stunned silence, his proclamation set off cries of joy from all over the room. Some of the nobles didn't really care who was in power, as long as their lifestyles didn't change; however, the vast majority of them hated the queen for one reason or another.

It took King Abrahams a couple of weeks to consolidate his hold on the kingdom, but it hadn't turned out to be as difficult as he'd feared. When he was sure that he had the country stabilized, he returned to see Governor Leopold.

"So you're back. I didn't think that I would ever see you again," Governor Leopold said. "Can you guarantee that the queen won't try to harm Linda or Billy West in any way?"

"I can," General, now King, Abrahams said.

"Well, convince me then."

King Abrahams didn't say a word as he threw a sack at the governor's feet.

"What's this?"

"Open it and see."

The governor opened the drawstring on the sack and

emptied the contents. He gasped as the half-rotted head of Queen Amanirenas hit the floor.

"Is that what I think it is?"

"It's Queen Amanirenas's head. I've seized power, and I'm now the ruler of the Nubian Empire. I give you my solemn word that no harm will come to any of the Earth people. Is this proof enough for you, and will you speak to King Peterovan for me?"

"It is, and I'll do better than that. I'll not only get you an audience with him, I'll guarantee your safety."

THAT NIGHT BILLY and Linda had identical dreams/visions. The next morning Linda asked, "Did you have any dreams last night?"

"I did, and if I understood it correctly, Queen Amanirenas is dead. Since you're asking, I assume that you did, too."

"Yes I did, although I don't know who the soldier was."

"I believe that was General Abrahams, although he's probably the king by now. I'm really surprised that he would take such a chance. I didn't think that anyone would ever have the courage to overthrow the queen."

"I don't know, but I think that we're about to meet him, so we can ask him when we see him."

A few days later a message from King Peterovan reached them.

"The king has asked that we come and meet with King Abrahams," Billy said. "King Abrahams wants to ask us to help with some sort of epidemic that's sweeping their country. Assuming that we end up helping them, do you think that William Robbins's team could handle it?"

"Of course they can, but why the worry? King Petero-van wouldn't allow them to pull anything again."

"That may be, but I'm not willing to take any more chances with your safety."

After more than a little discussion, they decided that they both should go and find out what was going on.

As they sat listening to King Abrahams, Billy immediately took a liking to him.

As much as he had learned to distrust Queen Amanirenas, he couldn't help but feel that he could trust King Abrahams.

Billy and Linda were sitting on a small couch as King Abrahams recounted their current troubles and the events that had led up to him seizing power. They had been really concentrating to make sure they didn't miss anything, when they both had a vision of the tragedy the king had found he had returned to his home.

They were sickened by what they saw, and the horrible loss that the king had suffered was almost overpowering. Nevertheless, here he was laying his life on the line for his new subjects.

When King Abrahams was finished, Billy told him, "Words could never properly express it, but we're very sorry for the loss of your family."

King Abrahams got a bewildered look on his face and said, "How could you know?"

"I can't really explain it, but sometimes God shows us things that we need to know.

"We've heard enough to know that your people are really suffering, and we'd be happy to try and help you out. When we're done talking, you can ride back with the medical team that we're sending to help your people.

"But before we go, there's one other thing that I would like to talk about. I tried once before to warn your people about the impending catastrophe, but if you'll bear with me, I would like to try again."

"There's no need. Priestess Ghia has already briefed me on what you said the last time, but I would like to share what we've discovered since then."

It took the king almost an hour to share the story of what they had found and their plans to try to replicate it in the other tunnels. When the king was finished, Billy told him about some of the things that they had found in the northern tunnels.

"It's quite a coincidence that both of your countries developed similar approaches to survival," Billy said. "The solar collectors are really quite innovative, given the general level of development here on Midgard. I don't suppose that it matters, but it almost seems like your two countries collaborated on it."

"I guess that anything is possible, but there's no mention of it in any of our history," King Abrahams said.

"Nor in ours," King Peterovan said. "However, I hope that all changes from this point on."

"I do too, and since we're in command, there's no reason that it can't."

ONCE THEY WERE on the ground, it only took William Robbins and his team a few hours to identify the cause of the epidemic.

When William called in his report, he made sure Linda was alone.

"Okay, I've asked everyone else to step out for a few moments," Linda said. "What's with all the secrecy?"

"We had expected to find another outbreak of the TB virus, but that's not what it is.

"We can't be absolutely sure until we get our lab results

done, but at this point, we're ninety-nine percent sure that we're dealing with an outbreak of the reengineered H1N1 virus. And if that weren't strange enough, I'm almost positive that it's the same strain that the terrorists were using against us."

"How can that be? We haven't had a single case of the H1N1 virus since we've been here."

"True, but we did keep several samples of it to make sure that we could treat it if we ever needed to. If you'll check, I'll bet you that at least one of the samples is missing."

"You can't believe that one of us could be behind this?"

"I don't think there can be any doubt of it. The variations we're seeing are identical to the strains we had, and I doubt that they could have occurred naturally."

After Linda had finished briefing Billy, they went to the lab to check out William's theory.

"He was right," Linda said. "One of the samples is missing. I just wish we could find out who took it."

"I'll be able to tell who it was in a couple of minutes. I had Nicholas install hidden cameras in several of the more sensitive areas of the base, and this is one of them."

Billy called up the video logs and started the search. He decided that he only needed to go back a few months, so it didn't take very long to find out who had taken the virus.

When the image of the perpetrator first came up on the screen, Billy hit pause on the playback and said, "I was afraid this was what we would find."

He hit continue, and they watched as Larry Sheldon walked across the lab and went straight to where the virus was stored.

"Why would Larry take the virus?" Linda asked.

"When I decided to allow the Nubians to retreat without attacking them, Larry was vehemently against it. I had thought that I'd convinced him that it was the right thing to do, but it looks like I was wrong."

Billy had John Tyler join them, and then he called Larry Sheldon in so that they could confront him with what they had found.

Billy hadn't known what to expect, but after he showed Larry the video, Larry looked at him, and with absolutely no emotion in his voice said, "Of course I took it. We needed to do something to make sure that the Nubians couldn't ever threaten us again. Besides, I believe that we're going to need to take over their country if we expect to survive here for very long. It was a simple matter to infect a few of the children that belonged to the Nubians."

"You, of all people, should have known how dangerous the virus can be," Linda told him indignantly. "It could have killed every one of the Nubians, if they hadn't asked for our help."

"That was something that I hadn't considered."

"You didn't stop long enough to consider that you might be killing all of them?" Linda asked incredulously.

"No, I didn't think they would ever reach out to us for help. I had counted on the virus killing them all."

John hadn't been shocked at Larry's words. He knew from bitter experience that they had both done many things over the years that would shock most people.

However, he knew that Billy and Linda would think that Larry was a monster.

Billy and Linda had been sharing their thoughts as Larry had been explaining his actions.

I know Larry has always looked out for us, but he's gone way too far this time. Linda said angrily. *But what*

*I can't understand is that I've never sensed that he was
an evil man. Have you?*

No, not evil, Billy remarked. *But I've always known
that he was capable of almost anything, if he believed that
it needed to be done. It's not for us to forgive him, but I
believe that we owe it to him to try to help him make his
peace with God.*

It was the most difficult thing that Billy had ever had
to do, but he turned and looked Larry in the eye. "What
you've done can't be excused. I'm going to have to ask
you to remove yourself from any form of leadership.

"I'm not going to tell anyone else about what we've
found, but I expect you to keep a very low profile until I
can decide what to do with you."

Larry didn't speak for a moment, as he considered
what he was going to say. "I understand, and I'll do as you
ask; however, you may find that you still need men like
me."

After Larry had left, John said, "Thank you for not
having Larry executed."

"That wasn't ever a consideration. He's done far too
much for us, and I know in my heart that he was only
trying to keep us safe from the Nubians.

"Besides, if King Abrahams hadn't seized power, his
actions might have been the only way for us to survive.
I just can't chance having him going off on a tangent
again. I expect you to help me keep an eye on him."

"I'll do my best, but you do need to be aware that the
majority of our people would follow his lead if push
came to shove."

22

THE NEXT FEW weeks went by quickly for Billy and the team, as they struggled to finish their preparations for dealing with the meteor.

"I'm taking the *Imagination* out to get some better tracking data on the comet," Billy said.

"Excellent timing," Nicholas said. "I've just finished calibrating the new sensor arrays, so you should be good to go. Look, I know that this is important, but once you've finished with that, we need to discuss the staffing plans for the mission."

"Alright, but nothing has changed."

As the *Imagination* was climbing through the upper atmosphere, Billy stood on the bridge admiring Midgard's beauty. Once the ship broke out into open space, he turned to the console to start collecting the sensor data he needed.

THEY HAD BEEN at it for several days, and they had already gathered thousands of sensor readings, when Billy spotted the first anomaly in the incoming data.

It had taken him over a day and a half to determine what had happened.

The meteor had been about a little over halfway on

its outbound pass, when a massive nearby sun had gone to supernova. Shortly afterward, it had imploded, forming a black hole.

The newly formed black hole's gravitational field had dramatically altered the meteor's path through the universe.

The course change had cut short its journey and had sent it back on a collision course with Midgard. Instead of the eleven months that they thought they had, they now had less than five.

Billy's team continued taking sensor readings for the next two days, but he had already sequestered himself in the ship's small lab to try to verify his initial findings.

At first he refused to believe what the data was showing, but he finally had to accept the fact that the data was accurate and that his first projection had been correct.

To matters even worse, the black hole had flung several of the smaller meteors out ahead of it.

He ran the tracking programs over and over, but each time they gave him the same result. The leading edge of the meteor swarm was going to hit them within a matter of months.

Now that he understood the gravity of the situation, he was struggling to understand why God kept throwing seemingly insurmountable challenges at them.

Frustrated by his inability to solve their problems, he pleaded, "Please God, haven't you already thrown enough at us. Show me how to save these people."

After he had spent several minutes feeling sorry for himself, he gathered his thoughts and returned to the bridge. "We can go back now. I've got all the data that I need."

When they landed, he didn't say a word to anyone as

he walked off the ship. As he walked in, Linda asked, "What happened? You look like you just lost your best friend."

Instead of telling her, he simply showed her what he had discovered.

"What are you going to do?" she asked.

"I'm not sure yet, but I've got to do something pretty quick. The first meteors are going to strike Midgard in less than three months. From what I could determine, they're going to strike the southern regions of Midgard in these locations." He took a moment to show her where he thought they were going to strike.

"Isn't that one going to be fairly close to where the Nubian capital is located?"

"Yes it is. The meteors aren't large enough to destroy the planet, but they're going to pack enough of a punch to cause an immense amount of damage. We'll need to relocate all of them, and I need to come up with some sort of solution that'll let us do it very quickly."

THEY SPENT MOST of the day lying in each other's arms, as Linda did her best to cheer him up.

Their parents had been after them to take a little time to visit, so that night, they met them for dinner. Linda's dad, Rob, was having a particularly bad day, so they stayed to watch an old movie with them.

They had digital copies of every movie that had ever been made, but Rob already knew what he wanted to watch.

One of Rob's all-time favorite movies was *Around the World in Eighty Days*. It was a Disney movie, and they had watched it many times while they were growing up.

As they sat watching the movie, they all found themselves caught up in the fantasy, and by the end of the evening, everyone was in better spirits.

That night, Billy dreamed of balloons and trips around the world.

When he woke up he was strangely reinvigorated, but the idea didn't hit him until he and Linda were eating breakfast.

"I've got it. I'm going to do just like they did in the movie last night. I'm going to use balloons to move the Nubians."

"Balloons? What in the world are you talking about?"

"You know that I've been struggling to come up with a way to move the Nubians.

"I'd thought about trying to rebuild their fleet of ships, but it would take far too long.

"Then I thought about trying to build more shuttles, but we simply don't have the time or the resources to do it.

"However, I'm fairly certain we can build enough balloons to get the job done."

He was so excited that he didn't even finish his breakfast before he rushed out to bounce his idea off of Nicholas.

"It's kind of crazy, but it just might just work," Nicholas said. "I actually built a few balloons when I was growing up. My father always believed that balloons made sense to move raw materials out of the Siberian plains, and he had me build some prototypes for him."

"I guess that we'll have to use hydrogen gas, since we don't have any helium."

"Actually, we struck several large pockets of helium when we were drilling test holes for the mine, so that's not going to be a problem."

"Great, now all we have to figure out is what to do with all of them," Billy said.

"As luck would have it, we got carried away when we helped King Peterovan renovate the old mines and tunnels, so space won't be an issue. We'll need to salvage as much of the Nubian food supplies as we can, but as long as we can pull that off, we should be able to get by."

When Billy looked back over at Nicholas, he was already busy sketching out his initial designs on his CAD/CAM computer.

"We'll make them semi-rigid blimps. Using a keel will let us evenly distribute the load and make it easier to add propulsion."

"Are you thinking jet power?"

"No, that would be too intense for the balloons. I thought that we'd use the fuel cells that we developed. That way we can use variable-speed electric engines with propellers to power the airships."

It took Nicholas's teams a little while to get started, but in what seemed like no time at all, they were producing up to seventy ships a day.

Billy had been amazed that each ship could carry up to a twenty-ton payload. Some of them were outfitted to carry passengers, and the rest would be used for cargo.

While they were busy building ships, John had set up a short training program for the pilots. They had designed the airships to be very simple to operate, so it didn't take very long to train one of the volunteer pilots to fly them.

Every morning at dawn, the airships they had completed the previous day would join the fleets of ships that were going back and forth to pick up the Nubian refugees.

The balloons had a maximum speed of fifty miles per hour, so the trip took over sixty hours one way.

Once they had gotten started, there was a constant stream of airships as they raced to get King Abrahams's people moved.

WHILE THE AIRSHIPS were struggling to relocate the Nubians, William and his teams had been working around the clock to try to stop the flood of new H1N1 infections.

But no matter how hard they worked, they were fighting a losing battle.

There had already been over two hundred and thirty thousand deaths, and there were so many others who were sick that they couldn't even guess at the number.

They had plenty of vaccine and medicine to treat people, but the logistics of treating that many people were overwhelming. At his wit's end, William decided to reach out for some help.

"We've simply got to have some more medical people," William pleaded. "There are far too many patients for us to handle."

"I'll send you the remainder of our medical personnel," Linda said. "Billy still won't listen to reason, so I'm not going to be able to come."

"Thanks, and don't worry about not coming. One more isn't going to make much difference. Besides, if you're sending everyone else, you're going to be needed there."

Linda got Billy to let them use the *Imagination* to move the rest of the medical personnel so that it didn't take so long to get them into position.

By then, the epidemic had spread to virtually every

area of the country, so they had to spread the medical teams out as much as they could.

None of them had ever experienced a disaster of this magnitude, and many of the other doctors were struggling to understand how it could be so virulent.

What they would never know, was that when Larry had infected the children, he had used a sample of the last, and most lethal, virus that the terrorists had created.

To make matters worse, the Nubians lacked any natural immunity, and the mortality rate was now very close to a hundred percent.

Robbins's teams worked day and night, but the virus had already spread too far for them to save a large portion of the population.

AFTER SEVERAL WEEKS, the rescue and the relief efforts were winding down, and they were ready to pull their people out.

"I think that we're about done here," William said. "We've already evacuated everyone that wasn't sick, and the rest of them will be dead by morning. I don't know how the other teams are doing, but you can pick us up in the morning."

"We've already picked up everybody but your team," Linda said. "I'll get John to send the *Imagination* for you."

A couple of days after William had returned, he met with the teams to do a postmortem on the operation.

"I've just finished the final tally, and it's pretty grim," William said. "As close as we can tell, there were over six million casualties. And I think that it's safe to assume that there were many more who died before they reached out for help."

"On the positive side of the ledger, we've managed to relocate almost two million Nubians," John said.

"So that's all we managed to save?" Linda asked.

"There's one more wave on the way, and if they are anywhere near capacity, there should be another thirty-five thousand on board. But that's all there is."

They continued discussing their successes and failures for most of the afternoon, until William finally brought up the topic that Linda had been dreading.

"I still don't understand how this could have happened. The only other occurrences of this virus, that we had ever seen, were in the last months before we left Earth."

Linda wasn't about to respond to William's statement, so she quickly changed the subject. "Have we gotten everyone to a shelter, and do we have enough supplies for the next eighteen months?"

William had started to press for further discussion, and then he realized that Linda had intentionally changed the subject on him. He didn't know why she didn't want to discuss it, but he respected her enough to let it go.

"Unfortunately several of the provinces that turned against King Peterovan have refused to evacuate," John said. "I think that they're afraid that it's a trap."

"I can understand why they might be worried," Billy said, "but we've got to convince them that it's not a trick.

"I'll have King Peterovan draft some amnesty documents to give to them. Maybe that will convince at least some of them to come in. Is there anyone else missing?"

"Only King Abrahams's final group," John said. "He insisted on coming with the last group, and they're still a day away from landing."

"I thought we were going to pick him up when we went to get William's group."

"We tried to pick him up, but he refused to come," John said. "He said he would ride with his people.

"At this point, it looks like he may have made a fatal mistake. The last group is about to run into a terrible storm that just appeared out of nowhere."

John put a satellite view of the storm up on the holographic projector.

The massive storm had come up so suddenly that the balloons never had a chance to try to go around it. By the time anyone noticed, it was already too late. Even if they had turned around, the storm was moving faster than they could go.

As Billy and the team watched, the storm was continuing to build in size and strength. Much like the storm that had killed General Staneus and his family, this storm was completely unexpected and out of character for the time of the year.

The storm clouds had already grown to over fifty thousand feet high, so there was no chance of them trying to get above them. Desperate for some relief, the fleet of ships dropped to fifteen hundred feet in an attempt to get out of the worst of the turbulence.

The lower altitude got them out of the worst of it, but the conditions were still simply horrible, and virtually everyone was terrified as the ships pitched wildly in the storm.

They had only been at the lower altitude for a few minutes when the winds strengthened again. The winds were now so strong that the fleet was actually being blown back toward the Nubian coast.

Even though they couldn't actually see the fleet of airships, Billy and the group knew that they had to be suffering terribly.

"Isn't there anything that we can do for them?" Linda asked.

"I might be able to save a few if you'll let me use the *Imagination*," John said.

"No problem," Billy said. "Do you think you could find King Abrahams's ship?"

"Probably. When we built the balloons, we installed transponders on every ship. I'll find out the code of the ship he's on before we leave. If he's still alive, we'll make him the first one we pick up."

Fifty minutes later, John had gathered his team and was on his way. They were at sixty-five thousand feet when they reached the area where the airships were supposed to be located.

The storm clouds had continued building, and they were already within a few thousand feet of their altitude.

"It looks pretty rough down there," Lieutenant Melrose said.

"It does at that, but we should be alright," John said. "Have you located the king's ship?"

"I have, and it's forty miles ahead. They're at fifteen hundred feet, but their altitude is varying by several hundred feet. They must be getting tossed around pretty badly. Do you have any idea how we're going to get them off the ship?"

"Billy worked it out for me, but I've got to say that I think it's iffy."

As the *Imagination* descended through the storm, they were awestruck by the sheer ferocity of it.

When they broke through the clouds, they could see what was left of the fleet of airships below them. They were being tossed about like leaves in the wind, and as they watched in horror, two more of them broke up in midair.

Most of the heavier-loaded ones had already broken up, and more were falling by the minute.

Once they were within a mile of the king's ship, John hit execute on the program Billy had put together. It immediately locked on to the airship's transponder signal and began an approach.

When they were directly in front of the airship, they slowed and matched its speed. The *Imagination* latched on to the airship's keel with one of its magnetic hull plates and began to pull it closer.

As the airship drew near, the program lowered the *Imagination*'s rear loading ramp. It continued pulling the airship in until its nose came to rest against the edge of the ramp. When the airship's keel made contact, it locked tight with the ramp.

When it had clamped on, it had helped steady the airship some, but the storm was still bouncing the airship around so violently that John feared that it could break up at any second.

He radioed Billy, "How secure is the magnetic connection to the airship?"

"It should hold through anything that you'll encounter."

"Good, I'm going to collapse the ship's balloon to lessen the wind's effect. Will it hold the entire weight of the gondola?"

"Absolutely. It was designed to hold a lot more weight than that."

John took a machine gun from the rack on the wall and walked to the back of the ship. He fired a couple of long bursts to collapse the airship's balloon, and as soon as it began to deflate, the winds ripped it to shreds.

As soon as the balloon was out of the way, John expanded the magnetic shields on the front of the ship to form a barrier to the wind.

Then he triggered the magnetic containment fields on

the edges of the ramp to keep people from being blown over the side while they worked.

When John was satisfied that they were ready, he sent a couple of men down the ramp to smash a hole in the nose of the airship. They had only gotten about halfway done when a gust of wind tore the weakened nose section off the ship, which left them staring at the terrified passengers in the gondola.

Even though John had managed to divert quite a bit of the storm's fury, the noise was so intense that they could barely hear anything. When John signaled them to begin, several more men rushed down the ramp with ropes.

When they reached the airship, they anchored the ropes to serve as handrails. Once they got started moving the passengers it only took them about twenty minutes to transfer them.

The last one to leave was King Abrahams, and as he walked on board, he took John's hand and yelled over the wind, "Many thanks, I thought we were goners. Do you think that you can help the rest of my people?"

"We're going to try. Let's go up to the bridge and see what we can get done."

The storm had continued to strengthen, and by now it was truly a terrifying sight. The clouds were rolling madly above them, and it was as bright out as a noonday sun. The lightning was almost constant, and it was flashing around them like a gigantic electric spiderweb.

As they peered out through the storm's fury to try and decide which ship to save next, they realized that there were only two ships left.

They immediately started closing with the nearest ship, but before they could reach it, the storm ripped its balloon to shreds, and it spiraled down into the ocean.

They realized that they might only have a few minutes left to save the last ship.

They were trying to hurry as much as they could, but the conditions were unbelievably bad, and they missed the first time they tried to capture it. After two more tries, they were finally able to latch onto it.

Normally, they would have had their shields up to protect them from the winds, but they couldn't use them while they were trying to capture the ship. By then the winds were so powerful that both ships were being tossed about so violently that several people had suffered broken bones.

The passengers were having a difficult time, so they had to send several more soldiers down the ramp to try to help them up; however, even with the help, it was taking much longer to get them moved.

They had managed to rescue most of them when a tremendous gust of wind splintered the bottom of the ship's gondola, and they lost the remainder of the passengers, along with two of the soldiers.

Frustrated at the loss, John slammed his fist against the ship's bulkhead. It was maddening to have been so close, and then to lose them. He took one last look at what remained of the wrecked ship, and then he released the ship's keel and let it fall into the ocean with the rest of the debris.

"I'm very sorry. I thought we were going to be able to save all of them. How many ships did you start out with?" John asked.

"There were four hundred and thirty when we left yesterday."

Not knowing what else to say, John turned to the command console and set a course for the tunnels where the rest of King Abrahams's people were being sheltered.

They had decided that King Peterovan would be in the old mines that John and Billy had explored, and that King Abrahams was going to be in the mines in the eastern mountains.

The thought was that if one of the facilities didn't make it, at least there would be one king left to take charge of the survivors.

As they had planned, Billy and his people were going to stay in their settlement.

IT HAD BEEN a struggle, but Billy felt like they were in as good a shape as they could be. Since they weren't ready to launch, Nicholas had used the extra power from the new ship's reactor to supplement the magnetic shield around the settlement.

The extra power had enabled him to expand the shields over all but one of the barracks. They were a little crowded, but they had managed to get everyone inside the magnetic shields.

As the meteors were approaching, their entire team was gathered around one of the holographic projectors to watch them hit the planet.

"It looks like our calculation was correct," Billy said. "The first meteor is about to hit just off the Nubian coast. I'm going to see if we can get a closer look."

He repositioned one of their surveillance satellites to get a better view of the impact zone.

They watched as the meteor cut a fiery trail through the sky. When it hit the water off the coast, it threw a mushroom cloud of dirt, water, and fire several thousand feet in the air.

At first they thought that might be the end of it, but

within a few seconds, they could see a thousand-foot-high tsunami rushing toward the coastline.

As it had moved inland, it swept away everything in its path. When it reached the capital, the wave was still higher than Queen Amanirenas's palace. Mesmerized by the destruction, they continued to watch until the wave played out, over four hundred miles inland.

They had been so intent on watching the first meteor that they had ignored the second one's impact. It was larger than the first, and it had struck within a thousand yards of the ancient shelter that the Nubians had discovered.

The shelter had been the salvation of their ancestors, but this time the meteor's impact vaporized it and much of the surrounding countryside.

By the time Billy switched satellites to see what it had done, the view was blocked by the massive cloud of debris that was already at thirty thousand feet and rising.

With all the dust that the impact had thrown into the atmosphere, they wouldn't be able to see what it had destroyed for several weeks. When they finally could, they found that the resulting impact crater was a little over five miles in diameter and over eleven hundred feet deep.

The sand around the edges had been fused into a bizarre sort of glass by the heat, and the shockwaves had extended out for over forty miles, flattening everything in their path.

Billy continued monitoring the meteors until they had all hit. When he was satisfied that the danger had passed, he said, "It's a good thing that we relocated the Nubians. It wasn't as bad as it could have been, but without a doubt, most of them would have perished.

"Now that we know what we're looking at from the

damage from the first round, I'm going to make a short visit to talk with King Abrahams. I would like to let him know what's happened so far.

"When I get back, I want us to all sit down and finalize the launch date of—" He paused and asked, "What do you think we ought to call it?"

"How about calling it the *Salvadora*?" Linda asked.

"Savior, that would seem appropriate," Nicholas said. "I know that you're getting anxious to launch, but I've just finished going over the numbers, and I'm going to need another twenty days."

"Why so long?"

"I've still got to fill the hull with the Pu-239, seal it, and then mount the crew module."

When they were finished talking, Billy and Linda went to see King Abrahams.

"How's it going?" Billy asked.

"How good can it be? We're living in a cave; however, I suppose it's all relative, because we're still alive. That's more than over half my people can say.

"Before you think that I'm ungrateful, let me say that I can't thank you and your people enough for helping us out."

"No thanks needed, I just wish we could have done better."

Billy spent the next three hours updating the king on the damage to his kingdom. When he had shown the king the video and high-resolution pictures of the damage, it had taken him a few moments to believe that it wasn't magic.

When Billy finished his briefing, the conversation turned to health issues.

"Are there any of your people who are still sick?" Linda asked.

"It seems like a miracle, but we haven't had any recurrences of the sickness since we've been here."

Unsure of how to ask his next question, the king hesitated for a second or two before he continued.

"I hope that you don't take this the wrong way, but I need to ask you a question that's been nagging at me for several weeks. When I was first talking with the team that you sent to help us, one of them made a comment that I would like for you to explain.

"He told me that they had seen the disease before, and he made the comment that it was the same strain that the terrorists on your world had been using. I'm not sure that I understand what a terrorist is. But more importantly, how could something like that suddenly show up here?"

Neither one of them said anything for several seconds. "I'm sorry, but I'm not going to try to explain how the disease showed up," Billy said.

The king's brow furrowed as he thought about what Billy had just implied, and what his response should be.

"Thank you for not lying to me. I wish you would reconsider, but I'm not in a position to try to force you to tell me. Can you at least assure me that we aren't going to suffer from it again?"

"I give you my word that it won't be an issue again."

"I'm going to take you at your word, and that's the last time we'll speak of it. Do have any idea how much longer we're going to be down here?"

"It all depends on whether we're able to divert the meteor. If we're successful, you should be able to return to your homes in a few months. If we're not successful, it may be a moot point, because I'm not sure that anyone will survive if it hits Midgard."

"You're just full of optimism today."

"I apologize if you think I'm being unduly negative, but I need you to understand the gravity of our situation. I still believe that we have a decent chance of success, but it's no sure thing.

"I'm sorry, but we've got to get going. I just wanted to check in with you and make sure you were getting settled in. We may not see you again, but the rest of the team will be delivering a couple more portable reactors to supplement your power needs. That should allow you to be self sufficient if you're cut off from the rest of us for any length of time."

"We'll be fine, and good luck on the mission."

23

THE NEXT FEW weeks flew by, and their window of opportunity was rapidly drawing to a close. If they didn't launch in the next eleven days, their mission would no longer be feasible.

"How much longer is it going to be?" Billy asked impatiently.

"We finished mounting the crew module last night," Nicholas said. "All that we've got left to do is a final system check and a short test flight. If everything checks out, the ship will be ready to go."

Billy spent the rest of the day mapping out the mission's flight plan. Once he had it done, he uploaded it into the *Salvadora*'s flight control computer. Nicholas was still finishing a few final details on the ship, so Billy decided to spend a little time with Larry Sheldon.

Larry had done as Billy had asked and kept a very low profile. The cover story they had used was that Billy had him working on a top secret project, and he wasn't to be disturbed.

Larry had spent most of his time recording the events of his life. It wasn't that he felt his life was terribly important, but he had witnessed and carried out many things that he wanted the survivors to remember so that they didn't repeat their mistakes.

He had decided to make two different versions, one for general consumption, and one for Billy and Linda's eyes only.

He had no way of knowing whether any of them would ever be able to rejoin their fleet, but if they did, he wanted Billy to have as much information as possible.

As soon as he had finished the public version he went to work on Billy and Linda's version.

Due to the sheer volume of information that he wanted to share, he had to break it into several sections.

The first section was a detailed listing of the Logos's membership, along with their ranks, roles, and responsibilities within the organization. He wasn't sure how many of them had survived, so he listed every one of the existing members.

He had made a special point to detail everything he had on President McAlister, so that Billy wouldn't be taken in by him. Toward the end, Larry had developed severe doubts about President McAlister, and he and the Logos's chairman had spent many hours discussing him.

Long before they had left Earth, they had both come to the conclusion that he wasn't a true believer, and that he was simply using his status as a member of the Logos to further his political ambitions.

Larry detailed everything that he had experienced, and he tried not to leave out a thing, no matter how disturbing some people might find it.

The very last section he worked on was the explanation he had promised Billy. He wanted to ensure that they would be the only ones who would ever view it, so he used the strongest encryption he had and keyed it to their retinal patterns.

He had taken over a week to detail everything he knew about what had happened to them. He knew that they had to hear the entire story, or they would never be able to understand who, and what, they were.

When he had gone to the Iraqi desert to retrieve the sarcophagus he had no way of knowing the events he was setting in motion.

After he had safely delivered the sarcophagus, he had been somewhat surprised when the Logos had asked him to stay involved with the project.

He hadn't really understood the enormous implications of the project until they had given him the opportunity to study the complete translations of the inscriptions on Adamartoni's sarcophagus.

As he wrote of the experience, he remembered how amazed he had been at their story. He possessed a perfect photographic memory, so he could transcribe the inscriptions word for word. When he had documented everything he had learned about Adamartoni and Evevette's background, he started to explain the rest of it.

He started by laying out the events that had led up to Billy being accidentally injected with Adamartoni's DNA. He even made sure that he detailed the theories that the other scientists had developed about the possible effects the DNA might have on Billy and Linda Lou.

It was harder for him to explain how and why he and his fellow Logos had coerced, manipulated, and guided them, and their parents, while they were growing up.

When he was finished, he had an immense amount of content for them. After he had verified that both versions contained everything that he wanted to share, he took a little time to contemplate what he needed to do next.

He knew that Billy and Linda truly believed that God was telling them to carry out the mission to divert the meteor. He knew in his heart, however, that the fate of all the Earth's survivors was in their hands.

As he had so many times before, he vowed to do whatever was necessary to make sure that they fulfilled their destinies.

"IT'S GOOD TO see you again my young friend," Larry said.

"Same here, but I wish that it could have been under better circumstances," Billy replied.

He looked Larry in the eye and said, "I'm at a loss on what to do about you. I've already decided that I can never let it be known what you've done. But, I don't think that I can ever allow you to resume your duties. This may sound strange, but what do you think that I should do about you?"

"I've been afraid that you might ask me that, and I've been thinking about how to answer. But I've got to tell you, I haven't come up with anything that would work for either one of us. In many cultures, I would've just committed suicide and solved your problem, but I'm afraid that's not my style."

"Nor would I ever want you to. Well, it's not something that we have to decide today.

"I was just talking with Nicholas, and he's finally done with the ship, and it's a good thing. We've only got four more days until we miss our final launch window."

"How long will it take you to reach the meteor?"

"If everything goes as planned, it should take forty-one days."

"That seems like a long time to be riding on a gigantic tube of plutonium. I thought that you had concerns about the radiation exposure to the crew?"

"I do, but Linda thinks she's developed a plan that

should allow us to make it. We're going to be taking Ca-DTPA treatments to enable us to continue functioning."

"A chelating agent like that should help, but it's still a long time." Larry didn't say what he was really thinking, because he knew that he wouldn't be able to change Billy's mind.

As they sat talking, Billy got the feeling that Larry was more at peace than he had ever seen him. They talked for over an hour before Billy got a call and had to leave.

The reason Larry had seemed more at peace was because he had changed his mind about several things while they were talking.

When Billy had first arrived, he'd intended to tell him about the video archives he'd created for them; however, as they had talked, he had decided to wait.

The bigger decision had come when he realized that Billy and Linda still intended to carry out the mission themselves. He'd always known it, but making the archives had reinforced it for him. They were still the only real hope humanity had for long-term survival.

After Billy had gone, he was sitting in his dimly lighted room thinking through what came next, and he realized that he felt more at peace than he had in years. He spent a few more minutes organizing his thoughts, and then he jumped up and started to put his plans into action.

Even though he had been keeping a low profile, he was still viewed as the man in command by most of the people on base. When he had made his list of things to do, he started contacting the people he needed to carry out his plan.

* * *

THE DAYS SEEMED to speed by, and before they realized it, they were preparing to leave. That night Billy and Linda were lying in bed talking before they went to sleep.

"I talked with Larry again this afternoon," Billy said. "It may sound strange, but he seemed to be more at peace with himself than I've ever seen."

"That could be good or bad," Linda said. "Oh, before I forget, Pastor Williams asked if it would be alright with us if he held a prayer service tomorrow night. He said that he would understand if we didn't want to mess with it, since it would be our last night before we leave."

"I can't think of anything that would be more appropriate. The only thing that I've got planned for tomorrow is a short morning meeting with our two volunteers. After that my day is free. I thought that we should spend the rest of the day with our parents, although I'm not looking forward to it."

"That's a good idea, and I know what you mean about dreading it. I love our parents to death, but they're going to continue badgering us not to go."

Billy was up before dawn the next morning, and he decided to take a walk out to where they had the *Salvadora* parked.

Even with all the extra shielding they had installed, it was emitting a tremendous amount of radiation. The risk of radiation exposure was so great that they had parked it as far away from the rest of the base as they could get it. Since it was well outside the base's magnetic shield, it was exposed to the brutal weather.

As Billy approached the ship, he could see the makeshift guard shack and the two young soldiers who were busy tending their stove as they tried to keep from freezing to death.

Seeing them reminded him of how much different their lives were since they had made peace with the Nubians.

Before the two kings had forged their informal peace treaty, they would have had at least fifty heavily armed men guarding the ship itself, and even in this weather their perimeter defenses would have been fully manned.

The soldiers hadn't seen him until he was within thirty feet of them, and when they did, he looked like a wraith when he suddenly appeared out of the blowing snow.

Startled by his early morning appearance, they both jumped up and saluted.

"We're sorry, sir, we didn't see you coming."

"It's alright, and you don't need to salute me. I'm just going to look around for a few minutes. You can stay where you're at, there's no need to be out in this weather."

Nicholas had kept just enough power to the hull plates to keep the *Salvadora* hovering above the snow. Even now, it was still an amazing sight to Billy as he stood staring at the ship.

It looked as light as a feather as it hovered there, but it weighed almost a hundred tons and was packed with enough plutonium to vaporize everything for miles around.

As he walked around the ship, he noticed the crew module that Nicholas had just mounted on the top of the ship. In between the waves of snow, he could see the faint glow of the console lights as they reflected off of the window glass.

Despite the terrible conditions, he stopped for a moment to contemplate what lay ahead of them. He knew in his heart that they were doing the right thing, but he hated that Linda was going to sacrifice her life as well.

We'll be together, and that's the only important thing to me, Linda said in his mind.

I didn't think you were awake yet.

I was awake when you left, but it just seemed like you needed some alone time. You need to stop worrying about me. God has given us both a mission, and we'll carry it out, no matter what the cost. Why are you standing out in the cold?

I don't really know. I just felt like taking a look at the ship. What time are we supposed to meet with our parents?

We're going to have breakfast with them, and then we're supposed to spend the rest of the day with them.

I'll have to catch up to you after breakfast. I've got a meeting with our two volunteers in a few minutes.

You did tell me that, sorry. I'll keep them entertained until you get there. But you're going to owe me big time.

BILLY SPENT ALMOST an hour with Manuel Vasquez and Jimmie Turner. They were only twenty-one years old, and he could tell that they were both very excited to be going with Billy and Linda.

Billy had tried to make it very clear to them what they were getting into, but they were both adamant that they knew what they had volunteered for.

He had started to tell them that they were too young to be throwing their lives away, when he realized that it was the same speech that Larry Sheldon and John Tyler had been giving them.

When he was satisfied that they knew what they were getting into, he thanked them both and told them to meet him at the ship at 0500 in the morning.

When he caught up with Linda and their parents, they were sitting in the cafeteria drinking coffee.

The day had gone just like they had feared, as their parents took turns trying to reason with them. They had tried literally everything that they could think of, but Billy and Linda stayed strong and never wavered.

They spent the entire day with their parents, and after dinner Billy told them, "We're going to get cleaned up before we go to Pastor Williams's service. We'll meet you there."

After they were gone, Ben said, "Alright, we've tried everything else, let's all pray that God will change his mind and let them live."

They all joined hands, bowed their heads, and prayed as they had never prayed before. Finally, they looked at each other and hoped that God would answer their prayers.

PASTOR WILLIAMS HAD decided to hold the service outside so that everyone could attend if they chose to. They were inside the magnetic barrier so the wind wasn't a factor, but it was still very cold.

When Billy and Linda walked up, the people parted to let them move to the front. The two young volunteers were already standing behind Earl Williams. When Earl saw Billy and Linda, he called to them, "Please, come on up and stand with us."

As Pastor Williams conducted the ceremony, emotions were running high. Several times he had to pause while the medics helped people who had passed out.

When he finally came to the end of the service, Pastor Williams asked, "Now I would like for us all to ask God to protect these brave young people as they carry out their mission and, at the proper time, receive their souls into his kingdom."

By the time they had finished their prayers, many of the people were openly weeping.

As the service broke up, there were hundreds of people that came up to shake their hands and to thank them. Even though they were all about to freeze, they stayed until the last well-wisher was gone.

When the last one had left, Pastor Williams put his arms around Billy and Linda. As he spoke to them, he, too, was trying to choke back his tears.

"I've known you two since you were children, and I can't tell you how proud I am of you. I just can't believe that this is the last time that I'll ever see you."

He hugged them even tighter and said, "I don't know why, but I feel that we'll meet again one day, although it may not be in this life.

"I'm going to say a prayer for you every night, but I already know in my heart that God has a plan for you, and that whatever happens is his doing."

When Billy and Linda got back to their quarters they were still shivering from standing out in the cold for so long. "Let's take a nice hot shower and try to get some sleep," Billy said.

They had just gotten dried off and were about to try to get some sleep, when they heard someone beating on their door.

When Billy opened it, there stood Larry Sheldon, and he acted like he was more than a little drunk.

"I just had to come by and tell you good-bye," Larry bellowed.

"Have you been drinking?" Linda asked.

"I have. It was the only way that I could bear to face you two, and I just had to say good-bye."

"You're always welcome here," Linda said. "I hope that you know that we think the world of you, and besides, you've always looked out for us."

"I've always tried in my own way, but enough of this. You've got to have a good-bye drink with me."

"You know that we don't drink," Linda said.

"I know, but you can make this one exception, as a favor to an old friend."

They talked for several more minutes, and Larry was being very insistent. Finally, they decided that if they were going to get any sleep, they had better humor him.

"Alright, just one drink, and then we need to get some sleep," Billy said.

Larry immediately produced three glasses and placed them on the table with a flourish. He quickly poured three full glasses of champagne and handed one to each of them.

"If I had ever had kids of my own, I would have wanted them to be just like you two. I can't begin to tell you what knowing the two of you has meant to me."

They touched their glasses together in a toast and drank them straight down.

Larry started to pour them another full glass, but Billy put his hand over his glass and said, "No, one is more than enough for us. We can never thank you enough for what you've done for us, but we need to get some sleep."

"Now that's touching, but weird," Billy said. "I've never seen Larry out of control before."

"There was definitely something going on with him, but I don't think he was as drunk as he was letting on. I'm going to bed; I'm exhausted, and we've got to get up at the crack of dawn."

It was unlike him, but Billy was suddenly feeling very tired as well, so they went straight to bed.

Once again, they both had the same dream about the meteor. They were holding each other as they watched it grow ever closer, but like before, they both woke up just before they hit it.

The next morning they slept right through their alarm, and when they finally did wake up, they both were covered in sweat, and their heads were throbbing.

As they both stumbled into the bathroom to get ready, Linda said, "I feel like crap. If that's what drinking does to you, I'm glad we don't drink."

After they had popped some aspirins and took a quick shower, Billy glanced over at the clock and said, "We'd better get going. I just can't believe they didn't come and get us."

They hurried to get dressed and rushed out to meet the rest of their crew. As they were walking out the door, they ran into John Tyler.

"What are you two doing back here? Did you have mechanical problems?"

"Mechanical problems, what are you talking about?" Billy asked. "We're just running late. For some reason, we overslept. Why didn't you come and get us? You know that we can't afford to lose any time."

"But the *Salvadora* left at dawn, over three hours ago."

"How's that possible? The volunteers didn't know how to fly the ship."

"They're not on board either. I just got done talking with them, and they said that the officer of the day had contacted them last night and said that you had scratched them from the mission."

They talked back and forth for several minutes until Billy said, "I've got to contact the *Salvadora* and find out what's going on. Maybe we can get it turned around and still salvage the mission."

It took him a few minutes to make contact, but he finally got the ship to answer his hail.

"This is the *Salvadora,* what do you need?"

"What do you mean, what do I need?" Billy asked. "Who is this, and why have you taken our ship? You need to turn around and return immediately."

"That's not going to happen. I'm well on my way, and I have no intention of returning."

"Larry, is that you?"

"Who else do you know that's stupid enough to take on a mission like this?"

"You know that it's not your mission to carry out. I'm going to get the *Imagination* and catch up to you. Then you can use it to return to the base, and we'll finish the mission like we're supposed to."

"I think not. I've disabled *Imagination,* and by the time you figure out what I did to it, I'll be too far away for you to catch me."

"Why would you do this? You know that we're the ones who have to carry out this mission."

"That may be, but I've had dreams as well, and I believe that God's given me a chance at redemption, and this is it."

"You can't carry out the mission alone. You're going to need help to operate the ship."

"Nope, I got Nicholas to fix it up so I could take care of everything that needs to be done. Stop worrying about it, I've got this covered. You two are needed there, and besides, I've already burned my bridges there, and this takes care of what to do with me."

Billy and Larry went back and forth at each other for over an hour before Billy finally came to the conclusion that there was no way to stop Larry from carrying out his plan.

It took some convincing, but he finally got Larry to agree to give them a call at least once a day until the mission was completed.

"How did Larry manage to do all of this without either one of us knowing about it?" Billy asked.

"You know Larry," John said. "Besides, everyone thinks that he's still in command. To be honest about it, had he asked me to help him out, I would have done it. I can't begin to tell you how relieved I am that you and Linda aren't on that ship."

LATER THAT DAY, Billy called the entire team together to try to piece together everything Larry had the different groups do. He wanted to understand what had been done so he could ensure that they had a plan to give Larry whatever support they could.

As the story unfolded, it was evident that Larry's actions hadn't been a spur-of-the-moment decision. As was his way, his attention to detail had been amazing.

He had been very careful not to draw any attention to what he was doing. He had limited his requests to one person in each of the areas where he needed work done, and he had sworn each one of them to secrecy.

Under the guise of not being able to sleep, he had even managed to con William Robbins into giving him the powerful sedative that he had used to spike their drinks.

Linda had been right when she had sensed that Larry wasn't as drunk as he had let on. In fact, the only drink he had had that night was the single glass of champagne he had had with them.

His only exception to the single point of contact had

been Nicholas Stavros's team. Larry had worked daily with the entire team. He had done it right under Billy's nose, and none of them had ever suspected a thing.

Nicholas Stavros had been the only one that Larry had taken into his confidence. Nicholas had fully supported Larry's decision and had even helped him keep his plans a secret.

Whenever Nicholas's team had asked about all the modifications, he would explain them away by telling them that they were contingencies, in case the crew got sick from the radiation.

When their parents had watched the *Salvadora* lift off, they had been resigned to the fact that they would never see their children again. At the time, they had been upset with them, because they hadn't taken the time to say good-bye before they boarded, but in a way they had understood.

They had stood out in the cold until the *Salvadora* was out of sight, and then they had gone back to the cafeteria to eat breakfast together.

They were still eating when they found out that Billy and Linda hadn't gone on the mission.

They were almost beside themselves with joy as they joined hands and gave their thanks to God for sparing their children. At that moment, they had never felt closer to God, and it had given each one of them the opportunity to recommit their lives to His service.

Once again, it seemed that God had heard their prayers, because that very night God started showing them what He had in mind for them. Both Ben and Rob had their first dreams of how God wanted them to help teach the people of Midgard new ways of farming.

* * *

AFTER A COUPLE of weeks, things had begun to return to normal. It had taken Billy over a week to find where Larry had sabotaged the *Imagination*.

When they had it fixed, he decided to take another tour of the Nubian homeland and see if they could get a complete damage assessment.

On the way there, John suggested that they stop by and get King Abrahams, so he could see the damage for himself.

24

King Abrahams had been more than ready to get outside again, and he jumped at the chance to see what had happened to his kingdom. After his previous experience with flying, the king was a little apprehensive about it, but this trip was a lot smoother, and he was enjoying the experience by the time they got to the Nubian coastline.

As they drew near, John brought the *Imagination* down to a thousand feet so they could get a better look.

Billy and the team had watched the tsunami on video when it had hit, but seeing the damage up close brought home the reality of the devastation. The massive wall of water had swept away virtually everything that had been on the coastline and, in some places, even the sand from the beaches was gone.

When they turned and followed the river up toward the capital, they found that there was nothing left of the numerous villages that had once lined it.

When they reached the capital, they could see that many of the buildings were still standing. They made several circles around the city to try to get an idea about what had survived.

When they were satisfied that they understood what

was left of the city, they landed in front of the queen's palace to take a firsthand look at the damage.

At first glance, the great pyramid didn't look like it had suffered any damage at all.

Its massive blocks of stone had withstood the wall of water with no problem, but when they went inside, they saw that the inside was a mess. Every inch was filled with mud, and virtually everything inside had been destroyed by the water.

"I'm very sorry, but it looks like the inside is a total loss," Billy said.

"No matter. In fact, it will make it easier," King Abrahams said. "This way I don't have to deal with any questions about why I'm changing anything. Are we going to have time to take a look at the areas where the other fragments hit?"

"Sure, I just thought that we should stop here first."

As they moved over the next impact area it was readily apparent where the fragment had hit.

The point of impact was surrounded by an almost perfect circle of total destruction that extended for several miles. But instead of the crater they had expected to find at the center, there was a brand new, crystal-clear lake.

The massive explosion had smashed through the bedrock into the aquifer below, turning the impact crater into a gigantic free-flowing artesian well.

The ancient riverbed that had once run through the area was now being fed from the lake, and it was once again flowing strongly.

As they flew around the area, they could even see several flocks of waterfowl that had already returned.

"Nature has an amazing way of healing itself," King Abrahams said. "I'd read that this area was once lush with agriculture, but I never believed it. When I was a young lieutenant, we did our survival training in this area, and I can promise you that it was anything but a paradise."

They spent the rest of the day flying over the Nubian territory to get a feel for the damage they would have to deal with if they ever returned. When they were satisfied they had seen enough, they returned King Abrahams to the shelter.

"Thanks for taking me with you. Knowing the truth about what's going on will make it easier for me to help my people. If we don't suffer too much more damage, we may be able to come out of this stronger than ever."

"We'll call you from time to time, but we probably won't be back this way until we know whether we've managed to divert the meteor," Billy said.

On their way back to base, they stopped to spend a few minutes with King Peterovan. They spent the first half an hour updating the king on what they had found.

"That's great news that the Nubians might be able to return home when this is all over," King Peterovan said.

"That's good to hear, because in the back of my mind, I'd thought that you might be hoping that they would all die," Billy said.

"I can't deny that it would have been true at one time; however, since I've gotten to know several of them, I've found that they're really not much different from us.

"It's much like the first time that I saw you. I didn't think that I could ever be friends with anyone that looked and acted like you did that day; however, I was wrong about you, and I've been wrong about them. We've been enemies for so long that none of us even remember what started it all. If any of us lives through this, I can promise you that it's going to be different."

As they were boarding the ship to leave, Billy told the king, "Good luck, and we won't see you again until the danger is past."

THE NEXT MORNING, Linda decided to sit in on Billy's daily call with Larry.

When Larry hadn't called in when he was supposed to, Billy had started trying to call him. After he'd tried several times, and they were becoming concerned, Larry finally answered.

"Sorry, I was in the head when you called."

As they were talking, Linda had just sat back and watched for the first five minutes. Finally, she asked, "You've been throwing up, haven't you?"

Larry hesitated before he answered. "Yes, I have. That's what I was doing when you first called. How did you know?"

"It's not that hard to tell. The picture is pretty grainy, but the resolution is good enough for me to tell that you've lost quite a bit of weight, and it looks like you might be sweating a little. Do you have a fever as well?"

"You're good. I do, but only a point and a half."

"Are you taking your daily shots?"

"I am, however, they don't seem to be working as well as they were."

"I'm sure that they're still working, but the cumulative effects of the radiation are only going to get worse. Do you have enough supplies to double up on your shots?"

"Sure, there's enough on board for four people at the normal dosage. Do you really think it's going to help?"

Linda hesitated before she answered. "It will help some, but all that you can hope to do is slow the progression. How long have you got until you reach the meteor?"

"At his current speed, it's going to take another thirteen days to reach the rendezvous point," Billy said.

She thought about it for a few seconds and said, "You need to start taking the vitamins that are in the supplies. The treatments you're taking can remove a lot of vitamins and minerals out of your system, which may be part of your problem. Other than that you should be fine for that long."

EVER SINCE LARRY had commandeered the *Salvadora*, Billy and Linda's dreams had changed.

Instead of the meteor, they were dreaming about the Earth's fleet and President McAlister. Unlike their dreams about the meteor, the dreams didn't ever seem to repeat, but they all had a similar theme to them.

After several nights of the dreams, they had come to believe that President McAlister was doing some truly awful things to the people of the fleet.

AFTER SHE HAD seen how Larry's condition was deteriorating, Linda made sure that she was always on their call. They talked about many things, and several times Larry had got so caught up in their conversations that he almost told them about the videos he had created.

A few days before Larry's rendezvous with the meteor, Billy and Linda were eating dinner with their parents. They hadn't spent much time with them since their abortive mission to the meteor, and their parents had been pestering them to spend some time with them.

As they sat eating, their parents told them about how they had joined together to pray that they wouldn't go, and how they felt like their prayers had been answered.

Their discussions soon turned to answered prayers and dreams/visions, when Ben said, "I know that you two believe strongly that some of your dreams are visions from God, so let me ask you a question.

"Rob and I have been having the same dreams for several weeks now. We keep dreaming that we're all living beside a crystal-clear lake, and that we're spending our days teaching the Nubians how to be farmers.

"In our dreams, the fields are laid out along a large river, and the land is so fertile that the crops seem to grow overnight.

"The dreams are very detailed and it all seems so real. In our dreams, we even have a good selection of farm equipment."

Ben and Rob went on to describe the area in great detail, and they seemed to agree on every part.

They could tell that Ben was nervous, because he had to pause and catch his breath before he continued, "Sorry, I don't know why, but I'm really nervous about this.

"My question is, do you think that the dreams could be God giving us a vision of what he wants us to do?"

Billy got a funny look on his face and said, "Just a minute, I'll be right back."

He was only gone for a few minutes, and when he returned, he was carrying a laptop and a miniature holographic projector.

When he got it set up, he started showing them several segments of the video they had taken on their tour of the Nubian countryside.

"Does this look anything like the lake in your dreams?" Billy asked, as he froze the video on a picture of the lake that had been formed by one of the meteorites.

"That's it, how did you know?"

"It wasn't that hard, your descriptions fit it perfectly.

Do you remember us telling you about when we went to get the uranium for the *Salvadora*?"

"Sure, but what does that have to do with the lake?"

"The lake is just a couple of miles away from the old quarry where we got the uranium; of course it wasn't a lake at the time.

"I don't believe in coincidences, so I'm going to agree that you're having visions from God. If we live through this, I'll make sure that you get equipment, and that you have the opportunity to carry out what God has asked of you."

"That would be wonderful. We'd love to be able to work on the land again."

The rest of the night went well, and they managed not to spend any time talking about the mission to the meteor.

Later that night Billy and Linda were lying in bed talking.

"Is it just me, or is God starting to speak to more and more people?" Billy asked.

"No, I'm seeing it as well. Do you think their dreams mean that we're going to be stranded here for the rest of our lives?"

"Who knows, but if our dreams are any indication, I would have to say no.

"This may be nothing, but I'm a little disturbed that I don't recognize anyone other than President McAlister, and I don't really know him."

"If the dreams are accurate, I don't want to get to know him. He's a horrible man."

"Let's make a point to ask Larry about him. I know that he's worked extensively with him over the years, and he should be able to give us some insight into what makes him tick."

The next day they were just finishing up their call with Larry, and it was evident that he was fading fast.

The additional treatments Linda had recommended had helped, but his health was still deteriorating.

She gave him a couple more things to try, but she knew that there was really nothing that would help very much. They were just about to sign off when Billy remembered to ask about President McAlister.

Larry knew that the videos he'd made for them would answer their questions, but he decided that he wasn't quite ready to share them yet.

"I do know quite a lot about him, but is there something specific you would like to know?"

"We've been having dreams about the rest of the Earth fleet, and we keep seeing him do some truly awful things to people. What are the chances that our dreams are true?"

"Obviously there's no way that I can know whether what you are dreaming is actually taking place, but I will say this about him: He'll do whatever he feels is necessary to achieve his goals. It's my belief that he's a man without any true beliefs, other than in himself."

"So you think that he's quite capable of the atrocities we've seen in our dreams."

"Without a doubt, but I wouldn't worry about it too much, they're probably just dreams. Besides, it's highly unlikely that you'll ever see any of them again. But if you do, you would do well to steer clear of President McAlister. Now if you don't mind I'd like to cut short our call today. I'm not feeling all that well."

"Larry sure didn't seem like himself today," Billy said to Linda.

"No, he didn't. I'm afraid it's because he's dying. It's a good thing that there are only a couple of days left in the mission, because that's about all the time he has left."

BILLY GOT UP early the next morning and went to find Nicholas Stavros and John Tyler. He couldn't be sure Larry was going to succeed, but he figured it couldn't hurt to get the rebuilding process started.

"I know that we're in the middle of a lot things, but I would like for us to start putting together our recovery plans. Here's a list of equipment and materials that I think we're going to need to start the recovery process."

They took a few minutes to look over the list, and then Nicholas said, "This should be simple enough. It'll take us a few months to manufacture the equipment, but everything else we can just pick up from the Nubian storehouses.

"They left all of their seed grains behind, and the chemicals for the fertilizers and insecticides shouldn't be a problem. But don't you think that you're getting the cart before the horse? We don't even know if Larry's going to succeed."

"We might as well stay busy. There's nothing more we can do about the meteor, so why not start planning for the future?"

The day before Larry was supposed to rendezvous with the meteor, he cut their call short again. After he had disconnected, they took a few moments to discuss how quickly he was going downhill.

"It's a good thing he's only got one more day," Linda said.

"He did look bad. Nevertheless, he's one of the toughest

people I've ever known, so if it can be done, he's the one to do it.

"When we talk with him tomorrow I would like to stay on with him until the end."

"It's the least we can do. I hope that we can give him some comfort by being with him at the end. I don't know the specifics of the plan, but I imagine the end will be quick."

"Without a doubt, it should be. The blast is going to be so unbelievably violent that it should be almost instantaneous. He may have suffered horribly up to this point, but his death, while very violent, will be very quick."

Neither one of them slept very well that night. But when they did manage to fall asleep, they dreamed about the meteor. It was the first time in weeks that they had dreamed about it, but the dreams were just as vivid as they had always been.

BILLY AND LINDA had anticipated that their last call with Larry was going to be very personal.

After they had talked it over, they decided to make the call from their quarters so that they could have complete privacy. When they got settled in, they placed the call, and Larry answered immediately.

"Thanks for being there for me," Larry said. "I've always believed that I would die violently, but I never thought that I would have the privilege of having friends with me when I did."

"We just wish we could do more," Linda said. "Did you take the pain shot like I asked you to?"

"I sure did, and it's helping a lot.

"I've had to make a couple of course corrections to

miss some of the outlying meteors, but now I've got a clear path to the big one. If my math is correct, it should be about twenty-five minutes before I intercept it.

"I've got several things that I want to share with you, and my time is short, so just let me finish before you ask any questions."

Even though he had taken a pain shot, Larry was so hoarse that he could hardly talk. He took a sip of water and continued.

"Before I left, I gave Nicholas Stavros a couple of laptops to give to you.

"The first one is intended for general consumption, and it contains a history of the events that led up to our evacuation of the Earth. I thought that it was important that people knew all the sacrifices that so many people made in order for the evacuation to succeed.

"There are some things in there that may not please some people, but the only thing that matters is that it's the truth, unlike what normally happens to history.

"The second laptop is intended for just the two of you. I've encrypted the data, and it's keyed to your retinal patterns, so you're the only ones that can access the data. It contains everything that I know about the Logos, as well as Adamartoni and Evevette's story.

"I've got to warn you that some of it is going to seem a little far out when you read it. I've read the original transcripts from the sarcophagus several times, but I've never been able to decide whether I believed them. I've included every line of what was on his sarcophagus, and once you've had a chance to study it, you can make up your own minds.

"I know that you must have thought that I'd forgotten, but the final section is the explanation that I promised you. It'll explain everything that has happened to you and, ultimately, Linda. I had intended to sit down and tell you the story, but it just never worked out.

"There's one last thing that I would like to share with you before I die.

"You already know that I intentionally infected the Nubians with the H1N1 virus. There's no way that I can ever atone for what I did, so I'm not going to try to explain why I did it.

"But what I wanted to tell you is that I believe that I've finally made my peace with God."

"For your sake, I hope that you're right," Billy said. "You've done so many good things for all of us, and particularly for Linda and me. I promise you that Linda and I will try to put in a good word for you in our prayers."

"Is there anything that you would like for us to do for you?" Linda asked. "Are there any messages you'd like for us to pass on?"

"Not that I can think of. I visited with Nicholas Stavros and John Tyler before I took off. You two were the only ones that I had left to talk with."

Larry paused for a couple of seconds, and they could tell he was struggling to maintain his composure. He took another drink of water and said, "There is one other message that you can pass along for me.

"You can tell Pastor Earl Williams that I can finally answer his question. Please tell him that there isn't any doubt in my mind that I believe in God, and that He has seen fit to give me forgiveness."

"We'll be honored to deliver your message."

"Thank you. I know that it may be disturbing, but if you don't mind, I'm going to keep the video channel open so that you can better judge the impact on the meteor."

Larry was clearly fading fast, but they could tell that he was determined to hold together until the end.

They had normally used a monitor for the video when they talked, but this time Billy had routed the video feed through a holographic projector, so they would have a better perspective of what was going on.

They were still sitting on their couch, and the holographic images filled one whole side of the room.

Billy had split the video feeds so that they could see the oncoming meteor while they communicated with Larry.

The images of the meteor were astounding, and as they watched the ship approach it, they realized that the images were identical to the ones they had been having in their dreams.

Billy put his arm around Linda, and they bonded their minds so they could talk without disturbing Larry.

They had gotten to the point where they could use their telepathy whenever they wanted, but they had never been able to reach anyone else.

They sat watching the *Salvadora* close on the meteor; their emotions were running wild as they waited for the impact.

The *Salvadora* was only a few seconds from contact when Linda and Billy's bonded minds reached Larry's. His mind was surprisingly lucid considering how ill he was and the circumstance he was in.

At first he hadn't realized they were touching his mind, but a couple of seconds later he said in awe,

This is unbelievable! I've always wondered what it would be like. I've heard you both describe it, but it's beyond my wildest imagination! I can actually feel both of your minds inside my mind!

They were about to respond when the *Salvadora* hit the meteor.

Even though they could sense everything that was taking place in Larry's mind, they didn't sense any additional pain. The next feeling they felt was Larry's feeling of calm and an almost indescribable joy.

It was gone almost as soon as it occurred. But they knew exactly what it was, because they had felt it on a much larger scale when the Earth had been destroyed. God had accepted Larry Sheldon into his presence.

25

THE NEXT MORNING, Billy and Linda were discussing the previous day's events over breakfast.

They were excited and a little apprehensive about what was on the laptops that Larry had left for them. Most of all, they were sad about having lost Larry.

They had both felt it, but they hadn't talked about Larry's final moments. Finally, Billy decided that they needed to talk about it.

I hate it that Larry's gone, but he's definitely at peace. I just wish that he could have made his peace with God a little earlier.

Their minds were fully bonded, and when Billy had brought it up, their memories of the previous day's events flooded through their minds.

Most of the time, it was a boon to be able to remember virtually everything, but in this case, the vivid memories were just as painful as they had been the first time around.

Several minutes later, Linda told him, *It doesn't matter when he made his peace with God. The only thing that matters is that he did make it, and the feeling was unmistakable, he's with God.*

They sat sharing their thoughts about what they had experienced for several hours before Billy told her, *I need to get back to work. I've got to try to figure out if Larry was successful.*

They had recorded every second of the *Salvadora*'s mission, and it amounted to several hundred terabytes of video, audio, and telemetry.

Billy knew it would take them months to go through all the data. For the time being, the only portions of the mission that he was interested in were the final seconds leading up to the impact and the tracking data they had gathered afterward.

Even though the final seconds of the mission were burned into his memory, he needed to determine the precise angle of impact on the meteor's. If they had been even a few degrees off on their calculations the meteor's course might not have been changed enough to save Midgard.

He worked straight through the night, but by morning he had realized that he needed some help analyzing the data. There was simply too much of it for him to do it alone. He didn't want to call the mission a success until he was absolutely sure, so he decided to get some help.

He took a few minutes to eat lunch, and then he gathered the entire team together so that they could discuss their next moves.

For the first time in a long time, the faces in the room had looks of anticipation instead of dread.

As he looked around the room, he flashed back to all the faces that were no longer with them. They had lost a lot of good men and women since they had left the fleet.

Their places had been taken by other good people, but Billy wanted to make sure that they would always remember their sacrifices. Before he started the meeting, he took a moment to print out the list of casualties.

"Before I cover what I've found out so far. I think it's appropriate that we take a few minutes to remember the men and women who have made the ultimate sacrifice so that the rest of us could make it through.

"Pastor Williams, would you mind leading us in a prayer of remembrance?" Billy asked as he handed him the list.

When Pastor Williams was finished, Billy kicked off the meeting.

"Now then, let's get to the matters at hand. I would love to tell you that the *Salvadora*'s mission has succeeded, but I simply don't have enough data yet.

"Now before you panic, I don't have any reason to believe that it wasn't successful. I'm just not going to call it a success until I'm absolutely sure."

He looked at Nicholas and said, "I need you and your teams to help me analyze the data that we collected. There's simply too much of it for me to do it alone.

"I'd like for us to get started by watching the final twenty minutes of the video together. When we're done, we'll break out into our teams to finish the analysis."

They spent several hours studying the video of the *Salvadora*'s approach. The meteor swarm stretched for hundreds of miles, but the sheer size of the main meteor was astounding.

When they reached the last few seconds before impact, he slowed the video to a frame at a time.

They had been so overwhelmed by the final seconds of the video that they asked him to replay the final minute several times.

By the time they called a halt to it, they were all emotionally drained by the experience.

"Judging from the size of the explosion and the amount

of interference we're experiencing, it may be three or four more days before we can get some decent readings," Nicholas said.

"That's about what I had figured," Billy said. "How do you want to split up the teams?"

"I've already taken care of it. I knew what you were going to want when you called the meeting, so I took the liberty of organizing the teams before we showed up."

"You're on top of it as always, although I don't know why that would surprise me. Have you made any progress on the farming equipment and the supplies?"

"I have indeed. I've got the first set of equipment ready, and if everything works out, we can build more.

"We've never done farm equipment before, so we may have to tweak the designs. On the supply side of it, we've already produced enough insecticide and fertilizer to last a couple of years."

FOR THE NEXT four days, they threw themselves into studying the meteor data. By the time they could get a clear view of the impact, they already had a pretty good idea of what they were going to find.

The force of the explosion had been even stronger than they had anticipated, so they were relatively sure it had been enough to deflect the meteor.

Once Nicholas had gotten the new observation data together, he and Billy sat down to go over it.

Neither one of them said a word as they went over the data. It had taken them almost an hour and a half, but they both finished about the same time.

When Nicholas looked up, he saw that Billy was looking directly at him, and that he had a huge grin on his face.

He grinned back at him, as they both acknowledged that their plans had worked.

The massive explosion had changed the meteor's path so significantly that Midgard would never even catch sight of the meteor again.

"God rest his soul, Larry got it done." Even as Nicholas had said it, he wondered why, because he was an avowed atheist.

"Yes he did, and his soul is definitely with God. Linda and I felt it when he met God."

Nicholas just shook his head in bewilderment. He had heard Linda and Billy talk of their experiences when the Earth was destroyed, but as brilliant as he was, he just couldn't bring himself to believe it.

After their excitement had died down, they sat and talked for several hours. They decided that their first order of business would be to let everyone know that they were going to be alright.

However, by the time they had finished talking, the sun had already set, so they decided to wait until morning to tell everyone.

When Billy walked in, Linda ran to him and gave him a big hug and a kiss. "I'm so glad that your plan worked. When are you going to tell everyone, and can we go and tell our parents right now?" she said, almost beside herself with excitement and relief.

He had started to ask how she knew, but then thought about it, and he realized that she had known at the exact same moment that he had. "Slow down, of course we can go tell our parents. I was going to try and tell everyone at the same time, but I suppose it doesn't really matter."

As they often did, their parents were eating dinner together. As soon as Billy and Linda walked in, Ben West stood, looked right at Billy, and said, "Congratulations, you've done it; we're going to be alright."

"I have no idea how you knew, but yes, Larry Sheldon got it done. The meteor will never threaten Midgard again."

"It's funny, but I knew a few hours ago. It's hard to explain, but I must have felt it when you first figured it out. I even knew that you were sitting with Nicholas Stavros at the time."

"I was, but it's beyond me how you could have known."

His comment set off a conversation among the rest of their parents. It seemed that they had all known. They had kept it to themselves, however, because they all thought it was just wishful thinking.

He had understood how Linda had found out, but it baffled him how the rest of them could have known.

But, as he thought about it, he realized that this was the second time that he had reached someone's mind other than Linda's. The only thing that made sense was that he had gotten so excited that his mind had reached out to their entire family.

They spent the rest of the evening with their parents, and they were happier than Billy and Linda had seen them in a very long time.

Billy decided to wait to tell them that Nicholas had their equipment ready, because he knew that as soon as he did, they would be chomping at the bit to get started.

The next morning they held town hall meetings to break the good news to the rest of the base. Once they had finished telling everyone at the base, they took the *Imagination* and went to brief the other shelters.

Their first stop was at King Peterovan's shelter deep in the ancient mines.

Billy made sure that they briefed the king before anyone else, so that he could be the one to make the announcement to his people. Once the king had finished thanking them, they left so that they could brief King Abrahams.

Like King Peterovan, they briefed King Abrahams first, and when they finished, he told Billy, "That's the best news I've had in a long time.

"But, if you've got just a minute, I would like to ask you a question. Even though you warned me not to, I've been going to the surface every day. I just couldn't stand not seeing the real sun. That doesn't matter, however. My question is, why is it this cold at this time of the year?"

"To be honest about it, I've been too busy to pay much attention to the weather. I'll have to get back to you with an answer. It's probably just an anomaly caused by the meteorites, but I'll see if there's anything to be concerned about."

They didn't get much done during the next few days, because they were so busy with all the people who wanted to come by and thank them. Finally, it started to slow down, and Billy got a chance to sit down with the team to talk.

"I think we've finished with everything on your list," Nicholas said.

"Great, we'll get started moving everything next week.

"I'd forgotten to ask before, but would you have one of your weather guys take a look at the weather patterns? King Abrahams asked me if it was supposed to be this cold already, and I had forgotten to ask you about it. I know that it's pretty hard to get any real feel for the weather where we're located, because it's cold all the time."

The storm that they had rescued King Abrahams from had destroyed a significant portion of their balloons, so they had to restart their homemade assembly line.

Since this was their second time around, it was a much easier task than before. In what seemed like no time at all, they were churning out balloons. Unlike the first time, they didn't have any real urgency, so they decided not to start moving people until they had plenty of ships.

Billy had forgotten all about King Abrahams's question, but a couple of weeks later, Nicholas called Billy over to meet with him.

"Molly Feinstein has finished the analysis on the weather that you asked for, and I've asked her to brief us both on what she's found out."

"I had to go back into some of the ancient records, but I think I've found the answer to your question," Molly explained. "It looks like the northern hemisphere is entering an ice age."

"Ice age? What would you call the mess we're in now?" Billy asked.

"I'm afraid that what we're experiencing is just the beginning. The meteorites may have accelerated it, but this whole region has been slowly cooling for several hundred years. The average temperature is going to go down another seventeen degrees in the next fifteen months. Once it has, there won't be a recognizable change of seasons anywhere in the northern hemisphere. In fact, it's going to become almost uninhabitable. When it's all said and done, it'll be very similar to the polar regions on earth."

"Your explanation seems fairly straightforward," Billy said. "If I've understood you correctly, we'll need to plan on relocating everyone to the southern hemisphere."

"I hadn't thought of it like that, but yes, I suppose that would be the proper course of action."

When they finished talking with Molly, they spent the next three days looking at their options.

Nicholas's teams had already managed to build several hundred new balloons and had more on the way, so they knew that they would have the capability to move pretty much the entire population of Midgard if that's what they decided to do.

The only other decision that they were struggling with was whether they should abandon their base. Finally, Billy came to his decision. He called all the teams together so that he could brief them all at once.

"As some of you may already know, we've been looking into a possible change in the planet's weather patterns. Molly Feinstein has prepared a comprehensive analysis on the issue. Her report details the changes that we can expect to see over the next couple of years.

"After looking over her report and weighing our options, we've decided that we'll need to relocate everyone to the southern hemisphere."

He paused for a few moments, so that his comments could sink in. He was a little surprised at the general lack of response, but considering what they had all just gone through, it just wasn't that big a deal.

"We're going to begin moving people next Monday. We're going to be moving equal percentages from the three locations. That way no one can say that we're playing favorites. Nicholas and John have already determined the first groupings for our people, and I've asked King Peterovan and King Abrahams to make their selections.

"Also, after several discussions with King Abrahams, we've decided to put King Peterovan's people and our people in the northern section of the Nubian territory. Since it was mostly barren desert before, the area was pretty much uninhabited, so he didn't have any problem with us settling there."

"I'm familiar with that area," John said. "So we're moving from an icebox into an oven."

"That would have been true not too long ago; however, it turns out that the meteorites' impacts changed the topography enough so that it's going to be a very nice place to live."

The meeting went on for several hours, and when everyone else had left, Nicholas and John stayed behind to talk with Billy.

"Have you made up your mind on what to do about the base?" Nicholas asked.

"I've got an opinion, but I would like to hear from you two first."

"Unless there's some overriding reason that I'm not aware of, I would recommend that we leave it where it is," Nicholas said. "We can always move it later if we see the need."

"I don't feel real strongly either way, but I agree that it's a decision that we can put off for later," John added.

"I agree, and we'll just leave it where it is, for the time being."

As they had planned, King Abrahams's group was the first to arrive.

When they landed in the capital, they had a very difficult time believing the carnage that greeted them. From the air, the city had looked pretty much as it always had, but the wall of water had ruined everything it touched.

Since he had already made a short visit to the palace, King Abrahams already knew what lay ahead of them.

He had tried to prepare the first group for what they would find, but his meager words couldn't do justice to the devastation that they found.

The damage was definitely a problem, but an even bigger issue for the king was the fact that over fifty percent of the Nubian population had died in the H1N1 epidemic.

King Abrahams really didn't have enough people left to repopulate all the different areas that they had abandoned.

When he had discussed it with Billy, they had decided to try to focus on the cities and not bother with the more rural areas, for the moment.

They had already decided that everyone else would relocate to the northern regions, but when King Peterovan and Billy had their final meeting before they started to relocate his people, the king had experienced a change of heart.

After talking with several of his advisors, King Peterovan had realized that many of his people had never lived anywhere but a city, and that they wouldn't be happy in a rural setting.

The king had decided that he needed to give his people a choice of where they settled. After hearing his concerns, Billy set up a meeting between him and King Abrahams.

There would have never been a chance of holding a meeting like that when Queen Amanirenas was alive.

Once the two kings had gotten past the first few awkward moments, Billy had been surprised at how well the two ancient adversaries had gotten along. They had both seen far too many of their people die, and they were willing to put their egos aside to try to reach a workable compromise. They met for almost three days, and by the end of the meeting, they had developed a plan that worked for both.

They agreed that almost half of King Peterovan's people would be allowed to relocate to the cities in the south. They were mostly artisans, metalworkers, shopkeepers, and they had spent their entire lives in the cities. Even more importantly, they could help King Abrahams more quickly rebuild their infrastructure.

When they had started moving people, it hadn't turned out to be one-sided. There was a fair amount of King Abrahams's people who wanted to relocate to the north with King Peterovan's people.

They hadn't set out to mix the groups, it just worked out that way. Once they had mixed in the Earth people, they had ended up with a nice mixture of the different cultures.

THERE WEREN'T ANY preexisting structures in the north, so Nicholas's teams constructed prefabricated buildings to use for housing. Once they were assembled, Billy and Linda decided to help their parents move into their new homes.

Instead of a balloon, they used the *Imagination* to ferry their parents, and as the ship descended through the clouds, they caught sight of the lake where they were building the new settlement.

Billy was amazed that in just the short time they had been working, they had already assembled enough buildings to house forty thousand people. They could see the village starting to spread out along the lake's shoreline, and the scene matched the images from their dreams.

Just to the west of the village, they could see where the lake flowed into the newly resurrected river.

"The river should provide us with plenty of water for irrigation," Ben said. "All we need to do is build some aqueducts to get it to the fields. Do you think that you could spare some of Nicholas's men for a few weeks?"

"I'm sure we can, but it may take me a couple of weeks to free them up," Billy replied. "It looks like they have got you set up pretty well."

When they walked down the ramp of the ship, a warm moist breeze greeted them.

"I don't care how hard this is going to be, this is much better than freezing to death all the time," Beth remarked.

Since Billy didn't have any projects that required his attention, he and Linda stayed with their parents for a couple of weeks to help them get settled in.

Finally, Billy decided that he had been goofing off long enough. "I've got to get back to our old base. I've still got a lot of work to do. We'll be back here in a few weeks, and you've got the satellite phones if you need to reach us."

"I was hoping that we could stay with them a little longer," Linda said.

"You can stay longer if you would like, but I've got to talk with Nicholas."

"I thought you and Nicholas had everything already planned out. I know how neither one of you likes to leave anything to chance."

"There's something that I want to get his opinion on."

"It's about the dreams we're having, isn't it?"

"Yes, I'm afraid it is, but I also want to get the laptops that Larry left for us. I'm not sure that I'm ready to see what he left, but we've got to at some point. It seemed very important to Larry, and frankly, I'm curious to see what he had to say about us."

His comments about the laptops piqued Linda's curiosity, so she decided to go back with him.

Nicholas was busy when they landed, but they set a meeting with him for the next morning. That night, they both had another nightmare about President McAlister.

If the dream was to be believed, the president had taken control of the Earth fleet and was ruling it with an iron hand. Even before they had left, he had shown signs that he might be getting ready to seize power.

The dream had seemed to go on forever, and when morning finally came, they were both exhausted.

"I'm completely drained," Linda said. "I can't believe that wasn't just a nightmare. Surely there's no way President McAlister can be that bad."

"I hear you, but you know as well as I do that our dreams are usually more than just dreams, particularly when we both dream about the same things.

"No need to put it off, let's go see what Nicholas has for us."

"HERE ARE THE computers that Larry left for you. I'll leave you two alone so you can take your time looking at whatever is on them.

"Please call me if you need anything, but from the way Larry talked, it's going to take you some time to get through all of it."

After he was gone, Billy hooked the laptop up to a holographic projector and they sat down to watch the video Larry had made for them.

It took them a full week to get through the first set of videos. There were Several times when they had both been near tears as they listened to Larry recount his exploits. As they watched, they could see that the things that he had done had been slowly wearing him down.

To make matters even worse, every night, after they had watched the videos all day, they would have nightmares about what President McAlister was doing to the Earth fleet.

When they got to the sections about them, they decided to watch the rest of the segments in their quarters. As they settled in on the couch to watch the final sections, Billy had his arm around Linda.

They sat motionless as they listened to Larry's explanation of what had happened to them. They were so spellbound that, at times, it seemed like they had forgotten to breathe.

As he talked, they thought back to all the times they had wondered why certain things had happened to them, and now they knew. As he had promised, he detailed how the Logos had guided and, at times, manipulated their lives.

When they were finished with the video, Billy asked, "Do you agree with Larry's belief that it was Adamartoni's DNA that made us the way we are?"

"I do, but there's no way that we'll ever know for sure; however, if it is true, it would explain so many things.

"We're the only telepaths that I've ever been able to document. If you combine that with our rapid healing abilities and our extreme intelligence, it would explain why we're truly unique in the history of mankind."

"Larry said that he included a word-for-word record of the inscriptions on Adamartoni's sarcophagus. I think that we should read it and see if we can glean any more information. Larry was a very smart man, but we'll have a different perspective on it than he did."

Billy opened the first file, and they started reading. The fastest speed readers of all time wouldn't have been able to keep up with them. Their immense intellects allowed them to devour the text a full page at a time.

Billy was changing the pages on the screen at about a page every three seconds and didn't stop until they had read every page of the transcript. By the time they were done, they were both exhausted from the effort.

Neither of them spoke for a few moments, and then Linda said, "That was the most incredible story that I've ever read, and it's all true. If I understood correctly what the Logos's scientists had theorized, a very large portion of our unique DNA is from an alien race. I've never even really seriously considered whether I believed that there was life on other planets, and now I've come to find out we're related to them.

"Think of it: in many ways, we're more closely related to an alien named Adamartoni than we are to our own parents. It's mind boggling."

"It's definitely hard to fathom, but it also explains a lot. Do you think that our life expectancies have been extended along with the additional abilities that we inherited from his DNA?"

"I'll have to do some more research, but I've got reason to believe that ours may be even longer than theirs. We may well see our abilities continue to evolve and grow as we get older. By their standards, we're still babies."

Billy asked, "What do you think we should tell our parents?"

"Absolutely nothing, because my dad would completely freak out if ever found out what happened. Don't you remember how upset he got when I said that I believed the blood transfusion you gave me caused the changes in me?"

"I do, and I'm not sure that my parents would be one bit better. Besides, what difference does it really make? We're still their children, and the fact that our DNA was altered doesn't change that.

"What sort of additional abilities do you think we might get?" Billy wondered.

"There's no way to know for sure, but I would think that telekinesis wouldn't be out of the question. We've already noticed that our telepathic abilities are growing stronger, so I think it would be a natural evolution."

"Boy, would that be cool, but I guess we'll just have to wait and see. I know that many of the things that we can feel and do are from the DNA, but I also believe that a lot of it is from God."

"I agree completely," said Linda, "but from what we read, Adamartoni and Evevette would have felt the same way. Now that I know what to look for, I should be able to determine which portions of our DNA are attributable to Adamartoni.

"Changing the subject, have you thought about what we're going to be able to do about President McAlister?"

"We aren't going to be able to do much of anything unless I can find a way for us to get back to the fleet."

"What are the odds of that happening?"

"I've been studying the problem ever since we were stranded here. Just before we lost the *Genesis,* I thought I had the solution, but I haven't spent much time on it since."

THE NEXT SIX months seemed to fly by. Once they had everyone moved to their new homes, life had started to return to normal.

Billy's and Linda's parents were happier than they had been in a long time. Their fathers were back in their element, working on the land. Once Nicholas's teams had gotten all the bugs worked out, they had managed to deliver all the farm equipment they would need for several years.

Ben and Rob were tutoring forty-six farmers. They were evenly split between King Peterovan's and King Abrahams's peoples, and Ben and Rob couldn't believe how hard they were willing to work at learning a new way to farm. Almost every evening, they had to force them to quit work for the day. It had been a long time since many of them had had enough to eat, and they were desperate to make sure that they could continue to feed their families.

WHILE EVERYONE ELSE was getting settled into their new lives, Nicholas tried to help Billy with his research. Billy already knew how to achieve faster-than-light travel, but he didn't want another disaster like the last time—although, he still felt that the last modifications he had designed would've worked if Vladimir Demetrius hadn't made unauthorized changes to the plans.

He had considered using their last remaining shuttle, but not only was it a complete mess, it was much too small for the new mission.

Short of building a whole new ship, the *Imagination* was their only real hope of returning to the fleet, but it was woefully underpowered.

After several weeks of work, they decided that the only way to address the power problem was to replace the entire power system.

When Nicholas had first seen Billy's new design for the ship's reactor, he immediately went to look for him so that they could talk about it.

"I would have never believed that this is possible," Nicholas said. "Are you sure this is going to work?"

"I'm as sure as I can be without building a full-blown prototype. It's really not as radical a change as you would first think. All I've really done is add an additional magnetic field inside the actual containment field. If it works like I think it will, it should increase the compression by a factor of three and raise the power output fifty times."

"No way. That would be more than the *Genesis* had after its last upgrade."

"I know that it's hard to believe, but I'm confident that's what we're going to see. I actually believe that there's a chance that it could be even more.

"Now that you've seen the plans, how long will it take you to do the upgrades?"

"We'll try to overlap the work, but it's going to take at least nine months."

Since the upgrades to the *Imagination* were going to take so long, they decided to take a look at the planet's transportation situation before they got started.

They had plenty of balloons, but with the weather the way it was, they wanted to be able to get over the storms.

Nicholas had just developed a new material for the balloons that would allow them to fly a lot higher; however, the additional altitude had made it necessary to upgrade the gondolas. They had switched over to hardened composites for extra strength, and they had added an oxygen supply and pressurization.

Once they had produced several of the new airships, they made one last flight in the *Imagination* to make sure that everything was alright with the two kings, and their parents.

After they had made sure that everybody was alright, they ripped the power systems out and started the upgrades.

26

NICHOLAS HADN'T HAD a real technical challenge for some time, so he and his teams threw themselves into the task at hand.

While they were working on the upgrades to the *Imagination,* Linda was trying to determine what additional abilities she and Billy should expect. She'd already determined that their minds were continuing to evolve. Their strengthened telepathic ability was the most obvious, but she suspected it wouldn't end there.

About six weeks into the process, Billy started to suffer from what Linda believed to be migraines. Neither of them had ever had so much as a cold, let alone a headache, so she knew that there something was going on with him.

She ran him through a full battery of tests, but couldn't find anything that looked abnormal. Finally, she used a combination of an EEG and an MRI scan to get a better look at what was going on in his brain.

Unlike most humans, his brain didn't have two halves; it was essentially one piece. She had expected to find the fused brain, because William Robbins had once done a similar scan of her brain and had found the same thing. She couldn't find anything wrong with him, but that next morning, she couldn't get him to wake up. When she touched his mind with hers, he didn't answer.

Linda could tell that his mind was still active, but she couldn't get him to communicate with her.

She was terrified that he was dying, so she contacted William Robbins and his teams of neurologists and got them to make the journey up to the base.

It took them a full day to reach the base, and by the time they got there, she was a mess.

"I know that you're worried sick about him," William said. "However, we don't believe that he's in any danger.

"We've already checked everything that we could think of, and there's simply nothing wrong with him, other than that his brain activity is off the charts and he won't wake up."

For the next eight days, Linda was in hell. Billy had been there for her from the moment she was born, and she had no idea how she could go on without him.

By the ninth night, she had spent every waking hour by his bedside, but there was still no response. Exhausted, she had gone back to their quarters to try to get a little sleep.

Before she fell asleep, she was praying to God, as she did every night. She was frustrated by her inability to help Billy, and was asking God for some help and telling Him that she couldn't go on without Billy.

Yes you could, if you had to, Billy told her. *But you're not gonna have to this time. I'll be over as soon as they can get me unhooked from all of these wires that you've got me hooked up to.*

THAT NIGHT, THEY spent their first night together since he'd been sick. When Billy woke up the next morning, he acted like it had never happened.

Linda and William did another complete brain scan on him, and they were shocked at the results.

"I don't see any physical changes to his brain, but the frontal lobe activity has doubled again," William Robbins said. "I've never seen anything like it. It's off the scale of our instruments, the energy is immense."

"Do you see anything that would concern you?" Linda asked.

"No, but I would continue to observe him for a couple of weeks. Otherwise, I think that he's going to be fine."

Linda babied him and monitored him very closely for a couple of weeks before she decided that whatever had been going on had at least stabilized.

Before Billy had gotten sick, Linda had been planning a whole series of tests to try to determine if he was developing any new abilities. When she was satisfied that he wasn't in any danger, she decided to proceed with the tests she had planned.

"WHAT'S THE PURPOSE of this test?" Billy asked.

"Now that I've got a baseline reading of your brain's activity, I'll be able to measure any changes. I'm trying to see if all the changes in your brain have given you any new abilities.

"Now then, I want you to concentrate as hard as you can and try to move this small block of crystal. I'm going to monitor your brain's activity so that I can see any changes as you attempt to move it."

"Alright, but I think this is a complete waste of time."

Once she had him hooked up to the machine, she had him begin. Neither one of them had ever thought of trying to move something with their minds, so Billy didn't really have any idea what to do.

He closed his eyes, and he sat there concentrating as hard as he could, but nothing happened. He had been growing frustrated, but then he suddenly told Linda, "I've just had the strangest feeling. I think that I'm actually starting to feel something in my mind. Are you seeing anything on your monitors?"

"I've been seeing it for several seconds, but I couldn't be sure that it wasn't just a machine malfunction. You've run the machine completely off the scale. See if you can move the crystal."

She could see the veins standing out on Billy's face and neck as he strained to move the crystal.

"Relax a little. The energy was stronger before you started trying so hard."

As he started to relax, he could feel the rough surface of the block of crystal.

When he was fully relaxed, he envisioned it floating above the table's surface, and he heard Linda say, "You've done it. The crystal is floating about six inches off the table."

He opened his eyes and saw the crystal floating in the air, just as he had imagined it.

"That's so cool, and it looks just like what I was seeing in my mind."

He started moving the block all around the surface of the table, and as he continued to play with it, he was getting more and more adept at controlling it.

Finally, Linda had him put it down, and said, "This is something else that we're going to need to keep to ourselves. Give me a few days to go over the data that I've gathered today, and then I'll devise some new tests to try out on you."

* * *

THE SHIP'S UPGRADE had progressed nicely while Billy had been laid up, and it looked like they were going to beat their self-imposed deadline. They were talking with the other camps daily, and they were heartened to hear how well everyone was getting on with their lives.

The integration of the three groups had gone far better than anyone could have hoped. In many ways, it almost seemed as though they had been reunited.

After everything that they had gone through Billy hoped that they would finally manage to gain a little peace and happiness, and that they would grow even closer as the years passed.

As they continued working on the new reactor, Billy had come to the conclusion that most, if not all of their people were going to live out the rest of their lives on Midgard.

Even if he was successful in rejoining the Earth fleet, he had no idea if they would ever be able to make their way back to Midgard.

What none of them had realized was that there was a faction of Queen Amanirenas's subjects that weren't pleased to see the blending of the different cultures.

27

THE REVOLUTIONARIES WERE being led Priestess Ghia and several of the other priestesses from the temple.

Their order had been controlling the lives of the Nubian people for centuries, and they weren't about to stand by and see everything they had believed in swept away by the newfound sense of unity.

Once she had decided to try to overthrow the new king, it had taken Priestess Ghia several months to gather enough support to try to carry out her plans.

Just as the queen had, she blamed Billy West for all of their troubles, and she intended to kill Billy and Linda during their first strike.

Once she had gathered her forces, she waited patiently for everyone to settle into a daily routine. She knew that once they felt safe, they would drop most of their security measures, and then she would make her move.

King Abrahams had kept a security force in place for several months, however, as the months had gone by without any incidents, he had become convinced that any danger had passed, and he sent all but two of his guards home to be with their families.

With the threat of a Nubian attack gone, and the fact that there wasn't anyone else left in the northern hemisphere, John Tyler had done away with almost all of the security measures around the base, but he had kept the electric fence energized. It wasn't because he was afraid of an attack, however, it was more to keep out the odd wild animal.

Priestess Ghia had spent the time laying out her plans to return the priestesses to a position of power once the king was out of the way. Her biggest problem had been finding a way to attack the base where Billy was.

They had used some of the younger priestesses to win a few of the king's men over to their side. Then they had convinced them to let them have three of their new balloons to use in their attack against the northern base.

A couple of days before the attack, they loaded their strike force into the balloons and moved them to within a couple of hundred miles of the base.

Once the balloons were in position, they waited until midnight to launch a simultaneous attack against the northern base and King Abrahams.

The balloons touched down inside the Earth base at just past midnight, and it was only by chance that they were spotted. One of the technicians had stepped outside to smoke a cigarette, and when he saw them land, he ran back inside and set off the alarm.

John Tyler hadn't kept any soldiers at the base, and when the alarm sounded, he knew that they could be in trouble if it turned out to be the real thing.

He threw on some clothes and grabbed the weapons that he always kept close at hand. As he was about to leave, he told Millie, "Get Adam and go over to Linda West's place. They'll take care of you while I'm taking care of whatever this is."

As he was running outside, Millie called after him, "Please, be careful, and don't do anything stupid."

When he got outside, he quickly looked around to see

what was going on. On his left, he saw the Nubians charging off the ships to attack the compound. On the other side, he saw the night shift technicians come rushing outside to see what was happening.

He needed to get the technicians out of the way, so he used his radio to call to them. "Get everyone back inside. We're under attack."

"What can we do to help?" Billy radioed him as he was getting dressed.

"Take care of Millie when she gets there. Since none of you are armed, you need to stay inside, but get everybody ready to run if I tell you to."

The insurgents immediately opened fire on the technicians, killing several of them before they turned and started running back inside the buildings.

When John saw the technicians taking fire, he immediately dropped to one knee and started shooting.

He had been in similar situations many times before, and his deadly accurate fire killed several of the attackers before they realized where it was coming from.

They hadn't been expecting much resistance, so when they started taking casualties, they panicked and hit the ground. But when they figured out where he was, they started returning his fire.

Their muskets hadn't been much of a match for John's weapons, and he had killed almost a quarter of them before one of their officers rallied them to charge his position.

They were still quite a distance from him, but he was running low on ammunition, and he knew that he couldn't kill all of them before they overran his position. He started retreating, firing as he went. As he moved back toward one of the base weapon lockers, he was hoping that he would find some additional weapons, or at least some more ammunition.

When he reached the door, he paused to kick it in and ran inside. They had already transferred most of the equipment, so there was very little left in the building.

His hurried search only netted him a few rounds of ammunition, but he did find a Heckler and Koch GMG (grenade machine gun) that Nicholas's group had salvaged before the *Genesis* was destroyed.

He had never used one, but he had seen one demonstrated while he was training a group of German rangers. He needed to buy himself a little time, so he stepped back out the door and emptied his rifle into the charging Nubians.

As he hoped, his renewed fire caused them to hesitate again. By the time their officers managed to get them moving, John had managed to drag the H&K out the door and open fire.

The H&K could fire three hundred and forty grenades a minute and the torrent of 40mm grenades resulted in absolute carnage among the massed insurgents.

When he had fired all the grenades he had, he drew his pistol and walked out toward what was left of the insurgents.

The scene of the battle hadn't been for the fainthearted. The pristine white snow of the compound looked a lot like a slaughterhouse kill floor, with blood spray and body parts everywhere.

John walked quickly through the area and made sure they were all dead. He found a couple of them that weren't already dead, so he shot each of them in the head and moved on.

It didn't really bother him that he had just slaughtered

over a hundred men. All that mattered to him was that he had kept his family and the rest of their group alive.

When he had finished his cursory inspection, he radioed in a status report. "It's all clear, and you can come out now."

"What happened to the attackers, did they already leave?" Billy asked.

"In a manner of speaking. They're all dead."

Billy and Linda came running out to see if they could help him with anything. They had almost reached him when they saw one of the attackers stagger to his feet. He was only a few paces behind John, and he had already taken aim before they had seen him.

Billy yelled, "John, look out behind you."

As John turned to face him, the man fired his musket at point blank range. He was so close to John that the muzzle flash almost blinded him.

Even though John was shocked that he wasn't already dead, he quickly put a round between the Nubian's eyes, killing him instantly. When they reached John, he was just standing there, looking at the man's body.

"I have no idea how he missed me," John said, shaking his head in disbelief. "I thought for sure I was a goner."

Linda glanced over at the man's body, and as she did, she saw the musket ball he had just fired lying in the snow at John's feet. Nobody else had noticed it, so as she moved over to congratulate him on a job well done, she stepped on it to hide it in the snow.

In his rush to get outside, John hadn't taken the time to put on very many clothes. As he stood there in only a tee-shirt and pants, he was starting to shiver from the cold.

"Why don't you go inside and warm up," Billy said. "I'll get some of the other men to clean this mess up."

After Billy had gotten the cleanup organized, he told

Linda, "I'd better call the other settlements and tell them we've been attacked."

THE GROUP THAT attacked King Abrahams had caught him by surprise. His two security guards had been overwhelmed almost immediately, but the sounds of the fight had given the king a few seconds to prepare himself for the attack.

When King Abrahams's men captured the snipers' M-25s, they had also gotten several of their sidearms.

When they were handing out the captured weapons, the king had taken one of the SIG Sauer P226s for himself. Its .40 SW rounds made it a fine combat pistol, and he had become quite adept with it.

He always kept it by his bedside, so when the attackers struck, he grabbed it and went to meet their attack.

The priestesses had all wanted to share in the glory of killing the king, so they were in the lead when they came through the door.

King Abrahams recognized them immediately, and as he opened fire, he thought to himself, "This is the same vermin that slaughtered my family. If I'm going to die tonight, I'm going to make sure that they all go with me."

The king quickly realized that he had no real chance of surviving their attack, so instead of trying to take cover or get away, he started walking straight toward them, firing as he went.

He managed to kill all the priestesses and several of the others before he ran out of ammunition. With his pistol empty, he turned to his sword, and he managed to kill a few more before they cut him down from behind.

As he died, he saw his wife and children waiting at the gates of heaven to welcome him home.

While their attack had succeeded in killing the king, they ended up losing the war. With all of their leaders dead, the rebellion had quickly fallen apart.

"I'm afraid that I've just gotten some bad news," Billy said. "King Abrahams has been assassinated, and it looks like Priestess Ghia was the one who organized the rebellion against the king and coordinated the attack against us.

"The one bit of good news out of this whole thing is that the king did manage to kill all the priestesses and fifteen of the others before they managed to kill him. I didn't know it, but he had one of our snipers' SIG Sauers, and it sounds like he put it to good use."

"That's too bad, he was a good man," John Tyler said. "Did you already check to see if King Peterovan is alright?"

"I did and, for whatever reason, they didn't attack him. My guess is that they were putting that off until later. When I talked with King Peterovan, I did find out that he and King Abrahams had made succession plans, and that they had it set up so that if either one of them died, the survivor would assume full control.

"I had started to say that it was a surprising turn of events, but he and King Peterovan had gained great respect for each other, so maybe it's not that surprising."

When the succession plan was announced, there was a lot of heated conversation among the Nubian nobles; however, when what was left of the Nubian army came out in favor of King Peterovan, the matter was quickly settled.

Even though he really hadn't wanted to, King Peterovan relocated to King Abrahams's newly renovated palace. When King Abrahams had redone the interior of the pyramid, he had done away with all vestiges of Queen Amanirenas. He had even gone so far as to remove all the various monuments to Isis.

With complete control of both armies, there weren't any credible threats to King Peterovan's rule. The combined population of Midgard was about to enter a time of peace and prosperity unlike any that they had seen before.

28

After King Peterovan had moved into King Abrahams's palace, he held a great feast honoring the dead king's memory.

When they walked into the great hall, Billy remembered the first time he had been there and thought about how much had changed since then.

That day it had been filled with members of the queen's court, and now it had people of all races and classes joining together to honor King Abrahams.

The event that excited Billy the most, however, was the secondary reason for their visit. In addition to a celebration of King Abrahams's life, the king was hosting the first meeting of his newly formed advisory council.

In an effort to ensure that everyone's needs were fairly represented, the council was made up of representatives from all three groups. The council's membership included two of the king's most trusted governors, the Earthlings John Tyler and Nicholas Stavros, and the last two surviving Nubian generals.

The king had learned his lesson, and this time he intended to make sure that he stayed in touch with what was going on.

* * *

BILLY AND LINDA had been so busy since the attack that they hadn't taken the time to discuss what had happened during the attack.

After they had gotten home from the king's celebration, they finally had a moment to themselves to sit down and talk about what had happened that night.

"I was pleasantly surprised by King Peterovan's willingness to form an advisory council," Billy said. "I guess our trip was worthwhile after all."

"He's definitely changed from the first time I met him," Linda said. "You've been a good influence on him, because nothing in their history would have led him to take a collaborative approach to ruling the kingdom."

"Speaking of cooperation and planning, I'm sure glad that the two kings thought ahead," Billy said. "If they hadn't set up their succession plans, this could have been a real mess."

"Very true, and my guess is that it was King Abrahams's idea. Planning ahead was what he did best. I took the time to read his biography while we were there, and he was quite a man. He never wanted to be king, but he certainly did an admirable job for the short time that he had the title.

"It's ironic that the priestesses chose to lead the attack against him. I know for a fact that he knew they had a hand in his family's deaths. I'm sure he made a point to kill them first. I just hope that God has reunited him with his family."

"I'm sure He did. Even though King Abrahams was a soldier his entire life, he was good man."

"Changing the subject on you, do you have any idea when Nicholas will have the new ship ready?"

"I haven't gotten an update from him in several

weeks; however, I'm supposed to meet with him in the morning to go over where they're at.

"I do know that the attack really slowed them down. Even though most of them didn't see a thing, the technicians have been having a hard time concentrating on their work. Nicholas said that any little noise would set them off."

"If anybody was going to be jumpy, it should be John Tyler," Linda said. "I can't imagine what he must be going through."

"From what I know of John, I doubt very much that it affected him. He's seen it all before, and none of what he did that night would concern him that much.

"I sure thought that he'd bought the farm. He must have told me fifty times that he couldn't believe that the guy missed him."

"Ah, but he didn't miss him," said Linda.

"What are you talking about? If he had hit him at that range, he would be dead."

"True, but the bullet never reached John. It fell at his feet."

"The soldier couldn't have been more than ten feet from John when he fired. How could you be so sure that the bullet fell at John's feet?"

"Because I saw it. At the time, I didn't want to try to explain it, so I stepped on it to hide it. My guess is that when you yelled at John, your mind reached out and stopped the bullet in midair."

"That's impossible. What makes you think that?"

"When you yelled, I felt a tremendous surge of energy, but it wasn't until I saw the bullet that I realized what must have happened."

When Billy didn't say anything for several seconds, Linda reached into his mind to ask, *Are you alright?*

I suppose so, but that's quite a bit to get my mind around. It's one thing to play parlor games with a cube of crystal, but quite another to stop a bullet in mid-flight.

Thanks for not letting John figure it out. We have enough trouble with people thinking we're freaks. This would have just proven it to them.

I doubt that John would have felt that way, but it's probably best that we hide it.

THAT NIGHT THE nightmares returned with a vengeance.

"Boy, that was the worst ever. We've got to try to help those poor people," Linda said.

"You're preaching to the choir," Billy said. "If the crews aren't about done, I'm going to try to light a fire under them. I don't care if the technicians are skittish; they need to get over it."

"How much longer is it going to be?" Billy asked Nicholas impatiently.

"If we have a good night tonight, we should be finished by morning," Nicholas replied.

"That's great, I sure didn't expect that. I'd better get with Linda and see what we have left to do before we go."

He paused and he thought back to Klaus Heidelberg's sage advice, and said, "I guess we'd better do a few test flights before we set off across the universe again."

Even though she wasn't in the room with them, Linda asked, *Can I come along?*

Sure you can, and we're going to do the first test flight in the morning.

* * *

THE NEXT MORNING, they met Nicholas at the *Imagination* just as the sun was coming up. The spaceship was hovering about three feet above the floor in the middle of the massive building.

It was the only thing left in the huge hanger, and it looked tiny, sitting there all by itself. The loading ramp was already down so they went straight on board.

Billy sat down at the control console, and when he turned on the holographic viewer the nose of the ship seemed to disappear.

Once they were clear of the building, he took the ship straight up, and he didn't slow down until they were just outside Midgard's atmosphere.

It had been a while since they had been in space, but the view was as awesome as they remembered.

At that altitude, they could see the entire northern hemisphere. The weather had been slowing deteriorating, as Molly Feinstein had predicted, and virtually all the land was covered by several feet of snow.

"Boy, talk about your winter wonderland, that takes the cake," Linda said.

"More like a winter nightmare," Nicholas replied. "We haven't had a day above freezing in months. I'll sure be glad when we can spend most of our time in the south."

"Speaking of the south, have you and your men decided where you're going to settle?" Billy asked.

"Sort of. Some of them want to live in the cities, and others want to try the country. Myself, I'm going for the country, at least until we can figure out where to move all of our stuff. I'll eventually go to whereever we relocate the labs."

"Good—so you and John have discussed moving the labs?" Billy asked.

"We have, and he has left it up to me. I don't think he intends to stay at the new lab for very long. He wants to move out to the lake with your parents and become a farmer."

"John Tyler as a farmer . . . I'm having a hard time envisioning him as a farmer. But for his sake, I hope it all works out.

"I'll never be able to repay what he's done for me. If it wasn't for him, I might have lost Linda.

"Do you want us to delay our departure so you can use the *Imagination* to help move the equipment?"

"No need. The new designs for the balloons are working out nicely, and we shouldn't have any trouble moving anything. I had been a little worried about moving the base's reactors, but I just saw the new designs for a heavy lifting balloon, and I'm sure that they'll be able to handle the job.

"Please don't take this wrong, but I've just got to ask. Why are you guys going to risk your lives to rejoin the fleet? Your families are here, and there's not much that you're going to be able to accomplish, even if you do manage to rejoin the fleet.

"I hope that you're not naïve enough to think that President McAlister is going to welcome you back with open arms."

"I don't have any illusions about how the president is going to receive us. Nevertheless, God has shown us that He expects us to return and try to help the people who are suffering under the President's rule.

"Honestly, now that things have settled down here, we would love to stay, but it's not to be."

"Look, I know that you think God has told you to go on this great quest, but I've got to tell you, I just don't buy into all that.

"I would love to believe that there's a God. My father was a deeply religious man, and after seeing what happened to him, I just can't believe that a just God would let something like that happen. So I'm afraid that all I'm going to believe in is my own abilities."

"I can't tell you how sad that makes me. You have no idea what God would add to your life. I just hope that one day we can help you find Him in your heart. But enough of that, let's try the ship out and see what she'll do."

Billy tapped the console's screen, and the ship accelerated away from the planet. In just a few short minutes it was going over two hundred thousand miles per hour.

He wanted to confirm that everything was working properly before they continued, so he put the ship on autopilot and took a few minutes to run some quick diagnostics.

After he was satisfied that everything was in order, he released the autopilot and let the ship resume its acceleration.

In what seemed like no time at all, they had passed one of Midgard's moons. By then the ship was doing just over three hundred and fifty thousand miles per hour. By most standards, they were really moving, but they weren't even close to the speed they needed.

But Billy didn't intend to try to break the speed of light on this trip. He simply wanted to make sure that the ship's systems were working as designed.

They continued to accelerate for the next two hours, and when they reached two million miles per hour, Billy put the ship into a slow turn and started back to Midgard.

He didn't begin to decelerate until they passed the moon again, and he had to apply a considerable amount of power in order to slow down before they overran the planet. As the ship slowed, he put it into orbit around Midgard.

"Wow, that was quite a ride," Nicholas said. "I didn't see anything that needs work, did you?"

"No. As usual, you and your men did a crackerjack job, but I want to make one more test flight before we go. I didn't want to test the magnetic projectors until I was sure the rest of the ship was in good shape.

"When we test them, I want for us to be prepared not to return, because I think that there's a fifty-fifty chance that once they are fully powered up, we'll be immediately sucked through, and we won't be able to return."

They had loaded several communication satellites before they took off, so as they orbited the planet, they placed them in their predetermined locations. When they were in place, they would provide worldwide communication and navigation services.

When they finished placing the satellites, they landed back at their base.

"Is there anything you need us to do before your last test flight?" Nicholas asked.

"There is one thing, if you think it's feasible. I would like you to install a pair of the Petawatt lasers in the nose of the ship."

"Going to war, are we? If you want them, you've got them, and unlike the shuttles, you should have more than enough power to operate them."

Billy decided to delay his last test flight until they had the lasers installed. When they were finished, Nicholas briefed Billy on the additions.

"We've finished installing the lasers, and while we were at it, we mounted two more in the rear of the ship. They're all on moveable mounts, and we added radar tracking.

All you have to do is identify the target, and they'll do the rest.

"The bow lasers are mounted on the top of the ship, and stern lasers are mounted on the bottom of the ship. That gives you the ability to cover all the angles of attack."

"As usual, you've gone the extra mile. Thanks, and I hope that we never need to use them, but it's comforting to know that they're there if we do need them. Linda and I will take it out this afternoon. If all goes well, we'll leave on Sunday."

BILLY FOLLOWED THE same course as the first test flight, but when they reached the end of their outbound leg, he didn't turn.

Ever since they had left the atmosphere, he'd been looking for a suitable target to test the lasers.

They were already several million miles from Midgard when they ran across a small swarm of meteors. Billy turned on the lasers and had the computer to target the meteors. When he hit execute, the computer immediately targeted and fired. In just a few seconds, the lasers vaporized the meteors in a brilliant flash of light.

"Wow, that was impressive," Linda exclaimed.

"As usual, Nicholas has outdone himself. I just hope the magnetic projectors work, as well."

They had used the magnetic projectors before, but Billy knew that they had been lucky to have lived through it. This time he wanted to be a little more cautious. Even though he had designed them, he still wasn't a hundred percent sure what to expect.

He knew that at full power, they would open what

was equivalent to a black hole, but he wasn't ready to let it suck them through. When it happened last time, it had been so rapid that they didn't have any chance to respond before they were sucked through into the dimension they were in.

When he was ready, he brought the *Imagination* to a full stop. He waited until there was nothing within a million miles of them before he started the test.

He slowly powered up the projectors. Once he had verified that there was plenty of reserve power, he slowly began to apply more power. He had programmed the computer to simultaneously add power to the shields and apply enough power to the propulsion system to keep them stationary.

By the time the magnetic vortex had formed in front of the ship, the computer had been pouring more and more power into the propulsion system to keep the ship from moving.

As the vortex gained strength, they saw it start to spin faster and faster, until it resembled a brilliant maelstrom of light. By the time the vortex had reached its full strength, the ship was using all of its reserve power to hold its position, but it held as steady as a rock.

As Billy and Linda stood in awe of what they were witnessing, they touched each other's mind.

That could be either the gateway to heaven, or the gateway to hell, but either way it's amazing, Linda said. *Do you think it's going to lead us back to our own dimension?*

I hate to say it, but I don't fully understand how it works, so we'll just have to take our chances.

He spent a couple of minutes gathering data, and then he switched off the projectors, and the vortex winked out of existence.

When they landed, Billy downloaded the data to the base's main computer, and he went to debrief with Nicholas.

"It sounds like it worked," Nicholas said.

"Perfectly. I've downloaded all the data we gathered so you and your team can study it after we're gone.

"I don't see any reason to put it off, so we'll be leaving on Sunday. We're going to spend the night with our parents, and then we'll leave from there. But I'll be sure to give you a call before we go."

After Billy and Linda had loaded what they were taking with them, they said their good-byes to Nicholas Stavros and his men.

As they were coming in for a landing at their parents' settlement, Linda remarked, "This so beautiful. The lake looks like a sparkling diamond, and the countryside is already green with this year's crops. Our dads have accomplished quite a bit. It's hard to believe that the meteorites actually ended up causing some good. This area is turning into a Garden of Eden."

They had let their parents know when to expect them, so they were waiting when they landed. It was a perfect night, so they decided to eat dinner outside beside the pristine lake.

They built a roaring fire, and while its light reflected off the crystal-clear water, its embers rose into the night sky like millions of fireflies.

"How great is this?" Ben said. "We're all together, and it's a perfect night. I just wish it could stay like this forever."

* * *

BILLY AND LINDA knew that their parents wanted to beg them to stay, but they weren't going to this time.

They sat around the fire talking until after midnight, when finally Billy said, "We've got to get a little sleep before we leave. We'll contact you before we try to make the jump back to the fleet."

There were lots of tears and hugs, but finally they made it back to their ship. They both woke up well before dawn, and after they had eaten, Billy said, "Let's go ahead and lift off. We'll give them a call before we make our try."

"You know they're going to be mad at us, don't you? They really wanted us to wait and let them see us off."

"I know, but I think this will be easier on them in the long run."

The ship didn't make a sound as they lifted off, and by the time their parents noticed, they were long gone.

As they had expected, their parents were very upset with them when they realized they had already left. Once they had gotten over the initial shock, they all gathered around the communication center to wait on their call. Just before lunch, Billy and Linda called in, as they had promised.

When the communication screen came alive, Billy and Linda were sitting at the flight control console. Behind them, the ship's holographic projector gave their parents a glorious view of space.

"That's quite a view," Rob said. "How long before you try it?"

"That's why we called," Linda said. "We wanted to say good-bye, and let you know that we've decided to let you watch as we make our attempt.

"The scene that you're seeing behind us is the space directly in front of the ship. I'm going to let Billy explain what you're going to see. I love you all, and we're going to be fine, so don't worry. God will take care of us."

After they had all said their good-byes again, Billy told them, "When I trigger the magnetic projectors, you're going to see what looks like a violent thunderstorm, only it's going to be spinning like a sideways tornado.

"When the vortex is fully formed, we'll accelerate directly into it. If everything goes as planned, we'll make the transition back to our dimension.

"I'm not sure how long you'll be able to follow us, but you should be able to see everything until we actually enter the vortex. Don't be alarmed when the picture cuts off when we enter the vortex."

None of them knew what else to say, so Billy put his arm around Linda and tapped the console screen to turn on the projectors. As they sat waiting for the ship to make its transition, their minds were fully bonded.

I'm a little scared, but I wouldn't want to be anywhere else but right here with you, Linda said.

I love more than you can ever know. We're going to be alright, I just know it.

Unlike during the test, he had the ship programmed to go to full acceleration when the vortex reached its full strength.

It took a few seconds for the vortex to spin up, and as it grew, their parents became quickly amazed and somewhat terrified of what they were witnessing. Rob was about to ask if it was supposed to be that violent, when the ship seemed to leap forward into the vortex, and then it was gone.

Even though Billy had warned them, they were all startled by the sudden ending.

"I sure hope they're alright," Ben said. "Was it just my

imagination, or were they glowing just before they disappeared?"

"I saw it as well," Rob replied.

They all talked excitedly for several minutes, and then they joined hands and asked God to take care of their children on their new journey.

TOR

Award-winning authors
Compelling stories

Please join us at the website
below for more information
about this author and other great
Tor selections, and to sign up for
our monthly newsletter!